"A fascinating tale of how Mickey and his little brother managed to survive a horrifying childhood. Once you start reading *Darkness Dwells in Dixie*, you'll have trouble putting it down until the very last word."

~Marilyn F.M. Meredith, author of over sixty books, including *Reversal of Fortune*, the *Deputy Tempe Crabtree Mysteries*, and the *Rocky Bluff P.D.* mystery series.

"Mike Reynolds has crafted a taut and tense narrative peopled with characters each wrestling with the peculiar demons of violence, loss, and identity. A family's hidden secrets, well preserved and tightly guarded, provide the background for an exploration of character and place. Well written, compelling, and ultimately uplifting, *Darkness Dwells in Dixie* is a singular piece of writing worthy of a careful read."

~Greg Fields, author of *Through the Waters and the Wild*, and Winner of the 2022 Independent Press Award for Literary Fiction

"On a very rainy day, curled up in my cozy RV, I began reading and could not stop. Just the diversion I needed. *Darkness Dwells in Dixie* is a riveting tale that blends the author's bent for storytelling with the very real tragedy of family secrets. The power of adults to both harm and provide stability for children is a thread that sharply reminds us all that even in chaos, love and faith make a difference. Reynolds' words weave an often difficult yet inspiring story that demonstrates the many ways we can care for children who we may not be able to fully protect—and the difference that makes for a lifetime."

~Janyne McConnaughey PhD, Trauma-informed Author and Advocate, author of *Trauma in the Pews, Brave, Brave Childhood*, and *A Brave Life*

"Mike Reynolds makes a bold showing on several fronts in *Darkness Dwells in Dixie* that clearly places him at the forefront of his generation. The feel of his story is so embracing and authentic of the Southern culture that he grew up in—it could almost be called 'Neo-Gothic' because this is a new South, not just a younger one. But it so clearly stems from Southern Gothic kinsmen like Faulkner who branded it long ago, and in which Reynolds is perfectly at home. The story unfolds with profanity so sensitive readers take note. Some situational depictions definitely fall in the adult category. I can confidently assert that Reynolds is authentic in these depictions. For a story that travels a very harrowing road, it does come full circle to a great and powerful redemption that realigns the situational parameters. And what a great conclusion to a riveting journey."

~Duane K Estill, Minister, Author of *A Tin Can Cosmos*

"*Darkness Dwells in Dixie* is a captivating read of a young, abused, and broken Mickey setting out at age eight to find the truth of his very existence. He coexists with half-truths and outright falsehoods for nearly two decades in his search. Surrounded by alligators and snapping turtles in the swamps of the deep South, young Mickey turns to his Mama to soothe jagged thoughts developing in his mind's eye. Unaccompanied, the maturing Mickey is eventually freed from the exhaustive pursuit for his legitimacy. In the end, after many personal struggles, the reader will marvel at the simplicity in which author Mike E Reynolds brings you so comfortably to a very self-satisfying and soft landing."

~Ron Hughart, author of *The Place Beyond the Dust Bowl, Déjà vu of a Skeptic*, and *Did I Meet Santa?*

"The street-level writing is not for the easily offended. Then again, neither is the Bible. This is humanity in God's unblinking spotlight. *Darkness Dwells in Dixie* is well worth the time."

~Jerry Wilson, author of *God's Not Dead (And Neither Are We)*, and host of "Cephas Hour"

"*Darkness Dwells in Dixie* is a gripping story full of real character- and emotion-driven storytelling. The historical and cultural context Reynolds provides audiences offers an intense read. Definitely a book worth reading!"

~Garrett K. Jones, author of *The Archives of Icínq-Régn*

DARKNESS DWELLS IN
DIXIE

MIKE E REYNOLDS

BERRY
POWELL
PRESS

Darkness Dwells in Dixie
Copyright © 2022 by Mike E Reynolds

First paperback edition November 2022
Cover Design by Kay McConnaughey

Published by Berry Powell Press
Glendora, CA

ISBN: 978-1-957321-00-4 (Paperback)
ISBN: 978-1-957321-01-1 (ebook)
Library of Congress Control Number: 2022909888

DEDICATION

This book is dedicated to Cora, Colee, and Patricia—
the three women who loved me most in this world.

CONTENTS

ACKNOWLEDGMENTS

It's humbling to realize that the story churning in my head for so many years is finally a book! But it would not be what it is without the hard work and commitment of so many others. I owe the following people an extraordinary debt, without whom this book would never have been written.

Thank you, Annette, my wife, who encouraged me to write this book before I died. Honey, I just might make it!

Many thanks to Carmen Berry, my mentor and publisher, who said I was a writer long before I believed it to be true. I still can't believe she was that gullible.

Thank you to Valeri Mills Barnes, my editor and publishing coach, who made this book readable—a truly remarkable feat of magic.

And my appreciation to the rest of the Berry Powell Press staff, who all had a hand in the creation of Darkness Dwells in Dixie: Marianne Croonquist, Abigail Dengler, and Kathleen Taylor. A special thank you for creating an amazing cover-reveal video goes to Carolyn Rafferty.

Last but not least, my gratitude to Kay McConnaughey for the coolest cover design ever!

I've been told I can rest now, but that next story is whirling around in my mind and beckoning me to write it down. After all, if it's not on the paper, it's not in the book.

PRESENT
FRIDAY, APRIL 21, 1972
1:18 P.M.

"Charlie is dyin', Mickey," Grandma Jean said softly.

Grandma Jean and I were sitting in old, faded red Adirondack chairs under the giant bean pod tree in front of the old white farmhouse she'd lived in for fifty years. Grandma Jean had been a pretty lady once, and she still looked wiry and tough. She was part Cuban and part Seminole Indian and usually carried a big old knife in a sheath around her waist when she was working the farm.

She and Grandpa Willie bought a hundred and twenty acres in 1922 in the small farming town of Greensboro, Florida—about an hour outside of Quincy, where I was born and raised. They built the house, planted a bean pod tree, and raised pigs, cows, and chickens together. And it was in that house they raised their sons, Charlie and Jimmy. After Grandpa Willie died in the late forties, Grandma Jean began selling off the land, a bit at a time, to Florida Power to enable them to build large transmission towers on it. She used the money to live on over the years and still kept a few pigs and chickens around, "…just for fun," she'd say.

Grandma Jean and I hadn't seen each other or had a real conversation since I enlisted in the Navy two and a half years ago. I signed up right after I graduated from Key West High School. After serving my two-year stint, I came back to Florida in September of 1971 to begin my college career at Florida State University, using my GI Bill benefits to pay for it. I rented a small house in Midway, a little village halfway between Tallahassee and Quincy, with the intention of reconnecting with my family. But in reality, I didn't come home often. I'd joined the Navy hoping it would give me perspective on my family and help diminish the anger and frustration I'd felt most of my childhood. It did not.

Grandma Jean had called me just the day before and said it was urgent she talk with me as soon as possible, so the following afternoon, after I finished my morning chores and ate some lunch, I made the drive out to the farm. We spent a few pleasant minutes catching up, but then, damn it all, Grandma Jean sucked me back into the nightmare that was my childhood.

She repeated herself. "Charlie is dyin', Mickey."

I looked down as my hands began to shake. In disbelief, I gasped before I could speak. "Grandma Jean, I wouldn't have come here if I'd thought, for even one second, you'd ask me to see Charlie again. I don't care if he's got cancer, or whatever else." The look on her face couldn't have been any more pained than if I'd physically slapped her.

"But—"

"No. How could y'all ask me knowin' what he did to us?"

Standing up from the chair, I started toward the door. "I don't wanna hear anymore. I gotta go."

"But Mickey, he just wants to make peace with y'all."

I looked her in the eyes. "Listen, I love you, Grandma Jean. We're family, but you can't really think that I wanna see that sumbitch after what he did to our family. Especially Mama."

A single tear ran down her left cheek. "I know he broke Dixie Mae's heart."

Trembling with anger, I nodded. "Yeah, he broke her heart, all right! He broke her spirit, her…" I struggled to find the words. "She's just a shell of the woman she could'a been."

My mind flashed back to when I was a young boy looking up at my mama, the young and vibrant woman everyone else called Dixie Mae. She had jade-green eyes that could sparkle with mischief, and then, without warning, turn as dark and disturbing as swamp water. Sometimes she'd look off into space as if watching a scene play back in her mind, and then she'd snap out of it just as quickly and pull you in with her infectious laugh.

Not only was Mama pretty, but she was also smart. She was the first woman in Florida to get her bartender's license. She sang like an angel and had a wicked sense of humor—and an extensive vocabulary, which consisted mostly of words used only by drunken sailors on leave and longshoremen on a Friday night.

Dixie Mae had a way of making you believe whatever she said, even though her stories didn't always have the ring of truth in them. It didn't matter, though, because when she flashed that brilliant smile in your direction, you believed everything she said.

Most of all, though, Mama was a vibrant woman who had a special way with men. She liked them, knew how to handle them, and they loved her for it. That made it difficult for me growing up, as I was both protective of her and in awe of the power she had over them.

The fact was, Mama never met a man who didn't want her. My mama could've had any man she wanted, but there was only one man for her—Charlie Crow, the man who raised me, the daddy I'd wanted to be like when I was a small boy, and the man I refused to call Daddy any longer. And I was outraged at Grandma Jean, the mother of the man I hated with every fiber of my being, for putting me in this position.

I attempted to maintain control. "Charlie has had plenty of chances to change his ways, to be the daddy that Harley and I needed, but he didn't. He just got meaner and nastier. Don't forget, he damn near killed us all! Now that he's about to meet his Judge, he wants me to act like nothin' happened? Ain't gonna happen!"

I turned to leave, then looked back over my shoulder. "I mean no disrespect to you, Grandma Jean. None at all. But Charlie don't deserve to die in peace after everythin' he's done. I'll never forgive the sumbitch, so please don't ever mention him to me again. When he dies, don't call me, because I honestly won't care."

CHAPTER TWO

"Y'all wake up, boys," Daddy whispered to me and my brother Harley. "Me and Bobby are gonna take y'all fishing this mornin'."

"It's dark, Daddy," Harley said from his bed.

"Shhh!" Daddy said. "Be real quiet, Harley. Don't wake up yo' mama." He looked up at me. "Mickey, get dressed and help yo' brother get dressed too."

"All right, Daddy," I said. Rubbing the sleep from my eyes, I started to get out of bed but hesitated a moment. "It's Sunday, Daddy. We're supposed to go to church with Grandmama this mornin'."

Harley nodded his blonde head. "Yeah, Daddy, she gonna be mad if we don't."

Daddy strongly protested. "That's too damn bad!"

"Shhh," I whispered.

Daddy quieted down. "Look, I'm y'all's Daddy, and I'm takin' you two fishin'. Yo' Grandmama will just have to get over it. Now get dressed and hurry before we get caught!"

Harley and I looked at each other knowing there'd be hell to pay come lunchtime. But, for now, there was probably nothing he and I would rather do than go fishing with Daddy and Uncle Bobby. They were both heroes in my eyes. Daddy had become a pilot in the Air Force, and Uncle Bobby was a Deputy Sheriff in our county. I tried my best to be just like them, even though I was only eight years old.

Harley and I quickly got dressed and snuck out silently behind Daddy. Uncle Bobby was standing on the curb next to our robin's egg blue Chevy Bel Air, waiting for us. He was always around and referred to us as "Dixie's boys" on account of our mama, Dixie Mae Crow. But I almost didn't recognize him because he was dressed in jeans, a t-shirt, and a jacket instead of proudly wearing his deputy's uniform like he usually did—on or off duty. He'd been doing that ever since he graduated from the sheriff's academy.

"Are you still a deputy today, Uncle Bobby?" I asked.

He smiled. "You bet, but today, I'm also a fisherman!" His red and white Wrangler bass boat was already hitched to the back of Daddy's car. With a big grin on his face, Uncle Bobby opened the back door so Harley and I could jump in. Daddy climbed into the driver's seat and Bobby rode shotgun.

Once the doors closed and we were all inside, Harley and I started giggling with delight. Daddy looked back at us. "To the swamp?"

"To the swamp!" Harley and I hollered in unison, and off we went to the Apalachicola River, about an hour southwest of Quincy.

I looked out the window and tried to forget how mad my grandmama was going to be when we got home. This wasn't the first time Daddy did something that Grandmama didn't like, and God knows it wouldn't be the last. Grandmama didn't like my daddy much anyway, and my Aunt Tootie, Mama's older sister, downright hated him. But I didn't care about any of that this morning. I looked up to my daddy, and, hell, we were going fishing in the swamp!

Life was pretty good—at least I thought so, considering every family I knew in town was a lot like mine. Harley and I lived with our mama and daddy in a small, two-bedroom house which seemed plenty big enough to me. My brother and I were just a couple of toe-headed, sun-tanned, little Florida crackers living the dream in Quincy, a small town in Gadsden County, Florida. I was stocky with strong arms. Harley was shorter and thinner, like Daddy. We were good Southern Baptists—except my Daddy, of course—blue-collar, hard-working folks of Irish descent, like most of the citizens of Quincy.

I don't think people paid me much mind in those days, seeing that I was only eight and kind of a quiet kid, but I knew more about what was going on than anyone seemed to think. I knew my mama was beautiful. I saw how the men around Quincy watched her walk by. She was a green-eyed, natural blonde with an hourglass figure. I heard more than one man say, "That woman is easy on the eyes." Some even compared her to Marilyn Monroe.

I'd figured out that Uncle Bobby liked my mama plenty. He and my mama and daddy had grown up together, starting with my daddy and Uncle Bobby being best friends in kindergarten. Uncle Bobby was always big for his age—built like a football player. My daddy was skinny and wiry and had lots of freckles. Kids picked on Daddy because of his size and made fun of his name, Charlie Crow. "Scrawny Crow" became his nickname until Uncle Bobby put a stop to it. He beat up a few kids on the playground and the teasing vanished. At least, as long as my daddy stuck close to his big best friend.

I'd overheard the grownups talking about how both boys had been smitten with my mama. Well, to hear them tell it, it seemed like *all* the boys at Gadsden High School, and maybe a few of the male teachers, had a thing for her. The story was that she had been somewhat attracted to Uncle Bobby, him being so big and strong. And it didn't hurt that because of his size and athletic talent, he'd been drafted onto the varsity football team as a freshman.

But all of that changed over the summer between their sophomore and junior years. My daddy transformed from a thin weakling into a muscular and very handsome young man. His black hair and summer tan made his green eyes stand out. Mama once told me about coming back to school that September.

"Mickey, on the first day of school, I met up with Bobby and yo' daddy. I almost didn't recognize him. I instantly fell ass over tea kettle in love with him!" I suspect that Uncle Bobby's heart was broken at that same moment. He must have realized that he'd just lost my mama to his best friend, Charlie.

But all of that was in the past. Uncle Bobby and my daddy were still best friends, and here we all were, on our way to fish in the swamp. I rolled down the window and let the cool air rush over my face.

"Why's it takin' so long?" Harley complained.

Daddy just grunted in response.

"Don't worry, Harley. We're almost there," Uncle Bobby said. And we were.

The boat was launched, and we hopped aboard. The sun was up, giving us a beautiful and warm spring day on the river. The birds were singing, and the fish were jumping as Uncle Bobby navigated his way to Daddy's favorite fishing hole. After we settled in, the cane poles came out from where we had stashed them under the seats.

"Mickey, y'all need some help baitin' that hook, boy?" Daddy asked.

"No, sir, I can do it myself." I loved cane pole fishing. Just the pole, a red and white balsa wood bobber and a hook with a worm firmly attached were all you needed.

Daddy leaned back and lit up a cigarette. We fished for a couple of hours, filling our bucket with perch and catfish. Taking a break, we all had peanut butter and jelly sandwiches for lunch. Daddy and Uncle Bobby washed them down with a few beers, and Harley and I filled our bellies with RC Cola and Orange Crush. It was heaven—it really was.

After lunch, Harley stood up in the boat and yelled out, "Mickey, look at that big ol' gator over there!" While we'd seen gators before, we had never seen one so large.

"Sit down, Harley, before y'all fall outta the boat," Daddy yelled.

Bobby pulled Harley back down to his seat. "Hell, Charlie, this boy won't even make a good snack for a gator that big."

Daddy's face turned dark. "What do y'all mean by that?"

"Sorry, Charlie. I didn't mean to bring up yo' daddy—"

"What y'all talkin' about?" I piped up. "Granddaddy was ate by a gator?" I didn't remember my granddaddy at all because he died when I was a toddler. I'd heard about him some, none of it good. But I'd never heard talk about how he died.

"Forget about it!" Daddy snarled.

Not a chance! My mind was racing, imagining all sorts of terrible scenarios. "Granddaddy got eat up by a gator?" I repeated. A look passed between Daddy and Uncle Bobby that I didn't understand, and nobody spoke for a minute or so.

Finally, Daddy broke the silence. "Yeah, y'all's granddaddy got eaten by a gator."

"But, how?" I wanted to know more.

"Charlie, they're gonna hear the story eventually. Might as well come from you."

Daddy nodded. "Okay, I'll tell you this one time, and y'all better never ask me again. You got that?"

Harley and I nodded our heads.

"Y'all's granddaddy took me and your Uncle Jimmy out fishin' not far from here when you were around three, Mickey. Harley, you were just a baby. My daddy stood up in the boat, just like Harley did, and he lost his balance. He fell in, and Jimmy and I tried to pull him out. I got a hold of his arm, but this huge gator came up out of nowhere and grabbed him with his huge jaws. That gator yanked your granddaddy right out of my hands." Daddy's voice trailed off.

"I was a volunteer with the search and rescue team," Bobby added. "I was one of those boys who searched for his body."

Harley and I made a face at each other.

"His body?" Harley asked.

"Yeah, we searched for 'im for more than a week but couldn't find 'im," Uncle Bobby said.

Harley and I sat in shock, our mouths wide open, staring intently at the giant beast swimming not more than six feet off the bow of our little boat. A chill ran up and down my spine. "Is this gator gonna eat us too?"

"He will if you boys stand up and fall in!" Daddy sounded really mad.

Harley started to cry.

"Oh, stop it, Harley," Daddy said.

Bobby interrupted. "It's time for us to leave, anyway. We've gotta get back in time for Sunday supper or else your Grandmama's gonna be pissed off."

"Oh, I bet she's been pissed off since she came to pick up the boys for Sunday school and they weren't there." Daddy laughed and slapped Bobby on the back. "Picturin' that woman fussin' will cheer me up all the way back home."

I didn't share Daddy's cheerfulness and didn't want to think about what was waiting for us back at Grandmama's house.

THREE

We dropped Uncle Bobby's boat off at his house and drove up to Grandmama Colee's just before one o'clock, the appointed time for Sunday dinner. Mama met us at the door, her blonde hair pulled up with a scarf and her hands on her hips, trying to look as angry as she could.

"Y'all cut it kinda close, don't ya think, Charlie? My mama's fit to be tied."

Daddy grinned mischievously. "Well, hell, Dixie Mae, yo' mama's always fit to be tied, ain't she?" He bent down and kissed Mama on the lips. She playfully whacked him on the shoulder, unable to stay mad at him.

"Dammit, Charlie Crow!" Grandmama shouted from the kitchen. "Them boys was supposed to go to church with me this mornin'!"

We all filed into the kitchen behind Daddy. He mumbled, "Cain't a man take his sons fishin' once in a while without y'all barking at 'im?"

Grandmama was uncompromising in her devotion to Jesus and mandatory weekly attendance to the Sunday worship service at Mt. Calvary Baptist Church on Stewart Street.

She looked around Charlie and caught me and Harley in her laser eyes. "Boys, y'all know that God don't like it when y'all miss church. He saw you fishin'." Scared us both half to death.

"They don't need that hell-fire preachin' every Sunday, woman."

"Please, Charlie, be nice," Mama whispered.

"You need that preachin' more than most, Charlie Crow." Grandmama's needling was nothing new—she and Daddy had been sniping at each other for as long as I could remember.

"I noticed yo' mama wasn't sittin' on her end of the pew this mornin'." Grandmama wasn't about to let up on Charlie keeping her grandsons away from the Lord's house. "Everthin' all right?" Grandma Jean was Charlie's mama and Grandmama's question wasn't out of concern, but rather to point out that her nemesis had the gall to miss church. I felt a quiver of anxiety ripple through the air, sure that everyone else felt it too.

The church we attended was small with a center aisle and wooden pews bolted to the floor. If you missed a Sunday, not only did God know it, but bless your heart, everybody else also knew it too.

I vaguely remembered hearing my Aunt Tootie tell someone on the phone that my two grandmas used to be the best of friends, sitting together every Sunday side-by-side. Everybody knew that the third pew on the left side was theirs.

Several years before I was born, a huge fight erupted, and they quit seeing each other, except neither would give up ownership of the pew. They moved as far away from the other as possible—on opposite ends of that same pew—forcing the rest of the family to sit between these two feuding matriarchs for years. Violence was avoided through Southern politeness, referring to each other as "sisters in the Lord." An otherwise scandalized congregation was able to sidestep the entire issue.

When Charlie ignored Grandmama's question, she asked again, trying to feign concern. "Mr. Crow, I'm askin' y'all, is yo' mama okay?"

"As far as I know, Colee." Daddy didn't make eye contact, but I could tell he was having a hard time keeping his temper under control. Mama shot Daddy a warning glance.

"Well, bless her heart. I'm glad to hear it." Grandmama's reply seemed nice enough, but we all knew what *that* meant.

Daddy, always the charmer, tried to steer the attention away from himself. "Hmmm, whatever you are cookin', it sure smells good! What's for dinner? Me, Bobby, and the boys are hungry." Grateful for the focus changing to food, I breathed deeply, taking in the delicious aroma of Grandmama's cooking.

"All right, Mama, that's enough," my mama said. "You, too, Charlie." She leaned down, and kissed Harley on the top of his head, and gave me a quick hug. "Did y'all have fun fishin' this mornin'?"

We nodded.

"That's good. Now y'all go wash up so we can eat."

"Yes, ma'am." Daddy bowed to Mama.

Harley and I ran toward the bathroom. I whispered to Harley, "Well, that wasn't as bad as I was expectin'. No one got mad at us!"

Harley wrinkled his nose. "Well, God is mad at us."

We shared a fearful look for a moment and then busted out laughin'. God was a scary old man in the sky who never wanted us to have any fun. But Daddy outsmarted God and Grandmama today. And we couldn't have been happier about that. I figured maybe this wouldn't be such a bad Sunday after all.

Sunday was my favorite day of the week because everyone gathered at my Grandmama's house for a huge dinner after church. Anyone and everyone were welcome, no invitation was required. As far as I remember, people from church or the neighborhood showed up at one time or another. For Harley and me, it was like a once-a-week picnic. I don't recall ever seeing Grandma Jean there though, and I never did ask why.

We filled up on fried chicken, green beans, mashed potatoes, and pecan pie. When we couldn't eat anymore, Harley and I would go hang out with my Aunt Tootie, my mama's older sister. She adored us, and we her. No one expected Aunt Tootie to ever get married. While the men swarmed around my mama, Aunt Tootie garnered no such attention. She wasn't ugly—you could see the family resemblance—but there was something about the way she hid her large body underneath drab, baggy dresses. Even her posture screamed, "Stay away." If that didn't work, the cold look on her face let everyone know she had no use for men. Fortunately, her disdain for men didn't extend to me and Harley.

Tootie always snuck us extra cookies and saved us a place next to her on the front porch whenever we dropped by. She was just fun to be around. Most of the kids in the neighborhood were in awe of her because she was the best shot in the whole damn county. Not even the toughest guys in Gadsden County would mess with her, especially after she won the State Championship Marksman Trophy four years in a row. When her daddy died, she'd found all of his guns and learned how to shoot. She could shoot the whiskers off a squirrel fifty yards away.

I always felt safe and welcomed by her. Sitting next to Aunt Tootie, munching on warm cookies just out of the oven—I couldn't have been happier this side of heaven. While pretending not to listen, I picked up every word shared by the grownups. No one told us kids anything about what was really going on, so I had to sneak around listening in on conversations if I wanted the latest gossip. Yep, Sundays were usually fun and relaxing, and though this one had started out tense, I was happy with the turnaround.

Grandmama and Mama were on the porch swing, and the gossip was abundant. I loved it and took note of it whenever someone said,

"Bless her heart," or "God bless him," or other such Southern zingers used for politely dismissing someone. Usually it was code for, "You're dumb, but you can't help it." I always wanted to know more about the terrible, unacceptable, and delicious things the other person had done.

While we rested in the shade of the porch, Daddy sat out back, out of earshot, smoking cigars with Uncle Bobby and Uncle Jimmy—Daddy's younger brother, who was usually hungover after a Saturday night bar crawl, and only came around once in a great while. The older men, including Grandpa Hank, were sitting under the big oak tree in the front yard playing cards. Me and Harley loved our Grandpa Hank, Grandmama's second husband. Tootie told us that our real granddaddy, Nash—who died before we were born—drank too much one night and killed himself by driving smack into a tree. "Bless his heart," she'd said.

Grandmama met Hank the day after Granddaddy died. He was the funeral director at the mortuary where Granddaddy Nash was buried. Tootie said some thought Grandmama married too quickly, barely two months after they put Nash in the ground, but no one dared say that where Grandmama could hear it. Oh, sometimes we'd hear comments like, "At least Hank ain't no drunk." Tootie said that in spite of the unseemly timing of their wedding, everyone agreed that Grandpa Hank was by far a better man than my real granddaddy.

I leaned up against Tootie and rested my head on her shoulder. Everything felt right with the world. It was turning out to be a perfect afternoon.

It was then that Mama made a fateful mistake.

"So, how many fish did y'all catch this morning, boys?" she asked, taking a short drag on her cigarette.

That question served to remind Grandmama that Daddy had kept us from church. "Them boys should'a been in Sunday School!"

"I didn't catch any, Mama, but we almost got ate by a gator!" Harley's eyes were as big as saucers.

"You what?" Mama shrieked. She angrily snuffed out her cigarette in a nearby ash tray. Everyone looked over at Daddy.

Grandmama yelled loud enough for my daddy to hear. "Charlie! Harley says yo' almost got him ate by a gator!"

My daddy took the cigar out of his mouth and stared back at Grandmama. "Relax, woman. We was never in any danger."

"Well, Harley stood up and almos' fell in, Mama," I said, trying to be helpful.

She stood up from the swing and walked across the porch closer to where Daddy and Uncle Bobby were sitting. "Charlie, what the hell were y'all thinkin'?"

Never able to read a room, I decided it was a good time to unburden myself further. "Mama, did y'all know that Granddaddy Willie got ate up by a gator?"

Everybody turned to look at me, no one saying a word. I knew instantly I never should've asked that question.

Mama turned towards me and looked me straight in the eyes. "Who tol' y'all that, Mickey? Huh? Who?"

"No one!" I tried to get up, but Aunt Tootie pulled me back down.

"It was yo' Daddy and Uncle Bobby, wasn't it?" Mama asked me. I nodded.

Harley, completely unaware that anything was wrong, said, "Yeah, they said he assdently fell in and a big ol' gator got 'im."

Aunt Tootie mumbled under her breath. "Couldn't have happened to a more deservin' sumbitch."

"Amen to that," Grandmama agreed.

Daddy stood up and walked toward the porch, pointing his cigar at them. "You wanna say that a little louder, ladies?" Aunt

Tootie and Grandmama stared back at him in defiance, but he was serious. "If y'all have somethin' to say about my daddy, then say it to my face."

Uncle Jimmy glared at Aunt Tootie and Grandmama through watery eyes. After all, they were talking about his daddy too.

Even though Grandpa Hank was a man of great patience and few words, we all knew that when he decided to take action, he never backed down. He pulled his considerable bulk out of the chair he'd been sitting in and started across the lawn towards Daddy and Uncle Jimmy. "Charlie, Charlie, Charlie! Do we have some trouble going on here?"

I got nervous when I saw Grandpa Hank get up because I knew it took a whole lot for him to get riled up enough to get out of his chair and onto his feet.

Uncle Bobby, realizing that Grandpa Hank was angry over Charlie's behavior towards his wife and stepdaughter, jumped to his feet and stepped in between Charlie and Grandpa. "C'mon, gentlemen, let's not spoil a perfectly good Sunday afternoon."

Grandmama wasn't done yet, and she tilted her head and pulled a stray hair from her face before opening her mouth. "I ain't afraid of you, Charlie Crow. You gonna hit me or somethin'? You gonna show us all that y'all are just like yo' good-fo'-nothin', wife-beatin' daddy?"

"Stop it!" my mama cried, turning on her own mama. "Charlie ain't never laid a hand on me. Never!"

She ran over to where the men were squaring off and put herself in the middle of Charlie, Uncle Bobby, and Grandpa Hank—the four of them now in a face-off. Finally, she smiled sweetly and said, "I just love to see my favorite three men together like this." She turned to Bobby and whispered, "Get us out of here."

Bobby nodded, turned to Daddy, and motioned with his head to back off. Daddy was still glaring at Grandmama and pressing forward. Bobby stood firm and blocked his way. "Charlie, knock it off, or I'm going to have to arrest yo' ass." If anyone else had said this to Daddy, it would have lit his temper like a match on a pile of dry grass. But there was a bond between the two men that ran deep. Daddy knew that Bobby always had his back. A smile spread across Charlie's face. I'd seen that smile before, and I didn't like it when he smiled like that. He had a mean streak in him that scared me to the bone.

"I was never goin' to hurt nobody but let me tell y'all somethin'." Pointing at Tootie and Grandmama, Daddy pushed for the last word. "Y'all may pretend to be good Christians, but I know who y'all really are. I've figured y'all out. Especially you, Tootie!" He edged a little closer to her and whispered something in her ear. I don't think anyone heard what he said to Tootie, except maybe Grandmama.

Tootie turned white as a sheet.

"You lyin' sumbitch!" Grandmama yelled at him. "Shut yo' filthy mouth!"

Mama pushed her way passed Bobby and put her face close to my daddy's. "Charlie Crow, you ain't figured nothin' out. Stop lyin' and causin' trouble."

"It's yo' sister who's trouble, Dixie Mae."

Mama paused, then twirled around as if she didn't have a care in the world and walked quietly into the house. We all froze, not knowing what to expect. Within a minute, she came back out with her sweater and purse. "C'mon, boys. We're leavin'."

"Stay where yo' at, boys!" Daddy barked.

Harley and I looked at each other, not knowing what to do.

Once again, Mama walked up to Daddy, only this time she ran her hands up his chest and played with a tuft of chest hair peeking out above his tee shirt. "Charlie, darlin', I'm so tired. Please take me home. I could sure use a nap." As if she assumed she'd get her way, Mama strolled to the car, swaying her hips with each step. A slight grin played at the corners of Charlie's mouth.

We paused for a moment, and then, one by one, like ducklings following their mother, the four of us trailed behind my mama to the car—first Harley, then me, followed next by Uncle Bobby. Daddy shrugged his shoulders and chewed on his cigar as he mumbled something inaudible to Uncle Jimmy, and then brought up the rear.

We piled in the car. Daddy with Mama in the front seat, and Uncle Bobby in the back with me and Harley. Daddy revved the engine, and Mama leaned out the window yelling sweetly, "I'll call y'all tomorrow, Mama!" We rode home without saying a word.

CHAPTER FOUR

That Sunday dinner in the spring of 1959 was one I'll never forget—even though none of us ever mentioned it again. But its impact was felt. I was just eight years old at the time, too young to understand it, but something shifted that Sunday afternoon. The thin covering hiding the intense animosity between the two sides of my family was ripped off that day and put out in the open. There was no way to stuff that genie back in the bottle.

My daddy and Aunt Tootie had always hated each other, but now they bickered more in public. Grandmama had been adamant about me and Harley going to Sunday school with her, but now she was all the more insistent. She made us promise that if Daddy ever tried to take us fishing again, we'd say no because "The Good Lord was watchin' us, and He'd know if we'd ditched church." Though Daddy would never admit to buckling to Grandmama's demands, Daddy took us fishing on Saturdays from then on, which helped us avoid getting into another public feud. Grandpa Hank was still his laidback self, but he stuck closer to Grandmama and Tootie when Charlie was around. Clearly, he wasn't going to leave them alone with Daddy if he could help it. Mama was more aware of any suggestion that Daddy was physically abusive to her. The slightest inference and she'd get in people's faces about it. Eventually, everyone avoided commenting on Charlie at all, just to be on the safe side. No one wanted to set off an even bigger, more unpredictable reaction.

We fell into a routine of going to church every week with Grandmama Colee. She would drive over from Shadeville and pick up Harley and me at 9:30 a.m. sharp for Sunday school. Though Mt. Calvary was only ten minutes away from our house, Grandmama drove her old Chevy Bel Air like we were already late. She only had two speeds— stop and go as fast as you can! No cop in town would give her a ticket, though. Hell, they wouldn't dare since she fed them all down at her truck stop, the Blue Star Café—especially Uncle Bobby, who stopped her occasionally, just to visit.

There were no seat belts in the back seat of her 1951 Chevy, so every time she made a turn, Harley and I slid from one side of the back seat to the other.

"What y'all laughin' at back there?" she yelled over her shoulder, one eye on the road and the other on us.

"Grandmama, I think Harley just peed himself on that last turn!" That sent Harley into a fit, laughing so hard he actually did pee himself a little bit.

"Well, knock that shit off, hear me? We on our way to church!"

The following Sunday, we were on our way to church when we heard a siren behind us. It was near the end of July, and I was really proud of myself because I was turning nine the next week.

When the siren screamed right behind us, Harley and I knew it was Uncle Bobby looking after us, and so did Grandmama.

"Damn it, Bobby!" Grandmama swore under her breath.

Grandmama pulled over, rolled down the window, and glared at him as he walked up to the car. "Damn, Mizz Colee! Y'all know how fast you were going?" Bobby loved Grandmama, almost like a second mother. He was always over at the restaurant or her house when he and Dixie Mae were kids. And though Grandmama wouldn't say it, she loved him like a son and was so proud of him for being a deputy.

"I don't know, Bobby. Me and the boys are on our way to church. We got an evangelist preachin' this mornin', and I don't wanna be late!"

"You got Dixie's boys back there, Colee?" he asked as if he didn't already know.

"Well, who else would be in my back seat, boy?"

He stuck his hand in through the open back window and tousled my hair. "Hey, Mickey, Harley. How y'all doin'?"

"We're good, Uncle Bobby. Just hopin' we all get to Sunday school alive." With that, Harley started giggling again.

"How's y'all's mama? How's Dixie Mae?" Uncle Bobby asked with genuine sincerity.

"I think she's good," I said. "She's workin' hard."

"Well, make sure you tell her I asked about her, okay?"

"If y'all want to tell her yo'self, come round for Sunday dinner," Grandmama said. "She'll be there."

Uncle Bobby blushed. "Thanks for the invite, ma'am. Cain't. I'm on duty today."

"All right, Officer Bailey, if y'all ain't gonna give me a ticket, I gotta go. Don't wanna be late for church, okay?"

"Okay, Colee, just keep your speed down."

Grumbling, Grandmama hit the gas as Uncle Bobby turned and headed back to his cruiser. Burning rubber for twenty feet before the tires finally gripped the road, she raced down the half mile to the church, turning into the parking lot with a minute to spare. Grandmama, with Harley and me in tow, headed for the main chapel where the adults' Sunday school was taught. "I'll see y'all right here after church. Don't mess 'round, y'all hear me?"

"Yes, ma'am," we said in unison and ran off to our class with Mr. Leon Mann.

All the kids loved Mr. Mann. He was a tall man, at least taller than any man I'd ever known, but then I was just a little kid. His fatherly demeanor and warm smile always made me feel welcomed and safe. He had a mustache worthy of a southern gentleman, and when he smiled, which he did often, it covered his whole face, always making his mustache turn up a bit at the ends. His eyes would always gleam whenever he launched into one of the great Bible stories, speaking in that high, soft voice he had, which didn't match his rugged looks. Before he started the lesson, however, he made an announcement. Looking at me he said, "Mickey has a special day coming up this week! He's turning nine!"

I stood up and took a bow while the other kids laughed and clapped. I have to admit that I felt pretty special.

Mr. Mann got serious. "Okay, settle down. Today's lesson is about Cain and Abel and how the brothers made sacrifices to God, but God favored Abel's sacrifice instead of Cain's. Cain got so jealous that he picked up a rock and snuck up behind Abel." Mr. Mann made us feel like we were standing over Abel while Cain picked up a stone and hit him with it.

He was describing, in detail, the final moments of Abel's life when Lila Martin, one of only three girls in the class, cried out, "Watch out, Abel!"

Mr. Mann said, "Cain killed his brother in a rage."

"What happened to Cain?" I asked.

"Good question, Mickey. Good question."

I beamed.

"God sent Cain away from everyone he knew. And he wandered around the desert for the rest of his life."

The thought of being forced to leave my family and friends in Quincy made my stomach turn. I looked at Harley and realized I'd miss him most of all. It would be awful.

"Remember, that anger is a powerful thing," Mr. Mann said. "It can cause a person to act and do things they'd never think of. So, guard y'all's hearts and minds, children, and don't let the devil into your life through anger, okay? It can lead to violence and even murder. It's a terrible thing, sometimes committed by otherwise good folks, who let the snake in through a small crack. Always, always, be on guard!" Just before the bell rang for church service, he smiled at us. "Well, that's it for today, boys and girls. I hope to see y'all back next week."

As we filed out of Mr. Mann's classroom, Michael, Janie, and Lisa Rice followed right behind Harley and me. They were a local family and had been at the church for years. Janie and Lisa were real sweet girls, but Michael was a bully with a mean temper, just like his daddy, from everything I heard. He tried to bully me one time, but I knocked him on his ass, so he never tried it again. Even so, he lived to cause trouble anywhere and anytime he could.

He sidled up next to me, close-like so the others wouldn't hear him. "Did y'all listen to the Sunday School lesson, Mickey?"

"What do you want, Michael?"

"All about murderin' people?" he sneered.

"What the hell y'all talkin' 'bout?"

"My mama told me that y'all's daddy murdered his own daddy in the swamp."

I pushed him up against the wall between classrooms and held him there. "You take that back, Michael, right now! My daddy ain't no killer. Yo' just a lyin', no-good jackass, just like yo' own daddy!"

He smiled, all venom and satisfaction. "Maybe yo' just like him with this bad temper and all."

I pulled back my fist to break his face. "It was an accident, you sumbitch!" He ducked his face to the side, and I got more of his ear than his nose, but at least I landed a punch.

Mr. Mann came out of his classroom and saw Michael up against the wall with my fist flying. "Mickey, what are you doin', boy? Let go of Michael, right now!"

"He said somethin' bad 'bout my daddy, Mr. Mann. Somethin' real bad."

"I don't care! Let him go right now!" I let Michael go, reluctantly and with murder in my eyes, thinking this must be what Cain had been feeling when he struck Abel with that rock.

Michael whined and rubbed his ear. "Oh, thank you, Mr. Mann. Mickey has such an awful temper." He gave me a vicious wink.

Mr. Mann turned to me and asked, "Where's y'all's grandmama?"

As soon as the words came out of his mouth, Grandmama came out of the double doors of the sanctuary. "What in God's name is goin' on here?"

I started to say something, but she held up her hand. "Stop! Just hold yo' tongue and say nothin'."

"Bu-but he said somethin' awful about my daddy."

"You got in a fight defending that…?" she caught herself before she said a bad word in the house of God. "Just get yo' ass into the pew, and don't say another word 'til the service is over! Understand?"

I turned around and pushed my way through the double doors and into the church, where I saw Harley sitting in our usual pew, right next to Grandma Jean. I snuck in, trying not to be seen, and plopped down next to Harley. I didn't know what Grandmama was up to, but eventually, she took her place at her end of the pew.

We sang The Old Rugged Cross, and the preacher did his best to scare us into heaven, describing the fires of hell if we didn't confess our sins to Jesus that very moment. He described the horror of Jesus dying on the cross for my sins, and it was all my fault for all that suffering. I sat through the entire service on the verge of tears. All the while, the Sunday School story was going round and round in my mind. Terror ran through my body. I'd lost my temper in God's house. I was going to be punished for it!

After church was over, instead of our usual after-service visiting, Grandmama immediately marched us to the Bel Air and got in. I barely shut the back door before she burned rubber out of the parking lot and headed home.

As we pulled into the driveway of our house, Grandmama said, "Harley, honey, go on inside. I want to have a word with your brother."

Harley ran off, not wanting to hear what was coming, and I got out of the car and stood at the driver's window, waiting and fighting back tears.

Calmly, Grandmama said, "I called your mama from the church office after I talked to Mr. Mann."

I gulped.

"I was really mad."

I nodded.

"I'm kinda sorry now that I did that," she confessed. She reached out the car window and patted me on the head. "I love you, Mickey. Good luck." And with that, she hit the gas and lurched onto the road, leaving me alone to face my fate.

I walked cautiously into the living room. Seeing the coast was clear, I ran into my room.

A few minutes later, Mama walked into the room with a long switch in her hand, her eyes ablaze. It looked like God wasn't going to waste any time in punishing me for hitting Michael in His House. I knew I was going to get a whipping.

"You know you're in big trouble, right?"

I nodded.

"Mama called from church this morning and said you got into a fight with Michael Rice after Sunday school. Said you really upset everyone, especially Mr. Mann." I knew where this was headed—a listing of my sins and then the wrath of Dixie Mae on my bare ass.

With nothing to lose, I launched into my defense. "Michael said that Daddy killed Grandpa Willie in the swamp. He said he was a *murderer.*" I emphasized the word for effect. "Mama, I had to hit him. I had to protect our daddy's reputation!"

Her grip on the switch tightened. That wasn't the effect I was going for. She snarled, "I'd like to get my hands on Michael myself. I'd show him what happens when people lie about our family."

"That's right, Mama. I had to stop his lies."

"Mickey, listen to me, for the last time, yo' daddy didn't kill yo' grandaddy, it was an ac-ci-dent!"

"That's what I told him, Mama, that it was an accident! Grandpa Willie lost his balance and fell in the water. Daddy tried to save 'im and almost died tryin' to fish 'im out." I was eloquent. I was passionate. I just made stuff up to make Daddy seem like a hero. Whatever it took to get that switch out of my mama's hands.

Mama was so furious she started shaking. "I hate it when people lie. Y'all's daddy might be a sumbitch at times, Mickey. He ain't perfect. But he ain't no murderer. You got that, boy? He ain't killed nobody!"

I nodded as she preached a mighty tribute to my ill-tempered daddy. She paused and gave me a steely stare. "Do you believe me, Mickey?"

"Yes, Mama! Yes!"

She slapped that switch against her palm, still deciding whether to beat me for fighting at church or anoint me as a hero for defending the family's name.

I cried out like one of the old ladies in church who gets the spirit of God on her from time to time. "Oh, yes, Mama. I believe!" Just in case she needed a little more divine inspiration.

She nodded her head. Convinced, she calmed down.

"Well, if you ever doubt that it was an accident, you go ask Uncle Bobby. 'Cause he knows."

"I don't need to ask Uncle Bobby, Mama. I believe *you*. Daddy ain't no killer."

She took a deep breath and pulled her hair back into place. "Let's not tell yo' daddy 'bout this, hear me? We don't need to get him all riled up."

"No, Mama, I won't. Never."

"Good, see ya don't." The beginnings of a smile began to creep across her face as she said. "I hear you only got Michael in the ear."

"Yes ma'am."

"Next time Michael says somethin' like that, I hope he goes home with missing teeth." She turned, swishing that switch through the air like a sword, chuckling as she left the room.

FIVE

FEBRUARY 1961

Nearly eight months passed without Daddy knowing anything about the fight I'd had with Michael Rice at church, then somehow he'd caught wind of it. He and Mama were sitting on the back porch, drinking beer, the blue smoke of their Winstons curling around their heads, like the journey of a lost soul seeking heaven. I could hear his voice get loud from the living room where Harley and I were watching TV.

"Why can't people at that damn church stop spreading lies about me, Dixie Mae?"

"I don't know, Charlie. Gossips, all of them."

I quietly got off the couch and snuck to the back door to listen in.

Daddy said, "I hear Mickey 'bout knocked that kid's ear off."

Mama chuckled. "He done right by you, Charlie. He stood up for 'is daddy."

"Good boy, that Mickey."

I was shocked. Daddy had never told me I was a good boy. Daddy went on, "I should teach 'im how to fight so he does some real damage next time someone lies 'bout me."

Mama got up, ready to change the subject. "Let me get supper started."

I got back into the living room just in time.

Daddy's was right. I gotta learn how to fight better so I can protect my family.

Yelling at each other was just something all of the families in the neighborhood did. The houses were small, built close together, so everyone pretty much knew everyone else's business. While it seemed that Mama and Daddy were crazy about each other, their arguments could be epic. Daddy always had a short fuse, but he seemed angrier after learning about my fight at the church. He thought almost everybody was out to get him, and that spilled over into their marriage. Whatever stable ground there was between them started to slowly crack, like a windshield hit by a rock.

Their voices grew louder and louder, doors slammed harder, and they began calling each other names. I hadn't noticed that before. But by the time I was nine, I was more tuned in to their fighting.

I also noticed that Uncle Bobby was coming over more often too. I liked him coming over because he always gave Harley and me a lot of attention, and we loved it. But I suspect Mama secretly called him, hoping he could calm things down when Daddy got angry. Otherwise, it was a true coincidence that Bobby showed up when the fights got bad. Uncle Bobby was the only one who could calm Daddy down; when Daddy was calm, he was much easier on Harley and me.

Every kid in our neighborhood got spanked by their parents from time to time, and some spankings were more dramatic than others. Mama's weapon of choice was a switch she'd pull off the tree in our backyard. She'd whip that branch through the air like a sword so fast you could hear it. I think she did it mostly to scare us, which it never failed to do. More often than not, though, she could be talked out of applying her "lovin' correction" to our bare asses.

Daddy, on the other hand, was never persuaded or deterred by any of my reasoning. He'd use his open hand, and it stung like a sumbitch. Sure, he might give little Harley a pass, but not me. I hated being spanked, and I'd do or say just about anything to avoid it. To be honest, sometimes I deserved them, but Daddy was quick to assume I was guilty, even when I wasn't.

To make matters worse, Daddy never struck Harley very hard, but Harley cried like one of his fingernails had been pulled out with a rusty pair of pliers. I might've had a few tears in my eyes, but I'd grit my teeth and defy him. I wanted him to know that I was just like him, strong and tough.

A couple of days before Easter in 1961, Daddy missed dinner and didn't call to say he'd be late. Mama was worried and called Bobby to see if there had been any accidents reported, but he said it had been a quiet afternoon and evening.

Bobby showed up at our house just as me and Harley were getting ready for bed. Walking through the door he told Mama, "I've looked at all the places he usually goes but couldn't find him. Sorry, Dixie Mae."

Mama was sitting on the couch, visibly worried and upset. Uncle Bobby sat down next to her. I distracted Harley by moving us into our bedroom to get our pjs on. We were headed to the bathroom to brush our teeth when we heard a loud crash as the front door flew open and banged into the wall.

My daddy's voice ricocheted through the house. "What the hell's going on here?" Peeking down the hallway I could see Daddy's eyes narrowing as he focused on Uncle Bobby, who was sitting right next to Mama on the couch, his arm across her shoulders, trying to comfort her. "Well, ain't this sweet. My best friend and my lovin' wife, together in my own house, behind my back."

Bobby scoffed, as he stood up to face Daddy. "Don't be stupid, Charlie."

"You callin' me stupid, Bobby—old buddy?"

Harley and I were both in the hallway when Mama stood to face Bobby. "Please, Bobby, just go. Please go now."

"But Dixie Mae. What if—"

"I'll be fine. But you gotta get out of here now, okay?"

Before Uncle Bobby could answer, Daddy lost his balance and fell onto the couch where Mama and Bobby had been sitting. You could smell the cheap whiskey and cigarettes all the way down the hall. "Yeah, Bobby, get the hell outta my house!"

Bobby hesitated for a moment, then realized he'd do more harm than good if he stayed. He left, reluctantly.

Daddy turned back to Mama. "You know that boy's still sweet on you, don't ya, Dixie Mae?"

"Come on, Charlie, we've all known each other since we was kids. You know I love 'im like a brother." She said as she sat down next to Daddy.

"Yeah, maybe so, but he's been in love with you since we was all in the tenth grade, and you know it, so don't pretend it ain't true." Daddy reached over and grabbed her arm. "You watch yo'self, Dixie Mae. Understand? 'Cause you don't always act like his sister when yo' around him."

Mama pulled her arm away. "Stop, Charlie. That hurt!"

Harley whispered, "Did you see that?"

I nodded. We'd never seen Daddy be physically rough with Mama before.

Mama stood up and stepped back. Without missing a beat, she switched to her sweet voice. "Charlie, darlin', y'all know yo' the only man I've ever loved, and ever will. There ain't nothin' to worry about—never has been. He was only here tonight 'cause I asked him to look for you when ya didn't come home. He came over to tell me that he looked everywhere but couldn't find you."

Daddy pulled a pack of Camels out of his pocket and lit one. "Don't ever let me find you alone with Bobby again, Dixie Mae. You hear me?"

Mama sat down next to him and snuggled up against his chest. "Where y'all been, Charlie? I been worried sick."

He mumbled something that I couldn't hear from the hall.

"You what?" Mama gasped. "That can't be true." Harley and I leaned forward to catch his next words.

"Yeah, I got fired today. I had to discipline one of my dumbass cadets today for nearly gettin' us killed on a trainin' flight, and my bosses didn't like me slappin' the sumbitch upside his head."

"What the hell are we gonna do now, Charlie? We need that money. We cain't live on what I make down at the Blue Star!" Mama was beginning to panic.

Daddy abruptly stood up. "I'm goin' to bed."

Harley and I scrambled down the hall and into our room. We made it just before Daddy entered the hall to their bedroom, slamming the door behind him.

I tiptoed into the living room where Mama stood, rubbing her arm. She knew we'd been listening in the hall. "What y'all doin', Radar Ears?"

"Nothin'," I stammered.

"If yo' daddy ever catches y'all listenin' in on us, y'all will get beat bad."

I knew Daddy had a temper, but that was the first time I'd ever seen him lay a hand on Mama. I pulled myself up as tall as I could. "Mama, y'all don't have to worry. I'll protect you."

"What ya talkin' 'bout, boy?" her face was a mixture of fear and anger.

I looked down at the red spot on her arm. She looked down and said, "Oh, that! I bumped into the door. Don't worry 'bout it." Her face was as innocent as an angel proclaiming a divine message. If I hadn't seen him grab her with my own eyes, I would have believed her. Smiling, Mama repeated herself. "Yo' daddy won't ever hurt me." She turned around and disappeared into the kitchen.

I couldn't believe that Mama lied to me, right to my face. Why did she pretend? Until that moment, I'd always felt safe with Daddy around because he was strong enough to fight off anyone who might try to hurt us. But now I was afraid of Daddy—and Mama trying to hide what happened added to the fear.

CHAPTER SIX

It can get hot living near a swamp in north Florida in August—as humid and wet as a sauna. It was one of those uncomfortably hot summer days in 1961. Daddy hadn't been able to find a job since being fired as a pilot trainer with the Air Force and was drinking more than ever. He was constantly sniping at Mama, Harley, and me every chance he got. Mama was working night and day at the Blue Star trying to make up for Daddy's lost income. Hoping to raise everybody's spirits and ease the tension in our little household, Mama announced that we would be having a barbeque on Saturday. Since we had yet to have a birthday party to celebrate my tenth birthday, Mama also said she'd bake me a cake.

Me and Harley were playing in the sprinklers, trying like hell to cool off, while Uncle Jimmy and Daddy were drinking beer and smoking those nasty cigars they always smoked on occasions like this. Uncle Bobby couldn't make it because he had to work. Uncle Jimmy—who looked like he'd already had a six-pack before he arrived—and Daddy were sitting in lawn chairs under the shade of an old swamp oak, laughing and talking sports, when the phone rang.

Wiping her hands on her apron, Mama yelled out to Daddy in the yard. "Charlie, can y'all keep an eye on this chicken while I get the phone?" Daddy grunted something unintelligible, and Mama ran off to answer the phone.

Suddenly, the loudest scream I'd ever heard erupted from the house. A moment later Mama came flying out the screen door in a rage. "You a lyin', cheatin' sumbitch, Charlie Crow!"

Running towards him, she saw my birthday cake on the table. Picking it up, she threw it at him like a pitcher looking for the strike zone. Quick as a seasoned fighter slipping a punch, Daddy dodged it as it fell to the ground in pieces, missing its intended target. "What the hell you goin' on about, Dixie Mae?"

She took a swing at him and made contact. "You sumbitch! I been working my ass off tryin' to support us, and you've been screwin' Sandy!" Sandy was the very pretty, very young waitress down at Grandmama's restaurant, the Blue Star Café, where Mama worked and was one of the truckers' favorites. "You cheatin' bastard! I work with her!"

Uncle Jimmy grabbed his beer and disappeared. We heard the engine of his car erupt, and I knew he had hightailed it out of there. Harley and I backed away, not knowing what to do. Daddy jumped at Mama and picked her up, carrying her into the house while she was doing her best to beat his brains out. Me and Harley followed them into the house and watched as Daddy threw Mama on the couch in the living room. He saw us standing there staring back at him in shock at the scene playing out in front of us.

"Get the hell outta here! Both o' y'all!"

I wanted to make sure Mama wasn't hurt so I paused a moment. "Dammit, Mickey, grab yo' brother and get the hell in y'all's room! Right now!"

I was standing there, defiantly, when Harley grabbed me by my arm and yanked me towards our room. I let him pull me a little way down the hallway but stopped him so I could see what was happening in the living room and be sure that Mama was safe.

She kept yelling at Daddy. "You think you can screw 'round, and I won't find out? You really are a dumb sumbitch, you know that?"

"Shut yo' goddamn mouth, Dixie Mae, befo' I shut it for you!"

Mama shot up from the couch where Daddy had thrown her and screamed in his face. "Get out, Charlie! I mean it, get out!"

"You'd like that, wouldn't you Dixie Mae? You think Bobby will ride in on his white horse and take care of you? You really are stupid!"

Mama picked up the glass ashtray sitting on the coffee table and threw it at Daddy's head, only missing him by inches as it shattered into hundreds of pieces on the wall behind him. He stormed at her, grabbed her by the arm, and pushed her to the floor. He raised his hand to slap her across the face, but then he caught my eye looking around the corner of the hallway. That gave Mama the chance she needed to wiggle out of his grasp and crawl across the floor. I slipped down the hall a bit further out of sight.

There was silence, and then I heard the front door slam closed so loud it shook the house and echoed into my soul. What if I hadn't been there? Daddy would have hit her in the face. Without me to protect her, Daddy could hurt Mama bad—*real* bad.

Moving back to the front of the hall, I snuck a peek around the corner again.

"Good! He's gone," I said. Suddenly I felt a push from behind me.

Harley looked frightened. "I don't want Daddy to go, Mickey." His eyes filled with tears. "You think he'll leave us?"

I shrugged my shoulders. "I don't know, Harley, I hope not, fo' yo' sake."

That night, lying in bed reflecting on what had transpired that day, I thought about my birthday cake and celebration. I imagined what other ten-year-old boys did for their birthdays. I was confident of one thing—it wasn't what my family did.

❧

When Daddy didn't come back that night, or the next—or the one after that—I held onto the hope that we'd never see him again. A hope, as it turned out, that was in vain, because a few days later Harley and I were in bed when our bedroom door swung open. I sat bolt upright as Daddy practically fell into the room, reeking of whiskey and cheap cigars.

"Boys, I got some bad news to break on yo' little asses. I'm leavin' yo' mama. So, I guess that means I'm leavin' you too." He said it breezily, like he was saying goodnight to dinner guests. "To tell y'all the truth, I don't know when I'll see y'all again." Harley and I promptly sat up on the edges of our beds, stunned into silence.

He continued in that same casual voice. "Yo' Mama don't deserve a man like me, so I'm movin' out. That woman will get what she deserves." I was bewildered that Daddy could be so cold and casual about leaving us. I looked over at Harley, whose face was twisted with shock. I felt bad for Harley.

Then it was over. No "I love you" or "I'll miss you boys." No hugs, kisses, or pats on the back—he just stumbled out of the room and slammed the door behind him. Harley looked at me and started crying. "Mickey, why's Daddy leavin' us? Did we do somethin' bad?"

I climbed into his bed and put my arm around my little brother. "It's okay, Harley, we didn't do nothin' wrong. Daddy did. We'll be okay. Just go back to sleep, buddy. Close yo' eyes." Harley lay back down and covered his head with his blanket. I heard sniffles for a while, and finally low, rhythmic breathing.

But I couldn't sleep. I shut my eyes and prayed real hard. *Dear God, I don't want Daddy to be my daddy anymore. He's a bad man, and he's mean to Mama. Can you make him go away?*

I knew it wasn't a nice prayer, and I thought praying this prayer should make me feel guilty, but it didn't. Besides, I figured God already knew how I felt, so it wouldn't come as a huge shock to Him anyway.

But an odd thing happened. I actually felt better. You know, like when someone pays attention when you tell a story or when someone laughs at your jokes. It actually felt like God was listening to me. I felt comforted, somehow.

I'll admit that it was a prayer with a lot of passion behind it but not much faith. I didn't actually expect God to answer it, so I was taken completely by surprise by what happened just a few minutes later.

CHAPTER **SEVEN**

PRESENT
FRIDAY, APRIL 21, 1972
3:28 P.M.

Memories overwhelmed me, racing through my mind like one of those carousel slide shows people use to share vacation photos with their friends.

On one hand, I felt guilty leaving Grandma Jean sitting alone under the bean tree as I headed back to Quincy. I could still see her bent over the pan of beans, clearly weighted down by her sadness and grief.

But I was overcome with anger—at Jean for asking me to meet with Charlie after all this time, at Charlie because of all the pain he'd put us through, and at myself, for thinking what I was thinking.

Charlie had never made any effort to make things right with us for what he did. And now he's dyin' and wants me to act like it's okay somehow? Even if I could forgive the sumbitch, why should I? Let him go to meet his Master carrying the full weight of what he's done.

I drove around for a while, going nowhere in particular. Another voice in my mind intruded into my thoughts. *You never wanted to be like Charlie. And look at you now. Angry. Bitter. Unforgiving. What makes you the better man?*

"Shut up!" I yelled aloud and hit the radio knob, turning the music up loud enough to drown out that voice. "I ain't nothin' like Charlie!"

I drove into Quincy, and without intending to, I cruised through familiar streets lined with blooming azaleas, purple cornflowers, and beach sunflowers. Somehow I found myself in front of Grandmama, Grandpa Hank, and Aunt Tootie's house. *Hell, I'm here. I might as well pop in before I drive back home.*

Grandmama was in the shade on the front porch swing that Grandpa Hank had built for her. I got out of the car, trying to silence the argument inside of my head, and headed up the red brick walkway. Grandpa Hank walked out the front door with a sweet tea in each hand. Handing one to Grandmama, he said, "Hey Mickey, just made some tea. Want some?"

"Yeah, Hank, love some."

"Take this one and have a seat in one of the rockin' chairs. I'll be right back." He turned and walked back inside, the screen door loudly shutting behind him like most old screen doors did.

"What ya doing here today, boy? Y'all a week early, aren't ya? My big party is next week." Grandmama seemed concerned.

"Wouldn't miss it for the world, Grandmama. I'll be at church next week, right on time, sittin' next to y'all on our family pew."

Grandmama smiled. "I don't know why they're makin' such a fuss."

"After all you've done for that church, for decades! They'd better appreciate you!" I said.

Hank walked out of the screen door with his own glass of sweet tea. Setting it down on the side table, he leaned over, put his arm around Grandmama, and said, "C'mon baby, give me a little sugar for gettin' you some sweet tea." Grandpa Hank was an affectionate man and didn't care who was watching.

Fussing, Grandmama declined. "Get off me, Hank!" She raised her arms in a defensive posture.

Not one to give up easily, Hank said, "C'mon sugar, just a little kiss. Just a little one, baby."

"Not now, Hank. Not with the boy here."

Hank removed his arm from around Grandmama and picked up his sweet tea. Glancing over at me, he had a gleam in his eye and a smile on his face. Winking, he said, "Got it! Later, when we got more time." Grandmama looked exasperated.

"What y'all doin' here today?" Grandpa Hank asked.

Grandmama nodded. "Just what I asked him."

"I'm just gettin' back from meetin' with Grandma Jean over in Greensboro."

"Jean! What the hell y'all doin' talkin' to her?"

"Jean asked me to come see her. She had somethin' important to talk to me about, so I went."

Before I could say anything else, Aunt Tootie rounded the corner and joined us on the porch. Before she sat down in the rocker next to me, she reached down and gave me a hug. "What the hell you doin' here, boy?"

I threw my hands up in the air. "Can't a guy come and visit his family without the third degree?"

"He just got back from seein' Jean," Grandmama said.

"Jean! What the hell you talkin' to *that* woman for?" asked Tootie.

I began my defense once again. "Grandma Jean asked me over to her farm. She had somethin' important to talk about, so I went."

"Well, quit stallin'," Grandmama said. "What was so damn important?"

"Charlie Crow has got paroled from prison and wants to talk to me."

"He's out of prison? So soon?" Grandmama asked.

I shrugged. "Don't know the details."

"He should be in there for the rest of his life for what he done."

"He's got cancer, and he's dyin' soon, so maybe they let him out early 'cause of that."

"Good riddance!" Tootie said.

Grandmama's face went dark. Hank kept quiet as usual.

"Y'all gonna tell that sumbitch to rot in hell, Mickey?" Tootie asked.

"Shut up, Tootie. It ain't yo' decision to make." Grandmama was giving me some leeway.

"I don't know. I told Jean there was no way I'd talk to 'im, but now, I just don't know." No one said anything for a long moment.

Finally, Hank spoke up. "That's a big decision, Mickey. I know why y'all feel that way, son, but for whatever it's worth, I think you should pray on it. Ask the Lord what you should do. Cain't go wrong with that."

I was taken aback a bit. Grandpa Hank never commented on things like this.

Tootie had an altogether different solution. "Well, if it was me, I'd tell the sumbitch to hurry up and die already. The world would be a better place without 'im!"

Grandmama stood up and set her half-empty glass of sweet tea on the side table. "Let us know what y'all decide, Mickey." She walked inside. The matriarch had spoken.

Tootie and Hank sat awkwardly for a few moments, and then followed her inside. As far as they were concerned, the conversation was over.

I sat there alone; my stomach tied in knots. I thought about what Tootie had said last. It was almost word for word what I said to Grandma Jean, but hearing it from someone else, it sounded harsh and unforgiving. After a few minutes, it was clear no one was coming back, so I walked to my truck, got in, and headed back home. As I drove, my mind drifted back to the night that Daddy had walked out on us as if we were trash to him, the turbulence of that night reeling through my mind once again.

EIGHT

AUGUST 1961

I finished my prayer and was listening to Harley sleep while my insides twisted and churned. Then, I heard Mama cry out, "No! Charlie! No!"

Sneaking down the hall, I stopped and slid down the wall to peek around the corner. I saw Daddy standing by the door with a packed suitcase in one hand and his golf clubs over his shoulder. "You're a bitch, Dixie Mae," he snarled, venom dripping from his tongue. "Just a good for nothin', white trash, back-seat Betty."

Mama fell to her knees and started crying. "I ain't never cheated on you, Charlie. Don't leave me."

"Yo' worthless Dixie Mae, always workin' and always too tired. Ain't no mystery why I'd find a woman that knows how to satisfy a man like me." Mama gasped at the insult.

"I'm done with you, Dixie Mae!"

Mama wailed loudly, full of grief. "I was mad, Charlie. I don't *really* want you to go."

I couldn't believe what I was hearing. Scared and in shock, I snuck into their bedroom and picked up the phone on the side table next to their bed. I quickly dialed the sheriff's station and asked for Bobby Bailey. After a minute, I heard Uncle Bobby's voice. "This is Deputy Bailey."

"Uncle Bobby, come quick. Daddy says he's leavin' us. They're yellin' and screamin'. I think he might hurt Mama."

"Is he drunk, Mickey?"

"Yessir, real drunk." I paused a moment. "And he cheated on Mama."

"Hang tight, Mickey, I'm on my way."

By the time I got back into the hall, Harley was waiting for me, his eyes huge with fear.

"Is he gonna hurt Mama?"

"I called Uncle Bobby. He's comin'. It'll be okay."

Harley took my hand and held it tight.

In the living room, Mama's groveling had turned to rage. She grabbed for daddy's golf bag, caught it, and pulled hard. "You ain't goin' nowhere you low-life bastard," she yelled at the top of her lungs. They struggled. The bag gave way, turned upside down, and spilled every last one of the clubs onto the black and white terrazzo floor. Daddy walked over to where Mama was standing and pushed her so hard that she fell against the sofa and hit the side of her face on the wooden edge of an arm of the couch. I heard a loud crack, and she slid off the sofa onto the ground—stunned.

"Dixie Mae?" He leaned over her, seeming concerned, but when she opened her eyes, he turned away in disgust.

He picked up his golf bag and recovered all the clubs. Mama groaned and rubbed her head while he placed the clubs in their proper compartments, and casually began to walk to the door, not looking back at his wife. When he opened the door, he ran directly into Uncle Bobby's big chest.

"What the hell you doin' here, Bobby?"

"We got a call down at the station from your neighbor across the street," Bobby lied. "They say there's all kinds of yellin' and fightin' coming from y'all's house, so I took the call. Looks like I was too late, though." He said, looking past Daddy and seeing Mama on the floor.

Harley stood frozen in the hallway, while I ran to Mama who was trying to get up but Uncle Bobby beat me to it. He got his shoulder under her arm and helped her back onto the sofa, gently pushing her hair off her face. "Dixie Mae, your nose and mouth are bleeding."

Uncle Bobby looked up at Charlie with murder in his eyes. "You hit her?" he said, more a statement than a question.

"Nah," Daddy snarled, "I pushed her."

Bobby held her head, and when he pulled back his hand, there was blood on it. He glared at Daddy. "You didn't need to hit her or push her Charlie." Bobby growled, "She's bleedin' all the same, ain't she? I never thought—"

"You never thought what, Bobby?" Daddy growled.

Bobby didn't answer. Through a half-closed and swollen eye, Mama looked at him. Confused, she mumbled, "Wha-what, Bobby? What y'all doin' here?"

He turned to me. "Mickey, go get a wet rag for your Mama and hurry back." Daddy just looked on, like a visitor who'd just walked in as the scene played out in front of him.

"She told me to get out, so I'm gettin' out!"

Dashing past Harley into the bathroom, I picked up a washcloth and ran it under some hot water like I'd seen Mama do whenever Harley or I got hurt. I hurried back to where she was sitting on the sofa and sat next to her. "Here, Mama, try this."

Mama looked surprised to see me. Then she glanced at the wet rag. "Oh, thanks, Mickey." She began wiping the blood from her split lip and nose, wincing as she did so.

Suddenly, Uncle Bobby moved. He shoved Daddy up against the door, and in a low, but very menacing voice, he said, "We've been friends for a long time, Charlie, but I'm done coverin' for you."

"What y'all gonna do, Bobby? Throw me in jail?"

Bobby poked Daddy hard in the chest. "I see your clubs and bags sittin' by the door. Best you take 'em Charlie and leave." Bobby stood back to give Daddy some room, but Daddy didn't budge.

Bobby leaned in. "Listen here, old buddy, you're not walkin' out of this house just for one night. I'm filing a restrainin' order against you first thing in the mornin'. This changes everything between us, Charlie. Don't get anywhere near Dixie Mae or her boys or I will throw your sorry ass in jail."

Daddy looked like he was going to say something else to Bobby, but instead, picked up his clubs and suitcase. He looked over his shoulder at me and Harley. "Bye, boys. This is the last y'all will ever see of yo' daddy."

Uncle Bobby sat down on the other side of Mama. She seemed oblivious to the blood slowly oozing across her lip. She put down the rag and lit up a Winston, exhaling some of the foul blue smoke. "Thanks, Bobby, for lookin' out for us."

Bobby put his arms around her. She leaned into his chest and burst into tears.

I held my breath, feeling scared that Daddy might walk back in and see Mama and Uncle Bobby together. But then I comforted myself. *Uncle Bobby could beat the shit out of Daddy if he ever wanted to.*

I let out a huge gust of air and realized that I was glad Daddy was gone and glad Uncle Bobby was there to help us. It seemed like God had answered my prayers after all.

A few minutes later, Mama pushed off of Uncle Bobby and sat up straight. "I think I'd like to go to bed now. I'm wrung out, you know?"

"Sure do, Dixie Mae." He helped her up from the sofa. "Do you know where Charlie was goin' tonight?" he asked.

"I don't know. He's been screwin' Sandy. Maybe he'll go stay with her for a while. Who gives a shit?" Mama looked at Uncle Bobby with suspicion. "He didn't talk to you 'bout this? You know, guy talk?"

Bobby looked offended. "No, we had lunch a few days ago, but he never said he was cheatin' on you."

"Humph!" Mama wasn't fully buying it.

As an afterthought, Uncle Bobby remembered something. "He did say he had some guy talkin' to him about flyin' in cargo from the Bahamas."

"That's news to me."

Bobby nodded. "You know he didn't like you payin' all the bills around here—said it seemed like you're the one wearing the pants in the family now."

"Well, looks like the bastard's been keepin' his pants under Sandy's bed." Mama turned and headed for her bedroom.

"Dixie Mae, I'll check up on you and the boys tomorrow. I'll need yo' signature on the restrainin' order so I can keep him away from you."

"Well, we'll see, Bobby," Mama said without turning around. She disappeared down the hallway.

Bobby finally noticed Harley leaning up against the hallway corner and walked over to him. "It's gonna be okay, Harley. Let's get you back into bed," he said. Harley took his hand and followed him silently down the hall.

I stayed in the living room. I wasn't ready to go to bed just yet. I wanted to ask Uncle Bobby a question. He returned and sat next to me on the couch. "Mickey, I'm sorry you and Harley had to go through all this tonight—no kid should see their daddy and mama fight like that."

"Can I ask you somethin'?"

"Sure, Mickey. You can ask me anything."

"Do you think my daddy is a murderer?"

Uncle Bobby's head snapped back like someone had slapped him across his face. Sitting there quietly for a moment, he finally asked, "You think your daddy's a killer?"

"I don't know. Maybe he killed Grandpa Willie, or maybe it was just an accident. But Daddy can get so mad and mean. I just don't know who to believe, 'specially after tonight."

"Look, Mickey, ain't no secret that your Daddy's got a nasty temper. Always has. But your daddy and I have been best friends since we was kids. I know just about everything there is to know about 'im. We've always told each other the truth."

I sighed. "But I never seen him like he was tonight."

"Mickey, I just don't think that Charlie could kill somebody. Lose his temper? Sure. But kill 'im on purpose? Nah, I just don't think so. He told me that Willie fell out of the boat when he tripped trying to hit Jimmy. Jimmy says that's exactly what happened, and I got no reason to think it was anything else. In a way, Willie did it to himself, trying to hurt Jimmy. He was a mean old man Mickey; I think he deserved what he got."

My eyes were wide open. I saw the scene in my mind as if it were a movie. "That's kinda how it was with Harley, huh? When he stood up and almost fell in."

"That's right, Mickey. Y'all's granddaddy had been drinking all day while they were fishing. He got mean, took a swing at Jimmy; he just lost his balance and fell in."

We sat there in silence for a moment. Then I continued the story as if I'd been there. "I'll bet he fell into that muddy water, and he just disappeared."

"That's exactly what yo' daddy said. He just disappeared under that black water. Charlie grabbed an oar and tried fishin' around for 'im but couldn't find 'im. Then Willie's head just popped up and when he tried to grab the oar, a huge gator sprung up outta nowhere and grabbed your granddaddy by the legs. Charlie says he and Jimmy grabbed Willie by the arms and for a minute, them and the gator were in a tug of war, until the beast started spinnin' and flailin' its tail—almost pulled them in too! The gator disappeared with Willie and that was the last they saw either one of 'em."

"The gator ate Grandpa Willie."

"Yep. When the water quieted down, Charlie said the silence was eerie until Jimmy started cryin'. Charlie started rowin' that jon boat as fast as he could to get outta there." I closed my eyes to shut out the image in my head.

"And Mickey," Uncle Bobby put his hand on my shoulder, "y'all's daddy was never the same after that. Y'all weren't born yet, so you wouldn't know what he was like before Willie died. Yeah, he was always a hellraiser, but not like he is now."

Bobby paused as if thinking things through. "Mickey, I never thought Charlie would hurt yo' mama like this. He's gettin' worse. I think seeing your granddaddy die that way really screwed both of those boys up. Jimmy's been a drunk ever since, tryin' to forget, I guess, and your daddy's been slowly sinkin' into some kind of horrible, private hell."

I almost felt bad for my daddy then, but only for a moment. *That doesn't give him the right to take it out on us.*

"For your mama's sake, Mickey, try to understand. Okay?"

"Understand?" All I felt was a cold, dark rage growing in the pit of my stomach, aimed at Daddy for hurting my mama, Harley, and me.

"I'll keep him away from you until I'm sure he won't do it again." Uncle Bobby kneeled down to look me in the eyes. "Once he sees what he did to y'all, he'll change, I know it. He loves your mama. I'm gonna give 'im another chance, Mickey."

I stared at his gentle eyes, hoping he didn't see the rage in mine. *I hate my daddy for what he did.*

He rustled my hair. "No matter what happens to Charlie, y'all's Dixie's boys, so whatever y'all need, you call me up. Okay?'

"Yes, sir, Uncle Bobby." I looked at his kind face and then blurted out, "I wish y'all was our daddy, Uncle Bobby!"

He gave me a hug and smiled tenderly. His voice broke a little. "I'm here if you need me, Mickey." He stood up and left, shutting the door quietly behind him.

I turned out the lights, headed for my room, and climbed into bed. Little Harley was fast asleep, but I lay there thinking for a long time. I wanted nothin' more than for Daddy to leave and never come back. Maybe he would leave us alone now. *I gotta grow bigger so I can take care of Mama and Harley. Bobby can give him another chance, but not me. It's up to me to protect my mama and Harley now.*

PRESENT

SATURDAY, APRIL 22, 1972

4:28 A.M.

I'd gotten back to my own place after the day trip to Quincy, fixed some dinner, and watched a little TV. I don't remember what was playing because all I could think of was Charlie. I finally went to bed, but sleep was hard to come by. I'd tossed and turned, and when I did sleep, I had a vivid nightmare about me as a boy asking Bobby if he thought Charlie had killed Grandpa Willie. Bobby's face mutated into Charlie's and the couch we were sitting on turned into a boat. Down at my feet was Grandpa Willie thrashing about while Charlie strangled him. I yelled "Stop!" but Charlie kept going until Grandpa Willie stopped moving, then he grabbed him up and started to dump his body into the black waters of the swamp.

I yelled "Stop!" again and woke myself with the sound of my own voice. I was covered in sweat, chilled to the bone, and shaking uncontrollably. It took me a few moments to fully wake up and pull myself out of the nightmare. I looked through a crack in the curtains and saw that it was just before daybreak. Giving up the idea of falling back to sleep, I got up, washed my face, and made some coffee.

By the time the sun came up, I'd decided that I would go back and talk to Grandma Jean again. I took a long shower, trying to get the sweat off my body and horror out of my head, then got dressed. I called Grandma Jean and told her I wanted to come out and talk to her some more.

"I'll be here, Mickey. Just c'mon out anytime," she said.

I stopped at a café in Greensboro, where Jean lived, and grabbed some breakfast before driving out to her farm.

She saw me coming when I turned into her long dirt driveway.

"I didn't think I'd see y'all so soon after our last talk, but I'm glad yo' here, Mickey. I really am. C'mon out here under the bean tree, and we'll sit and talk a spell. You can help me snap some beans. Think y'all still 'member how to do that?"

"Hell, yeah, Grandma Jean, I still remember."

We sat down and made small talk for a while, and Grandma Jean handed me a bag of beans to work on while we did. Snapping those beans was a blast from the past. They smelled so fresh—I could just imagine them smothered in butter with some bacon pieces in them, the way Grandmama used to make them for Sunday supper. It was cool, and breezy, and part of me wanted to just enjoy the sweet, slow rhythm that was part of life in the South and forget about the real purpose of my visit. But I knew I had to get to it.

Before I could say anything, though, Jean said, "You know he's livin' over in Gretna. Did y'all know that? It's only a half hour away."

"No offense, Grandma Jean, but honestly, I was hopin' the sumbitch was dead. I was kind of sorry to hear he's not." I felt anger rise up again and wasn't thinking at all about what my words might do to Grandma Jean. I cringed a little at how it sounded coming out of my mouth.

"I take no offense, Mickey. I surely don't. I have an idea what he did to yo' mama and to you." She spoke softly and kindly and with what I thought might be some regret. "It was terrible. I knew he beat yo' mama and slapped y'all 'round some, and I'm sorry. I should'a tried to stop 'im, but I didn't know how."

She sat there for some time, silently snapping beans in half and tossing them into a paper bag.

"Mickey, I know Charlie's done a lot of bad things in his life. It wasn't all his fault though. His daddy was one mean ol' sumbitch. He beat Charlie within an inch of his life. Many times. He'd even made him watch while he beat me with a strap, when he was just a small child. And he made him watch while he beat his brother. I should'a left the bastard, but I was too 'fraid he'd kill me if I did."

It was my turn to be silent, as I took all this in. "Damn, Grandma Jean, I had no idea. None."

"No way for you to know it, Mickey. Charlie had come home from servin' in the Air Force and it was obvious he wasn't gonna take any more of Willie's crap."

I paused for a moment. "Grandma Jean, do you think that Grandpa's death was an accident or—"

"I don't rightly know, Mickey. I know what the boys tol' me—that it *was* an accident. But I cain't tell you if that's the whole story or not. Charlie hadn't been home from the service but a couple of weeks. He came home tougher. Angrier. Like I said he wasn't gonna take shit from anybody, especially his Daddy." She paused and looked at me for a moment.

I had a sense of how Charlie must have felt. The Navy hadn't calmed me down—only made me angrier and all the more determined to stand up for myself. Looking into her eyes, I wondered if she sensed the same thing in me that she saw in Charlie all those years ago.

She went on with her story. "Charlie tol' me and Jimmy that Willie was never gonna lay another hand on any of us. I'm tellin' you, boy, he meant it. To be honest, it scared me some—it really did."

"Charlie already had a mean streak befo' he left, but it was worse after boot camp and all that military trainin'. He grew up around guns, ya know. We all did. But when he was servin' in the Air Force, he was on their High-Powered Rifle Team. Jimmy tole me once that he and Charlie was messin' around with Willie's gun out by the cow pins, shootin' at some ol' bottles and cans. He said the way Charlie handled Willie's ol' Colt scared the holy shit outta him. All I know for sure is that Charlie told us the truth. Willie never got another chance to hurt us."

She kept snapping beans as if that would spare her the feelings she was having.

I sat back in my chair. "I think that's a hell of a coincidence, Grandma Jean. You know, I had a dream that Charlie killed Grandpa Willie."

She looked up. "You saw him do that in a dream?"

I nodded. "Last night."

Grandma Jean stopped and put her hands in her lap. "I believe the Lord speaks to us through dreams, Mickey." Her eyes filled up with tears. "I just don't want to believe Charlie could do somethin' like that."

"I understand. I want it to be an accident too."

Grandma Jean went back to her beans. "Maybe he did. Maybe he didn't. If he's asked, he'll say what he already tol' me, so if he did, we'll never know." She had to ask. "So, will you see 'im Mickey, befo' he dies?"

"I don't know, Grandma Jean, I just don't know. But I promise that I'm thinkin' about it, I really am. I'll let you know what my decision is soon, okay?"

"Well, okay then, let me know. But Mickey? Don't wait too long."

I said my goodbyes and got back into the truck. Driving off, my heart suddenly filled with rage for what Charlie had done to all of us, and maybe to his own father.

There were a lot of questions I had for Charlie—questions I needed answers to. If I decided to meet with him, this could be my last chance to get those answers. But then, again, I couldn't trust Charlie to tell me the truth about anything. What was the point? Would I square off with the man I hated with every fiber of my being? I just didn't know—not yet, anyway.

TEN

| AUGUST 1961

The morning after Charlie left, Mama got drunk, gathering up as many bottles of booze she could carry, then locked herself in her room. Harley and I could hear her crying, then screaming with rage, then crying some more.

Early that evening, Uncle Bobby came over with the papers Mama needed to sign for the restraining order. He asked us where she was, and I pointed to her bedroom door.

"She's in there cryin' and drinkin' and won't come out." I said it matter-of-factly. I had no faith Mama would sign those papers.

Walking over he yelled into the closed door. "Dixie Mae, I've done all the work for you. All you need to do is come out here and sign these papers, and then Charlie will have to stay away from you and the boys."

She screamed through the door. "What's that damn paper going to do to protect us? If he wants to come in here, he'll just knock the door down."

"But then I can put him in jail, Dixie Mae."

She laughed a wicked laugh. "Yeah? How long's it gonna take you to get here, Bobby?"

"Open the door, Dixie Mae. At least talk to me about it." No luck. Uncle Bobby tried for over an hour to reason with her, guilt-trip her, and scare her, but, as I expected, he lost that battle. Exasperated, he finally left, slamming the front door behind him.

The next day, Aunt Tootie finally called. "What's goin' on over there, Mickey? Dixie Mae didn't show up for her shift at the Blue Star today."

"I don't know, Aunt Tootie. Mama's locked herself in her bedroom and won't come out."

"I'll be right over."

I'd made me and Harley peanut butter and jelly sandwiches for dinner, and we were eating in front of the TV when Tootie burst through the front door. She wasn't happy. In fact, she was livid. "Where's y'all's mama?"

"In her bedroom with the door locked." Harley confirmed with satisfaction. My response was a nod of agreement, then we went back to watching TV.

"How long?"

I shrugged. "A couple of days."

"She drinkin'?"

I rolled my eyes. "What do you think, Aunt Tootie?"

She went down the hall and banged on Mama's door. "Open up, Dixie Mae! Get the hell outta that bed! Y'all missed your shift!"

Mama yelled something I couldn't quite make out, but I'm sure it wasn't particularly polite. Tootie kept pounding. "Y'all want to know what people are sayin' about you at the café?" No answer. "Well, I'll tell you, whether you care or not. They sayin' y'all always been the fool when it comes to Charlie. He's rotten to the core, but y'all the fool in this story."

Mama yelled something I still couldn't understand.

"That's right, Dixie Mae. Everybody's laughin' at you behind your back. It's embarrassin' to me and Mama. But there's nothin' we can say, is there? Yo' playin' the fool, cryin' your heart out over that bastard."

Silence.

Tootie paused. She hadn't expected that. "You okay, Dixie Mae?"

The door swung open and smashed into the wall. "Why the hell should I care about what they're sayin' about me?" Mama flew out of her room, past Tootie, and into the living room.

Tootie shrugged. "Don't bother me none, Dixie Mae. But everybody knows yo' missin' work, and that yo' cryin' and drinkin' in your bedroom. Boo-the-hell-hoo!"

Mama held her head up high. "I don't give a good goddamn what those bitches think of me." Mama did whatever she wanted, so I knew that was true. She never gave a damn what other women thought about her. She knew they were all afraid she could take their men, if she wanted to.

But one thing she couldn't abide was anybody thinking a man had gotten the better of her. "Bitches!" Mama declared and stormed into the hall.

Aunt Tootie sat down beside us on the couch and smiled. "She'll be okay now."

We nodded.

Aunt Tootie looked at what we were eating. "You boys cain't live on this shit." She got up and headed for the kitchen. "I'll fix y'all something worth eatin'."

"Y'all the best, Tootie!" Harley and I said it at the same time, and we meant it.

By the first week of September, Mama had completely sobered up. She held her head high and strutted back to work at the Blue Star during the day. She also began bartending at night at the swanky Savannah Country Club, or, as the locals called it, "The Savannah." She said she could make more in two days at The Savannah than she could all week at the Blue Star, and with Daddy gone, we needed the money.

One afternoon in late September she met a real estate broker named Mel Harris at The Savannah. He was impressed with her people skills and thought she would make a great real estate agent, so he encouraged her to get her real estate license and spent a lot of time helping her study to pass the exam.

"Boys!" Mama yelled from the living room. "Y'all seen my keys?"

I was getting ready for school. "Nope, why would I know where they are?"

"Y'all watch yo' smart mouth, Mickey. Yo' daddy may be gone, but I can still beat yo' ass."

"Yes, ma'am."

"Get yo'self and yo' brother off to school. I got a big day today. Takin' the real estate license test."

I shrugged.

"You don't get it, do ya, Mickey? It's real important that I pass this test. It could mean more money for all of us—a lot more money."

"Sorry, Mama. I hope you pass!"

"Found 'em," she said, grabbing her keys from between the couch cushions. "Tootie's comin' over tonight to celebrate me passin' the test."

"You sure y'all gonna pass, Mama? Tests are hard—at least they are for me."

Mama's face lit up with a beautiful smile that glowed with confidence. "Damn right, I'm sure. Don't y'all know I always get what I go after?"

Tootie showed up early to fix dinner, knowing that Mama wouldn't want to cook after taking the real estate exam and working an afternoon shift at The Savannah. Right at dinner time, Mama sailed in and took a bow. I hadn't seen her smile like that in a long time. "Y'all are lookin' at an official real estate agent who's gonna make a shit load o' money! I also got a secret to tell y'all after dinner."

"What secret, Mama? What is it?" Harley jumped in.

"No, not now. After dinner."

Looking at Aunt Tootie, I asked, "You know what the secret is, Tootie?"

She shook her head no, looking at Mama with confusion on her face. "I ain't got no idea, so y'all go wash up and get to the table so we can all find out. Scoot, boy, run!"

I was on my third biscuit when I looked over at Tootie and Harley. It was clear they were both thinking about the same thing I was. *What was Mama's secret?*

Harley blurted out, "We gonna get a dog, Mama? Mickey, we gonna get a dog!"

Mama shot that down in a hurry. "Sorry, Harley, but we ain't gettin' a dog."

His face fell. "I sure wish we had a dog."

Aunt Tootie's face lit up. "Maybe she takin' us all on a summer vacation—someplace excitin' like Miami Beach!"

Mama grinned. "Well, yo' close, Tootie!"

I gasped with hope. "Does it have water?"

"Even better than that, Mickey." I couldn't imagine anything better than a vacation on a beach.

"I bought a house on a lake, and we're movin' there!"

Harley and I jumped out of our seats and spun around the kitchen, squealing with delight.

"What, Dixie Mae?" Aunt Tootie was stunned. "What y'all been up to?"

Mama confirmed. "Like I said, I'm buyin' a house out on Lake Irene, off Highbridge Road right outside of Quincy. Nice little neighborhood, right on the water. Y'all will love it!" She was preaching to the choir as soon as she said lake.

"How did you do that?" Aunt Tootie wasn't convinced. "Ya just got your license today, right?"

"That's right," Mama said.

"How'd ya get enough money to buy a house?"

Mama stuck her chin in the air. "Mel lent me some money against future commissions. He believes in me. He knows I can do it."

"Mel lent you some money?" Tootie said suspiciously.

Mama laughed. "Hell, yeah, he did! That boy knows a good thing when he sees it."

Aunt Tootie smiled. "Well, if anybody can get a man to do what she wants…" Her voice trailed off. "So, when you movin'?"

"*We* are movin', Tootie. I want you to quit the Blue Star and come live with us! It'll help me if you'd watch Harley and Mickey while I was workin' these long hours."

Harley and I couldn't believe our ears. "Say yes, Aunt Tootie! Say yes!"

Aunt Tootie grabbed us into her arms. "Damn, Dixie Mae. Y'all ain't gotta ask me twice! I been lookin' for an excuse to quit workin' at the café. I love bein' with these rascals! Boys, it looks like we all movin' to the lake!"

Mama and Tootie stood up and hugged and cried for a long time—two sisters clinging to each other like it was the end of the world. At last, they let go and wiped their eyes.

Aunt Tootie looked at her sister again, but with a serious expression. "Now, you promise me that you'll never take Charlie back again. I ain't gonna move in with you only to have that sumbitch show up at the door."

Mama put her hand up in the air as if swearing in court. "I'll never take him back. Ever!" I wondered if that was a promise she would keep. I hoped so.

Tootie looked at us boys with a big grin on her face. "Okay, then. Boys, let's finish off the rest of this chicken-fried steak. Who wants another biscuit?" We spent the rest of the evening making plans for our new house on the lake.

Later that night, after supper, Tootie pulled me aside. "What y'all think about this, Mickey? And don't bullshit me, boy!"

"Well, ya know Mama's been real sad since Daddy left."

"Yeah, I know."

"The thing is, Aunt Tootie, so has Harley. He's really missin' his daddy."

"What 'bout you, boy?"

"Naw, I'm glad he's gone, Tootie. Really glad."

"I understand," she said softly, pushing my hair from my sleepy eyes. "Time for bed, Mickey. I'll be movin' in with y'all real soon."

Somehow, I felt safer knowing that Aunt Tootie would be living with us. I knew that she couldn't protect us physically from Daddy if he decided to break into our house, but there's safety in numbers. Four against one seemed like the best odds we'd had in a long time.

CHAPTER ELEVEN

We moved into our new home on Lake Irene in late October. Fall was in the air and the leaves were turning that orange and red color that said Halloween was just around the corner. When Harley and I got out of the car we were immediately caressed by the begonias, blue daze, and night blooming jasmine, that filled the front yard of our new home. We laughed with delight as we made our way down to the lake's edge.

"This is so great, Mickey!"

"You bet it is, Harley! I think this is gonna be the best time of our lives!" Having Tootie around made it all the better. It was like heaven, it really was.

The house was much larger than what we'd been used to living in and it made us feel like we were living in a fancy summer resort. While it wasn't new, it was so clean and bright white that it felt new. It had these cool, deep green awnings over the windows and doors in the front the of house. It had a great patio with a cover and the lake was right there. It was so close that we could hear the water lapping against the shore from our porch. I knew right away that I never wanted to leave this place.

As Tootie, Harley, and I worked to get settled in our new home, Mama spent her time showing model homes to wealthy people looking to buy in a ritzy part of Gadsden County. She shared how much she liked working for Mel at the real estate office and at The Savannah because she met so many influential people. Being who she was, most folks just warmed right up to her, especially the men, who liked looking at her long, tanned legs. Their wives were, let's say, less warm, and it didn't help her reputation with the ladies when they found out she was newly separated. Mama said she didn't care what they thought—she was determined to launch a "real career," as she called it.

Aunt Tootie said to me and Harley, "Y'all might not know this about yo' mama, but once she puts her mind to somethin', ain't nothin' gonna get in her way." We believed it.

Our new home was just on the outskirts of Quincy, in the county, and was only fifteen minutes from Grandmama and Grandpa Hank's place, still close enough that Grandmama insisted we attend Mt. Calvary Baptist church every Sunday. Harley and I liked going to church though, especially Sunday School where Mr. Mann made his Bible stories come to life. And we got to see our friends from the old neighborhood, at least the ones that attended Mt. Calvary.

Mama loved her Sundays off and stayed behind while Aunt Tootie took over driving us to church on Sunday mornings. It was a safer trip, but Harley but I really missed Grandmama's thrill rides.

I don't think Aunt Tootie liked going to church much because she would drop us off and come back a couple of hours later to pick us up. I asked her one time why she didn't come in. "I don't fit in with these people, Mickey. They look down on me."

"No, they don't!" I insisted. "Who cares about them anyway? It's God's house, not theirs."

Tootie got a sad look in her eyes. "God don't have much use for me either, Mickey."

"That ain't right, Tootie! Mr. Mann says God will forgive you of your sins if you just confess."

Aunt Tootie mumbled, "I won't be doin' that any time soon boy, no sir."

I was scared my Aunt Tootie would end up in hell, and I'd be heartbroken if we weren't together. "Aunt Tootie, God loves everybody, and everybody means you too."

"No, not everyone. Not people who do more wrong than God can forgive."

"Tootie, you ain't done nothin' wrong!"

Her sad eyes were replaced by an icy stare that I'd never seen before. Something inside me said it was time to shut up about it, so I did, and didn't bring it up again.

Even though Grandmama insisted we go to church, Mama said it was too far for us to go over to Grandmama's for dinner every Sunday. I didn't think that was true, so at first, Harley and I were really mad about that. But Mama created a Sunday tradition of her own, and in some ways it was better. By the time we got back from church, Mama would have our old metal drum grill fired up, with the coals red and hot—ready for action. She'd stack it with ribs and chicken and let it cook all day. Aunt Tootie wasn't to be outdone. She whipped up her mac and cheese, collard greens, biscuits, and pecan pie to supplement Mama's smoked ribs and chicken. And Uncle Bobby showed up most Sundays bringing some kind of treat for us boys—a box of Cracker Jacks or Bazooka Bubble Gum.

Both Mama and Aunt Tootie enjoyed Uncle Bobby's company, even though he only had eyes for my mama. He seemed to be the only man that Aunt Tootie was comfortable around, and she let her guard down around him. There was plenty of laughter and relaxed conversation.

After supper, it was time to dance. Mama would turn on her beloved console stereo and ask, "Which one of you gentlemen is gonna ask yo' mama to dance?"

"I will," I'd yell as I jumped up and took my position.

"You a fine dancer, Mickey. A fine dancer." She shook and shimmied her way across the old wood floors in the living room.

"I wanna dance too!" Then Harley would take his turn in our mama's arms.

Mama would dance with both of us at once sometimes and it was great fun. Uncle Bobby wasn't much of a dancer, but he volunteered to oversee the record selection and did a damn fine job of it too. Tootie loved to dance though, especially to her lord and savior, Elvis Presley. She had every one of his records and knew the words of every one of his songs. She was so funny and made Harley and me laugh until we fell on the floor with tears streaming from our eyes, as she pretended to be "the great one"—swivel hips and all. Harley and I always felt loved and safe when the five of us were together.

Mama fought hard to keep her Sundays free. She came home from the real estate office one Saturday looking like the cat who swallowed the canary.

"C'mon, Dixie Mae," Aunt Tootie called out as Mama stepped through the door. "We just started supper. What's makin' y'all so happy?"

Please, don't let it have anything to do with Daddy.

She set down her papers and purse, went into the bathroom to wash her hands, and joined us at the table.

"Ah, Mel tried to sweet talk me out of my only day off." She made her voice deep. "He said, 'Dixie, yo' the best salesman I got 'round here. I need y'all to start workin' on Sundays—startin' tomorrow.'"

"I said, 'Cain't do it, Mel. Y'all know that.'"

"He wouldn't give up. 'Why not, dammit? Don't pretend like you go to church or somethin'!'"

"I laughed. 'Church? Nah. Look, Mel, I got two hands, two legs, two boys, two jobs, and one day off, and that's Sunday. Sorry, Mel, but no can do.'"

"Mel was incensed. 'Well, Dixie, if you cain't work on Sundays, then I'm gonna have to let you go.'"

"You gettin' fired, Mama?" I asked.

Mama smiled. "Hell no, Mickey. I said to him, as sweetly as I could, 'Mel, bless yo' heart. You and I both know that you ain't gonna fire me. Y'all just said I'm yo' number one salesman, didn't ya?'"

"Good one, Dixie Mae!" Tootie laughed, almost choking on a biscuit.

Mama continued. "Mel just bobbed his head up and down. Bless his heart, he knew he'd lost this one. He just fell back in his chair and yelled, 'Dammit, Dixie Mae! Okay, see y'all next Saturday.'"

CHAPTER TWELVE

Harley, now in the third grade, and I, in fifth, walked the few blocks to our new school, Gadsden Elementary. Even though it was a new school for us, we knew some of the kids there because they went to Sunday School at Mt. Calvary Baptist Church too. With their help, we made friends quickly. School days were full of dodgeball and kickball games when we weren't in class. All the kids looked forward to Friday afternoons when Principal Stephens would show serial movies the last hour of the day in the cafeteria. *Flash Gordon*, *Gunfighters of The Northwest*, *Pirates of the High Seas*, and *Zorro's Black Whip* kept us all on the edge of our seats and longing for the next Friday afternoon when the cliffhanger from last week would be resolved.

After-school hours were filled with marbles contests, football games, and anything else our fertile little minds could come up with. Aunt Tootie took good care of me and Harley, while Mama worked hard at her jobs. Sundays were the best, of course. It was Mama's day off, so barbequing, dancing, and Tootie's desserts were always on our Sunday itinerary.

While the memories and bruises of my daddy's violence began to fade away like the autumn leaves falling from the trees around our house, my hatred of him became a cold, hard lump in the pit of my stomach. "Why didn't he love us?" I'd ask myself while waiting for sleep to take me somewhere far away. "Why'd he have to be such a mean sumbitch?" It just never made sense to my ten-year-old brain or heart.

But all in all, our little family was happy, and, most importantly, we felt safe. I began to feel like it would always be that way, and I leaned into it, hoping it was so.

APRIL 1962

Fifth grade passed easily and happily, and we'd just returned to school after Easter break. It was cooler than usual that Spring when I awakened to the heavenly aroma of bacon. After I finished my bathroom ritual, I headed for the kitchen. As I got closer, I heard Mama and Tootie talking about Daddy. No one had mentioned him for months, so it surprised me. I stopped at the end of the hallway and listened to their conversation, peeking around the corner just enough to see that neither one of them looked happy.

"Damn, I hate that man, Dixie Mae. I told y'all he was a bad apple 'fore you married the bastard."

"Yeah, I know, Tootie. You've mentioned it a time or two over the years. It's old news."

"But after Charlie killed—"

Mama cut her off.

"Goddamnit, Tootie, why do ya keep bringin' this up? Let it go!"

Tootie sighed. "I ain't thought about him for the longest time, but the other day I was looking at Harley. Don't he look a lot like his Daddy?"

Mama agreed. "He does. All the more reason to stop sayin' Charlie is a murderer. If y'all gonna stay here, I don't wanna hear that shit again. You got it?" Mama's face was hard, and she was clenching her teeth, "I mean it, Tootie. Tell that bullshit lie again and you can go on back and live with Mama. I don't want the boys to think their daddy is a killer, 'cause he ain't!"

I walked in and the talking stopped. "I asked Bobby."

"Asked Bobby what, shithead?" Mama looked confused.

"I asked Bobby about the accident, just like you told me to. And Bobby said that Daddy didn't kill Grandpa Willie."

My mama turned to her sister with a triumphant look on her face. "There, see Tootie? Bobby knows the truth."

"Hmmph. What y'all expect Bobby to say?"

I didn't much like defending my daddy, but I was more than willing to stick up for my Uncle Bobby. "Aunt Tootie, are you callin' Uncle Bobby a liar? Are you sayin' I cain't trust 'im?"

Tootie froze in place, seeing that she was caught between a rock and a hard place. To condemn Daddy, she'd have to take Bobby down with him. She turned to me with the sweetest smile and said, "C'mon over here, Mickey."

I did, and she put her arms around me. "Y'all's Uncle Bobby is a good man, Mickey—a real good man."

"I know he is, Aunt Tootie. That's why I trust 'im. Don't you?"

She patted me on the head. "He done scared yo' daddy away, so I got nothin' bad to say 'bout Bobby."

AUGUST 1962

It didn't stay cool for long once summer forced its will on us with a vengeance. Being sick in the winter is awful enough, but there's nothing worse than suffering with the fever, aches, and pains of the flu in the summer when the air is hot and humid and you're too miserable to play. In the height of the heat of August in 1962, not long after my eleventh birthday, I came down with whatever flu virus was going around and was stuck in bed for the better part of a week—absolute torture for an eleven-year-old!

On Sunday morning, Aunt Tootie felt my forehead and announced, "Sorry, Mickey. No church for you."

"C'mon, Tootie!"

"Nope. Stay in bed where you belong."

It was the day Mt. Calvary Baptist Church was having its annual summer picnic, and I felt sorry for myself for not being able to go. But I knew there was no chance of talking Aunt Tootie out of her decision. Mama came in after Tootie and Harley left and sat on the side of my bed. "Why don't y'all come out to the livin' room and watch some TV?"

"Nah. Ain't nothin' on but church shows."

She smiled. "Well, that's true. If ya need me, I'll be outside washin' my car."

Angry with the entire situation, I told God how annoyed I was at being sick in the summer and missing the picnic at His house. After a while, I got bored and wandered into the living room. For lack of anything better to do, I decided to see if there was anything on TV after all.

I walked by the big plate glass window in the living room, glancing outside as I passed. I froze dead in my tracks and just stared at what was before me. Not believing my eyes, I closed them, shook my head, and reopened them slowly. Yep, Mama was washing her most prized possession—her VW Bug—but not in a way I'd seen anyone else's mama wash their car. She was lathering up the car in the front driveway wearing a very small, very pink, very revealing bikini. Mama looked like a car-washing goddess with water cascading over the windshield as well as her body. Never in my life had I seen a woman move with such grace and allure. I didn't know if I should run outside and throw a beach towel over her or call my friends and charge admission.

I wasn't the only one mesmerized by the sight of the suds and sun. Our street was off the main road, rarely traveled by anyone except those of us who lived there. But today, a parade of cars slowly rolled down our street. At first, I wondered if they were families out for a Sunday drive. But I soon realized that each car had only one person on board—a male driver taking his sweet time maneuvering his car past our house. I'd hear, "Hey, Dixie Mae. How y'all doin' this fine Sunday?" To which Mama would wave and greet each one by name in that smartass way she had. "Hey, Jake, what y'all doin' all the way over here?" or "Mornin', Roger. Lisa and the girls with you today?"

I realized in that moment that Mama's car was *always* freshly washed whenever we came home from church on Sundays. Come to think of it, Mama's hair was always wet and her skin warm and tanned too! Who could've imagined this? I don't think even Aunt Tootie knew what Mama was up to while we were at church, and I suspected Uncle Bobby would've been quite upset if he knew, but he was always working on Sundays. While none of us in the family were the wiser, it seemed like everyone else in town was more than aware of Mama's car-washing abilities and penchant for cleanliness.

I felt embarrassed and very unsettled, so I went back to my room. Mama spent the rest of the morning washing, waxing, and buffing that car until the shine of the chrome bumpers blinded all the men in the neighborhood as they watched her work her magic on that Bug.

Right before the hour Mama expected Tootie and Harley back from church she waved to her admirers and came inside. Earlier, she had set fire to the coals in our oil-drum-turned-barbeque-grill before she began washing the car, so by the time she finished, had a quick shower, and got dressed, the coals had burned down to the exact right temperature for cooking the ribs and chicken. It was going to make for the perfect evening meal.

Right on schedule, Harley came into our room and plopped on his bed. Aunt Tootie poked her head in the door. "Y'all feelin' any better, darlin'?"

"Yeah, a bit, I guess."

"Yo' mama and I are fixin' a little lunch. You feel good enough to eat something? Anything interestin' happen while me and Harley was at church?"

Thinking about it for a moment, I slowly shook my head no. I had no intention of saying a word about what I had seen. I wish the rest of the neighborhood hadn't seen it either.

THIRTEEN

NOVEMBER 1962

A little over a year had passed since we moved to Lake Irene, and I was doing well in the sixth grade. Life was a happy rhythm of school days, playing by the lake on Saturdays, and Sunday church followed by Mama and Tootie's barbeque feast. Uncle Bobby was a regular fixture in our family. Harley was growing up fast, having turned nine in August. When Daddy first left, Harley mentioned him a lot, saying how much he missed him. But he hadn't brought him up at all lately. And with Daddy out of the picture, Mama was a different woman. Kinder. Happier. And her wicked sense of humor was back in full force.

The day before Thanksgiving, our school decided to let us out early. Honestly, the cheering could be heard all over town. It didn't take long to vacate the premises as my classmates and I stowed our books and supplies inside our desks. No homework was given over the Thanksgiving holiday.

I met Harley and my friends waiting on the blacktop so we could all walk home together. The euphoria we felt because of the upcoming four days off from school was only matched by the anticipation of the roasted turkey, gravy, biscuits, and sweet potato pie we would all enjoy the next day.

"Hey, Mick, y'all wanna play football after we change our clothes?" my friend Eric asked.

"Okay, I'll grab my ball and meet y'all at the field in ten minutes."

"Hey, I wanna play, too, Mickey! I can play as good as you." Harley sounded perfectly sure about his skills.

"Okay, Harley, but don't go cryin' when you get hit, y'all hear?"

"I ain't gonna cry, Mickey. I'm as tough as you."

I was a little worried because even at nine, Harley was a small kid. I ruffled his hair as we turned the last corner to our house.

"I know it, Harley. Y'all is tough as nails."

Just then, I looked up and saw Mama's car in the driveway. "What's Mama doing home so early?" She usually worked until five at the real estate office, then came home, had some dinner, and got ready for her job at The Savannah.

"I dunno. Maybe she don't have to work today 'cause it's Thanksgivin' tomorrow."

"What's that red car doing in our driveway?" I asked.

"I dunno that either, Mickey. How's I s'posed to know that?"

"Just strange is all."

Not knowing why, I began to have a really bad feeling as we ran the rest of the way to our door and slowly walked in.

"Daddy!" Harley exclaimed.

"Oh shit!" I said, under my breath.

Right there, sitting on the divan with my mother, was the man I hated most in this world—my daddy, Charlie Crow! To make matters worse, the bastard was holding Mama's hand!

"C'mon over here, boys, and hug yo' Daddy. I ain't seen y'all in forever." Smarminess dripping from his smile like honey from a spoon.

Harley didn't hesitate. He ran over and launched himself into Daddy's outstretched arms. "Gawd, I've missed y'all, Daddy." Harley was beginning to cry. "Where y'all been, Daddy?"

"Boy, I've been everywhere, but I'm home now," Daddy said, and then, looking at Mama, "If your mama says so."

Mama, also smiling her brightest, shook her head yes. Looking at me she said, "Go on, Mickey. Go on, now, and welcome yo' daddy home."

I couldn't move. My feet felt like they were stuck in cement. Finally, I slowly worked my way over to where Daddy sat with Harley. "How have y'all been, Mickey?" He put his arm around me and pulled me in. "Damn, boy, looks like you've grown six inches since I last saw you." He looked me up and down. Good thing he didn't take a closer look, or he would have seen my skin crawl.

"Yessir," was all I could manage to say. Looking at Mama, I asked where Tootie was.

"She's in her room." Mama was looking at me with suspicion. She knew that Tootie and Daddy hated each other, and she knew I knew it too.

"Well," Daddy said standing up, "I'll be going now. I know y'all have a lot to talk about. I'll be back in the mornin'." He looked down at Harley. "I promise."

Mama walked him to his car, where I saw her kiss the sumbitch goodbye.

I ran into Tootie's room, not even knocking on the door, and found her crying on the bed. "Don't y'all know how to knock, boy? I know I taught you better." She sniffled.

"I cain't believe that sumbitch is back, Tootie! I just cain't believe it!" I practically shouted at her.

"Keep yo' voice down, Mickey, you hear me? He's your daddy, and he's back, so y'all better mind yourself. Understand?" She sounded concerned.

"I don't *understand*, Tootie! How can Mama take him back after all he's done to us? How?"

"Mickey, I know y'all don't understand now, but you will someday. Y'all's mama loves the man—always has, though none of us know why. But she does." Tootie was right. I sure as hell didn't understand.

"But she promised to never let him back in our lives again!"

"Mickey, don't matter what she promised. I believe y'all's daddy will be movin' in here in a few days, so I'll be going back home to Mama's on Friday."

"What? Why?" I was on the verge of tears.

"Y'all know me and your daddy don't get along. Truth is, we hate each other, so I gotta go."

Letting the tears fall freely now, I begged her to stay. "Please, Aunt Tootie, don't leave me and Harley alone with him. You know he ain't changed any. He's the same mean ol' sumbitch he always was!"

"I'm sorry, Mickey, I truly am, but I cain't live in the same house as that man, and he won't let me anyways."

Right then I heard the front door open, and Mama came back in. She walked over to Tootie's bedroom door and leaned against the doorjamb.

"Why, Mama, why?" I yelled. "Why'd you let him back after how he's treated us? Ain't you been happy, Mama? We all been happier than ever without him. Why let him come back?" I was so angry the tears just started to flow.

She turned around and walked back into the living room. "Come in here, son, and sit down." I shuffled over to the divan where she was sitting and sat beside her. "He's y'all's daddy, Mickey, and we're still married. I still love 'im, and he still loves me."

"How, Mama? How can you love somebody who hurts you and makes you cry? I don't love him! I hate 'im, and I'll never love him again! Never!" I bolted and started running through the kitchen and out the back door.

Mama yelled after me. "Y'all come back here right now, Mickey. Right now!" I could still hear Mama yelling at me as I ran down to the lake. I fell to the shore, crying angrily. I kicked my shoes off and dug my toes into the cool sand below the hot surface, hoping to stave off the angry heat coursing through my body. Nobody was on the lake, so the quiet and peaceful calm of the water was a drastic contrast to the hell I knew was building inside our house. I wished I could stay right there forever.

I was interrupted sometime later when Harley joined me on the sand. We sat that way, shoulder to shoulder, feet in the sand, for a long time, watching the egrets fly in and feed on the minnows that inhabited the shoreline. Little Harley put his arm around me and said in a low, slow voice, "Mickey, it's all gonna be all right. I just know it will. You'll see. Mama and Daddy gonna be fine, and we gonna be a family again."

I couldn't have loved my little brother more than I did right then. I really couldn't. But I knew in my heart he was wrong. Even in my young heart, I knew Daddy hadn't changed, although I didn't know all the reasons I felt that way. I simply felt it, deep down in my bones.

"You pro'bly right, Harley." I put my arm around his shoulder. "You pro'bly right." I hated lying to the person I loved most in this world.

On the Friday after Thanksgiving, Mama, Harley, and I drove Tootie back to Grandmama's house in Shadeville. There were lots of tears as we said goodbye. "It's only eight miles away," Tootie said. "It ain't like I won't be seein' y'all again. Y'all will come over for Sunday supper and all, right?"

"Not if *he* has anything to say 'bout it," I said.

Hugging Tootie, Mama said, "Tootie, thank you for helping me and the boys. I never could have made it without y'all's help these last couple a years. Truly, I couldn'a done it."

"Dixie Mae, you promised me that you'd never go back to that man if I moved in, 'member?"

"I know, Tootie. I love him, God help me. I still love him."

"I know you do Dixie Mae. It's a cryin' shame, it truly is, but I know you do."

Mama looked down at her shoes, knowing it was true, but before she could say anything else, Aunt Tootie said, "Even so, if thangs don't work out like y'all hope, call me. I'll come back here in three shakes of a lamb's tail. Y'all hear me?"

"You'll be the first one I call," Mama assured her before releasing her.

Tootie turned to Harley and picked him up off the ground. "Y'all be a good boy, won't ya, Harley?" She enveloped him in her big arms and kissed both his cheeks.

"I will, Aunt Tootie. Promise I will." He hugged her neck and softly wept.

Letting Harley down, she turned and pulled me into her open arms. Whispering in my ear, she said, "Mickey, y'all keep an eye on your daddy, hear me, boy?" She pushed me back a bit and then gazed over at each one of us. "I love y'all so damn much. I'm gonna miss seein' y'all every day. Don't wait too long to come see yo' Aunt Tootie."

She turned and walked into Grandmama's little white house. Harley and I cried all the way home.

When we pulled up into the driveway, Uncle Bobby was waiting for us on the porch. Mama got out of the car and looked over at him. "Don't start in on me, Bobby," she yelled across the yard.

"Wouldn't think of it, Dixie Mae. You're a grown-ass woman."

She breezed past him, unable to look him in the eyes. "That's right, Bobby."

He didn't follow her in but waited for us to get up to the porch. I wiped tears from my eyes, not wanting him to see me crying. He looked at me with mournful eyes. "Hey, Mickey, you don't look very happy."

"I ain't happy, Uncle Bobby. I ain't happy one little bit."

"He's y'all's daddy, Mickey. Y'all gotta give him a chance, son."

"Uh-uh."

"Boys, I just came by to tell you that I won't be comin' around like I have been."

Even more loss and it was too much to bear. I ran to him, putting my head on his shoulder while he patted my back. "It's okay, Mickey. It's the way it should be. Y'all together as a family again."

My sadness turned to anger, and I backed away. "This ain't right, Uncle Bobby, and you know it. You're just sayin' that 'cause you have to."

Harley leaned up against him. "Why can't you keep comin' on Sundays, Uncle Bobby?"

"He and Daddy ain't friends no more, Harley. Don't you get it?"

My brother looked wounded by my outburst, and the thought of not seeing Uncle Bobby anymore. His eyes filled with tears.

"I'm sorry, Harley," I said.

"Boys, don't you worry. You'll see me around plenty. Just…" he paused.

I finished his sentence. "Just when Daddy's not around, right?"

He stood up realizing that there was no easy way out of this conversation. He started to walk down the steps, and then turned around and got down on his knees. We both ran into his arms. Wrapping us up in his strong embrace, he held us close. "You're Dixie's boys, and I'll always be here for y'all." He stood up. "If y'all ever need me, for any reason at all, call me. Okay?"

We both nodded, tears staining our faces.

"Promise?"

"Promise," I whispered. Harley went inside, but I stayed and watched as Uncle Bobby's truck disappeared around the corner.

After he left, a heaviness fell over the place. For me, it was a soul-sucking emptiness, an unrightness if you will. It's difficult to express the anger, sadness, and loneliness I felt that day. I'm sure the anger was exacerbated by the fact that I didn't understand the kind of love that would make Mama stay with a man who hit her, and us, and emotionally hurt me and Harley. How could my mama choose my daddy over Aunt Tootie and Uncle Bobby? Sadness choked me with its bony fingers that day and for many days afterward. I kept asking God, "Why? Why would you let Daddy come back here? Why won't you protect us?" But I heard no answer.

The despair came and went, depending on the circumstances, in waves of grief. No one seemed to understand, or care, how I was feeling. Maybe Aunt Tootie or Uncle Bobby, but they weren't coming around to act as a buffer. Even around others, I was lonely—lonely for someone who could say, "I feel just like you about this." But there wasn't anyone who seemed to really understand or care.

FOURTEEN

PRESENT
SATURDAY, APRIL 22, 1972
11:28 A.M.

After leaving Grandma Jean's farm, I drove around aimlessly, not knowing where I was headed. I was so angry, confused, and conflicted that I could hardly see. Having grown up here, I knew all of the highways but decided to try out some of the back roads just to give myself more time to think.

After a while, I found myself in the Apalachicola Swamp, at the boat launch where Charlie and Uncle Bobby used to take Harley and me fishing when we were little kids. I pulled up under an old cypress tree, rolled down the windows, then cut the engine.

I thought I'd put Charlie behind me.

The thought of seeing him again actually scared me—not because of what he might do to me but because of what I could do to him. But I knew what Grandma Jean actually wanted—not just a meeting with him but to actually forgive Charlie so he could die in peace.

That wasn't possible. I grew up in the church, and it had been pounded into my head that I was *supposed* to forgive other people. Saying the words "I forgive you," was easy. Truly forgiving that bastard wasn't something I knew how to do, even if I wanted too, and

I didn't. I had no idea how to truly forgive Charlie Crow for what he'd done.

I tried to pray, but instead, I just raged. With that, I burst into tears—not just crying, but weeping uncontrollably, desperately sobbing from somewhere in the depths of my soul. I don't know how long I went on like that, for a long time, I think. When I was done, I was totally exhausted. Yet, the memories of my history with this man flooded my mind in living color.

CHAPTER FIFTEEN

Daddy didn't waste any time moving his belongings into the house the next day.

While he tried to make nice, I could only mutter "Yes, sir," or "No, sir" whenever he spoke to me. Harley and Mama, on the other hand, were absolutely giddy with delight—bless their little pea-picking, traitorous hearts.

Mama called Mel and let him know that Daddy was back in town. They had a short talk and when she hung up the phone, she was beaming. "Charlie, I think I got you a job!"

He grabbed her around the waist and kissed her hard on the lips. "That's my Dixie Mae."

"All yours," she cooed.

I would've laughed out loud if wasn't for the fact I wanted to puke all over the floor!

She told Daddy that Mel was developing swamp land near Pensacola and Tallahassee and hit on a great idea to take potential buyers on a "bird's-eye" view of what would soon become dry and developed land. Seeing an opportunity to capitalize on Daddy's Air Force training, Mama made Charlie get showered and took him over to introduce him to Mel.

It must have gone well, because a couple of days later, Daddy took a check ride in Mel's four-seat Piper Cherokee. Daddy told Mama when he got home after the flight, he was hired on the spot. These "swamp flights," as Daddy liked to call them, were very popular, as was Daddy. Don't get me wrong, he was meaner than a blind spider, but he was smart and could be very charming and erudite when the occasion called for it. It didn't hurt that he was movie star handsome either, so those swamp flights translated into big bucks for Mel.

Daddy got to do what he loved—fly around without anyone looking over his shoulder. His charm and intelligence was a perfect match for his wealthy, worldly-wise passengers. I knew that now that he had a job, he was here to stay.

I continued the politeness to a fault, saying "yessir" and "no sir" every time Daddy spoke to me, and I did my best to stay out of his way, even though every cell of my body oozed disgust for him. I was surrounded by an energy field of utter defiance. The model child on the outside, and the enemy on the inside. One night, Mama came into our bedroom and said, "Mikey, it's so good to see you gettin' along with yo' daddy." I smiled innocently but the smile never reached my eyes.

At breakfast one cold and windy Saturday morning in January, 1963, Daddy said to me, "Mickey, how 'bout y'all taking a ride with me this mornin' over to the golf shop? I need to pick up some new balls and thought I'd hit a bucket."

It wasn't a question, more like an order, so I had no choice but to say, "Yessir." I wasn't too upset about it though, because Daddy had just bought himself a red 1958 Mercury Turnpike Cruiser with a retractable rear window. That car was seriously cool and made my eleven-year-old heart skip a beat, although I tried not to show it. Any excuse to ride it in made my polite responses much easier.

On the way over to the golf shop, Daddy suddenly got all serious. "Mickey, what the hell is goin' on with you, boy?"

"Nothin'."

"Don't bullshit me, boy! You've been acting all perfect as if you're glad I'm back."

I didn't respond.

For a moment, I think Daddy hoped I really was happy to see him. He looked at me sideways. "What? Y'all don't want me back?"

In a moment of insanity, steeped in hatred, I said, "No, sir, I don't."

He laughed. "You got balls, Mickey, I'll give y'all that."

We drove in silence until he pulled off the highway and into the parking lot of the little golf shop and range, not far from our house. He put the car in park, turned the ignition off, and turned to me. The gloves came off, and he was angry. "Y'all listen up, you little shit. I'm back, and I'm staying. You got it?"

"Yessir, if you say so," I said defiantly.

"Y'all don't have to love me or even like me, but you're gonna have to—" then, poking me in the chest to emphasize every word, "—Accept. That. I. Am. Back. Got it!"

"No, I don't love you, I hate you. I wish y'all was dead!" I screamed at him, and all the anger and cold rage bubbled to the surface. "Y'all ain't changed, and you better never hit Mama again!"

In the blink of an eye, the sumbitch slapped me on the side of my face, knocking my head back into the window. The world spun around, and I thought I was going to pass out. He grabbed me by the shirt and pulled me towards him. "Listen up, shithead. Y'all ever tell yo' mama about this, or anyone else, I'll kill all y'all and hide yo' sorry asses in the swamp where only the gators will find you! Don't test me, boy!" His face was inches away from mine. "Y'all understand me, Mickey? Do you?"

"Ye-yessir," was all I could say. Whimpering, I slid over as far as I could to the car door, shaking with fear and rage.

He got out of the car, slammed the door behind him, and walked into the golf shop. I couldn't stop shaking, seething with hate, and trembling with fear so palpable that it felt like a vice gripping my heart. *He just threatened to kill me—Mama and Harley too!*

Deep down, I had never really believed that Daddy was a murderer, or at least I never wanted to. I'd hoped that Uncle Bobby had it right. But now I realized that he hadn't.

Daddy was capable of killing, just like he killed Grandpa Willie. He didn't try to save him. He killed him and fed him to the gators. I was sure of it now. He was going to do the same thing to me, Mama, and Harley if I pissed him off. Aunt Tootie had been right all along.

A few minutes later, I watched as he came out of the shop, walked over, and climbed back in the car like nothing ever happened.

We drove home in silence—me scared shitless and shaking all the way, and Daddy grinning like a possum eating a sweet potato. I was petrified that he would kill us all and there was no one I could tell, not even Uncle Bobby—especially not Uncle Bobby. He might say something to Daddy, and that would be the end of us all.

Mama was already out working her real estate job by the time we got back home, and Harley was outside catching minnows in the shallows of Lake Irene. I ran into my bedroom, slamming the door behind me. I stayed there the rest of the day, with my only visitor being Harley. He came bouncing in and jumped next to me on the bed, but my back was to him.

"What's a matter, Mickey? Where y'all been all day?"

"I went to the golf shop with Daddy, and when we came home, I wasn't feelin' good. Still ain't."

"Y'all gonna puke, Mickey?" He seemed to take a little too much delight in the question.

"Naw, I ain't gonna puke. Just leave me alone, okay?"

"All right. Yo' not eaten' supper tonight, then?"

"No! Just get out, okay?"

"You don't have to yell! I'm goin'." He sounded hurt.

"Harley, I'm sorry. I didn't mean to yell at 'cha. I'm just not feelin' good right now."

"I understand. Y'all want some saltine crackers? Always makes me feel better when I'm sick."

"Ya know, that sounds good. Will you get me some, buddy?"

Harley sprinted to the kitchen and returned a few minutes later with the saltines and an RC Cola. I was half asleep, so he left them on the dresser. I didn't see him again until the next morning. I'd been asleep when Mama came home from her job at The Savannah and Daddy hadn't said a word to me since we got back from the golf shop. Thank God he didn't have a reason to.

The next morning, I sauntered into the kitchen with more than a little trepidation. Harley was still asleep, so only Mama and Daddy were sitting at the breakfast table. "C'mon over here and give yo' mama a hug, boy." Mama said it with real affection.

Daddy eyed me with suspicion. "Yeah, Mickey, get on over there and hug yo' mama."

I did as instructed, bent over and hugged Mama—harder and longer than usual.

Mama pushed me up and away a bit, looking me over, and then gasped. "What in the hell happened to the side of yo' head, Mickey?" Reaching up, she touched the lump residing there.

I flinched because it still hurt some. "Nothin', Mama. I fell off my bike yesterday and bumped my head. I'm okay."

"Are y'all sure, baby? That's a pretty big dinger you got there."

"It was just a dumbass mistake." I looked at Daddy as I said it. He gave me a little smirk and a quick head nod as if to say, "Smart move, boy."

"Watch yo' mouth, Mickey," Mama said. "Get a bag of peas out the freezer. Lie down and put it on that knot for a little while, hear me?"

"Yes ma'am." I did as I was told.

I have to say, it did feel better after a few minutes with that bag of peas on it. After a little while, I got up. Putting on my coat, I yelled, "I'm going over to Tommy's to play," and escaped before anyone could stop me.

School let out for two weeks for Christmas vacation and things hadn't gotten any better with my Daddy, but not any worse either. We just stayed out of each other's way and didn't speak to one another unless we had to. Mama noticed, quizzing me a few times, but didn't really push that hard. I could feel she wanted me to tell her that I was happy about Daddy being home, but I couldn't. I hated him and I wanted him gone, the sooner the better.

SIXTEEN

APRIL 1963

Spring was here and the country was celebrating Neil Armstrong's X-15 flight, which had resulted in a human being flying higher than any human had ever been before.

West Side Story won the Academy Award, and Arnold Palmer had just won his third US Masters Tournament at Augusta National. For all the victory and celebration going on throughout our country though, I could only feel loss and defeat.

For obvious reasons, the noteworthy fashion in which Mama used to wash her car came to an end—much to the disappointment of the men in the neighborhood. The all-day barbeques we'd enjoyed ever since we'd moved to the lake house vanished after Daddy came back. There was no more Sunday afternoon music and dancing, and no more of Tootie's delicious pies.

Instead of the peace and joy we'd had before Daddy came back, our house was now full of yelling and cussing, like it was before Daddy had left. The only good part was that Charlie seemed to be able to walk away when he got mad. When he was just about to lose control, he'd storm out of the house and disappear, sometimes until the next day. When he came home, he always smelled of alcohol, and occasionally he was full-on drunk. But he'd sleep it off and things settled into a low, mean simmer. Don't get me wrong, I still hated Daddy. But I figured if this was the worst it got, I could tolerate it.

Sunday night was "Couple's Night" down at Star Lanes, where drinks and frames were half-price. Daddy had a late afternoon Swamp Flight this particular Sunday, so Mama was going to meet him at the Star—that way, he wouldn't have to come all the way home to pick her up. Before she left, Mama made fried chicken and mashed potatoes for me and Harley's supper. "Mickey, you and Harley clean up after supper and make sure y'all are in bed by nine, hear me?"

"Yes ma'am," we both said in unison.

It wasn't unusual in those days to be left alone at night—most of our friends had done the same many times. Nobody I knew even locked their doors at night. We did as Mama said and cleaned up the supper dishes and then took our baths. Later, we watched *Lassie*, *The Jetsons*, and *Ed Sullivan* on our old black and white TV. Soon after, we were off to bed.

"I love Lassie, don't you, Mickey?"

"Me too," I agreed. "Y'all go to sleep now, okay?"

"Okay." He was yawning one moment, and just like that, we both drifted off.

Looking back, I think what woke me up that night was the slamming of the front door. It was loud, like a gunshot, and I lurched upright in bed. My heart was racing, unsure about what was happening. I jumped out of bed, heading for our bedroom door, but stopped when I heard Mama yelling. "I don't know why I let you back in our lives!

Y'all nothing but a cheatin', lyin', son-of-a-bitch! You're a bastard, Charlie; you ain't nothin' but owl shit!"

"You better shut yo' mouth, Dixie, before I shut it for ya!" Daddy sounded dangerous to me, but I didn't know what to do at that moment.

"What y'all gonna do, shit for brains? Run off with that red-headed piece-o'-ass, Charlotte?" Charlotte was the pretty secretary who worked with Mama at the real estate office. "She's just a common whore! Y'all two are made fo' each other!"

"Y'all think you're so high and mighty. Well, you ain't! Y'all ain't no better, Dixie Mae."

I stood there shaking with anger. I tried to move but couldn't. Daddy wasn't done.

"Yo' whole family ain't nothin' but white trash. Why do y'all let Tootie anywhere near our boys? She's nothin' but a slut. Everybody knows she started screwin' around befo' she got out of junior high!"

I was livid. *How could anybody lie about Aunt Tootie like that?!*

"You bastard, you better shut yo' filthy mouth," Mama screamed. "You don't know nothin'. My sister never screwed anybody, you ignorant shit! She's the only one in this goddamn world I trust 'cause I sure as hell cain't trust you!"

Charlie laughed, mean and loud. "Yo' not much better. What about Jack, huh?" He amped the volume up to the max and yelled at the top of his lungs. "What about Jack?"

"Shut up about Jack, you sumbitch. You disgust me!"

Jack? Who's Jack? Could it be that my mama went out on Daddy with some guy named Jack? A deep sense of satisfaction moved through me. Daddy certainly deserved to know what it felt like to be betrayed, and up until that moment, I thought Mama didn't have it in her to give him as good as she got.

I was abruptly shocked back into the present when I heard a loud slap, and Mama cried out in pain. I slung the door open and ran into the living room, where I found Mama laying on the floor, dazed and bleeding from her mouth. Remembering my promise to not let anyone hit my mama again, and not caring about the consequences of my actions, I ran screaming at my daddy with all the force an eleven-year-old kid could muster.

"Get away from her, ya old bastard! Leave her alone!"

The force of me running into him knocked him over the sofa table, but he quickly recovered. As I ran over to help Mama off the floor, he caught me by the arm and backhanded me so hard I saw stars and lost consciousness for a few seconds.

When I came to, I saw Mama trying to get up, screaming at the top of her voice. "He's just a kid, ya worthless piece o' shit!" Getting her feet under her, she went after Daddy with a vengeance—all fingernails, teeth, and little fists swinging and occasionally connecting. During that hurricane of struggle and violence, Daddy somehow had stripped the clothes off Mama, and they lay in shredded pieces on the floor leaving her nakedness in full display. Before I could reach him again, he hit Mama in the face with his fist. She crumpled back down to the floor, out cold.

"You killed my Mama, you sumbitch!" I started running over to Mama to see if she was all right, but Daddy grabbed my arm and threw me into the wall. I hit my head with a loud thud and dropped to the floor like a ten-pound sack of flour.

"Stay down, ya little bastard, or I'll make sure yo' ass stays down for good!"

Dazed, I reached back and felt something wet and warm running down the back of my head. Through the confusion, I watched Daddy open the front door and drag Mama's unconscious body outside. Dumping her on the cold, damp, front lawn, he reentered the house, slammed the front door, and disappeared down the hallway. He went into their bedroom, slamming and locking the door behind him.

A minute later, Harley snuck a look around the corner. He had been hiding in the hall. Seeing me on the floor, he was clearly alarmed. "Mickey! What y'all doin' on the floor? Yo' head's bleedin' bad!"

"I'm fine. Harley, help me up and get the blanket off yo' bed and bring it outside."

"What? Why? What ya need a blanket for?"

"Daddy beat Mama, and she's outside with no clothes on! Go get a blanket and bring it outside, now!"

I ran outside to find Mama lying on the grass, bleeding and moaning in pain as she searched for lucidity. Harley, coming outside holding the blanket, immediately started crying when he saw the condition she was in.

"Harley, help me get Mama up, okay?" Struggling, we finally got her up into a sitting position. Tears streaming down my face, I placed the blanket around her bare shoulders, shamed at seeing her nakedness. "Can you get up, Mama? Me and Harley will help you, but we need y'all to help too."

"What? Mickey, what am I doin' out here, son?" Mama's voice was shaky, and her body was shivering from the trauma and the cold.

"Come on, Mama, stand up and let's get inside," I said gently.

Little Harley chimed in through his tears, begging, "Mama, please get up. Please get up!"

Mama looked up at us through swollen and ugly bruised eyes. "Okay, boys. Ready, lift."

At last, the three of us stood up, Mama still shuddering from the ordeal and Harley and I trembling from the exertion of lifting her.

I felt a trickle of Mama's blood hit the back of my neck, mixing with my own. Finally, we slowly walked her back to the house and closed the door. Mama, recovering her senses and her rage, suddenly ripped herself from our grasp and screamed at the top of her lungs. "I'm gonna kill you, Charlie Crow! I'm gonna kill you, goddamnit!"

She screamed, "I'm not taking any more shit from you, you bastard!" as she ran into the kitchen and came out with the biggest butcher knife we had. She raced down the hall, with Harley and I following close behind. Mama tried to open her bedroom door, but Daddy had wisely locked it.

"Open this goddamn door, you coward! I'm gonna cut yo' heart out and watch you bleed!"

"Shut up, bitch. Y'all are just a cheap, back seat whore—just like Tootie."

Dear God, how I hated him for what he did to my Mama. He turned her into a killer! If she was married to a good man like Uncle Bobby, she'd never act like this. I didn't think it was possible, but her rage kicked into a higher gear. She stabbed the door with the butcher knife, all the while kicking it as hard as she could. Pulling out the knife, she stabbed it again and again and again. "Open this door, you coward! Come out! I'm gonna kill yo' sorry ass!"

Suddenly, the thought struck me that if Mama killed Daddy, she'd go to jail and we wouldn't have anybody to take care of us. That scared me to the bone, so I began yelling and grabbing her arm that held the knife.

"Please, Mama, please stop! Don't kill 'im. Please don't kill 'im!"

Harley, seeing all this, started to cry in earnest. He grabbed Mama's leg, trying to help me get the knife away from her. Mama stopped banging on the door and looked down with wild eyes at her youngest, little, towheaded boy. Seizing the opportunity, I tried to disarm Mama, grabbing again at the hand that held the knife.

During the struggle for the weapon, Mama's hand was cut and bleeding badly. She dropped the knife, and as blood spurted from the wound, she froze at the sight of her bleeding hand. Her eyes fluttered and a cruel angry look spread over her face. Looking down at Harley as if he were the devil, she rubbed her bloodied hand over his little face until it dripped with her blood. She screamed maniacally to Daddy, "I got yo' boy out here, ya sumbitch! I got yo' boy out here!"

She glanced in my direction, so I pulled back not wanting to be next to get smeared with blood. But it was like Mama didn't see me. Instead, she grabbed the knife from the floor and thrust it deep into the wood of the door. It held strong. When she couldn't free it, she slammed her bleeding palm again and again on the offending door, smearing it with her bloody handprints and spraying us with red droplets. Harley, stupefied, fell back against the hallway wall, wailing as if he was the one who was actually cut.

I didn't know what to do next. I didn't know what Mama was going to do. Terrified of who my mother had become, I was afraid she might hurt Harley. The phone rang in the living room. I jumped at the sound and ran to answer it. "Hello!"

"Mickey, is that you? What the hell's goin' on?" Uncle Bobby's voice blared from the phone. "The crazy lady next door called and said that a murder is goin' on at y'all's house."

"Uncle Bobby, Mama and Daddy is fightin'. Daddy beat her and threw her outside, and when she came to, she grabbed a knife and now she's tryin' to kill Daddy!"

"Are you boys okay?"

"Mama's gone crazy! He's locked himself in their bedroom. She's bleedin' bad and so is Harley! Please come now! Please, Uncle Bobby." I broke down in tears.

"I'll be right there, Mickey. Don't let Dixie Mae get in that door, understand? Don't let her get in that door!"

Uncle Bobby hung up, and I ran over to Mama, who had somehow gotten the knife out the door. I started screaming for her to stop and put the knife down, but she didn't respond. She just kept stabbing the door, over and over again. A few minutes later, I heard Uncle Bobby's siren and his patrol car drive up, so I ran out to meet him. He gasped when he saw me covered in blood.

"What happened, Mickey? Are you bleedin'?"

"Don't worry about me. Stop Mama befo' she kills Daddy or Harley. She's gone crazy." We both ran back inside. The scene that awaited us when we got there was something out of a nightmare.

There was so much blood, it looked like someone had surely been killed. Mama was slumped down the wall next to her bedroom door, holding Harley in her arms and rocking back and forth. She appeared to be in a trance. Harley was whimpering now, looking wild-eyed and in shock. The knife was stuck in the middle of the door again, and Daddy could be heard on the other side taunting Mama. "Y'all gonna kill me, bitch? Y'all gonna kill me?"

Uncle Bobby knelt next to Mama. He spoke so gently that it almost hurt to hear it. "Dixie Mae, it's Bobby. I'm here now, okay? I'm here now."

Mama looked up into his loving eyes. "Bobby?"

"That's right, Dixie Mae, it's me. I'm here to help you and the boys. Y'all come to my house tonight, and we'll clear all this up in the mornin'. Is that okay?"

Daddy, hearing Bobby talking to Mama, yelled through the door, "You taking her back to yo' place? Y'all been screwin' my wife, too, Bobby? You been screwin' Dixie Mae while I was gone, old buddy?"

Looking at me, Uncle Bobby took charge. "Mickey, take y'all's Mama and help her to my car. I'll get Harley, okay?"

"Yessir, Uncle Bobby." I walked Mama, who was wrapped in the blanket, out to his cruiser.

Uncle Bobby picked up Harley, who grabbed onto his neck, and said to Daddy through clenched teeth, "I'll be back, Charlie. You'd better not be here when I do, *old buddy*. You understand me? You'd better be long gone and far away, and don't come back, Charlie. Ever!"

"Fine, take 'em, Bobby. Just leave me the hell alone!"

"Listen up, Charlie!" Uncle Bobby bellowed. "I'm takin' yo' family to the hospital. As soon as I know they're okay, I'm comin' back for you! Believe this, Charlie! When I'm done, there won't be nothin' left to arrest, but if by some miracle there is, I'm gonna arrest what's left of you for assault with intent to kill, and nobody down at the station will question a goddamn thing. I've always protected yo' ass, Charlie, since we were kids. But not ever again. You and I both know I can take you down, so if y'all want to see the sun tomorrow, y'all better not be here when I come back!"

Daddy didn't say another word.

CHAPTER SEVENTEEN

I held the blanket around Mama in the backseat next to me. Uncle Bobby carried little Harley and put him in the front passenger seat before he hit the siren, and as we sped through the streets, he radioed ahead telling the emergency room staff that he had three patients in immediate need of care.

When the sheriff's car arrived at the entrance, there were three gurneys waiting for us and a slew of medical personnel. Bobby yelled to get Harley out of the front seat while he helped Mama out on his side. By the time I stumbled onto the pavement, they had whisked Mama and Harley inside. Arms grabbed me and put me onto the gurney, and the rest was a blur. I must have passed out because the next thing I remember, my head was bandaged, and an ice pack was up against my face. A petite brunette nurse gave me a worried smile, "You back with us, Mickey?"

"Yes ma'am." She reached up and touched my face. "Ow."

"You're going to be fine, but you'll have quite a shiner to show off to your friends for a while. I hear you tried to protect your Mama."

"My Daddy is a..." I stopped. I didn't want to cuss in front of the nurse.

"Don't worry about your Daddy. He can't hurt you anymore."

I wished that were true, but I knew that he'd likely kill us and throw our bodies in the swamp, just like he promised if he got the chance. But I did think that Uncle Bobby had scared him out of town—for now anyway.

Uncle Bobby popped his head in the door with Harley on his shoulder, holding onto Bobby's neck for dear life. "You okay, boy?"

"Yessir."

The nurse filled him in. "He's got a mild concussion and a small cut on the back of his head, but he doesn't need stitches." Pointing to my face, she said, "Make sure you keep ice on that bruise. It's gonna hurt for a few days, okay?"

"Got it. Can he come out here with me now?" Bobby asked the nurse.

"Yes, the doctor signed off on his treatment."

I walked slowly behind Uncle Bobby and Harley into the hall and to the waiting room. He sat Harley on one of the seats and told me to sit next to him. "I'll be right back, I'm gonna call Tootie." He pointed to the pay phone on the wall.

"How's Mama?" I asked, scared of the answer. "Is-is she alive?"

"Oh, yeah, Mickey. She'll be okay." I gave him a skeptical look. Uncle Bobby looked me straight in the eyes. "Trust me, Mickey. I won't ever lie to you."

I nodded and sat next to my brother. Harley had been taken in first since the nurses thought, due to the amount of blood on his face, he'd been cut badly. But that was Mama's blood smeared on his face. He had no injuries, thankfully. Now he sat, wearing a stained shirt, staring through unseeing eyes—clearly traumatized.

Bobby walked over to the pay phone in the ER and called Aunt Tootie. He asked if she could meet us in the emergency room at Quincy Memorial.

"What the hell's goin' on, Bobby? Are the boys all right? Is Dixie Mae hurt?"

"They're all okay, Tootie—just meet us at the hospital, and I'll tell y'all everything."

"On our way!"

Uncle Bobby sat down. "Okay, I'll tell y'all about yo' Mama. She has a broken rib that punctured her lung, cuts, and bruises all over her body, and a concussion. She's got seven stitches in her hand where she cut herself with that knife." I felt guilty for that cut on her hand.

It took some time for Aunt Tootie, Grandmama, and Grandpa Hank to get to Quincy Memorial. Harley and I were stretched out on the seats in the waiting room. Harley was sleeping, but my pounding head kept me awake. Bobby kept one eye on us and the other on the ER door in case the doctor came out with any more news.

The trio ran into the waiting room. "What the hell's goin' on, Bobby? Where's Dixie Mae?" Grandmama was beside herself. "Oh, God, is she dead? Did that sumbitch kill my baby?"

Raising his hands up in surrender, Uncle Bobby said, "Now, hold on, Mizz Colee. Dixie Mae's gonna be fine." For ten minutes Grandmama and Tootie hammered Uncle Bobby with questions, their voices rising and falling like a boat on a big wave in a storm.

"Calm down, ladies!" Grandpa Hank stepped in. "Let the boy talk."

When he could get a word in edgewise, Uncle Bobby said, "She's gonna be okay and so's her boys." He leaned his head in our direction.

They hadn't really noticed us before that moment. Tootie ran over and burst into tears when she looked down and saw my swollen cheek, the bandage on my head, and the blood spattered all over my clothes. "Oh, my God! I'm gonna kill that bastard for this! I'm gonna kill 'im! Then I'm gonna cut his balls off and feed 'im to our pigs!"

Grandmama grabbed up Harley, waking him abruptly and surprising him. She cried, "Whose blood is this? It's all over this boys' clothes." She pulled him to her bosom and held him close where he leaned in and cried softly.

"All right, all right, everybody, just calm down now. Y'all hear me?" Uncle Bobby was frustrated and loud enough to be heard over the commotion. Everyone stopped talking. He told them what he knew about her condition.

"Oh, my God!" Grandmama gasped.

"The doctor said he'd come out as soon as he got a handle on everything and let us know how she's doin'," Uncle Bobby said.

"I wanna see my baby, and I wanna see her now!"

"Y'all can't see her right now, Mizz Colee. The doctor will be out soon and fill us in on what's next, okay? Listen to me! You're upsettin' the boys. Get yo'selves under control." His voice was authoritative and strong. Just strong enough to jolt them back to their senses.

Grandpa Hank put his hand on his wife's shoulder. "Put the boy down, darlin', and let him sleep."

She did as she was told, and Harley fell back into a deep, but fitful sleep.

Aunt Tootie sat down and put her arm around me. "It's okay, Mickey. I'm here now." Feeling her warmth next to me gave me a sense of safety I hadn't felt since Daddy came back. I leaned into her.

Bobby pointed down the hall. "Y'all want some coffee while we wait? There's some freshly made right around the corner. I can get some for y'all."

Grandmama said, "That'd be nice, Bobby. You want some, Tootie?"

"Yeah, I'd like some, if y'all don't mind."

"All right," Bobby said. "I'll be right back."

When he came around the corner with the three cups of coffee, he found the doctor talking with Grandmama, Grandpa Hank, and Tootie.

"We've got her stabilized. We've got her lung patched up, and she's breathin' just fine right now. We wrapped her broken rib, but that's gonna take a while to heal, and it's gonna hurt like hell for a while too. We can give her some pain medication for that. We also cleaned and stitched up the cut on her hand. Because of her concussion, we're gonna keep her in the hospital for a couple of days, just as a precaution." There was an audible sigh of relief from everyone.

Grandmama spoke first. "Can we see her, doctor? I wanna see my baby."

"I'm sorry, Ma'am, but the answer is no—not right now. We've got her on some pretty powerful painkillers, and she's sleepin', which is another reason we want her here for the next couple of nights." Seeing the disappointment and worry on her face, he quickly added, "Call us in the mornin', and if she's awake, you can come and see her then. Okay?"

Uncle Bobby spoke up before Grandmama could protest. "All right, now. Let's all get home and get some sleep. I can take the boys to my house—"

Grandmama cut him off. "I wouldn't dream of lettin' these precious babies out of my sight tonight, Bobby. They're comin' home with us."

"Don't try and stop us, Bobby!" Aunt Tootie said, putting on her best warrior-woman voice.

Uncle Bobby smiled in defeat. Turning to Grandmama. "Okay, get the boys home and in bed. You get some sleep, too, Mizz Colee. No need in fussin' anymore tonight. I'll check in on Dixie Mae first thing in the mornin' and give y'all a call. I promise."

I fell asleep in the car and don't remember Grandpa Hank carrying me into their house. But when Uncle Bobby showed up early the next morning and rang the doorbell, I woke up to find myself and Harley tucked into the big bed in their spare room. My head throbbed and my face felt fat and sore, but I was relieved to be exactly where I was. I heard someone knocking on the front door, so I got out of bed and ran to open it.

CHAPTER EIGHTEEN

Uncle Bobby was standing at the front door holding a grocery bag filled with clean clothes for me and Harley and talking to Aunt Tootie who beat me to the door. She was wrapped up in a blanket talking quietly to Uncle Bobby so as not wake the rest of us.

Bobby smiled when he saw me. "I should've known you'd be the first one to find out what's goin' on."

I grinned back, and Aunt Tootie put her arm on my shoulder. "Radar ears!" She grinned at both of us.

Uncle Bobby told us he went back to the house last night once we all left the hospital, and Daddy's snazzy new car was missing from the driveway. "I went inside and checked. The place is a mess, but he cleared out all his stuff. He's gone."

"Good!" said Tootie. "I hope we never see that low-life sumbitch again."

"How's my mama?" I asked.

"From there I went to the hospital, and your mama is fine. She was sleepin' so I haven't talked to her yet, but I wanted to check on you boys. I'll go back soon and see if I can't get into her room."

Tootie's eyes filled with tears. "Oh, thank you, Bobby. I don't know what we'd do without you." She threw her arms around him and hugged him, then stepped back as if surprised at herself.

Bobby smiled. "I'm always here for y'all—you know that." Then he looked down at me. "And, of course, Dixie's boys."

He looked back at Aunt Tootie. "Tootie, the house looks like a murder scene. I was wonderin' if you could meet me over there and help me clean it before Dixie comes home. I don't think the boys should go back to that mess either."

Without hesitation, Tootie agreed. "Don't worry 'bout nothin', Bobby. Go on and visit Dixie Mae. Me and Mama will go to the hospital later this mornin'. After that, we'll go over to the house and clean it up."

"Y'all talkin' like I'm not here," I said. "I know what it looks like. Y'all do know I was there, right?"

The grownups continued to ignore me,

"That'd be great, Tootie," Bobby said. "Let me know what time y'all will be there, so I can help."

"Ain't no need, Bobby. Me and Mama can handle it. You'll only get in the way."

Handing me the grocery bag, Uncle Bobby said, "Y'all get dressed, and I'll take you and Harley to the hospital to see your mama. I got you and Harley some fresh clothes when I was there last night."

"Thanks, Uncle Bobby!" I grabbed the bag and ran into the bathroom to change. I couldn't wait to see Mama with my own eyes and make sure she was okay.

Uncle Bobby and I got the okay from the head nurse to see Mama. I didn't know what to expect, so I braced myself as we walked through the door. Mama was propped up in bed smoking. Uncle Bobby exclaimed, "I can't believe they let you smoke in here!"

She smiled sweetly when she saw us enter and stubbed out the smoke. "Let 'em try and stop me." She winced in obvious pain. "C'mon over here, Mickey."

I rushed over to her and hugged her. She cried out in pain. I jumped back. "Oh, I'm so sorry, Mama!"

She grabbed her side with the cracked rib and tried to give me her best poker face. "Oh, don't worry, Mickey. I'm fine. Are you okay?" She held my face in her hands and looked me over.

"I got a 'cussion or somethin' like that. What they call it Uncle Bobby?"

"Concussion."

"Looks like we both got one of those," Mama said as she rubbed the back of her head.

Bobby seemed worried. "You really all right, Dixie Mae?"

"I'm fine, Bobby. Almost time for some more painkillers is all."

"Well, if you don't mind me saying so, you don't look fine. You got a nasty cut on your forehead." He drew closer and brushed her hair away, gently, to take a better look.

"Stop fussin', Bobby. Really. I'm fine, I really am." She touched his arm affectionately. "I know I don't look so good, but everythin' is fine on the inside."

"You mean other than the collapsed lung and broken rib?" Uncle Bobby asked. "Just because you say yo' fine, don't mean much to me at the moment. I want to hear it from the doctor."

Mama looked offended. "Well, there was no blood in my pee this mornin' when they took all those tests. They said I'd be fit as a fiddle soon."

"After a few days here."

"Yeah, that's what the doctor tol' me a little while ago. I'd like to go home now, Bobby. Can you make that happen?"

"Nope, you need to be here, so you're stayin'. Sorry." He looked at me. "Mickey, can you sit out in the waitin' room for a few minutes? I'd like to talk to Dixie Mae alone. I'll come get you when I'm done, okay?"

I hated being treated like a child. There were always secrets being told that no one wanted me to hear.

"Okay," I trudged outside. "I'll see you in the waitin' room." I rounded the corner but didn't go far. Instead, I ran back down the hall and stood just outside the door where I could hear most everything.

Uncle Bobby said, "Dixie Mae, Charlie's taken all of his stuff and he's gone."

"Good, I never want to see that bastard again."

"I don't want to leave it at that, Dixie Mae. Will you press charges?"

"Hell, yeah, I wanna press charges. He nearly killed me. Let's put 'im in jail and throw away the key!"

"All right, I'll put out a statewide arrest warrant for Charlie. I want to drag his ass back here and bring him to trial. Get him locked up for what he did to you and the boys."

Mama was silent for a long time. "No, wait. Bobby, I don't want 'im back here."

"After what he's done, Dixie Mae? You owe him nothin'."

"Thanks, Bobby. But I just want 'im gone. Out of our lives altogether. If you arrest 'im, he'll end up back in town madder than he already is."

"But Dixie, he needs to be in jail and kept away from you."

She laughed. "You think he'll be put away long enough to keep us safe? Hell Bobby, this is Florida. He'd be home by supper. No jury will put him away once they hear that I tried to kill 'im."

Bobby sighed. "But Dixie."

"No, forget it. We was both wrong. He was just wronger than me."

"Ya gotta let me help you and the boys, Dixie Mae."

Her voice took on that sweet tone she used when she was determined to get what she wanted from a man. "Bobby, you *do* help me. You *do* help the boys. Somebody would'a ended up dead last night if it wasn't for you comin' in time. Best way to protect us is to let Charlie go as far away as he can get."

Bobby was quiet and thoughtful for a moment. "I hate that he'll get away with it. Maybe you're right, Dixie Mae. I'll let 'im go. I'll be back later to see you."

Bobby came out of the room faster than I expected, and he ran right into me. Disgusted at having no way to hold Charlie accountable and realizing that I'd heard the entire conversation, he walked quickly down the hall without a look back to see if I was following behind. I ran to catch up.

We got in Uncle Bobby's cruiser and drove off in silence. *Should I tell Uncle Bobby about Daddy's threat now? Would Daddy come back and kill us if I told that secret? Would he come back and kill us, anyway, even if I didn't?*

Bobby's voice broke through my thoughts. "I should've done somethin' to stop it before now—before it got this far. I should've done somethin' to make sure Charlie never came back here. Then none of this would've happened. But I didn't. I'll tell you one thing, Mickey. I'll never let y'all's Daddy do this again. Y'all can bet on that!"

"You was just tryin' to protect us, Uncle Bobby."

"Right, some good that did, huh?" He patted me on the shoulder. We drove for a while in silence.

"Um, Uncle Bobby? I gotta' tell you somethin'."

"Sure, Mickey. Anything."

"I think Daddy killed Grandpa Willie."

"What? Why?"

"I probably should'a told ya this before. This ain't your fault, it's mine."

Bobby pulled the car to the side of the road and turned all his attention to me. "Listen, Mickey. None of this is yo' fault. None of it, ya hear me, boy? None of it!"

"You don't understand. Member' when Daddy first came back—'round Thanksgivin'?"

"Sure, Mickey, I remember."

"Well, he threatened to kill me, Harley, and Mama."

"He what? What'd he say, Mickey? Exactly?"

"He was mad 'cause I didn't want Mama to take him back, so he hit me and told me that if I ever tol' a soul 'bout it, he'd kill Harley, Mama, and me."

Uncle Bobby shook his head. "After last night, I think he could get mad enough to kill someone. But Charlie has always been straight with me, Mickey. I don't think he'd lie to my face after all these years."

I looked out the car window. "Uncle Bobby, he told me he'd shoot us in the head and feed us to the gators. I'm tellin' y'all the truth. I wouldn't lie to y'all, Uncle Bobby."

Uncle Bobby's hands gripped the wheel until his knuckles were white and his face was red with rage. "That sumbitch! He lied to me. And so did Jimmy. Those…Agh! I cain't believe you been dealing with this on your own. Look at me, Mickey. You gotta promise me somethin'."

"Yessir."

"Promise me that you'll never keep a secret like this from me again."

"I promise."

"I mean it. No matter what anybody says, you gotta always tell me the truth."

"Yessir."

He started the car. "But…umm…I wouldn't tell yo' mama about this—not right now, anyway."

"No, sir. I know better than that."

NINETEEN

APRIL 1963

Uncle Bobby wanted to swing by our house to see if the cleanup had started. Aunt Tootie and Grandmama hadn't arrived yet. Uncle Bobby was about to drive on when I begged him to stop and let me get some comic books for me and some toys for Harley to play with.

"I shouldn't do this, but okay." He parked the car. "Cain't have you boys without somethin' to do 'til you get back home."

We found the door still unlocked from last night. He went in first and I followed behind. I gasped. It did look like a murder scene from the movies, just like Uncle Bobby said. The living room was a mess with broken lamps, a broken coffee table, and an easy chair lying on its side. There was a hole in the living room wall where Daddy had thrown me. No wonder my head hurt.

Then there was the hallway. The knife was still stuck in the door, looking like a scar on the Mona Lisa. The terrazzo floor was sticky with blood, as were the walls. I thought I might be sick. Uncle Bobby slowly pulled the knife from the bedroom door and walked inside. It, too, was a mess. There were empty clothes hangers all over the floor and dresser drawers pulled out and left on the bed. As Uncle Bobby had hoped, Daddy had packed all his belongings and slithered off like a rattlesnake escaping to the protection of swamp grass.

We heard noises at the front door.

"Hey, Bobby! That you in there?" Aunt Tootie yelled out. She walked into the living room. "My God, it looks like a war zone in here! Humph. Thought you didn't want the boys to see all this mess."

Grandmama walked in the door. "Dear Jesus!" She fell, more than sat, on the couch. "What a holy mess!"

Aunt Tootie looked down the hall. "Look at all this blood! Is it all Dixie Mae's?" Before Bobby could answer, she turned around, white as a sheet. "This is way worse than I thought it would be."

Grandmama got angry. "We'd better never lay eyes on that bastard again, or God forgive me, I'll kill him myself!" And then she started to cry.

Aunt Tootie looked at Bobby. "You ought to take Mickey out of here, don't ya think?"

He agreed. "I'll drop 'im by your place and come back to help clean up." The first time he volunteered, Aunt Tootie had rejected his offer. This time, she said, "Thank you, Bobby. We gonna need a lot more bleach and cleanin' supplies. Can y'all pick those up for us on yo' way back?"

"Sure. I'll be back soon as I can."

Tootie moved back in with us. She showed up with her stuff and moved back into her old room. Harley stayed close to her. He seemed extra weepy, with the fighting and all. I think he missed his daddy, but I didn't ask.

Uncle Bobby drove Mama home from the hospital two days later. If the terror of that night hadn't still been hanging over us, it would have been a celebration. While Uncle Bobby got Mama settled into her room, Aunt Tootie whipped up a great dinner and before we knew it, the five of us were back to the way it had been— before Daddy had come back to ruin our lives.

Mama stayed home the rest of that week and the next before she went back to work. Rumor was that Daddy had quit his job flying for Mel. He disappeared from town, as far as I knew. Harley had nightmares the first few nights, cryin' out for help. But he soon settled down. I showed off my shiner to my friends, who were duly impressed.

The outward evidence of Mama's ordeal was healing and could be covered up by her artful makeup skills. Harley's wounds, and mine, were covered by bandages. However, the inner wounds and scars we all suffered from that night would take much longer, if at all, to heal. I tried my best to pretend that Daddy had never come back and that living at the lake was just the same. But it never was the same. The magic was gone.

Before we knew it, the last school day arrived. Harley and I chattered on about our expectations of the summer—swimming in the lake, Little League Baseball finals, the All-Star Tournament (and I was one), Fourth of July, and, of course, my twelfth birthday. It was going to be great, and it was all we could talk about.

We rounded the corner to our house and saw Mama's car in the driveway and a car I didn't recognize in the street in front of our house. "This cain't be good, Harley."

"What y'all mean, Mickey?"

"Seems like ever' time Mama's car's here after school instead of at work, it ain't nothin' but bad news."

Turned out I was a prophet.

As we got closer, I could hear yelling coming from inside.

"Mel, you cain't do this to me!" Mama raged.

A man's angry voice responded, "I can, Dixie Mae, and I am."

Harley and I walked into the living room to see Aunt Tootie sitting on the couch with shock all over her face while my mama and her boss yelled at each other. Mama saw us and said, "Boys, go to your rooms right now. This ain't none of y'all's business." Looking over at Tootie, she snapped, "Ain't none of yo's either. Why don't y'all get out of here while I work this out with Mel."

Aunt Tootie stood up. Indignant, she motioned to us, "C'mon boys. Let's get out o' yo' mama's way." She stormed from the room, and we followed her down the hall like obedient puppies.

Mama and Mel's yelling was so loud, I didn't need to sneak to eavesdrop.

"Mel, if you fire me, you know I cain't make the rent payment. You said this house would be mine someday."

Tootie looked up and said, "Rent, hell, I thought Dixie Mae owned this house."

"Don't you put this on me, Dixie Mae," Mel said. "I been coverin' your fine ass for months now. I told you I've been gettin' complaints from our lady clients about your car washin' demonstrations in your driveway every Sunday mornin'. But now everybody's sayin' you tried to kill Charlie!"

"It was self-defense, Mel!"

"Your neighbors ain't deaf, Dixie Mae. They heard you screamin' that you were gonna kill Charlie. There's some who says he locked himself in a room while you tried to beat down the door."

Mama's voice got hard. "You gonna fire me from my job even though I'm the best agent you got? You gonna take my house away from me 'cause Charlie Crow is a lyin', cheatin' bastard who was screwin' that slut Charlotte?"

"Yeah, that kinda sums it up."

Her voice softened significantly. "Mel, cain't we work somethin' out?" I knew what that tone meant. Mama was trying to work her magic, that as far as I'd ever seen, had gotten her whatever she wanted from the men in her life.

"Dixie Mae, you know I like you, always have. And as much as I'd like to take you up on your offer, it ain't about you. It's about business. I cain't tell you how many phone calls I've gotten from clients asking me if one of my agents attempted to murder her husband. They're startin' to cancel their listin's 'cause of what's happened." He opened the front door. "I'm sorry, Dixie Mae, I really am, but I cain't afford to keep you on. You're fired. You got thirty days to move outta *my* house."

The door closed, but Mama stormed after him and threw it open again. "What offer, you lyin' bald-headed fat bastard? Don't flatter yo'self. You the last man on earth I'd screw!" She slammed the door so hard it shook the house and knocked one of the pictures off the wall.

We found Mama sitting in the backyard on a lawn chair, a Winston in one hand and a glass of vodka in the other. Aunt Tootie sat down on another chair, and me and Harley sat on the grass.

Tootie was blunt. "Y'all told us you bought this house."

Mama shrugged her shoulders. "I did buy this house. I mean, sort of. It's called rent with an option to buy. Mel bought the house and agreed that part of our rent would go to the down payment." She gave her sister a glare. "How did y'all think I could come up with a down payment on what I make, huh?"

I didn't understand. "Mama, are you sayin' we don't own this house? We're just rentin' it?"

Mama took a drag on her Winston and slowly let the foul blue smoke waft over her head.

Aunt Tootie stated the obvious. "So, you lied to us."

"It wasn't a lie. It's real estate stuff that you just cain't understand."

"Well, Dixie Mae, I know I ain't as smart as you, but I know this much. We gotta move in thirty days 'cause Mel owns this house, not you."

"No!" Harley and I yelled at the same time.

"Ain't there some other way, Dixie Mae?" Tootie was not happy.

"'Fraid not, Tootie. There ain't no other way to keep up the payments. I made good money workin' for Mel. Without that, we just cain't afford to stay here."

"Cain't you find another job sellin' real estate?"

"No, Tootie, not in this town. Me gettin' fired will be all over town by tomorrow—hell, it probably already is." Mama snuffed out her Winston on the arm of the lawn chair and downed what was left in her glass in one long swig. Standing with as much dignity as she could muster, Mama walked toward the house.

"Where we gonna live?" Aunt Tootie called after her.

"Don't know, Tootie," Mama yelled back. "But we'd better start packin'."

CHAPTER

TWENTY

PRESENT
SATURDAY, APRIL 22, 1972
6:48 P.M.

I looked up and saw that the sun was beginning to set, the western sky ablaze. I hadn't realized how long I'd been sitting on the ramp, but hours had passed in what seemed like moments. My stomach was making noises that translated into hunger, so I started up the truck and noticed the needle on my gas gauge was near empty. Driving back to the highway, I saw an old Sonoco station and pulled in.

Stopping at the pump, a high school kid walked over. "How much y'all need, sir?" He said through my rolled-down window. Looking at the pump, I saw the price was thirty-six cents a gallon.

"Fill 'er up."

I got out and headed to the bathroom as the kid moved to the pump and plugged the nozzle into my tank. When I finished my business, I walked out to my truck and noticed the kid was cleaning my windshield. When he moved around to clean my back window, I asked, "Do you know of a good place to get a bite to eat?" My stomach was getting a little more insistent.

He smiled, braces shining against his white teeth. "There's Billy's Café down the road a ways." Pointing, he said, "Ya cain't miss it."

I didn't get very far before I passed a sign that said, "Billy's Café—Best Burgers in the Panhandle, Next Exit." I pulled off the highway and coasted into a parking spot for the diner that reminded me a lot of the Blue Star, only smaller and seedier. I hoped the food was as good as promised. As I shifted into park and opened the door to step out, Billy's neon sign came to life, reminding me of that other diner that was open tonight. I wondered if Aunt Tootie was working the evening shift. My thoughts returned to the summer we moved back in with my mama's family because we had nowhere else to go.

CHAPTER TWENTY-ONE

While we lived at the lake, Grandmama and Grandpa Hank had bought a four-bedroom house in Rolling Hills Estates—a new subdivision out on King Street near the Quincy Airport. "This a big house, Dixie Mae, with plenty o' room fo' all y'all," Grandmama said. "There's a bedroom for all o' us—one for Tootie, one for Hank and me, one fo' you, and one fo' the boys." Though Mama didn't want to move back into her mama's house, it was the best deal she was going to get, so there was no question that she would have to take Grandmama up on the offer.

Four weeks later, we said goodbye to the best place I'd ever lived and moved into Grandmama's new house. Rolling Hills was only eight miles from our lake house, but it might as well have been on another planet. Mama still had her job at The Savannah and went back to working part-time at the Blue Star. We were going to live with Grandmama until Mama saved enough money to rent another place.

I missed the lake house, for sure, but Grandmama and Grandpa Hank's house was the biggest, newest, and grandest one I'd lived in. And the outside was just as exciting to me and Harley. The house was situated on a large corner lot with pine woods across the street. It was a deep, thick grove of trees with a large creek running through it. We wasted no time exploring every tree-covered inch of the woods and creek.

Most days that summer, Harley and I could be found in the woods. We hunted all sorts of game in those woods with our BB guns—deer, rabbit, possum, raccoon, bobcat, and turkey—*especially* turkey. Never hit a thing! No animal could've been safer than when the two of us were hunting it, but it was a great adventure trying. We had better luck in the creek where we fished for catfish, bass, and shad. We kept the catfish for Tootie to fry and threw everything else back. We made a few friends in the new neighborhood, but none shared our love of the woods and creek.

Grandmama started taking Harley and me back to church again. I was surprised at how much I'd missed it. Mama stopped talking about moving out on our own as if resigned to the fact that the three of us couldn't make it alone. And we also got to join in with Grandmama's Sunday dinners again. Uncle Bobby came around once more, and we all picked up where we left off—as if nothing had ever happened to any of us. Another lie we were telling ourselves.

On the first Sunday dinner back, Grandmama stood up and said, "God is so good! It's a real blessin' to have y'all around my table again. So, no mo' talkin'! Let's get to eatin'!"

Taking her words to heart, we dug in. By the time we were done, there wasn't much left, except for the pies. Apple, cherry, banana cream, and peach pie—oh my! They all made it to the table with lots of homemade whipped cream. After dinner, we retired to the Florida room, where Harley and I sat in quiet rapture as we listened to stories of days gone by.

One afternoon, the group was sitting around the porch after a feast of food. Uncle Bobby said, "Mickey, I think you're havin' a growth spurt!" I had turned twelve in July, growing a little bit every day, it seemed.

Aunt Tootie smiled. "C'mon over here, boy." She took my face in her hands and examined me carefully. "I believe this boy is gonna need a razor real soon!"

"Aw, Aunt Tootie!" I pulled away, acting embarrassed. Secretly, I was proud of those new hairs growing on my chin. My voice sounded different too—deeper somehow. I guess I was growing up some.

Harley and I were still very close. We stuck together through thick and thin. He was my best friend. Oh, don't get me wrong, we both made friends at school and around the neighborhood, but there was no one on the planet that I trusted more than Harley.

In September, Harley and I attended yet another school. Neither one of us warmed up quickly to Rolling Hills Elementary. The kids were nice and so were the teachers, but the sudden move from everything we loved and everyone we called friends left us feeling like we didn't really belong there.

The best part of living with Grandmama was the chance to feel safe and secure. Grandpa Hank was quiet, but we knew he loved us. We enjoyed Aunt Tootie's cooking and life became predictable. Even Mama seemed happier and more relaxed, and that made me happy.

Eight months later, on a Friday evening in early February 1964, Mama was working at The Savannah and Grandpa Hank was deer hunting with a couple of his buddies for a few days. Grandmama and Tootie were cleaning up the kitchen after dinner. Harley was working a puzzle, and I was nosing around in the bookshelves looking for something to read. I found a stack of picture albums, took one out, and started looking through it. I found some of me and Harley when we were kids.

"Come over and look at these, Harley!" I called. I thought he'd enjoy these old pictures of us when we were younger. They were all typical kid shots—us sitting on horses in our cowboy outfits with six-shooters strapped to our waists; pictures of us in our swimsuits, running and jumping through the sprinklers on a hot summer day; and running around the yard naked when we were toddlers—that kind of thing. As we looked through the album's pages, we came across lot of pictures of Mama and Daddy in happier times. There were shots of them water skiing, sitting at a picnic table, and on the hood of a car.

Tootie came in from the kitchen and noticed we were looking at the album. "What y'all boys doin' with that picture album?"

"Nothin'," I said. "Just looking at these old pictures of the family."

"Who said you could look at 'em?" Tootie snapped.

"Why cain't we see these albums? There's only some old pictures in the damn thing," I snapped back.

"Y'all watch yo' mouth, boy. We don't talk like that in this house!"

Well, hell, that was news to me, but I wisely decided not to bring that up.

She turned off the TV and came over to the couch. "Here, scootch over and let yo' ol' Aunt Tootie take a look."

We found another album with pictures of Mama and Tootie when they were little girls.

Harley looked up at Aunt Tootie with a wide grin. "You and mama were so pretty!"

I was surprised that they looked so much alike when they were young—although it was obvious that Tootie was older. But their faces were the same shapes, their hair blonde and curly. It was hard to believe that the cute little girl in the picture had grown into Aunt Tootie. She wasn't pretty at all anymore. I felt guilty thinking that way because I loved her so much. But she was a large, heavy woman who wore no makeup, with long, stringy hair, and she hid her shape under big, oversized muumuus. How could they look so similar then and so different now? They actually looked happy, with big smiles on their faces. It was a bit startling, actually. Aunt Tootie hardly ever smiled at anyone unless it was me and Harley.

I kept flipping the pages until we were on the last page. Both Tootie and Mama were sitting on a man's lap.

"Who's that, Aunt Tootie?" I asked.

My aunt frowned. "Oh, that's me and Dixie Mae's daddy, Grandpa Nash. He died when I was in high school."

"How come nobody ever talks 'bout 'im? What was he like?"

I was startled when Aunt Tootie slammed the album shut and said, "Enough of these pictures. Let's look at somethin' else."

"But—"

"My turn!" Harley declared as he dashed toward the bookshelf. "Here's a really old one!"

Aunt Tootie laughed. "This thang's nearly as big as you, Harley."

I took the album from Harley and placed it on the coffee table. Upon opening it, a small picture slipped out onto the floor. I picked it up and held it closer to my eyes. I realized it was a man with his arm around Mama's waist. She had a small baby in her arms.

Aunt Tootie gulped and tried to snatch it out of my hand, but I was too fast for her. "Gimme that picture!" Aunt Tootie yelled.

"No!" I shouted. I grabbed the album, jumped to my feet, and tried to run. I had no idea who this guy was, but if it upset Aunt Tootie enough to try to stop me, I was determined to find out. Tootie made another grab for the picture and latched onto a corner. The album went flying into the air, pictures floating down around us like dead leaves falling off a tree in autumn.

Grandmama heard the commotion from the kitchen and stormed out to see what happened. "What the hell is goin' on in here!"

"He found a picture."

"Of what?"

Aunt Tootie looked genuinely scared. "Not what, who."

"Dammit, Tootie, of who, then?"

"Of *him*."

Grandmama looked down. "Nobody move! We don't want to step on these photos." We all froze in place. It felt like we were surrounded by landmines waiting for some unsuspecting soul to step on one and set them all off.

"Boys, y'all wash up for dinner and me and Tootie will pick up them pictures."

Harley was only too obliging, but I wanted to get my hands on that picture again. "I wanna help pick up!" I started to grab as many pictures as I could.

Aunt Tootie spoke loudly and firmly. "Do what your Grandmama says. Wash up for dinner." She tried to intercept me.

I stepped out of reach and frantically flipped over photos.

"Stop that, Mickey!" Grandmama bellowed.

Harley, who had wisely remained silent through all of this, said, "Aw, Mickey, you gonna get us in trouble."

Aunt Tootie lunged again, but she was too late. I held up the picture in triumph so they could see it, but kept it out of Aunt Tootie's reach. "Who's this man next to Mama, holdin' a baby?"

Tootie and Grandmama stood there for a minute like trapped animals with no way out. Tootie finally spoke in a soft tone, like a police officer trying to talk a jumper off the ledge. "That's nobody y'all know, boy—no one to concern yo'self about. So, hand it over, okay?"

I guess I didn't hand it over fast enough because Grandmama reached over and snatched the picture out of my hands.

"Is that Jack?" I asked.

They shared a look of horror. Grandmama asked, "How do you know about Jack?"

"One time, when Mama and Daddy were fightin', Daddy said Mama cheated on him with some guy named Jack. Was that true? Is this Jack?"

It was so quiet that you could hear Tootie and Grandmama's panicked breathing. Grandmama just looked back and forth between me and the picture. And then Mama walked in.

"What's this shit?" Mama asked, looking at the pictures still strewn all over the floor. She spied the picture in her mama's hand. "What y'all got there?"

"It ain't nothin', Dixie Mae," Aunt Tootie said.

Grandmama started to put the picture into a pocket in her apron when Mama held out her hand and demanded to see it. With a heavy sigh, the picture was placed in her hand. Her eyes got wide with fear and then narrow with rage. She swung around so she could see both Aunt Tootie and Grandmama at the same time. "Where'd this come from?"

"It's Jack, ain't it?" I confronted her.

My mama's eyes fluttered like a struggling butterfly as she realized the Pandora's Box that had just been opened.

Suddenly, as if the heavens opened, a thought filled my mind. "You're with Jack, and you're holdin' me." I paused. "You're holdin' me." Then another thought. "Is Jack my daddy? Is he Mama!"

Mama turned white as she turned her gaze to her mama. "You told Mickey that Jack was his daddy?"

Grandmama said quietly, "Dixie Mae, Mickey found this ol' picture and asked if it was Jack. That's when you walked in. We didn't tell them nothin'. You're the one who let the cat out of the bag."

CHAPTER TWENTY-TWO

Chaos ensued. Mama, Aunt Tootie, and Grandmama were all yelling at each other. Cussing and accusations filled the room in a deafening rush of acrimony. I fell back onto the couch, completely stunned, attempting to take it all in, while Harley cried.

As I watched the tempest boiling over in front of me, I began to think that I might not be Charlies Crows son. I mean I *couldn't* be Charlie's son, right? We looked nothing alike. Harley, yes, he looked just like him. But I didn't at all. And I didn't feel for Charlie what a son should feel for his daddy. In fact, many times I'd wished that Uncle Bobby was my daddy, but no, it was someone named Jack.

I always thought it was wishful thinking, but now? *What if Charlie isn't my daddy? What if this Jack guy is? Grandmama said the cat was out of the bag. What cat was that?* And finally, everything made sense. "Jack's my daddy." No one heard my realization.

Slowly, a grin spread across my face. That sumbitch Charlie Crow was *not* my daddy. Praise God and thank you Jesus! I didn't care that some man named Jack was my daddy. I was giddy with the possibility that Charlie was not! My heart danced. My soul rejoiced! Impulsively, I stood up, spread my arms out in proud declaration, and yelled, "Charlie Crow is not my daddy!"

The tempest sputtered and came to a complete stop at my outburst. Grandmama and Tootie's mouths dropped open, but Mama's face was dark and fierce.

"Jack's my daddy!" I shouted again and burst into tears—not tears of sadness or anger, but tears of relief.

Harley paused in shock. "What? Daddy ain't Mickey's daddy? Who's my daddy then? Is Jack my daddy too?"

Aunt Tootie put her arms around Harley. "No, Harley. Charlie is still yo' daddy."

The pennies were dropping in Harley's mind, and he turned to me. "Mickey, if my daddy ain't yo' daddy, does that mean we ain't brothers no more?"

Grandmama jumped in, bless her, and assured Harley we were. "Don't y'all worry about that none, ya hear? Mickey's still yo' brother cause you and him have the same mama."

"Really, we still brothers and all?" He was still sniffling but seemed encouraged by this news.

Aunt Tootie affirmed it. "You betcha, Harley. Y'all as much brothers now as y'all were five minutes ago, before y'all saw those pictures."

Harley wiped his tears on his shirt and looked down. "Good, 'cause I don't want no other brother than Mickey."

Harley, still trying to piece it all together, turned to Mama and asked, "You still me and Mickey's mama, right?"

Mama had been silent through all of this, her eyes dark and wild like an animal trapped and terrified. But when Harley questioned if she was his mama, she came undone. Mama grabbed the picture, ripped it into tiny pieces, and walked out of the room without a word. We heard her stomp down the hallway and into her bedroom, slamming the door so hard it shook the whole house.

⚬

No one dared to speak. Grandmama and Tootie headed down the hall to their bedrooms.

Harley turned pale as ghost when Mama slammed the door. He looked at me with pleading eyes and said, "Did I say somethin' wrong Mickey?"

I went over to him and whispered, "You ain't done nothin' wrong, Harley." Pointing down the hall I said, "They did."

Shortly, Grandmama retuned from her hideout and spoke up. "Boys, why don't y'all let me talk with yo' mama before you say somethin' to her, okay?"

"Good idea, Mama." Tootie said as she entered the room, nodding her head with enthusiasm, relieved not to be the first to encounter Mama's wrath. Hell, no one *wanted* to talk to Mama right now.

"Okay, then," Grandmama smoothed her dress down the front in preparation for the encounter. "Pray for me," she said as she left the room. We knew she meant it.

We watched as she knocked on Mama's bedroom door. "Dixie Mae, can I talk to y'all for a minute?" There was no reply, but the door opened. We heard footsteps, then the door softly shut behind her as she disappeared into the lion's den.

I didn't move, I knew better than to try and eavesdrop, not this time, though it was disappointing to miss the gist of their encounter. All we could hear was muffled sounds, although I was sure there was plenty of cussing and crying going on. The door abruptly opened, and Grandmama walked out, looking ashen and shaken. She walked past us and into the kitchen. Saying nothing, she sat down and covered her face with her hands.

Mama yelled down the hall, "Tootie, get in here! I wanna talk to y'all." Now it was Tootie's turn to face Mama's wrath.

Stricken, Tootie looked like a mouse cornered by a couple of hungry cats. "Me?"

"Yes, goddamnit, you! Is there another Tootie out there?"

Tootie mouthed to me, "Fo' God's sake, I wish there was."

Standing up, she straightened, took a deep breath, and walked into Mama's room. I swear, if I didn't know better, I could have believed she was headed for the gallows, preparing to swing for her crimes. Thirty more minutes passed with more muffled cussing and crying. Finally, the door opened, expelling Tootie, who looked a lot like a whipped dog.

"Mickey, come in here!" Mama barked.

"Yo' turn." She pointed at me as she walked by, headed for the sanctuary of her room.

I walked in and sat on her bed.

"Mickey, I was gonna have a talk about this with y'all one day. Well, I guess today's the day. It's true. Charlie Crow ain't yo' daddy."

I relaxed and smiled.

"What ya smilin' 'bout, boy?"

"Nothin', Mama."

"You best not be smilin', Mickey", Mama barked. "Charlie's been the only daddy you ever knew."

That was something I wished weren't true. "So, you cheated on Charlie with this Jack?" I asked, not really knowing what that meant.

"What kind o' dumbass question is that?" She glared at me. "Course not. Shut up and listen, shithead, there's more. Charlie ain't yo' daddy, and he ain't Harley's daddy neither."

"He's not?" I didn't think I could've been more shocked than I already was, but I was wrong.

"No, Jack McCarthy is both y'all's daddy."

"But Mama, Grandmama and Aunt Tootie said that Jack's *my* daddy, and Charlie is *Harley's* daddy." Someone was lying to me.

"Who yo' gonna believe, boy? Me or them? Don't y'all think I would know, since I was the one havin' you babies? Y'all don't think I know who y'all's daddy is?"

"Yes, ma'am," I said, but I wasn't sure I believed her. I was old enough to know about where babies came from, and if Mama had been with both men, even she might not know for sure.

"Look, I can prove it. Just sit there and keep quiet."

Walking over and pulling out one of her chest of drawers, she grabbed a small, worn, wooden box. Opening it, she took out two pieces of paper. "Y'all need to see this. This here is yo' birth certificate." She unfolded the document and handed it to me.

I took it, handling it like it was the original stone tablets given to Moses by God himself. Looking at it, I saw my name, the date I was born, and the city and hospital I was born in. My mama was Dixie Mae McCarthy, and my daddy, John Jack McCarthy. More proof Charlie Crow was not my daddy. Then she handed me the second document, saying, "This 'un is yo' brother Harley's birth certificate."

I took it from her, handling it in the same reverent manner as my own. It had the same kind of information as mine. I silently mouthed the words as I read them. "Baby Boy: Harley Charles McCarthy. Mother: Dixie Mae McCarthy. Father: John Jack McCarthy."

"Y'all believe me now, shithead?" Honestly, I didn't know what to believe. I was still shocked to find out that Charlie Crow wasn't my father, and now he wasn't Harley's, either? Harley looked exactly like Charlie. It made sense to me that he was Charlie's boy.

And Grandmama and Tootie had said that Jack was my daddy and Charlie was Harley's. Why lie to us? Nothing made sense, and my head was spinning. I decided I needed further assurance about the main point. "Okay Mama, but you're sure that Jack is *my* daddy?"

She smacked me upside the head. "Ow!"

"Dumbass."

I was feeling vulnerable here alone with her, but I pressed on, believing I'd never get another chance like this. "So, you lied to me and Harley our whole lives?"

She sat back on the bed. Maybe she was getting confused as well. So many daddies and sons to keep up with. She shoved the birth certificates back in my face as if that ended the discussion. But for me, it was just the start.

"How come our last names are Crow then?"

"Because, Mickey, Charlie adopted you. That's why."

I sure could've used a chart to keep all of this new information in order, but as it was, I was totally confused.

"Mickey, y'all need to forget Jack McCarthy. He's gone, and he ain't never comin' back. Never, y'all hear me? Never!"

"Mama, is he dead?"

"He is as far as yo' concerned, so forget 'bout 'im. He was an awful man. He left us right after Harley was born, and I was destitute. He tricked me and stole all the money I'd saved up when he was away in the Air Force. That sumbitch left me with two small kids and not a pot to piss in!"

Cain't Mama ever find a good man? Aloud, I asked, "He just left us?"

She nodded. "And if it wasn't for Charlie, I would'a never known what to do. I got a quick divorce and Charlie married me and told me he would raise both you and Harley as his own boys. That was the deal. So, we filed the paperwork and we got married, and he promised to take care of us as long as we never spoke about Jack McCarthy again."

"So, yo' sayin' that Charlie was a better man than my real daddy?"

She smacked me across the top of my head again.

Mama shot back, "Listen here, smart ass. You better believe Charlie is a much better man. Jack was a sumbitch, and I ain't gonna talk about 'im no more and that's final!"

Raising my voice I said, "Okay Mama, but I'll tell *you* this. I'm not gonna call that sumbitch daddy anymore. He's just Charlie to me now." Then I turned to leave.

Mama's face distorted into a stare of calculated coldness. She grabbed me by my wrist. "Here's how this is goin' to happen, you little shit!"

She was hurting me, but I didn't resist. "We're gonna say that Jack is yo' daddy, but Charlie is Harley's."

"Why?"

"'Cause I said so! He's too young to understand it all." She dug her nails deeper into my wrist. "So, keep yo' mouth shut, got it? Don't tell him that Charlie's not his real daddy."

I lost my temper and pulled free of her grasp. "Mama, why does *everybody* in our family lie?"

Her eyes got dark and scary mean. "You callin' me a liar, boy?"

I was confused by the question. "Ya told me and Harley that Charlie was our daddy our whole lives. Now yo' tellin' me he's not. If I said somethin' like that to you, would ya call me a liar? I know you would, 'cause it ain't the truth." *Oh shit, I just called Mama a liar to her face!*

She stood up in defiance, or reality, I didn't know for sure. She put her face so close to mine I could feel her breath. "Don't you *ever* call yo' mama such an awful thing again, Mickey, or you'll be pickin' yo' teeth up off the floor! Y'all hear me?"

I didn't say anything.

"Well, do ya?" she said, seething with anger. I nodded yes, because I was too scared to speak. Having made her speech, she sat back down. "And don't y'all ever tell Harley or anybody else what I told ya today. I mean it Mickey. Yo' the only one that knows the whole truth. And as far as everyone else outside the family is concerned, Charlie is both of y'all's daddy."

My head spun trying to make sense of what Mama was saying. "Aunt Tootie and Grandmama don't know? Just me?"

She grabbed me by the shoulders and emphasized each word as she stared into my eyes. "I said, don't ya ever tell anybody that Charlie ain't Harley's daddy, do you hear me?"

I was trapped. "Yes, ma'am, I won't say nothin'."

"Now get on outta here and tell Harley I want to see 'im."

In a flash, I remembered my Sunday School teacher, Mr. Mann, telling us all that lying was a sin. I knew then that both me and Mama were going straight to hell when we died.

CHAPTER TWENTY-THREE

FEBRUARY 1964

Mama and Harley weren't in the bedroom for long. He came out with a smile on his face and headed to our room. Mama walked to the back yard where Grandmama and Tootie had retreated after their sessions. I heard her arguing with them again, then she stormed through the house and out the front door. A few seconds later the Bug started up, and I saw Mama pull out of the driveway onto Beverly Street and disappear.

I walked out to the back porch where Grandmama and Tootie were sitting in old rocking chairs. Grandmama was crying and Tootie was trying to comfort her. I started to say something, but Tootie cut me off. "Mickey, we done talkin' 'bout this today—maybe fo'ever—so don't ask any mo' questions right now, okay?"

Headlights of a car coming into the driveway caught our attention.

"Maybe Dixie Mae came back." Aunt Tootie didn't look happy. I wasn't sure right now if that would be a good or bad thing. But instead of Mama, Grandpa Hank sauntered up the driveway into the backyard.

"How y'all doin'?" he asked innocently.

I let Grandmama and Aunt Tootie field that question.

Walking back inside, I headed to our room where Harley was stretched out on his bed.

"Mama's real mad, Mickey."

"Yeah, I know it."

"What was y'all talkin' about in there with Mama?" he asked.

"My daddy."

Harley pulled himself up on one elbow. "So, my daddy's Charlie."

I nodded. "And my daddy is Jack."

Harley got very serious. "But ya can't tell anyone. Me neither."

"Mama told ya to keep this a secret?"

He nodded. "I promised on the Bible, Mickey. Ya know what that means?"

I shook my head yes.

"I promised God I'd obey my mama, like they say at church. Y'all can't break a promise to God, ya know."

It was the first time I'd witnessed someone twisting the Bible around to say whatever they wanted it to say. And Mama knew her Bible well, so she had plenty of ammunition at her disposal.

Mama's plan still wasn't clear to me. "So, Harley. We're both supposed to say that Charlie is our daddy, right?"

He nodded. "But we know the truth."

The truth, now that's an interesting concept.

He continued, "But no matter what, we're really still brothers, right?"

"We sho' the hell is, Harley. Nothin' on God's green earth will ever change that— nothin'!" I patted him on the shoulder.

"Mama said that as long as we got the same mama, we're still brothers."

I nodded.

"And we got the same mama, right?"

The thought of that being in question made my stomach turn. Harley was just ten, and because Mama wouldn't be honest, she made an even bigger mess out of things. Why should he have to navigate her convoluted lies? I nodded again, then said, a little irritably, "Yeah, Harley, we still brothers so let's stop talkin' about it, okay?"

"Okay, Mickey, okay."

Lying there on our beds, we both pondered the situation in silence. I was angry at Mama for manipulating both of us to keep her secrets. I knew that Jack was Harley's daddy, but I couldn't tell him. He thought Jack was my daddy, while Charlie was his, but he'd promised not to talk about any of this. She got us both to keep different secrets, pulling us into her web of bullshit.

It shook me to the core that Grandmama and Aunt Tootie had also lied to me, over and over again. They had to have seen those birth certificates, even though Mama said they hadn't. Damn, they were there when she gave birth to both of us and was married to Jack! They had to have known the truth all these years but never said anything. Even now, they both would lie to Harley without hesitation. But why would they go to such lengths?

And then it dawned on me. Maybe Mama was terrified of what Charlie would do if she defied him. He'd married her on one condition—that everybody would say that he was the father of us both. Everyone had to know she'd been married to Jack. And no one said a word to me or Harley.

My gut twisted into a new formation. Uncle Bobby must also be in on this whole deception. Not even Uncle Bobby was straight with me. The bottom dropped out of my world.

I rolled over on my bed, hiding my face under my pillow. I didn't want Harley to see the hot tears of rage spilling over onto my cheeks. *What other secrets are being kept from me? I'm on my own now.* There wasn't anyone I could completely trust anymore to tell me the whole truth—and now here I was keeping secrets from Harley. Damn it all, I was no better than the rest of them.

⚬

Two days later, on Sunday, Mama still had not returned home. We were all frantic with worry about where she'd gone, wondering if she was okay or if something bad had happened to her. After dinner, Grandmama finally had enough and called Uncle Bobby.

"Bobby, Dixie Mae's been missin' since Friday night. You gotta find her, boy. You gotta find her, please. I'm 'fraid somethin' bad has hap'n to her!"

He was at our front door so fast Grandmama barely had time to hang up the phone.

When he walked into the living room, Grandmama hollered, "We're in the kitchen, Bobby."

With a couple of large steps, he found us sitting around the kitchen table. Worried, he asked, "Mizz Colee, what's goin' on?" He didn't bother to sit down. It was as if he was ready to jump into action.

"We ain't seen Dixie Mae in a couple o' days, and we worried as hell 'bout her. That's what's goin' on, Bobby"

Uncle Bobby chewed his lip. "Two days? And she left the boys behind?" With me and Harley sitting at the table, it was pretty clear she had.

"We had a big blow-up when Mickey found a picture of Jack, but yo' gonna need to get that story from Dixie Mae," Grandmama said.

Yeah let's see what version of "the truth" she tells Uncle Bobby.

He paused and looked at me. A wave of guilt passed over his face. I looked away.

Uncle Bobby sighed. "Oh, my God Mizz Colee, Dixie Mae must've been crazy mad about that. She swore she'd kill all of us if we ever uttered a word around the boys about Jack."

"So, ya admit you knew 'bout Jack?" My anger was swelling.

"I knew yo' Mama was married to him before she married Charlie."

I got up and stormed out of the room in a display of disgust. "Wait, Mickey," he called after me.

Aunt Tootie interrupted. "Bobby, don't mind Mickey right now. We're all sick with worry."

"Alright, I'll get on right on it. We'll find her, I swear we will. Okay?"

He ran past me in the living room. Dashing out the front door, he yelled back to me, "We'll talk about this later, Mickey."

I said to an empty room, "The hell we will."

A few hours later, we heard the screen porch door open. Bobby had Mama in his arms, sleeping and looking like a small child.

"Let's lay her down on her bed, Bobby," Grandmama whispered, then led him back to Mama's room. I followed. After he'd gently laid her down, Grandmama pulled a quilt over her—the one she'd made Dixie Mae when she was a child. The three of us walked quietly out Mama's bedroom door, gently shutting it behind us.

Back in the living room, Uncle Bobby looked at all of us with great concern etched on his face. "Mickey, Harley, why don't y'all go outside for a minute. I need to talk to Tootie and y'all's Grandmama, alone."

"Right," I said. "More secrets."

"Get out of this room," Grandmama snapped. "Your snoopin' around is what caused all this to begin with."

Yo' lying is what caused all of this to begin with! I wanted to say it out loud, but I knew that would get me a whipping, so I grabbed Harley by the arm and took him into the kitchen. We never made it outside, though. I pulled Harley down to the floor, and put my hand over his mouth. Whispering, I said, "Shhh, don't say a damn thing. Let's just listen, okay?" Harley nodded his head up and down.

We heard Uncle Bobby talking first. "I found her car at that seedy little bar out there just off highway two-sixty-seven and the ten. Y'all know the one?"

"Yeah, we know it. There's a dumpy little motel on the other side of the road where some of the truckers stay now and again. They say it ain't much to look at, but it's cheap," Grandmama said.

"Yeah, that's it, alright. Anyways, the bar was closed so I walked over to the motel and talked to the clerk in the office. Described Dixie Mae and he showed me her room and gave me a key. Said she came in a couple nights ago so drunk he had to help her to her room. He saw her come out of her room 'bout nine last night and walk across the street to the bar. Said he didn't see her come back."

Tootie started to cry. "Oh my God, it's all my fault! It's all my fault! We can't blame Mickey. I should've never tol' those boys nothin'!"

"Hush, now, Tootie," Grandmama said as she pulled Tootie close. "It's as much my fault as yours, so hush, baby, okay? It'll be all right."

Uncle Bobby stood up. "I think she's gonna be out for a while—maybe all night. Just let her rest, and I'll check in on y'all in the mornin', okay?"

Grandmama got up and gave Uncle Bobby a big hug. "Thank ya, Bobby. Thank ya for bringing my little girl home." She had tears rolling down her cheeks. As an afterthought, she called to him as he walked toward the door. "Yo' always there when we need ya, Bobby. Praise God, yo' always there."

"Mizz Colee, when it comes to Dixie Mae and her boys, I always will be."

When Mama finally came out of her room the next morning, no one said a word to her about where she'd been over the weekend. We were just happy that she was home and safe.

I think we were all expecting this to die down, but it didn't. She gave us all the silent treatment for the longest time. Then one night after dinner, she looked at Aunt Tootie and Grandmama and said, "You both broke yo' promise to me. Me and my boys are moving outta this house."

We all gasped in the same moment, sucking the oxygen out of the air.

"I already found a place. We'll be outta here on my day off—next Sunday."

CHAPTER TWENTY-FOUR

The Friday before we moved out of Grandmama's house was cold—damn cold for Florida—with temperatures in the mid-thirties. All of us were tucked in our warm and cozy beds, except for Mama who was working the ten-to-six shift down at the Blue Star. Harley and I had a hard to going to sleep because we were real sad that the only place Mama could afford was a single-wide mobile home she'd found somewhere out in the county. We were mad too, we didn't want to move. Finally though, we drifted off to sleep.

In the wee hours of the morning, unknown to us as we slept, a Stranger came in through the back door. The door was unlocked because nobody locked their doors in 1964. Finding himself standing in the breakfast room, near the kitchen, he noticed Mama's console stereo cabinet against the wall. The stereo, and the expensive heavy-leaded glasses displayed on top of it, were Mama's most prized possessions.

He grabbed the biggest and heaviest of the glasses from the cabinet and then began surveying the home he had just invaded. Very quietly, the intruder slowly began making his way into the kitchen until he saw the adjacent hallway harboring a closed bedroom door. Not making a sound, the Stranger walked over and opened the door.

Looking inside, he saw two twin beds filled with two little boys. Disinterested, he carefully closed the door.

Looking farther down the hall, he saw another door, only this one was open. Again, walking softly and carefully, like a lion stalking a clueless antelope, he worked his way down to the door opening. Hearing light snoring and other night noises, he glanced around the room to see what prey might be taken there, in the darkness of the night. He walked over and stood next to Grandmama's side of the bed. He must have decided that Grandpa Hank wouldn't prove to be a deterrent to assaulting the old woman who lay next to him.

"C'mon, Hank, I'm tired." Grandmama said as she tried, and failed, to remove the hand that was beginning to grip her neck. "Not now—" The man roughly turned her over onto her back and threw his leg over to sit on top of her. He pulled her nightgown up with one hand while threateningly holding Mama's leaded glass in the other. Grandmama realized it wasn't Grandpa touching her and screamed as loud as she could.

"Lord Jesus! Hank, wake up!"

Grandpa Hank, startled out of a deep sleep, immediately sat up, ram-rod straight, eyes open wide.

"What the hell!" he yelled as he saw the Stranger sitting on top of his wife.

Not saying a word, the Stranger hit Grandpa Hank with the heavy leaded glass, splitting his forehead wide open.

Punching Grandmama in the face, he tried to continue his assault, but Grandmama was stronger than he expected, and pushed him off balance.

Harley and I, awakened by the screaming, dashed into the hall just in time to see the door at the end of the hall swing wide open. Aunt Tootie stood there for a moment, looking like the Angel of Death with her double-barreled shotgun in hand, trying to comprehend what the screaming was about. The Stranger, hearing a door open and the slide of a shotgun being racked, jumped off Grandmama and ran out into the hall looking for an exit. He took one look at Tootie holding the weapon in her hands, and pushed past Harley and me, slamming us up against the wall and headed for the door where he'd entered. No one in their right mind would have entered our house uninvited, had they known about Tootie's expertise using a "thunder-stick."

When Grandmama yelled, "He done killed Hank! Oh my God, he done killed Hank!" Tootie ran after the Stranger, now fully grasping what she'd interrupted. Harley and I watched the dark form run out the door with Tootie in hot pursuit behind him. Running after her, I saw her lift the "Righteous Arm of God" and point it at the foul thing as he opened his car door. As the poor bastard scrambled to get in his vehicle and flee, Tootie screamed at the top of her lungs, "I hope y'all die, ya bastard!"

She pulled the dual triggers. Thunder roared and fire erupted from the twin barrels, splitting the silence of the night like an exploding bomb. The rain of shot struck the Stranger's now moving car. The back window was blown into a thousand little pieces of retribution, some of which reached the front seat and found their target. She was still the best shot in Florida, and had the trophy to prove it.

The Stranger let out a scream of pain so loud that neighbors told us later they'd heard it in their bedrooms. His tires spun on the wet grass, but before Aunt Tootie got another volley off, the car jumped off the lawn and into the street, nearly swerving out of control as the horrid creature screeched around the corner and disappeared.

I turned and rushed back into the house. Grandmama was screaming for help. "Mickey, call yo' Uncle Bobby! Right now!" I saw Grandpa Hank bleeding all over the bed. Shaking with adrenalin and fear, I called the Sheriff's office. I didn't ask for Uncle Bobby by name. I yelled into the phone our address and said, "Y'all gotta come now! Somebody done broke into our house and attacked Grandmama and Grandpa Hank. He's bleedin' real bad—real bad!"

By that time, Aunt Tootie was back in the house. Taking the phone from me, she gave them the address then ran back to Grandmama's room to help Grandpa Hank. Grandmama was holding a pillowcase to his forehead trying to stop the bleeding, but it wasn't near enough. Tootie ran for the closet and returned with several white towels to wrap around his head.

Handing the towels to Grandmama, Tootie said, "C'mon, boys, we gotta get Hank to the hospital, and we cain't wait for the police. He won't make it if we don't go now! Get y'all's shoes and coats on, hear me? Right now!" I had never heard her speak so forcefully as she did that night. I slipped on my sneakers and sweater and got Harley dressed. "Hurry up, boys!" Aunt Tootie shrieked.

I heard sirens and vehicles pulling up and into our driveway. Dressed, Harley and I stepped out into the hallway and into hell. There was Tootie trying to hold up Grandpa Hank, but he was too heavy, and he fell from her arms. Grandmama was holding a red towel around his head, only we didn't have any red towels. They were all white in Grandmama's house.

All three of them were covered in Hank's blood as they struggled to get him into the living room. It was everywhere—dripping from the towels covering his head, down his night shirt, into his slippers, and puddling onto the floor. He was so pale, due to the loss of blood, that Harley cried, and I thought I'd be sick.

Before I had the chance, Tootie shot me an order. "Mickey, come over here and help me carry Hank to the car." But before I could comply, two sheriff's deputies came through the door, guns drawn, then two more behind them. One of them was Uncle Bobby, and my relief almost caused me to pass out.

"Lay him down on the floor and move off. We'll take it from here," Uncle Bobby said. We did as he instructed and backed away.

Grandmama started wailing as she crumpled to the floor. "He done killed Hank! He done killed my husband!" Tootie grabbed me and Harley and held us close, unintentionally smearing us with Grandpa Hank's blood. Harley kept crying, but I went into a state of shock.

Uncle Bobby came over to talk to the three of us. "Tootie, what the hell happened here?" She began to relay the events of the evening as another officer bent down to help my Grandmama. Just then, the rescue squad came rushing in with a gurney and took over the care of Grandpa Hank. As I watched the scene unfold, I couldn't help but remember the night Charlie beat my mama and threw her on the front lawn. All the blood. The memory of that night, still fresh in my mind, caused me to shake uncontrollably.

Harley moved closer to me and took my hand. "Mickey, is Grandpa Hank gonna die?" His voice was hoarse and shaky. He looked and sounded so small and scared. I lost control and cried. "I don't know, Harley. I hope not."

We just stood there—two brothers holding onto each other—sobbing.

The Rescue Squad got Grandpa Hank on the gurney, moving him outside and into the waiting ambulance that had arrived a moment earlier. Returning, they focused their attention on Grandmama, who had been examined to verify that the blood belonged solely to Grandpa Hank. She described what had happened, in between fits of tears, to another deputy as best as she remembered them. They led her out and into a waiting cruiser for the trip to the hospital.

I overheard Aunt Tootie telling Uncle Bobby that she was pretty sure she "shot the sumbitch" with her shotgun as he was trying to drive off. He asked her to show him where she had fired and where she thought the bastard was hit. Following her to the door, she showed Uncle Bobby where she'd pulled the trigger. He began a search of the area where the Stranger had parked his car. After a few minutes, he came back in and confirmed that there was glass all over the area. The extent of her artful blasts was yet to be confirmed.

"Tootie, it's a good chance ya hit 'im. Might have done some serious damage too. I found a bit of blood mixed in with that broken glass. I'm gonna call this into the dispatcher so they can begin a search of local hospitals. If he was hit, he'll probably require medical attention to survive. After that, I'll give y'all a ride down to the hospital where they took your mama and Hank. Is that okay?"

They both looked around to see where Harley and I had ended up in this disaster. "Oh my!" Aunt Tootie cried out as she saw us clinging to each other. She ran over to us and threw her arms around us.

"It's okay, now, boys."

Uncle Bobby put his hand on my head. "You're safe now." I looked up at him, hoping he was right.

CHAPTER TWENTY-FIVE

Mama arrived home in the midst of all this chaos. As she told her side of the story, she said she'd been tired—dog tired. It had been a long shift at the Blue Star, and all she wanted to do was get home and go to bed. When she turned onto our street, she couldn't help but notice the police car and firetruck's emergency lights blazing with their blue and red strobes, cutting through the night like a knife. As she got closer to the house, she saw neighbors standing around in their pajamas and housecoats. While the firemen and police were going in and out of the house, her wonder quickly became panic, as she drove her little Bug up onto the lawn, not taking the time to turn off the lights. Running in the side door, she was stopped by a deputy she'd seen many times at the Blue Star.

"Hold on, Dixie Mae, where y'all think you're goin'?" He blocked her way.

"Let me pass, goddamnit! I live here!" She pushed past him.

She stopped in her tracks when she saw all the blood and bloody towels in the hallway. "Oh my God!" Mama practically fell into the deputy's arms. "Where's my boys? What's happened to my boys?"

Catching her, he tried to reassure her. "They're fine, Dixie Mae."

She was beginning to hyperventilate. "What the hell happened here, and where's Mickey and Harley?"

"It wasn't your boys. Some sumbitch came in that side door there and attacked your mama and daddy."

"Mama owns this house with my stepdaddy, Hank. Ar-are they dead?" Panic started to rise again, and she was doing her best to keep it at bay.

"I don't know the whole story yet, Dixie Mae. From what I understand, your mama wasn't hurt bad, but your stepdaddy was hit in the head and cut bad, and that's where all this blood come from."

"What 'bout my sister, Tootie? Is she okay?"

He smiled. "She's better than okay, so I've heard. She shot the sumbitch with a shotgun while he was trying to get away in his car. Blew out his back window with both barrels blazing. Must be quite a woman." There was admiration in his voice.

"She is," Mama replied. "Where're they now?"

"The ambulance took your mama and stepdaddy to Quincy Memorial. Deputy Bailey took y'all's sister and boys down there too."

"Bobby's with 'em?" Mama told us later that she was immediately relieved to hear that.

"Yes, give me a minute, and I'll take you down there too. I just gotta check out with the sarge." After a few minutes, he escorted Mama out to his cruiser and drove her down to the hospital to meet up with me, Harley and Tootie. She said she prayed all the way there that Hank would still be alive when she arrived.

Thanking the deputy for the ride, Mama got out of his cruiser and sprinted to the hospital's emergency entrance. Tootie, seeing her come in, ran up to her, crying and taking Mama into her ample arms. "Dixie Mae, it was just awful—the most awful thang I ever saw."

"The boys?"

"We're here, Mama!" I called out. Once again, me and Harley were stretched out on the seats in the ER, the same place we'd been several months before.

"Thank the Lord," Mama said. She began to cry. "How's Mama? Is she hurt? And how's Hank? Is he still alive?"

"Mama's fine, though she got a big shiner where the bastard hit her. She's 'round the corner talkin' to the doctor 'bout Hank. I don't know nothin' else right now, but Dixie Mae, he lost a lot of blood—I mean a lot. He was white as a sheet when they put 'im in the back of the ambulance at the house. Oh, here comes Mama now."

Taking one look at Grandmama's bruised and bandaged face, Mama broke down. Grandmama did, too, as they fell into each other's arms.

"Oh my God, Mama! Are y'all all right? Are y'all hurt anywhere else besides yo' face?"

"I'm fine, Dixie Mae, I'm fine."

"Okay, Mama. What's goin' on with Hank? Is he gonna make it?"

Grandmama nodded her head. "I was just talkin' with the doctor over there, and he said Hank was gonna pull through. Said he just made it here in time 'cause there weren't much blood left in his body."

"Thank God," Mama said. "Thank God Almighty!"

"Amen to that," Grandmama agreed. "Doctor said he's gonna have to be in here for 'bout two weeks. He had a bad hit to the head, so we don't know if he'll have some brain damage. He's gonna have a steel plate put in his forehead 'cause the sumbitch hit him so hard, he cracked his skull!"

"Who is he, Mama?" Dixie asked. "Do they know yet?"

"Never laid eyes on 'im befo' tonight. I don't know why he chose our house, Dixie Mae. I just cain't understand it. Truth be told, I was so scared when he climbed up on me, I'm not sure I could pick 'im out of a lineup. It was real dark in our room when it happened."

Just then, Uncle Bobby came around the corner directly toward the family. When he reached the little group, Mama fell into his arms. "Y'all got to get that sumbitch, Bobby. Ya hear me? Y'all got to get that sumbitch!"

"Well, y'all ain't gonna believe this, but the man that attacked your mama and stepdaddy tonight was just arrested at the main entrance to this hospital! I shit you not!" Looking at Tootie, he said, "His right shoulder was almost shot off, it was so full of buckshot!"

Tootie, hearing that, raced over from where she was sitting with me and Harley. "I knowed I hit that sumbitch—I just knowed it!" No doubt she was pretty proud of herself.

"I hope he dies," Mama said. "Do y'all know his name now, Bobby? I want to know who did this to my mama and Hank!"

"I don't think he's gonna die. They didn't say, but they got 'im under lock and key in the criminal ward, patchin' 'im up right now. Dixie Mae, they've identified him, so I can get his name for y'all, but there are procedures in place right now. Not much you can do at this point."

"I hope to hell he dies, but not befo' I get my hands on 'im. I'll make that sumbitch wish he was never born!" It was clear that Mama had something very graphic in mind.

An hour later, the doctor came out to update us. "Folks, y'all might as well go home for a spell. Hank will be out like a light for the next eight hours because of the medication we gave him." He looked at his watch before continuing. "It's about five a.m. now, so come back this afternoon, say two o'clock? He might be able to talk with y'all by then, but I can't promise. It might be a couple of days before we get the results from some tests to know what the toll will be. Maybe he'll be coherent enough to carry on a conversation, maybe not. Go home, get some sleep, and come back later."

"I ain't leavin' 'im alone," Grandmama said. "I want a chair in his room, next to his bed, so if he wakes up, he'll know I'm there." She was glaring at the doctor, daring him to deny her request.

"Okay, okay, I'll tell the head nurse. Give us a few minutes to get it set up."

"Y'all go on home," Grandmama said. "Y'all need to get these boys to bed, Dixie Mae."

"I can stay for a bit. Tootie can take 'em home."

"No, there ain't no need for y'all to wait around out here for hours. Ain't nothin' you can do, anyway, Dixie Mae. So go home!" Mama and Tootie hugged and kissed Grandmama goodbye and assured her they'd be back in a few hours. Then she packed me and Harley up and headed for home.

On the way out, Bobby stopped them. "Dixie Mae, why don't y'all stay at my house for a while?" he offered. "There's still a bunch of people over at y'all's house, and it's a mess. You won't get any rest there. What ya say?"

"That sounds great, Bobby, let's go." Tootie agreed.

CHAPTER TWENTY-SIX

We stayed with Uncle Bobby for a couple of nights, long enough for the house to get cleaned up, and then we all moved back in. Mama put off moving us to the trailer for a few weeks until Grandpa Hank came home from the hospital and got settled in. The day Grandpa Hank was released, Mama got us out of school early, so we would all be there when he walked in the door.

I hadn't seen much of him while he was in the hospital, because they didn't like kids visiting in the critical care ward. When he walked through the front door, I was shocked at his appearance. Grandpa Hank had always been a big, strong man. Gentle as a lamb but as hard as steel.

He might have been tough in the past but not today. He looked old and frail—his hair and whiskers grayer than before. I had tears streaming down my face when his eyes found mine.

"Mickey, don't cry, boy. Hear me? I know I look like an old, wet hen right now, but the doctors all say I'll be right as rain in a few months. Okay?"

"Yessir."

"Now help me over yonder to my chair, if y'all please."

"I can help too," Harley said.

"I know you can, Harley. Looks like you grew three inches since I been gone, and stronger too!"

Beaming, Harley ran over and helped guide Grandpa Hank to his chair. Shortly after he settled in, he fell asleep.

Grandpa Hank seemed to be the only one of us getting much sleep. We were all on edge after the attack. I created an alarm on our bedroom door by putting a chair close to the door with an old metal world globe resting on the back of it. The globe leaned against the door in such a way that if someone opened the door, it would fall off the chair and hit the tile floor. I knew that would wake us up!.

It worked great too—right up until the time my mama came home from working at The Savannah at two o'clock in the morning and opened the door to our bedroom to check on us. The clang from the globe striking the tile floor was so loud, it startled everyone awake, including my Grandmama and Aunt Tootie! Both Mama and Grandmama screamed, and Tootie came out of her room carrying the Angel of Death, once again ready to exact vengeance on whichever demon dared disturb our peace. The globe, dented and abused as it was, found its way back inside the closet from whence it came—never to be used as guardian again.

Grandmama was especially distressed about the entire situation. One morning I heard Mama, Tootie, and Grandmama talking at the kitchen table. "Girls, this thing with Hank has showed me that life is short. Anythin' could happen to any of us, anywhere and anytime."

I peeked around the corner at the three most important women in my life.

"I cain't stay in this house much longer, though," she confessed. "I'm scared all the time—cain't sleep none either. Just too many bad memories, I guess. Everywhere I look, all I can see is Hank's blood—in our bed, on the walls, on the floors—everywhere!"

Aunt Tootie nodded. "Yeah, me too."

"Y'all know I want to move out." Mama sounded so cold.

Grandmama started crying, "Dixie Mae, I cain't stand that yo' still mad at me and Tootie."

Aunt Tootie nodded in agreement. "Really, Dixie Mae. I'm so sorry for tellin' the boys anythin' that you didn't want them to know. It wasn't right, an' I'm sorry. I really am."

There had always been an unspoken bond between Grandmama and her two daughters that no one had ever been able to penetrate. But that deep connection snapped the day I found the picture of Jack. It had been agony to see the rift that formed between them. There was a gaping hole in my family when these women weren't united.

Mama said quietly, "Y'all promised to never tell the boys."

Grandmama wiped her eyes. "Yes, we did, Dixie Mae."

Tootie said, "We've always kept our word to each other."

Mama looked up quickly, as if she'd been slapped. "You're right, Tootie. We always did, until that day."

A painful silence fell over them. Grandmama put her arms around Mama. "Dixie, please don't move away from us. Not yet anyways. If somethin' was to happen to you or the boys, it would kill me. It surely would."

Thinking about it for a minute, Mama said, "Alright Mama, I won't. We're a family and we gotta stay strong for each other."

That wasn't what I expected to hear.

Grandmama smiled for the first time since the attack. "Oh, Dixie Mae. Thank you. I need us together. Dixie Mae, yo' my baby girl, and I need y'all with me—at least for a while. Can you forgive me, baby? Can ya?"

Mama started to cry. "Oh, Mama, yes, I forgive y'all." She grabbed Aunt Tootie and pulled them both in for a hug. "I forgive ya both! It's in the past. Let it stay there."

I was so relieved that we weren't going to move out in the country to some trashy single-wide. But why were Grandmama and Aunt

Tootie apologizing to Mama? Mama should have been apologizing for asking them to lie. It was so twisted, but right then I didn't care.

When they stopped crying, Mama put her chin up, sat up tall in her chair, and said, "From now on, we cain't let nothin' come between us. We gotta always stick together."

"That's right, praise God, I promise," Grandmama exclaimed.

"Me too!" said Tootie.

They sat back and drank their tea.

Grandmama said, "After Hank gets better, hopefully in a few months like the doctors say, I'm gonna sell this house and move us closer to the Blue Star."

"Are you sure, Mama? Yo' ain't gonna find nothin' as nice, or as big as this closer, to the café."

Grandmama agreed. "I know, Dixie Mae. I know. This here's been the best house I ever lived in, let alone owned. I just cain't stay here any longer than I have to!"

Aunt Tootie agreed. "Mama, I think movin' from here is best."

The discussion continued and they all decided that it was best to wait to move until the end of the school year so me and Harley wouldn't have to change schools again so soon. The three of them chatted and laughed and made plans as if nothing had ever been wrong between them.

I wasn't sure what I'd witnessed—three women admitting their wrongs and forgiving each other? I didn't remember my mama admitting to any mistakes or wrongdoing. And what did Tootie mean that they'd always kept their word to each other? Were they simply three co-conspirators who had just renewed their vows to present a solid front on an agreed-upon story, regardless of its truthfulness?

These questions were to haunt me for years to come. I had no idea if I'd ever be able to put them to rest.

TWENTY-SEVEN

PRESENT
SATURDAY, APRIL 22, 1972
7:24 P.M.

I walked into Billy's Café. There were only two other customers in the place—a couple of teenagers sitting in the back booth exploring each other's tonsils. I was about to sit at the counter, but I wasn't in the mood to talk, and waitresses in diners always talk to people at the counter. I chose a booth in the front at the far end of the big front window. On my way over, I caught the eye of the waitress and asked for a menu.

Ruby showed up at my booth with a cup of coffee accompanying the menu. I smiled. "You read my mind."

She smiled back. "I can tell someone who needs coffee when I see 'im." Ruby looked about fifty; a woman that life had rode hard and hung up wet. I'd seen the look before. She was wearing a uniform that seemed a size too small, white nurses' shoes that had seen better days, red lipstick, and gave off the faint odor of stale smokes.

She gave me a minute to look over the menu, then asked, "Whatcha gonna have sugar?"

"The sign says y'all got the best hamburgers in the Panhandle. Guess I'll try one of those."

"It's your life," she said. Her smile hinted at the beauty she once was. Ruby placed my order and wandered back over. Lonely, I suppose.

"Y'all from around here? Ain't never seen y'all in here before."

"I'm visiting family in Quincy."

"What y'all doin' out this way?" she asked.

"I was visitin' my Grandma Jean. She owns a little farm out in Greensboro."

"Really, what's her name? I know a lot of folks out there."

"Jean Crow," I said reluctantly.

"Jean Crow? I don't know her, but I've heard about her." She paused glancing over to watch the teens disappear through the front door. "Don't she got a boy named Charlie? I think I 'member him being in jail or somethin' " Her eyes got wide. "So, if y'all's Jean Crow's grandson, is Charlie yo' daddy?"

Dear God. I can't believe this, but hey, this is rural Florida.

I smiled sadly. "Ruby, that's been the biggest question of my life. Is Charlie Crow my daddy?"

The cook rang the bell, alerting Ruby that my burger was ready. "I'll be right back, sugar."

Ruby talked with the cook for a moment then brought out my burger and a pot of coffee to freshen my cup. Filling up my mug, she asked, "Wanna talk about it? I'm told I'm a good listener."

"Is it okay with your boss?" I asked.

She grinned. "Oh, yes. I own this place. My daughter's working the kitchen tonight. She can cover anyone else who comes in."

I laughed. "I thought it was Billy's place."

"It was. Billy's my ex. I had a very good lawyer." Ruby slid onto the seat across from me. I don't know why, but I started to tell her about Charlie and my mama, Dixie Mae.

CHAPTER TWENTY-EIGHT

In the middle of April, we heard that the stranger—Morris Winters—had pled guilty to his crimes, seeing he was nearly caught red-handed. There was no trial. Uncle Bobby said Winters thought he'd get less time if he confessed, but the judge, in his infinite wisdom, gave him the maximum fifteen years in Gadsden Correctional Facility.

My mama didn't agree with the sentence. "That sumbitch should'a got life for what he done!"

"I wish they'd take the bastard behind the courthouse and shoot 'im," Tootie said.

All Grandmama would say is, "He got what he deserved, so it's time to let it go and thank God above nobody died. Hank ain't no dumber than he was before that night." She winked at him.

Grandpa Hank smiled and nodded his head, before getting up and walking over to Grandmama to say, "C'mon, sugar, give me a little kiss."

"Get off me, Hank. Don't slobber all over me." She raised her arms in mock defense.

"C'mon, baby, just a little kiss."

"You want somethin' sweet, Hank? There's leftover ribs in the fridge."

Forgetting all about his original intentions, he said, "Really? Well, let's have some then. I need to keep up my strength if I'm gonna heal." Grandmama obliged.

We all waited until the end of the school year to move so that Harley and I could complete the year at Rolling Hills Elementary. And, let's face it, moving in the summer had almost become a family tradition. So, at the end of May 1964, we moved again. Though the new house Grandmama and Grandpa Hank bought on Cherry Street near downtown Quincy was a little smaller than the one in Rolling Hills Estates, it still had four bedrooms, which meant that Harley and I would have our own bedroom and wouldn't have to share with Mama. The setup wasn't much different from the place we'd just left.

Cherry Street was a beautiful, tree-lined wonder with jacarandas on one side of the street and moss-covered oaks on the other, and a Dixie Ice Cream warehouse at one end of the street next to the A&P market. We spent many a weekend, spoons in hand, waiting underneath the freeway overpass that bordered the back of the place for someone to toss a crushed ice cream container in the bin behind the warehouse. Damn, that was some good ice cream.

Aunt Tootie and Grandmama were busy running the Blue Star and didn't have the time to watch us much. Grandpa Hank finally got back to work, trying to catch up on the time he had missed while recovering. And Mama was working two jobs and was rarely at home.

Harley and I spent most of our time alone that summer. I guess Mama figured since I was going to be thirteen in a few weeks, I was old enough to take care of Harley, who would be eleven in August.

Mama took on as many hours as she could at The Savannah and the Blue Star. Even though she, Tootie, and Grandmama had made up, Mama didn't want to live with them forever. She told me that she was working as hard as she could to save money so we could eventually get our own place again.

Mama still had Sundays off but was no longer interested in attending family Sunday dinners as had been our tradition in the past. Instead of spending her time off with family, she began to date. Since she worked as a bartender, that was the primary place she met men. The guys drank while she was working and when they took her out on dates, she drank with them. Before long, she started coming home later and drunker.

I didn't like it much and I don't think Uncle Bobby did either. Occasionally, he'd take Harley and me hunting or fishing. Or he'd just drop in from time to time to check up on "Dixie's Boys," as he always called us. But it was rather remarkable that no matter when he dropped by, Mama was never at home at the time. It was as if she had some kind of Bobby radar because he picked different days of the week and different hours to drop by.

One day in early July, we were out fishing, and no one was catching anything. Harley had nodded off with his pole balanced between his legs. I got to thinking about what I'd heard at Sunday School—that God will forgive us for the ways we've hurt other people. But also, how we can't keep doing the same bad things over and over.

Bobby looked over at me. "What's with the serious face, Mickey? Looks like y'all thinkin' deep thoughts over there."

I smiled. "Uncle Bobby, do y'all think keepin' a secret is the same thing as lyin'?"

A dark look came over him. "Damn, boy, y'all really are thinkin' some deep thoughts for a kid your age."

"I'm twelve, gonna be thirteen in a couple of weeks! That's old enough!"

"Sorry, Mickey. I'm not criticizin'. Actually, I'm impressed. So, what's got ya askin' a question like that? Ya keepin' a secret? Or are y'all talkin' about me?"

My stomach lurched. "Well, Mama told me that Charlie wasn't my real daddy."

"She did? That's news to me."

I was stunned. "You didn't know? Truly?"

His cheeks flushed red. "I honestly don't know who yo' daddy is, Mickey."

"How can ya not know?"

"I know what I been told, but only yo' mama knows for sure."

I knew what he was saying. Just because she was married to Jack at the time I was born, that didn't mean that he was my daddy. Hell, it could have been any man in the county.

"Is my mama a slut?"

Bobby sat up straight with anger flashing in his eyes—for a second, I thought he might hit me. "Don't y'all ever say that about yo' mama again, boy. Hear me?"

I pulled away, surprised. He said, "C'mon, Mickey. Y'all know I'd never hit ya."

Relaxing, a bit, I said, "No, I don't think ya would, but I got nervous there for a minute."

He put his arm around my shoulders. "Hell, no. Never. But I mean this, Mickey. Don't ever say that about your mama again, understand?"

"But—"

"Dixie Mae has her problems. She surely does. But mostly, they're all due to how much she loves Charlie. If she just let herself love a good man..." his voice trailed off.

"Like you, Uncle Bobby."

This time his face flushed bright red. "No, not me, Mickey. There's only ever been one man in her heart. And it's always been Charlie."

We sat side by side, letting the weight of that fact sink into our hearts like a suffocating blanket. Life would have been completely different for both of us if that weren't true.

I confided in Bobby. "I always been afraid that I'd turn out like Charlie, havin' the bad blood from both Grandpa Willie and Charlie. I'm relieved that Mama told me he's not my daddy. I just don't wanna be like Charlie, in any possible way."

"Don't blame yo'self, Mickey. Charlie wasn't always bad, but the friend I used to know is gone." Uncle Bobby surprised me with that admission.

"Yeah, I guess he is. You lost a friend, and I got rid of a sumbitch." We both laughed.

"I will admit to you, that I promised your mama to say that Charlie was your daddy. But it bothered me to wonder what the truth was about Jack and Charlie. That's why I always called y'all Dixie's boys. No matter what else, that was the God's honest truth."

I felt a swell of trust come over me toward Uncle Bobby again. I guess I understood why he did what he did. Maybe I truly forgave him. I was just about to tell Uncle Bobby about how Mama got me to agree to lie to Harley, how much Mama was drinking, and how many assholes she was dating, but right then, Harley was awakened by a tug on his pole. Our attention was diverted to cheering him on as he landed the only fish caught that day.

When he dropped us off for the day, Uncle Bobby said what he always said. "Well, tell Dixie Mae I dropped by and to call me if she needs anything—anything at all."

"Yessir, I will Uncle Bobby, and thanks for taking us fishin' today—and the talk."

I felt bad for him and would often daydream that he was our daddy. I asked Mama about it once. "Why don't you ask Uncle Bobby over to Sunday dinner like ya used to? You mad at him or somethin'?"

She shook her head no, but I wasn't convinced. So, hell, I decided to jump into the deep end. "Why don't y'all marry Uncle Bobby? I bet he'd be a good daddy."

"What?" She laughed as if that thought had never crossed her mind. "We just ain't meant to be together—me and Bobby. I love Bobby, I really do, but not like that. It's more like how y'all love Harley, ya know? Like a brother."

"He loves ya Mama, and I don't think he loves ya like a sister."

She just smiled and walked away.

CHAPTER TWENTY-NINE

On the Sunday after Valentine's Day, Grandmama, Tootie, Harley, and I got home from church, and Mama was there to greet us. This was a little unusual, as she generally slept in late on Sundays or she hadn't come home from wherever she'd stayed Saturday night. She was all smiles. "Mama, I'm takin' the boys out to lunch today, okay?" But it didn't sound like a question—more like a statement.

"They yo' kids, Dixie Mae. You don't need my permission." Grandmama said it in a way that seemed to question that assumption.

"Boys, go change outta y'all's church clothes, and we'll take off."

As I headed toward my room, I heard Grandmama say, "Dixie Mae, this ain't like you. What's goin' on?"

"Mama, I just wanna spend some time with my kids. Is that okay with you? Besides, I got to talk to them about some things."

"What things?" Grandmama was now very suspicious.

"I promise, I'll tell y'all when me and the boys get back. I wanna tell 'em first."

Grandmama and Tootie looked like they'd just taken a big bite out of a lemon. Raising her hands in surrender, Grandmama repeated herself. "Like I said, they yo' kids. We'll talk when y'all get back."

"We will, Mama, I promise."

Changing into our everyday clothes, we heard Mama yell that it was time to go.

"Comin', Mama," Harley yelled back, and a minute later, we were out the door headed towards Mama's Bug.

"Where we goin' to eat, Mama?" I asked.

"Oh, it's a surprise, boys—a good one, I hope." There was that word again—hope.

We headed downtown and a few minutes later, we pulled into the parking lot of Mama's favorite place to eat in Quincy—Matty's Italian Restaurant. Empty Chianti wine bottles littered the walls like stars littering the heavens. White linen and candles adorned the tables, and the aromas coming from the kitchen caused a kind of Venetian enchantment as soon as you walked into the place.

Harley and I had never been in a place this nice. It was like something out of a movie and didn't seem real—especially in Quincy, Florida. A man dressed in a tuxedo, carrying a white cloth over one arm, told us to follow him. He led us to a table located in a small alcove near the back of the restaurant, away from the main dining room. Of all things, it had a curtain that separated us from the other diners.

The man in the tuxedo closed it after seating us, saying in an Italian accent, "Luigi will be your waiter tonight. Please, make yourselves comfortable, and he will be with you shortly."

Harley and I sat there grinning from ear to ear.

A few minutes later, a handsome young man opened the curtain and addressed Mama in a deep Italian accent. "Ciao, Bella, my name is a Luigi, and I have the honor of being your waiter. How may I help you tonight?" He had the biggest and brightest smile I'd ever seen!

Mama blushed. "Luigi, I'll have a glass of Chianti. In fact, just bring the bottle, and my boys here will have a sweet tea. Is that okay, boys?" We both said yes, and Luigi departed to get our drinks, closing the curtain behind him. It went on like that for a while. Luigi opening the curtain, taking our orders, closing the curtain behind him. Opening the curtain, placing bread on the table, closing the curtain behind him. Opening the curtain and placing plates of goodness Harley and I had never tasted before, then finally, closing the curtain to let us enjoy it all, without interruption.

In due course, Luigi opened the curtain and removed the evidence of our gluttony. Mama sat back and smiled. "Well, what y'all think of that, boys? Was it good?"

"Yes ma'am!" we said in concert.

Just then, Luigi stuck his head through the curtain. "Excuse me, Bella, may I bring you or your fine sons anything else right now?"

"No, Luigi, not right now. Maybe in a few minutes. Can y'all check back with us then?"

"My pleasure," he said and ducked out of the curtain.

"Boys, I brought y'all here today to talk about somethin' important." Harley and I sat up straighter, so as not to miss anything. We hadn't a clue what Mama wanted to talk about. Turning, she looked us both straight in the eyes. "I've been talkin' to y'all's daddy for the past few weeks. Not yo' daddy, Mickey. Yo' daddy, Harley." Keeping the lie alive.

My mouth dropped open, but nothing came out. She continued before I could recover. "Mickey, before y'all start, just listen a minute, okay? Charlie and I been talkin' to what they call a marriage counselor."

"A what?" I managed to croak out.

"A marriage counselor—a woman that's supposed to help mamas and daddies work out their problems, so they have a good marriage. Lots of people do it."

My stomach turned as the Italian food revolted. I thought I might be sick. As the wave of nausea passed, I tried to keep my cool, but then, I couldn't help myself. "Mama, I ain't changed my mind none about Charlie. He's mean, and he's dangerous. He don't like me none, never has, and now I know why. I ain't his boy."

Harley just sat there, tears welling up in his eyes.

"Mickey, keep yo' voice down. Yo' upsettin' yo' brother."

"I'm sorry, Harley, I don't mean to make y'all cry. Mama, what 'xactly are y'all trying to tell us?"

"Boys, Charlie has changed. I mean it. He's really changed. He's got a great job with lots of money, and he's buyin' us a new house, and it's gonna be completely different than it was befo'." She was talking so fast, I couldn't get a word in edgewise. "And he and me are gettin' back together befo' summer. We gonna renew our weddin' vows and everthin'."

I sat there shaking my head, working hard to push down the rage I was feeling to a manageable level, and failing miserably. "Mama, I don't get it. Ever' time you and him get back together, things turn to shit."

"Mickey, y'all watch yo' mouth, boy. I ain't gonna tell ya again." Now she was angry.

"No, I ain't gonna watch my mouth 'cause you know it's true. Mama, I'm thirteen now. I'm not a kid anymore."

Harley wiped his eyes. "Mickey, I think we should give 'im another chance—just one more chance."

"What? Are y'all nuts?"

I was amazed at what meek little Harley said next. Looking at Mama intently, he said, "Mama, I'm okay with givin' Daddy one mo' chance."

"Oh, Harley, that's great, just great."

"He's my daddy, and yo' my mama, and I love both y'all."

"I know ya do, Harley."

"But, Mama, if Daddy hurts you, me, or Mickey again, then I never, ever wanna see 'im again. If y'all stay with Daddy after that, I'll run, Mama. I'll run as far away as I can and never come back."

Mama and I both sat there in silence. For my part, I was never prouder of my little brother than right then. I knew how bad he wanted our family back together—needed it back together—but he'd just laid down the gauntlet.

Mama started to cry. "Harley, it would break my heart if either of y'all ever left me. It surely would. I'm tellin' y'all now—both of y'all look at me—Daddy has changed. Even the marriage counselor thinks so, and she's a professional and all. Y'all need a daddy in yo' lives—now more than ever. Ya know, to teach y'all how to be men; things I cain't teach y'all."

I wanted to scream. *No way in hell would I live with that sumbitch again!* But I didn't. I simply couldn't leave Mama and Harley alone with that man. I just couldn't do it, no matter how much I hated and feared him.

"Okay, Mama, let's give it another try, but I ain't gonna be part of no weddin'."

"Thank y'all, boys. I really do believe it's gonna be great this time. Y'all wait and see. Don't worry, Mickey, ya won't have to be part of the weddin' if ya don't wanna."

Hell, no, I didn't want to, but what choice did I really have?

The next day, when I got home from school, the house was empty. I called Uncle Bobby.

"Hey, Uncle Bobby, it's Mickey. You told me to call if I ever heard that Charlie was back in town."

Uncle Bobby let out a big sigh. "I know he's back, Mickey. And I wish there were somethin' I could do about it."

I'm sure you do!

"So, you knew?"

"Yeah, he actually called me before he moved back. He said he didn't want any trouble with me or with the law. He went on and on about how he'd changed, and that he and Dixie Mae were actually gonna see a counselor or some such. Said he wanted to make sure I wouldn't enforce that restrainin' order we've got on the books."

"Charlie cain't change," I declared.

"Probably not Mickey, but yo' Mama also met up with me and begged me to give Charlie another chance. She loves him, Mickey. Makes no sense to you or me, but that's how it is. Ya know I can't say no to your mama."

Unconvinced, I asked, "Where'd he get all of his money? He's buyin' us a brand-new house!"

"I don't know, Mickey. But..." he paused, "...now, Mickey, we talked about keepin' secrets, but if I tell you this, you gotta swear never to tell anyone."

"I promise, Uncle Bobby. You can trust me."

"I've been contacted by the FBI about a drug smugglin' operation based in the Bahamas, with one of its US locations being near Quincy. Out in the Apalachicola swamp, somewhere. Ya know, Charlie has been livin' in the Bahamas ever since he left."

I interrupted him. "Y'all mean the last time he beat the hell outta Mama and me?"

Without missing a beat, Bobby said, "Now he's apparently made lots of money down there because he told me he was buyin' Dixie Mae a new house, with cash. Now, look, I don't know if Charlie made his money legally or illegally. It's just somethin' I'm looking into, and if you tell anyone what I'm doin', you could blow the whole investigation."

"The FBI? Damn, that's big. I promise, Uncle Bobby. I won't tell nobody. If he's involved, I want him to burn for it."

Uncle Bobby warned me. "Now, Mickey, at this point, I got nothin' at all that ties Charlie to this smugglin' outfit. Nothing at all. So don't go gettin' ahead of yo'self. I just want you to know that I'm suspicious. If you see anything odd about Charlie, or see anybody you don't know talkin' to 'im, let me know right away, okay?"

"I'll be happy to help y'all nail that sumbitch."

Uncle Bobby laughed. "Mickey, we gotta be men about this. We both want yo' mama to be happy, right? So y'all gotta give Charlie a chance, okay?"

"He ain't got no chance with me, Uncle Bobby, but I won't be the one who breaks Mama's heart, either."

We hung up. I felt like Uncle Bobby had talked to me man-to-man for the first time. I was going to be watching Charlie like a hawk. There would be nothing sweeter than to be the one responsible for having the bastard thrown in jail for the rest of his life.

THIRTY

APRIL 1965

Mama kept Charlie and me apart for as long as she could while she was planning the renewal ceremony. I'd made it clear that if I had a choice, I'd never lay eyes on him again for the rest of my life. But seeing as how we were all going to be living together in some big house, for the sake of Harley and Mama, I'd do my best to pretend we were one big happy family. Charlie and I were like oil and water, we just didn't mix. The best we could hope for was an uneasy peace until, at some point, we stopped pretending.

Wasting no time, Charlie and Dixie Mae Crow renewed their wedding vows at Grandmama's church, with the Right Reverend Snowden presiding, in April 1965. Mama wore a light pink dress with lace in all the appropriate places, and I have to say, she was beautiful. Aunt Tootie stood next to her, the look on her face revealing her true heart about it all—her hatred for Charlie was almost as deep as mine. Harley was the ring bearer, and I sat next to the double doors in the back, trying hard not to be seen. Grandma Jean was there with a sour look on her face.

The crowd wasn't large, mostly family and a few friends of theirs, most of whom witnessed the original vows. I was told Uncle Bobby had been the best man the first time, but now he was standing next to me in the back. He didn't look happy either. In fact, I'd have to say he looked downright miserable. I couldn't imagine how he felt, as the woman he'd loved most of his life was up at the altar marrying the man who used to be his best friend—again.

Thankfully, it was over quickly. A small reception followed in the church's multi-purpose room. The next day, Mama, Harley, and Charlie packed his new sedan and headed up to Atlantic City for their vacation-honeymoon for two weeks. I refused to go, opting to stay with Grandmama, where I'd be for as long as I could.

Two weeks sped by all too quickly, as far as I was concerned. On the Friday they got back in town, at the end of April, Charlie officially got the keys to our new house, located in the small town of Crawfordville, about forty-five minutes south of Quincy. He'd recently gotten a job as a supervisor with Mason Dixon Agricultural Services, just outside of town, managing their fleet of crop dusters and the pilots who flew them. He and Mama moved over the weekend, but Harley and I stayed with Grandmama until the end of May, so as to finish out the school year. It didn't take Mama long to pack. She really didn't have that much, but she made damn sure she took her cherished stereo console.

At the end of May, Harley and I packed our meager belongings and joined Mama and Charlie at the new house in Crawfordville. When we arrived, Harley and I were surprised to find brand-new furniture in every room. Charlie had bought it all, with Mama's approval, with the cash he was always bragging about—ever the attentive and caring husband, don't you know? Mama showed us to our new rooms, each with a new bed, side table, lamp, and chest of drawers. This was the first time Harley and I ever had separate bedrooms or new furniture.

"Well, what y'all think? Y'all like 'em?" Mama asked.

"I love it, Mama." Harley gave her a big hug.

"Mickey, what you think, boy?"

"It's okay, I guess," I said without enthusiasm, still not happy about living with Charlie Crow. But inside, I couldn't help but think how nice it would be to have my own room. To top it all off, Charlie had bought us a parakeet. Sam was a cool bird, and we all loved to watch his crazy antics. I was attempting to be positive. *Maybe, just maybe, this was going to work out.* But it didn't take long to see the cracks that were already forming in this new-normal relationship.

The day we moved to Crawfordville, I met Ronnie Ripley. He caught me as I was moving some boxes into the house. "Hey there, my name is Ronald Ripley, but you can call me Ripley—everybody does."

"Hey, I'm Mickey."

"I live right across the street." He was pointing to the house directly across from ours. "When y'all are done there, come on over. I'll tell ya everythin' ya need to know about Crawfordville."

"Thanks, Ripley, I'll do that soon as I'm done here."

"Okay." And a friendship was struck.

When I was done, I told Mama, "I met a boy livin' across the street from us. I'm gonna go over and talk to 'im, okay?"

A smile spread across her face. "Sure, Mickey. That'd be fine."

"Hey, Harley, y'all wanna come too?"

"Really? Yeah, sure would. That okay with you, Mama?"

"Go on ahead, Harley. Y'all go on and make some new friends. See y'all at home later."

We walked across the street and knocked on Ripley's door. He came out and saw me standing next to Harley. "Hey, Mickey, who's this?"

"Ripley, this is my brother, Harley. He's gonna visit a while, too, if that's okay."

"Okay, sure! Hey, Harley, nice to meet 'cha."

"Nice to meet you too."

Ripley began his description of our new hometown. "This is a small town—less than five thousand folks 'round here, even though we ain't that far from Tallahassee. Most people 'round here are pretty nice. Our neighborhood is new and all, so most of the folks at school are new, just like me and you, Mickey. Harley, you'll be goin' to Crawfordville Elementary, just across the street from Wakulla Junior High. Y'all wanna walk down there and see it?"

"Cain't right now," I said. "Me and Harley gotta finish unpackin'. How 'bout tomorrow mornin'?"

"Sounds great! See y'all tomorrow."

The next morning, I met Ripley out front of his house. Harley decided not to come, which was a good thing because my education about the opposite sex was about to begin in earnest. Ripley, at fourteen, believed himself to be the consummate expert, and thus my perfect guide into the mystery of women.

"I got two older sisters—Sharon's seventeen and Suzy's sixteen. Whatever you wanna know 'bout girls, I'm y'all's boy!"

To my inexperienced ears, his Ripleyisms fell and found purchase on the fertile ground of my young life. He quickly became the best friend I'd ever had, and we did everything together. Ripley was a good-looking kid, with a sharp-edged wit and a quick smile. He was a bit taller and slimmer than me, and very fast. He seemed to know something about everything.

I learned a lot from Ripley during our time in Crawfordville. I tried hard to include Harley in our activities, but Harley was making his own friends and so we spent less and less time together—really, for the first time in our lives—although we still remained close. Now at different schools, it was inevitable that we would spend more time with the friends that we didn't have in common, but I was still so proud of him. He was making friends like a champ and seemed happy.

CHAPTER THIRTY-ONE

Charlie and I didn't speak much from the day Harley and I moved in. I didn't trust him one bit, and he flat-out didn't like me, but we worked the uneasy truce between us as best we could. He wanted Mama to quit working and stay home, but that was never going to happen. Due to the move, Mama had to quit her jobs at the Blue Star and The Savannah Country Club, but before she had even made the move to Crawfordville, she was offered a job as the head bartender at the exclusive Southwood Country Club, halfway between Tallahassee and Crawfordville.

Her work and references from The Savannah in Quincy preceded her, as did her reputation as beautiful and personable, so obtaining a position like that was easy for her. She managed to work the day shift during the week and only worked weekends when there was a special event. She refused to work nights so she could be home when Charlie came home. Even so, he didn't like her working, mostly because he was jealous of the attention she always got.

Things were lurching along, like a car with a bad spark plug—drivable, but not smoothly. It didn't take long for Charlie to start making comments about my "bad attitude" and how ungrateful he thought I was for all he was doing for the family. I'd given him all I was going to give and had no intention of acting like he was the butter on my toast. He hated it when I called him Charlie instead of Daddy, it really pissed him off, but I just didn't give a damn.

One Saturday afternoon, a couple of weeks after we'd moved in, Mama was out working on one of those rare Saturdays, and Harley was off doing something or the other with his buddies. It was just me and Charlie alone in that big house.

I was watching TV in the living room when Charlie came over and plopped down on the chair across from me. "Y'all wanna go to the store with me, Mickey?" He had a malevolent grin on his face.

I laughed. "Hell, no, Charlie. I ain't never gettin' in a car with you by myself again. Y'all think I forgot about what happened the last time we took a drive together?"

Stunned that I would speak to him in this manner, he got angry. "Ya little shit!"

"Takes one to know one, *Charlie*."

He stood up and quickly closed the distance between us, raising his hand to slap me.

"Go ahead, hit me. I won't be tellin' Mama I fell off my bike again, that's for damn sure. It'll just prove to her I'm right about you. I told her you ain't changed and y'all never will."

I guess he realized that his entire plan, whatever that was, would fall apart if he laid a hand on me, so he backed up and sat down. "Y'all think yo' so smart. You better watch yo'self, ya little shithead. You outta yo' league, and you call me Daddy!"

Anger coursed through my veins. "Really? Well, I don't think so. I know y'all ain't our real daddy. Jack McCarthy is our daddy."

He started laughing. "Y'all's Mama told ya that Jack was yo' daddy? And Harley's too?"

"That's right."

"Don't tell me. She showed y'all the birth certificates, right?"

I nodded lazily, but my interest was piqued.

"I can tell by the look on yo' face that she did."

I felt my lungs deflate, as if Charlie had punched me in the chest. "So, what about the birth certificates? I saw 'em with my own eyes."

Charlie shook his head. "Damn, Mickey, yo' really are one dumbass cracker. Who do ya think filled out those certificates?"

"I don't know, and I don't care."

"Listen up, dumbass! Yo' mama filled out those papers, and she wrote down whatever the hell she wanted. She was mad at me both times she had a baby. She knew it would piss me off if she wrote down Jack's name, so she did. Hate to tell you this, boy, but I'm yo' *real* daddy, whether you like it or not."

I countered. "Grandmama and Aunt Tootie said that Jack is my daddy, and I believe 'em."

"Shit, boy, you can't believe a word that slut Tootie says. Don't ya know that yet?"

He finally pissed me off. "You stop talkin' 'bout Tootie like that. Y'all ain't half the *man* she is." I was furious.

Laughing, he said, "Yo an ignorant sumbitch, you know that? I cain't believe y'all never heard about yo' Aunt Tootie. When she was younger, befo' you was born? Damn, son, she screwed any boy that wanted it."

I stood up and shouted, "Stop it!"

He didn't. "Yo' Aunt Tootie is nothin' but a common slut. She ain't nobody y'all should admire, much less love. She's just white trash, is all."

Shaking with anger, I was trying hard to keep myself from jumping on him and pounding my fists into his smug face. "Yo' a liar!"

"I'm not lyin'. She even got an abortion."

"What? What's that?" I had no idea what an abortion was. Never even heard the word before, but the way he said it, there was no doubt it was a bad thing.

"Some low-life loser screwed yo' precious Aunt Tootie, and she got pregnant. Y'all do know what that means, right?"

Aunt Tootie had a baby?

"She was too young to have a baby, so yo' lovin' Grandmama got some back-alley doctor to kill the baby inside her and pull it out. The bitch almost died."

"Yo' a goddamn liar, Charlie!"

Charlie snarled, pure evil in his eyes. "My own mama told me. You callin' yo' Grandma Jean a liar?"

Stunned, I felt my world starting to spin. But he wasn't finished yet, wanting to rub salt in my wounds.

"Nobody tells you nothin', do they Mickey? It's pathetic, really, how much y'all don't know. Everyone lies in your mama's family. All of them. Grandmama Colee, Tootie, and even Grandpa Hank."

"Grandpa Hank?" I was stunned by that name. "He doesn't ever say nothin'."

"Yeah, that's right, Mickey. He never tells y'all the truth. He goes along with all of it. But, then again, Dixie Mae is yo' mama, and the biggest liar of 'em all." And with that, he turned and left the room.

My head spun so fast I thought I might throw up. My fragile reality cracked like a walnut hit by a hammer. The threads of existence that held my place in the world unraveled, one at a time. Charlie was right about one thing for sure—I didn't know who I could trust. At one point or another, they'd all lied to me—either straight out or by their silence. Uncertainty consumed me, and for days I proceeded to disconnect with nearly everyone I had ever loved or trusted. I fell into an angry depression.

Harley and Ripley were the only two fragile strings left, tying me to any certainty. Still, Harley believed whatever Mama told him, and Ripley was an outsider looking in. No one knew the truth but

Mama, and it seemed entirely possible even she couldn't tell what the hell was truth or a lie. At last my anchor broke loose, and I was set adrift with no land in sight.

Everyone noticed that something was different about me, but no one knew how to get through to me. I didn't want them to—I welcomed the numbness and the soft-focus view of my life. Mama worried about me. So did Harley. He did his best to break through the fog I was in. Ripley tried to entertain me and keep me moving with talk of his sister's escapades, sports, and the like. Uncle Bobby asked if I wanted to talk about anything. I didn't. Aunt Tootie cooked my favorite meals, but I kept losing weight.

Charlie took great delight in my anguish, smiling that smug, evil smile at me whenever he got the chance. He knew what he'd told me had crumbled the foundation of my young life and wanted to grind it into dust. I felt like I didn't know who Aunt Tootie was anymore. Did she do what Charlie said she'd done in her past? It seemed like everyone had lied to me at one point or another, so there wasn't anyone, not even Uncle Bobby or Grandmama, who I could trust to tell me *all* of the truth.

Charlie had methodically destroyed my faith in the people I relied on and revered the most. It was worse than getting hit, because at least then there would have been a bruise or cut to prove he'd hurt me. But there was no outward injury to point to the inward destruction. What he'd done was invisible to everyone except me and the devil himself.

With no place else to turn, I prayed. Whenever I was alone, I prayed. *God, help me get through today. God, help me get through dinner this evening. God help me get to sleep tonight.* The more I prayed, the more strength I felt. The more I prayed, the more I trusted God. It felt like

He was hearing my prayers. Before long, I was adding to my prayers. *God, you're the only one I can trust. Help me find the truth.*

The things that Charlie had told me hit me hard, they really did. But like a boxer who's been knocked down and hears the referee counting *One. Two. Three. Four.*—through the fog and confusion in the ring, I swear I heard God say to me, *"Get up, son, get up. You're not alone. Just wait and see."* I clung to that voice. It was like a lifeline thrown to a drowning man. I grabbed hold of it before the referee counted *Ten* and let it pull me to safety.

If I hadn't fully known before, I was certain that Charlie had not changed one iota. He was still the snake that had threatened to kill Mama, Harley, and me and throw our bodies in the swamp.

The fog and despair slowly lifted, and having more clarity of mind, I was convinced that if I could just hold on long enough, Charlie would implode on his own. I knew I'd lose if I fought him physically, and clearly, he had the upper hand emotionally. But if I just waited it out, the tide would turn and everybody would see the snake for what it really was.

Turns out, it didn't take very long for the implosion to begin.

THIRTY-TWO

The day before the Fourth of July, Charlie and Mama's arguing was in full force. The argument of the day was about her working at the Southwood. Charlie had visited the club one afternoon when Mama was bartending, hiding in the shadows like a snake stalking a rat.

There was a tournament in progress, and many early participants were already in the bar, recounting the day's successes and failures while waiting for the final foursome to finish and the winner to be determined. Spirits were high, and Mama was right in the middle of it, joking and flirting with the club members as she served them the adult beverage of their choice. Mama could always work a crowd and knew just what to say to keep her tips high.

Charlie, watching all of this without Mama knowing he was there, was furious and left without saying a word to her. When she got home a few hours later, Charlie was nowhere to be found.

She knocked on my bedroom door. "Mickey, y'all in there, boy?"

"Yes ma'am."

Opening the door, she asked, "Y'all seen yo' daddy?"

I answered like the smart-ass I sometimes could be. "Nope, I ain't seen *Charlie Crow* all day." At least with her, I could claim to be Jack's boy, regardless of whether or not it was true.

Mama walked out the front door and drove off in her new Bug—the one Charlie had only recently bought her as a wedding gift. She came home a few hours later, stinking of vodka and cigarettes, stumbling down the hallway to her room where she stayed the rest of the night. Charlie never did make it back home.

The next day was the Fourth of July, and Grandmama, Grandpa Hank, and Tootie were going to drive the forty-five minutes to our house for an early supper, and then we'd all go on to the park in downtown Crawfordville for the fireworks show.

Mama got up late, hungover and angry, but after she'd had some breakfast and a pot of coffee, she seemed to settle down a bit.

"Y'all heard from yo' daddy this mornin'?"

Before I could answer, Harley said, "Naw, ain't seen him today. He must've left early."

"I don't think Charlie came home last night, did he, Mama?" I couldn't help myself.

She ignored my jibe. "Don't forget, ever'body's comin' here today for supper and fireworks."

"Yes ma'am. What time they comin'?" I asked.

"Pro'bly 'bout five. I'm gonna need some help cleanin' up 'round here before they come, okay?"

"Yes, ma'am." Harley and I both agreed to help.

After she finished breakfast, Mama instructed us on the jobs we each had. When we finished, we were free to do whatever we wanted until five o'clock. Later in the afternoon, Mama got busy frying chicken for the Independence Day feast—her part in the event.

Grandmama and Tootie were bringing the rest of the food with them. Harley was rolling chicken in flour and handing them to Mama. I was sitting at the counter that divided the kitchen from the dining room, on the phone with Linda Clark, a girl I liked. Sam, our parakeet, chirped and chattered in his cage, which sat over the countertop next to the wall that held our phone.

The front door suddenly flew open with a bang. Charlie was home. He'd been drinking, and he was mad.

Marching into the kitchen, Charlie yelled at me, "Mickey, get yo' ass off that phone! I wanna talk with yo' Mama!"

"Okay, I'll be right off." I said pleasantly, not wanting a confrontation with him. "Linda, I'm gonna have to go now. Are y'all goin' to the fireworks show tonight?"

"We sho' are, Mickey. Wanna sit together when we get there?"

I began to answer, but Charlie jerked the phone from my hands and pulled so hard that the entire device flew off the wall, creating a little explosion of dust and torn wallpaper. I leaped back toward the middle cabinets, far enough to prevent Charlie's heavy shoes from crushing the phone, and missing my bare feet by inches.

"What y'all do that for? I was gettin' off!" I yelled.

Kicking the shattered pile, he walked over to where Mama was cooking chicken in an old cast iron skillet—her favorite.

I was standing next to Sam's birdcage when Charlie picked up the skillet by the handle and flung it, splattering hot oil and fried chicken all over the counter. Fortunately, I was quick enough to leap out of the path and avoid most of the scorching oil, though some of it did splash on my face and arms. Sam was not as fortunate.

"I told y'all to get off the goddamn phone, boy! Shut that smart ass mouth of yours next time I tell y'all to get off the phone!" Harley screamed as he ran to the birdcage. At the bottom lay a scalded, dead parakeet. "You killed Sam!" he yelled.

Mama just stood there in shock, looking at me, then at Harley staring at his dead pet and finally, at her ruined chicken. "Yo' a sumbitch! Yo' a crazy sumbitch!" Mama screamed at the top of her lungs. "Y'all burned Mickey!"

My arm was hurting something awful and was already blistering even as I ran cool water over it in the sink. Charlie got in my face. "You little pussy. Yo' not burned." He turned the water off and pushed me away from the sink.

Right then someone banged on our front door. Recovering quickly, I started for the door, but Charlie got there before me. He flung open the door to yell at the visitor and came face to face with one extremely angry Grandmama.

"What in Satan's hell is goin' on in here? We could hear y'all before we even parked the car. And so can y'all's neighbors!" Grandpa Hank and Tootie were right behind her holding the side dishes and desserts they had brought for the Fourth of July festivities.

"Colee, I'm gonna shut yo' mouth up once and for all!" From there, everything seemed to move in slow motion. I watched in horror as Charlie stepped back from the open door and picked up the heavy mosaic candy dish from our coffee table. He pulled back his arm to hit Grandmama with it, but before he could, Aunt Tootie lunged in front of her mama and threw a large wooden bowl of coleslaw at his head. It was solid teak and knocked him back towards the wall. Cabbage and mayonnaise dripped from his face down onto his shirt.

Charlie was so incensed, so livid, so out of his mind enraged that he looked like a wild animal, almost frothing from the mouth. He grabbed Aunt Tootie by the arm. "You whore!"

"I ain't no whore!" Aunt Tootie leaned in rather than pull away. She screamed in his face. "Yo' a lyin' bastard."

"My mama tol' me about the abortion. Ever'body knows who you really are, Tootie." Charlie smiled, thinking he'd just landed a knockout punch.

Harley looked up at me. "What's a 'bortion?"

Grandmama's face froze for a moment as she took that in. "Yo mama told y'all that? She's the one who been spreadin' that ugly rumor?" She looked stunned. "I never suspected her."

The depth of Charlie's cruelty seemed limitless. "That's why she won't sit with you at church! Y'all's just white trash."

Grandpa Hank dropped the sweet potatoes and took a step toward Charlie. But before Hank could get past Grandmama, I raced over and threw myself at Charlie, knocking him away from Aunt Tootie, Hank, and Grandmama. Charlie fell to his knees and the mosaic candy dish flipped from his hand into the air and landed on the hard terrazzo floor. It came apart like shrapnel from a grenade, striking Grandmama, Charlie, and me on our arms and legs.

Charlie had his back to me, so I grabbed him in a chokehold and fell on the sofa, me on the bottom, and Charlie landing backward on top.

Choking him as hard I could, I wrapped my legs around his waist in a scissor lock and squeezed. I began to feel Charlie weaken, so I squeezed harder, and in that moment, I realized that I could kill this bastard. I wasn't going to be his victim anymore. I screamed in his ear as loud as I could, "I told ya, you ain't never gonna hurt nobody I love ever 'gain!"

He tried frantically to pull my arms from around his throat, making unintelligible gurgling noises, but I was stronger and bigger than he was now. Looking up, I saw Mama, Grandmama, and Tootie screaming at me to stop. I eased up a bit, allowing Charlie to take a breath, but as I did, my left ring finger found its way into his mouth. He took the opportunity to bite down on it as hard as he could. I felt his teeth cut deep into my flesh. I screamed in pain and released him from the human vice I'd become.

He rolled off the top of me, trying to catch his breath, wheezing and sucking in air for all he was worth. I sat up and saw the bone exposed at the end of my finger and the meaty flesh that was supposed to be covering it, hanging by a small band of skin. Holding my finger together with my other hand, blood ran down my arm and off my elbow onto the rug.

Mama raced to the kitchen for a cloth to wrap around my finger to stop the bleeding. Charlie stumbled toward her screaming that he was going to kill us all, but she ran back into the living room with the rag. Then he lunged at her.

"No!" I screamed and quickly found myself between the two of them, blood from my finger flying everywhere. He grabbed my t-shirt and ripped it off my body. When the t-shirt came apart, we both fell backward to the ground.

Almost like a dance, we both jumped to our feet and charged one another. Mama grabbed a vase from a nearby shelf and whacked Charlie on the side of the head. It stunned him long enough for me to yell, "Everybody get outta here! Get out now!"

Grandmama, Tootie, Harley, and Hank were all out of the door in a flash. Mama jumped over Charlie and was out the door with the others. I stepped over him too, but he grabbed me by the leg and pulled himself up.

"Not you, boy!" he raged. "Not you!"

We grabbed onto each other, too close for either of us to get a good punch. My finger spurted blood in every direction as we fell, then rolled down the porch stairs and onto the lawn. Neither of us could get the advantage, so we rolled down the grass, across the sidewalk, and over the curb into the street. When we hit the asphalt, our grips slipped, and we struggled once again to our feet. We stood there glaring at one another.

As I took a moment to catch my breath, Charlie looked at me— his face distorting into an ugly, horrible mask, like those you see in horror movies or nightmares. "Yo' gonna die today, boy. Hear me? Yo' dead."

Charlie let out a primal scream as he attacked me, pushing me to the cement and jumping on top of me. He hit me in the face and head. Sharp pain exploded in my mouth. I spit blood and teeth in his face, and he recoiled just long enough for me to roll away and jump up. I grabbed the bastard, lifted him over my head, and body-slammed him onto the asphalt.

All the years of fear and rage exploded from inside me and became something terrifying and tangible. I growled like some rabid wolf, "Yo' wrong, Charlie. If anybody dyin' today, it's gonna be you!" I banged his head on the curb a couple of times. Blood came oozing out of his nose. Sitting across his chest, I wrapped my hands around his neck and squeezed.

In the distance, outside my distorted reality, I heard Mama voice. "Mickey, stop, for God's sake. Stop! Yo' killin' 'im. Sweet Jesus, stop, boy!"

Aunt Tootie's voice screamed, "Help! Someone stop 'em!"

I was grabbed by each arm and yanked off of Charlie with a force that left me in a heap on the gravel-filled street. Uncle Bobby's voice pierced the buzzing in my ears. "See if Charlie's still breathing! I'll take care of Mickey."

I tried to sit up, but my head swirled. I rolled to the side and threw up vomit laced with blood. Bobby knelt down beside me. "He's down, Mickey. You can stop now. He's down."

I looked over at Charlie, ashen and still, and then into Bobby's face. I threw my arms around him like a little child and sobbed into his chest. "It's okay, son. It's all over now. It's all over now."

"Is he dead?" I asked.

Uncle Bobby looked over to the two officers attending to Charlie and saw Charlie move. "Not yet."

THIRTY-THREE

CHAPTER

JULY 1965

The sun was setting, just enough for the flashing lights of police cars and ambulances to surround us with a surreal light show. Four patrol cars and two ambulances had arrived by that time. Officers yelled instructions to each other as they dashed around the yard and street to quickly set up a perimeter. In the process, my family was cut off at the lawn. Bobby pulled me further away to make more room for the officers working on Charlie. Behind them came the ambulance drivers. I lost sight of Charlie as they prepared him to load into the ambulance.

I tried to stand, but fell to my knees, weeping uncontrollably. Kneeling in the middle of that road, in the little town of Crawfordville, I released all the hate, rage, and fear I'd built up over the years for that man. I must have lost consciousness for a moment or two. All I remember was a big wave crashing on top of me, releasing all of its power and energy on the shore, finally pulling its remaining waters, and me, towards the peaceful depths of the sea.

Bobby signaled the second ambulance in my direction. Both Charlie and I were covered in each other's blood, so it was hard to locate the points of injury. But it was easy to see that Charlie had knocked out my front teeth and my finger was mangled. It was quickly wrapped in white gauze. Within seconds, the wrap was soaked red.

Bobby kept speaking to me softly and tenderly. "It's okay, Mickey. You're safe now. It's gonna be okay."

One of the ambulance attendants said, "I don't think this kid needs your sympathy, Deputy. It's the other guy who may not make it."

Uncle Bobby pushed him away from me, and said, "Keep your mouth shut. You got no idea what's goin' on here."

Bobby got himself under control. I was scared. "Did I kill Charlie? Tell me the truth!"

We watched the other team lift the gurney carrying Charlie and push it into the back of the ambulance. "He's still breathin', Mickey. I don't know if he'll live or not—we'll just have to wait and see. Ya know he's a tough old bird."

I heard my Mama screaming, "Get outta my way! That's my boy!"

A deputy lifted the tape and said, "Okay, ma'am. You can come in. But the rest of you, stay back—" The entire family pushed through as a single unit, as if joined at the hip. The deputy didn't even try to keep them back. Rushing over, they surrounded me and Bobby.

Another deputy showed up with a notepad in hand, yelling, "All right, folks, quiet down. What the hell is going on here?" Everyone started talking at the same time, each trying to explain the events of that day.

"Everybody just shut the hell up, please!" The deputy said, raising his voice above the din. He pointed to Tootie. "Why don't you start, Miss."

She took the deputy through the whole sad story, but before she finished, I was put on a stretcher and carried to an ambulance.

"I'll be right behind y'all, Mickey." Uncle Bobby continued to assure me, and I felt better knowing he would be there for me.

I heard Mama yelling too. "Don't worry, Mickey! We'll all meet ya at the hospital!" Then the doors closed, and I felt more alone than I ever had in my life.

The deputies took Charlie Crow to the same hospital as I was taken to, but he was already in a room being treated when I arrived. I'd just been put in a room nearest to the front door when Mama and the others exploded through the entrance with a horrible racket. I was behind a curtain, but I could hear Uncle Bobby speaking to them authoritatively. "Y'all settle down, now! Dixie Mae, come up to the front here and talk to the receptionist."

"Let her through!" Grandmama commanded.

The receptionist spoke to Mama. "Hello, ma'am. You cain't go back to see yo' family just yet. But who would y'all like to see first? Yo' son or yo' husband?"

Mama couldn't contain her anger. "I don't ever wanna see that sumbitch husband o' mine again! Ever! He tried to kill my mama, my sister, and my son! I hope he dies."

"He killed our bird, too!" Harley added from the rear of the group.

"As soon as the doctor has a chance to examine yo' son, I'll let you know and y'all can go in and see 'im."

"Excuse me? I will see my son *now*." Nobody was going to keep Mama from seeing me. Before long, she was escorted into my stall by Uncle Bobby, who motioned her to a chair by the door. "Sit here, Dixie Mae, and keep quiet or they'll kick ya out."

She nodded in compliance but walked directly toward me instead. She touched my shoulder. "Oh, Mickey."

Tears rolled down the sides of my face.

She kissed me lightly on the forehead and sat in the chair he was pointing to. In the seat beside her sat another deputy from Uncle Bobby's station.

The doctors and nurses descended upon me, slowly tending to my many injuries. There was an eerie silence, as they spoke only when necessary.

I had second-degree burns on my arms, no visible top teeth in the front of my mouth, a finger that might have to be amputated, and a bad concussion. I was covered with more bruises and small cuts than they could count. I also had asphalt burns from rolling and dragging Charlie over the pavement, so I assumed the same was true for him. They stung like the fires of hell.

They sewed my finger back on, packed my gums to stop the bleeding, applied ointment and wrapped my burns, then stitched up the biggest of my cuts. The adrenaline from the fight and its aftermath was ebbing, leaving me painfully aware of every inch of my tattered body. Pain meds were prescribed, and it was clear that I wasn't going to make it home in time to watch the fireworks.

I called for Mama and she jumped to her feet and rushed to my side. "What y'all need, Mickey? What can yo' mama get y'all?"

"I wanna get out of here, Mama. There's fireworks down at the park, and I'm supposed to meet Linda there."

"Sorry, Mickey, they ain't gonna let you outta here tonight, so forget about it. Ain't gonna happen." Seeing my downtrodden face, she switched to Dixie Mae mode. "But let's see what I can do."

Turning to look over at the attending doctor, Mama fluttered her eyelids and flashed her most electrifying smile. I thought I saw the man's knees actually buckle some. "Doctor, thank ya so much for all y'all's help tonight with my son. You know, he was protectin' me and the rest of my family from a vicious attack. Y'all think you can let him go home tonight to see the fireworks in the park?"

The nurses looked at each other, then at the doctor, and they all became visibly more relaxed. "I'm sorry, ma'am, but with that bump on the head he's got, we gotta keep 'im overnight. I'm real sorry."

"He's only thirteen, and he just loves the Fourth of July. Since he has to stay the night, ya think it'd be all right if I brought 'im some food from home and watch the fireworks from the hospital roof?"

A smile broke across the doctor's face. "Yes, ma'am." The nurses all rolled their eyes in unison.

"Thank you, doctor." She gave him a wink. "You know, my son's a hero."

He nodded. "I know. I saw what happened to the other guy."

Grandmama and Tootie went back to the house and salvaged what they could of the meal. They returned to my room and took me by wheelchair up to the top of the elevator for a Fourth of July rooftop picnic of mashed potatoes, collard greens, biscuits, and Grandmama's delicious pies. Unfortunately, being pumped full of pain killers, plus the emotional trauma of the entire event, I don't remember much of it as I kept dozing off.

It wasn't until I opened one of my blackened eyes the next morning and saw a deputy sitting at the door of my room that I realized that Uncle Bobby hadn't been quite right about this all being over. It wasn't yet—not by a long shot.

I was really out of it the next day and couldn't tell you who visited me or where I was most of the time. I felt very little pain, though, which I was glad about. The following morning, however, I woke up sore and grumpy. Uncle Bobby came into my room with a worried look on his face and closed the door. "You look like shit, boy."

"Thank you, Uncle Bobby. I feel like shit."

"Don't let yo' mama hear you talkin' like that."

We both chuckled. "Yeah, let's don't tell her that I cuss. Only that I just about killed her husband." I paused. "He ain't dead, is he?"

"No. He's really messed up, but he's still breathin'. The doctors released him into our custody. Some boys are gonna drive him to the infirmary at the Wakulla County Jail."

"Good."

"I did visit Charlie yesterday, though. He's definitely banged up. Two broken ribs, a severe concussion, a broken nose, and a split to the back of his head that required twelve stitches. I guess he wasn't payin' attention to how much you've grown."

I let out a sigh of relief. "I was so afraid he'd die. I would've killed 'im if you hadn't shown up."

"Then it's a good thing I showed up." Bobby was dead serious.

I asked the question that had been haunting me through the medicated stupor I was it. "Am I gonna be arrested for hurtin' Charlie, Uncle Bobby?"

"The boys at the Wakulla County Sheriff's office want to arrest you for what you did to 'im, Mickey."

My voice quivered. "I was only protectin' Mama, Uncle Bobby. He would've hurt her bad if I hadn't stopped 'im—maybe even killed her. I seen Charlie mad—real mad—before, but I ain't never seen 'im that mad. He was like a crazy man."

"I know, boy, that's what I told those deputies. I vouched for you, Mickey. Do you know what that means? Means I stood up for ya, told 'em you were a good boy, and when ya grew up, you'd be a good man."

"Thank you," I managed to say in spite of the emotion swelling my throat.

"Listen up, Mickey. I just need y'all to know that nothin' like this can ever happen again, with anybody. You understand?"

"Yes, sir."

"If it does, I won't be able to help you again. I used up all my chips on this one."

"I understand, Uncle Bobby, and it won't happen again. Ever! I promise."

"Good boy."

I guess I should've been happy about the outcome, but I felt unsettled—guilty somehow. The level of violence that flowed out of me that day reinforced my fears about becoming just like Charlie, and it would probably haunt me forever. I feared the poison he'd injected into our lives had infected me, somehow. I vowed to never let that happen again.

Uncle Bobby stopped by again later in the day to tell me he'd spoken with the deputies over at the county sheriff's office in Wakulla. He explained to me what they'd worked out. "So, it will be officially declared as a case of self-defense. I talked with the District Attorney also, and they agreed. That's the final decision."

I sighed with relief. "But what about Charlie? Is he gonna walk free again? Is Mama finally gonna press charges so y'all can throw his sorry ass in prison?"

Bobby took a seat and leaned back in the chair. "No need, Mickey. I contacted a judge this mornin' and got a warrant to search y'all's house. We found a receipt for a storage unit he had out near the interstate."

"Our house? Did you scare the hell out of Mama and Harley doin' that?"

Bobby smiled. "No, I went ahead and let her know what was gonna happen. When we searched the storage unit, we found a trunk. Searchin' through that trunk, we found documents with receipts, flight plans, and enough evidence to put Charlie away for a long time. I've already contacted the FBI this mornin' and they've got federal agents comin' down here to arrest Charlie for transportin' drugs to Miami from the Bahamas. He'll be moved to a federal facility in Miami."

"He actually smuggled in drugs?" I was stunned. I knew he was violent, but to become a drug smuggler seemed more extreme than

I ever expected. *That explains where the cash came from to buy our new house,* I thought.

Bobby told me everything. Turns out Charlie was approached by some Columbians in Nassau who needed a pilot to fly their stuff into America. Charlie had been working for another real estate developer down there, flying potential customers looking to build around the islands.

"He said he also took tourists around for a fee, from time to time. One of the tourists he was flying around was recruiting pilots, like him, to do some work for the Columbians. At first, he said no, but those boys just kept right on raising the amount of money they'd pay, and finally, he said yes. He got in deeper and got scared. He tried to get out, but got a visit from a very scary Columbian that told him once yo' in, there ain't *no* way out."

My eyes grew wide. "So, he was still smuggling when he came back here?"

"That's right. He brought the danger back here to yo' family."

"That bastard."

Uncle Bobby said, "Accordin' to my buddy over at the Wakulla County Sheriff's office, a judge will have to decide how long he'll spend in the county lockup for his fight with you, and then he'll go to trial for the federal crime of drug dealing. Y'all won't be seein' him any time soon, if ever, if I have anything to say about it."

Mama walked in and came over to my bedside. "Sweet Jesus, Mickey. I'm so sorry." She tried to hug me but couldn't find a spot that didn't hurt. She turned to Bobby. "This boy saved all of our lives the other day, Bobby. I really think Charlie would'a killed all of us if Mickey didn't do what he did."

"Mickey's big enough now to stand up to Charlie," Uncle Bobby said.

"Charlie Crow is rotten to the core, and it's not that he won't change—he can't change." Her cheeks flushed red. "I feel like a first-class jackass, allowing myself to be fooled by that sumbitch again. What the hell is wrong with me?"

Neither of us knew how to answer that question. Bobby finally said softly, "Some loves die hard, Dixie Mae."

"Well, Charlie beat it to death last night. Forever, and that's a promise."

Bobby brought her up to date on Charlie's situation. Mama held out her hand to show us it was steady. "I'm stone-cold sober right now, so I know what I am sayin'. I'm divorcin' the bastard, and that's final."

I didn't believe her, of course. She'd always given in to his persuasion before, but he was going away for a long time, so who knows? I didn't say anything. Neither did Uncle Bobby.

She walked to the door. "I know y'all don't believe me. Well, you watch me. I'll never lay eyes on Charlie Crow again."

I was released right after Mama showed up. It was a painful ride. Everything hurt. That night, Harley came into my room and wanted to talk.

"Mickey, did y'all really wanna kill Daddy yesterday?"

I didn't want to answer that, so I said, "Harley, all I did was try to keep Charlie from hurtin' all of us, understand?"

"I understand, Mickey. Thanks for not killin' Daddy, though. I 'preciate it." He paused for a minute, and then said, "And thanks for keepin' Daddy from hurtin' Grandmama."

"Welcome. Now go to sleep, buddy."

After Harley went back to his room, I lay there a long time waiting for sleep to come, but it didn't. Finally, I got up and kneeled my aching body down beside my bed to pray.

Dear God... I stopped. I didn't know what to say. I knew I was supposed to be sorry for what I'd done, and I was, but part of me wasn't. A big part. Charlie deserved everything he got. He'd attacked me, killed our poor parakeet, tried to hurt Grandmama, and almost bit off my finger. I wasn't sorry for protecting them one damn bit.

But deep in my heart I knew now what it felt like to actually want to kill somebody. I thought of the Bible story of Cain and Abel that Mr. Mann had taught us years ago. Somewhere in that fight, I'd turned a corner. I'd started out trying to stop Charlie from hurting my family, but then, I just wanted to stop him forever.

I'm scared, Lord. I really did wanna kill Harley's daddy. I would've, I know it. Lord, if Bobby hadn't shown up, Charlie would be dead now, and I'd be in jail for murder.

I'm just as bad as Charlie Crow, damn it all, just as bad.

I climbed back into bed. Putting my head under the pillow, I tried to muffle my sobs. *I can't be forgiven, not for something as bad as this.* A sense of despair and loneliness pressed down on me. I remembered what Tootie had said, when I asked her why she didn't go to church with us. She'd said, "God don't have much use for me..."

I'd been emphatic about God loving everybody. But now, I wasn't so sure. Maybe Tootie knows something about life that I was just finding out. Maybe God can't love everyone, not when you have murder in your heart.

THIRTY-FOUR

PRESENT
SATURDAY, APRIL 22, 1972
9:45 P.M.

My face was wet when I finished my story. Suddenly, I found myself embarrassed for talking so long, telling so much, and exposing my deepest fears to a stranger in a café.

Ruby sat there silently for a moment. "Damn! That's one hell of a story, Mickey!"

I looked at my watch. "I've been talking for over two hours."

Ruby smiled. "Y'all ready for some dessert?"

I nodded, and she got up and walked over to the counter and cut two pieces of pie. Coming back with a refill of coffee, she set the plates down on the table, then sat back down to join me.

"And I thought *my* family was screwed up, but hell, we're like the Cleavers compared to y'all!" I got the reference to *Leave It To Beaver* and chuckled.

"It don't seem real, sometimes, and believe me, I wish it weren't. My Grandma Jean wants me to meet up with Charlie. He's dyin' of cancer."

"That's a tough one alright."

"I just can't forgive him for what he's done."

She leaned forward. "I just met 'cha, but after that story, I feel like I know ya. Mind if I give ya some advice?"

"Sure, go ahead."

"I think you're askin' the wrong questions. It's ain't whether or not you can forgive Charlie for what he's done. It's whether or not you can forgive yo'self for what you've done."

I sucked in some air. Damn, she nailed it.

"Wanna hear some more?"

"Alright." I wanted to hear if she had some wisdom to help me make this decision.

"Y'all are worried that you've become just like Charlie. But ya really need to ask whether or not yo' becoming the man yo' meant to be. I don't know you, but it seems to me that you been carryin' a burden around that I don't think ya' need to carry anymore. When are ya gonna forgive yo'self?"

I stared at her. "I don't know that I can."

Ruby nodded sagely. Maybe she'd had similar feelings.

I looked at my watch. Close to ten. Before I could say I needed to go, Ruby got up and said, "Stop in anytime yo' in the area, Mickey. I bet there's lots more to yo' story, and I'd love to hear about it, if ya need someone to talk to."

We walked to the counter, and I paid my bill. Ruby gave me a big hug. As I walked outside, the night was dark and matched my feelings. Obviously, it was too late to go see anybody at this point, so I headed for home.

Damnit all to hell! Talking to Ruby dug up all those unanswered questions about forgiveness I'd struggled with for years.

How could Charlie think that he could do or say anything that would rectify what he'd done to us? Mama would have been a completely different person if he'd left and actually stayed away. And I'd be different, too. I wouldn't have had to fight him to protect my family. I wouldn't have experienced what it was like to lose control the way I did.

As I drove through the night, I tried convincing myself that everything I felt guilty about was Charlie's fault. *Ruby was wrong after all. I don't need to forgive myself. I'm a victim of Charlie's evil, like everyone else in my family. No way in hell I'm going to go see that bastard. No way in hell!*

THIRTY-FIVE

Mama, Harley, and I reacted to the "Big Fight" and Charlie being arrested in extremely different ways. I felt guilty and relieved he was gone. Harley felt grief and still longed for his daddy. And Mama's reaction to filing for divorce to end her marriage to Charlie was as unexpected as it was logical—in some weird, Dixie Mae way. Mama had invited the family over and included Uncle Bobby. After the meal, she declared, "I'm over Charlie. I cain't be with a man who smuggles drugs! That makes him a *criminal!*"

I sat next to Aunt Tootie who looked over at me and rolled her eyes. She whispered, "Like tryin' to kill y'all wasn't a crime."

I tried to pretend Aunt Tootie's comment didn't bother me, but it pierced through me like a knife. It was true. Charlie had tried to kill us. But God knows, I'd wanted to kill him, and tried my best to do it.

"What-cha say, Tootie?" Mama asked.

Grandmama shot us an angry glance. "Don't mind them, Dixie Mae. We ain't ever gonna let that man anywhere near us again. Do y'all hear me?"

Mama put her hand in the air and said, "In fact, I'm swearin' off men completely!"

Uncle Bobby looked devastated. Aunt Tootie, rolling her eyes again, glanced at me, and I almost laughed. Grandmama kicked me under the table.

Harley had been sitting quietly, glaring at his plate while this chatter was going on. He looked up and said, "That's great. How y'all think I feel about this? No matter what he's done, he's still my daddy!"

That shut everybody up.

Grandmama stammered, then sweetly said, "That's right, Harley. Charlie will always be yo' daddy, bless his heart."

He stood, shocking us all with his outrage. "That's right. Y'all can make fun of 'im and talk bad about 'im all y'all want, but I'll always be his son!" He stormed out of the room, leaving us in stunned silence.

In spite of how Harley felt about Charlie, Mama was true to her word. She initiated the divorce proceedings and much to Uncle Bobby's disappointment, she did something none of us would have guessed. For the first time in her life, rather than get drunk and stay out all night with some loser with a red car, she stopped dating altogether. Instead, Mama started going out with her new girlfriends.

It was a heroic effort to change her ways. Even though she'd never gotten along particularly well with women—other than her sister, Tootie—she now went out of her way to meet the other women in the neighborhood who were either separated or divorced. And while she wasn't out drinking with some sailor, pilot, or marine, she and her girlfriends enjoyed their liquor. They were out enjoying their "adult beverages" more often than any of us would have liked, especially me and Grandmama, who hated her drinking more than I did.

Four of them developed what can only be described as some kind of exclusive social and drinking club. This presented a real opportunity for me to earn some money, as they all had young kids and needed someone to babysit their little darlings whenever they participated in the "club's" regular Saturday night "meetings." I'd just turned fourteen and saw myself as a budding entrepreneur.

One Saturday night, I was watching Lila McFee's kids. It was quite late by the time she came home, and she was very drunk, although that wasn't unusual. All the members of the club were in that condition when they came home from their "field trips." I had fallen asleep on the couch watching Gunsmoke when I was awakened by Lila trying to open the door and failing miserably. I got up, opened the door, and watched her stagger in.

"Why, hey there Mickey. Cain't believe y'all still up." She stumbled and fell against me. "Oops! Sorry 'bout that." She pushed herself off me. "I might've had too many martinis tonight, but who the hell's countin', right?" She giggled at her own joke, which wasn't funny to me, but I smiled anyway. "How'd the kids act tonight? Those rascals give y'all any trouble?"

"Naw, they were good kids, like always. I let 'em stay up a bit longer than usual, and they fell asleep on the floor watchin' TV."

Placing her arm on my shoulder to steady herself, she made for her bedroom. "I'll be right back, darlin'. I got y'all's money in my room. You wait right here, okay?"

"Okay."

A minute later, the good Lila McFee came out of her room with the cash in her hand, naked above the waist. I'd be lying if I said it didn't set my little fourteen-year-old heart a flutter! I'd once seen my mother dancing on top of our living room table without any clothes on at a party she and Charlie hosted at our house. I'd gotten up to go to the bathroom and saw her in all her naked glory. I thought my eyes would burn into my brain. No boy should ever see his mama that way. Seeing Lila like this was all kinds of different. I didn't know what to do, so I just stood there, flabbergasted.

Ms. McFee stopped in front of my frozen body holding out the money for me to take. "Here y'all go, Mickey. Here's five dollars. That enough, sweetie?"

"Yes, ma'am." I was still in shock.

"Yo' a good boy, Mickey—a real good boy." She moved closer.

I could smell her intoxicating perfume, mixed with cigarette smoke and booze, as she kissed me on my lips and put her hand on my crotch. Startled back to reality, I jumped back like I'd just been shot. I couldn't say anything. I mean, nothing would come out. She just laughed. "Just shut the door on yo' way out, okay, darlin'?" She turned around and headed back to her bedroom like nothing happened.

It was late when I got home, and Harley was asleep. Mama wasn't home yet, so I went to bed. I barely slept that night, what with all the mixed feelings I was having. Shock, horror, disbelief, and something else I'd never experienced before—lust.

What should I do? Tell Mama? Forget about it? She'd just say I was lying, like usual. I wrestled with those questions all night, but in the end, I decided to forget about it as best I could. The problem was, I couldn't forget about it.

The next day, Sunday, Ripley and I were hitting golf balls down in the open field at the end of our street using a couple of clubs he had borrowed from his dad. I told Ripley everything that happened with Lila the night before.

"You a damn liar. A goddamn liar!"

"I ain't lyin', Rip. Every word of it is true."

"Y'all telling me that you saw Lila McFee's jugs?"

"Yep. Saw 'em all. And they was big."

"Damn! I knew it! I knew they was big! Did y'all touch 'em?"

"Hell, no!" I mean, I'd just kissed a girl for the first time less than a month ago, and that didn't really go very well. Ripley had told me I was supposed to open my mouth when I kissed a girl, so I did. Linda said I kissed like a fish with my mouth opened like that. He failed to tell me you were supposed to touch her tongue with yours, though that was probably a blessing!

"No, I didn't touch 'em. To be real honest, the whole thing scared the hell outta me."

"Y'all such a sissy, Mickey. I'd a touched 'em."

"I ain't no sissy. Just inexperienced is all."

"I'd a touched 'em, is all I'm sayin'."

"You just full o' shit, Rip." I may have said that, but in my heart, I knew he would've.

"You gonna tell yo' mama about what happened?"

I shook my head no. "I don't think so. I'm not sure. Maybe. I just don't know."

Lila asked to me to babysit the next Saturday, but I told her I had something else to do and couldn't watch her kids. The same thing happened the following weekend, too, and the next. Frankly, I was too embarrassed to face her after what happened. After the third time, Mama got suspicious. That Sunday, she sat me down after dinner.

"Mickey, what the hell's goin' on, boy?"

"What y'all mean, Mama?" I had a pretty good idea what she meant.

"Lila said y'all turned her down for babysittin' three weeks in a row. What the hell is goin' on?"

"Nothin'." Oh, boy, I was not at all comfortable with this.

"Bullshit! Now what in the hell is goin' on?"

I took a deep breath, blew it out, and looked at the table as I spoke. I told her the whole story, everything, leaving out nothing. After I finished, Mama looked at me like I was crazy, and she was irate. "What the hell you talkin' 'bout, Mickey! Y'all' cain't go 'round tellin' lies 'bout Lila that way!"

"I ain't lyin'!" Now I was offended. "Everythin' I told you is the God's honest truth—every word!"

"No, yo' lyin', Mickey. Lyin' through yo' teeth. Y'all know that boys who tell lies go to hell when they die, right?" she asked, then slapped me hard across the face. That truly hurt—but not as much as her refusal to believe me.

"Fine! Don't believe me, then, but I'm tellin' y'all right now, I'll never watch Lila's kids again. Ever!" I stood up, knocking over my chair, and started for my bedroom.

"You get yo' lyin' ass back here right now, shithead!"

"Go to hell!" I entered my room and slammed the door. Telling my Mama to go to hell was not the smartest thing I'd ever done. It was absolutely the wrong thing to say. It was like throwing gasoline on a fire.

She chased after me down the hall, beat on my locked bedroom door, and screamed at me to get my "lyin', sorry, ungrateful ass" out of my room "Right now! Or else." *This must be how Charlie felt when Mama came after him with that knife. Damn, she's scary!*

After five more minutes of that, I'd had enough. I opened my bedroom window, removed the screen, and left the building. I could hear her screams all the way over to Ripley's house.

When I got home, around eleven, Mama was already in bed and dead asleep. Harley was still up and stopped me in the hallway.

"Whoo, boy, Mama's madder than a wet hen at you! Wha'd y'all do?" He was whispering, hoping she wouldn't wake up.

I wasn't going to say anything but changed my mind and told him all about it. After I finished, he looked at me in amazement.

"Did y'all touch 'em, Mickey? How'd they feel?"

"Good grief!" I said and went to bed.

THIRTY-SIX

SEPTEMBER 1965

Something changed between Mama and me after the whole Lila McFee incident, and it really bothered me. I told Uncle Bobby about it and how it made me feel. "Mickey, I think it's just because yo' mama is startin' to realize that her boy is growin' up."

"So?"

"Yo' mama has been through so much, you know that. And with so much change, she might be havin' trouble acceptin' the fact that yo' not a little boy anymore. Hell, Mickey, think about it. She saw you beat the shit out of Charlie, a grown man."

It didn't make sense to me until a few nights later when we were heading for bed. She'd kissed Harley goodnight on the top of his head and said, "You my good boy, right Harley?"

"Yes ma'am!"

Mama looked at me. "Y'all grown up, aren't ya, Mickey?"

I didn't know what to say.

"Y'all don't need yo' Mama no more, do ya?"

"What ya talkin' about, Mama? O'course I do."

Looking a little sad, she just walked away as if the matter was settled. It was as if I had transitioned from the world of "lovable little boy" into the violent realm of men. Charlie and Mama always argued, and most of the time, she could give as good as she got. Now that he was gone, it seemed to me that I had become his replacement in some weird way. And in doing so, she became increasingly demanding and critical of me.

Mama started drinking heavily again. It was slow, at first. One or two nights a week she'd come home clearly drunk, stumbling and disoriented.

I didn't know what to do. I worried about her all the time, but I was afraid to say something—until one night when she came home blind drunk, and belligerent as hell. I'd failed to wash the dishes after dinner that night, and they were piled up on the counter by the sink. Harley and I were dead asleep when she came home. But that didn't matter.

She turned on the light saying, "Get up, shithead, and get 'dem dishes done like I tol' y'all to 'fore I left." She slurred her words, listing about like a sailboat in rough seas. Glaring at me she began to pull me out of bed.

"Whaa-what's goin' on?"

"I tol' y'all to do those goddamn dishes in the sink after supper, and y'all ain't done it!"

Finally coming fully awake, I stood up. "Mama, what the hell are ya goin' on 'bout? I'll do 'em in the mornin'!" With that, she took a swing at me, but missed.

"What did y'all do that for?"

"Yo' a real smart ass, Mickey, y'all know that?"

"Mama, I'll do the dishes first thing in the mornin'. They'll be done before y'all get up." I knew that she wouldn't be up until noon.

"Yo' gonna do it now, or I'm gonna beat yo' ass!" She grabbed the belt I'd set on the chair at the end of my bed and began to hit me with it across my back and shoulders.

Jumping back, I grabbed for the belt and pulled it from her hand. "Mama, stop it. I'm fourteen years old, and you ain't never gonna hit me with that belt again. Y'all hear me? Never again!" I shouted.

She lunged at the belt in an attempt pull it from my hand, but stumbled and fell on the floor, hard, and began to sob, mumbling incoherently. "I'm y'all's mama! Y'all gotta do what I say, cause I'm y'all's mama."

"C'mon, Mama, I'll help you get into bed, okay?"

"Yeah, okay, it's time to go to bed now. What the hell y'all doin' up so late, Mickey?"

I helped her off the floor and walked her into her room. I got her into bed, pulled up the sheet to her neck, and began to walk out of her door when I heard her say, "Mickey, did y'all do the supper dishes like I tol' y'all to?"

"Yes, Mama, they all done and put away."

"Good. You a good boy, Mickey, Yo'still my little boy, right?" I closed the door behind me without answering.

When she finally got up at noon, she found the dishes done and put up. I sat across from her at the kitchen table.

"Mama, we gotta talk 'bout somethin' serious, okay?" I relayed the events to her, just like they happened. When I finished, she just sat there slack-jawed, a look of disbelief all over her face.

"Why yo' lyin' like that, Mickey? Why?"

"Mama, I ain't lyin'. Look here." I showed her the belt marks on my legs and back.

"I did that?" She appeared astonished.

"Yeah, you did."

Tears welled up in her eyes. "Mickey, I'm so sorry, son. I'm so sorry." She began to weep, now inconsolably.

I pulled my chair next to hers and put my arms around her. "Mama, you been drinkin' an awful lot lately, an awful lot. I'm worried, scared, mad, and sad about it, all at the same time. It's only us, Mama—you, me, and Harley. What if somethin' happens to y'all, Mama? What? What will happen to me and Harley? They teachin' us in school that kids who don't have parents wind up in foster homes, or worse. So, what happens to us if somethin' happens to you?"

She stopped crying and wiped her eyes.

"I'll do better, Mickey. I swear I'll do better." Then she gave me a big hug.

"I love you, Mama," I said it and meant it. I was understandably skeptical, but I hoped she would be better. Honestly, I didn't really believe she could change, but I wanted to hang on to that hope.

A few days after the conversation with Mama about drinking, things seemed to get back to normal, or as normal as it ever was in our world.

I figured it might be safe enough to talk to Mama about the taboo subject of paternity. It wasn't.

"Mama, I got ask you somethin'."

"What is it?"

"Remember when we was livin' with Grandmama, and she told me about who my real daddy is?"

"Yeah," she said, suspiciously. "What of it?"

"You said that Jack McCarthy was both my daddy and Harley's daddy, remember?"

She tensed up. "Get to the point, Mickey. What ya tryin' to say?"

"You told me at the time not to say anythin' to Harley about Jack being his daddy, 'cause he was too young to understand. Remember?"

"Yeah, so what?"

"Mama, Charlie told me that he was our real daddy and that you'd faked those birth certificates." I let that settle in for a minute. "What's really the truth?"

"You gonna believe Charlie over me?"

"I didn't say that, Mama. He just got me confused again. You got those birth papers provin' it, right? I mean if Jack McCarthy is my daddy and Harley's daddy, why cain't we tell Harley about it now that he's older? In fact, he's older now than I was when I found out. He can handle it. Might be a mercy for him to know that Jack is his real daddy, 'specially after all that's gone on with Charlie, right?" Dropping the bomb, I finally said, "Unless Charlie Crow *is* Harley's real daddy. Is he, Mama? Is Charlie Harley's real daddy?"

I needed to know the truth—all of it. To get all the cards out on the table, so to speak. I'd concluded that Harley really was Charlie's son, not Jack's, no matter what those certificates said. I didn't know why, but I believed it. It was hard to deny that Harley was looking more and more like Charlie the older he got. Not only his looks, but his mannerisms were much like Charlie's. And Harley's voice was beginning to sound more like Charlie's too. It was eerie. It did not, could not, and would not make one iota of difference to me who his daddy was. He was my brother, period. I just wanted Mama to admit it, to confirm it for me. It was important to me that she did.

"What the hell y'all mean by that?" Mama was sitting up straight, obviously getting angry. "That's a goddamn lie, Mickey, and y'all know it. Why do y'all always lie like that, Mickey?"

"Mama, I don't know nothin' for sure. That's the problem. Grandmama and Tootie said Charlie is Harley's daddy that day I saw the pictures of Charlie when he was a boy, and he looked 'xactly like Harley does now, 'xactly."

"You callin yo' mama a liar, boy?"

Backtracking a bit, I said, "No, ma'am, I'm not callin' you a liar. I just think if Charlie is not Harley's daddy, you should tell 'im that

Jack McCarthy is, 'specially after all that's happened. Why would Harley want to be the son of a convict like that sumbitch?"

She literally growled. "We ain't gonna tell Harley nothin'. Not right now, hear me, Mickey? Nothin'. He ain't ready yet."

I stopped short of calling Mama a liar to her face, but I was certain now, more than ever, she was lying about this. I didn't know why she was lying, but she was.

"Okay, Mama. I don't understand why, but I won't say anythin' to Harley right now."

Giving me the evil eye, she said, "Make sure ya don't!"

It wasn't until years later that I found out that I wasn't the only one in the family who listened in on other people's conversations. Unbeknownst to me or Mama, Harley had been just around the corner and heard the entire conversation.

THIRTY-SEVEN

SEPTEMBER 1965

Over the summer, Rip and I decided to try out for the Crawfordville High School junior varsity football team. Uncle Bobby was an assistant coach for the varsity team and encouraged me to try out, reminding me that he and Charlie had been football stars at Gadsden High back in the day. "I'll train y'all if you want before 'Hell Week.' Might help ya make the team."

We couldn't say no and got to work, learning as much as we could from Uncle Bobby. He schooled us in the basics of the game—catching, tackling, throwing, and blocking. He was a hard taskmaster, working with us whenever he wasn't on duty, but he was an outstanding teacher, and we both learned a great deal from his training.

"Hell Week" was actually two weeks long and included both junior varsity and varsity players from the year before, and hopefuls like me and Rip, trying to earn a place on the roster.

Those two weeks lived up to the name and in an attempt to separate the "men from the boys," as Uncle Bobby put it, the coaching staff did everything in their power to cull the herd.

"Get yo' goddamn, maggot-lovin', fat ass up those bleachers, Crow," Coach Patton, the varsity head coach, yelled. "How y'all think yo' ever gonna make this team if y'all can't get yo' fat ass up those bleachers?"

The temperatures reached ninety degrees, with the humidity level reaching eighty percent. The last week of August and first week of September were brutal. We did our best to stay hydrated, drinking lots of water and taking salt tablets. Even so, most of us threw up our guts two or three times per practice, which was two hours in the morning and two hours in the evening.

When the last day of Hell Week finally arrived, Coach Patton and Coach Pickett, the JV head coach, posted the rosters for the two teams on the board outside of their offices. We were not allowed to look at them until after the final practice. I was never known for my speed, but I was scary quick. As soon as the final whistle blew, I was off like a shot and the first in line to see the results with Ripley just behind me. Looking for my name outside Coach Pickett's door, I was deeply disappointed to find that my name was not listed, nor was Ripley's.

Stepping back to let the others check the list, Ripley and I looked like rented mules beat with a big stick.

"What the hell Mickey? Y'all look like yo' dogs just died," Uncle Bobby said.

"Didn't make it, Bobby—neither of us," I said, tears of defeat in my eyes.

"Yeah, we didn't make it," Ripley said.

"What the hell y'all talkin' about?"

"Our names ain't on Coach Pickett's list. We didn't make it," I said.

"Damn boy, y'all are lookin' on the wrong list." Uncle Bobby pointed down the hall where Coach Patton's office was.

The only two Freshmen to make the varsity line-up in 1965 were Ronnie Ripley and Dixie Mae Crow's boy, Mickey Crow. Uncle Bobby was smiling so hard I thought his face might split in half. "I'm proud of ya, Mickey. You too, Rip. You boys worked hard and earned it!"

I knew why we made it. "Uncle Bobby, thank you for training us. No way we would'a made it without you."

"Mickey's right, Mr. Bailey," Ripley said. "We'd never have made it without you."

Uncle Bobby sucked in some air, his chest bursting with pride. "Thanks, boys, that means a lot, but all I did was teach y'all a few things. You did the work, and it paid off."

School was good, football was great, and both me and Harley had a lot more freedom than any of our friends, though I would've traded it all if it meant Mama was around more, and sober. Between working and spending time with her *club* members, we didn't see her much.

When we did see her, more often than not, she'd been drinking—maybe not to the point of being drunk, but certainly feeling no pain. At least she didn't have that sumbitch Charlie hitting her all the time, and I was thankful for that.

As for Harley, without making a fuss, he started writing Charlie in prison. Every so often, a letter would come in the mail for him with Charlie's scrawling handwriting. He'd snatch up the envelope with a look in his eyes that said, "I dare ya to talk about this." Whatever relationship he had with Charlie was private, and he wasn't going to share it with me. I was good with that.

Harley didn't care that much about sports, except judo, which he'd been taking through an after-school program for short while, so he stayed busy with that and schoolwork. Even though he was only twelve, girls were calling the house all the time for the boy, but he seemed oblivious to their attentions.

I came home from school one day in December to find a flyer in our screen door. I grabbed it and took it into the house with me, stopping to read it while I drank a glass of cold water. It was about this little Baptist Church around the corner from us. The flyer said they'd hired a new youth pastor who was looking to build up their "teen outreach" program, whatever that was. They were having the first meeting of the First Baptist Church Teen Club the next Wednesday and were inviting any interested teens in the neighborhood to come and visit.

I hadn't been to church much since we moved out of Grandmama's house, but I was wanting someone to talk to about what I was feeling, regarding Charlie, Mama's drinking, and my concern that I was more like Charlie than I wanted to be.

I walked over to Ripley's house to see if he'd go with me, but before I could knock on the door, he snatched it open. "What the hell you want, white boy?"

I shoved the flyer at him, and he shoved it away as he beckoned for me to come in. "My sister's in the shower. Y'all wanna see?"

"Which one, Suzy or Sharon?" I was hoping for Suzy. She was the youngest, but, oh my God, she was beautiful—stacked, racked, and packed. Just seeing her with clothes on made me sweat. I couldn't imagine what she looked like naked.

"Suzy."

"Hell, yeah!" I was delighted.

"C'mon, but stay quiet, okay?"

"No problem." My anticipation was growing.

We crept down the hallway towards the bathroom like a couple of thieves trying to steal the Mona Lisa in broad daylight. Reaching the bathroom door, we could hear the shower running. In my mind's eye, I could see the wet, pearly drops from the shower head roll down Suzy's beautiful, tanned, smooth, naked skin. The thought of it caused my heart to pound hard in my chest.

"You ready?"

"Yep." He pushed the door open just enough for us to see the shower.

Standing up a little straighter so I could see better, I exhaled in disappointment. There, behind the shower curtain, in silhouette, was—someone. It could have been Suzy, Sharon—hell, Ripley's daddy, for all I could tell!

"Well, that's disappointin'."

"You should've seen the look on yo' face." Ripley was laughing so hard; he fell on the floor. "Y'all think I'd let y'all see my sister naked?"

"Yeah, I do! Y'all talk 'bout it all the time."

"Whoo boy, the look on yo' face was priceless. Wish I had a camera. Damn, I wish I had a camera!"

I jumped on him, and we wrestled around on the floor for a few minutes.

"Hey, let's go down to the school and hit some golf balls before it gets too dark," Rip said.

"All right, let's go." I jumped up from the floor, we grabbed a couple of his dad's clubs, and headed down to the school, laughing all the way.

Later that night, lying in my bed, I remembered the flyer about the Wednesday church meeting next week. I'd left it over at Ripley's house earlier and had forgotten all about it, but decided I'd get it back the next day.

The next morning, I met up with Ripley for our daily walk to school. "Hey, did you find the flyer I left at y'all's house yesterday?"

"Yeah, somethin' 'bout some church thing. Why?"

"I dunno. Thinkin' 'bout goin' next week. Wanna come with me?"

"To church?"

"Yeah, I was thinkin' it might be fun."

"Naw, I'll pass. I didn't know y'all was religious."

"I used to go to church with my Grandmama when we lived there, and I liked it. Ain't been since we moved here, though."

"We're Catholics—only go to church on Easter and Christmas—but we ain't done that since Mom died."

"Well, come with me then. Let's check it out. If y'all don't like it, then don't come back. What ya say?"

"All right, guess it won't kill me to go one time. Besides, there might be some cute girls there." A big ridiculous grin grew on his face.

"Cool." I was looking forward to it. Maybe someone could help me sort out my questions.

We walked the short distance to the First Baptist Church on Wednesday evening. There were a few kids milling around the grounds at the front of the church, just talking and stuff. To Ripley's relief, there *were* also girls there. We walked up to the little crowd, but before we could say anything, one of the older looking boys approached us. "Hi, my name's Eddie. Thanks for comin' tonight."

"Hey, I'm Mickey and this here's my best friend, Ripley."

"Hey," was all Ripley said.

Turns out Eddie was the new youth pastor and the author of the flyer I'd found on my screen door. "Y'all come on over, and I'll introduce you to the others." As we walked over to the group of kids, I realized I'd seen most of them at school.

"Mickey, Ripley, I'd like to introduce you to Patty, Ernie, Jenny, Billy Joe, Mike, Bobby, and Ella." As he called out their names, each one stepped forward and shook our hands. "I'm expectin' a couple more, but why don't we all go inside and get started, okay?"

We followed Eddie into a classroom annexed to the main church building. After we all found a seat, Eddie gave us a big warm and welcoming smile. "Y'all might think that everyone but you has been here before, but that would be wrong. I know Jenny and Billy Joe because they go to church here, but tonight is the first time I've met the rest of you, so welcome to the First Baptist Church Teen Club." Just as he said that the door opened, and two more kids came in—a good-looking boy I'd never seen before, named John, and to Ripley's and my surprise, Linda Clark!

Linda and I hadn't seen each other as much as we used to because I had started playing football, which had taken up a lot of my time and focus. Also, most of my Saturday nights were taken because of my babysitting duties for the Mama's club members. She was in the school band and that took up a lot of her time as well. We managed to go out once in a while, but not like we used to, and over time we just sort of drifted apart, headed in different directions.

It seemed to me that all the girls in the room perked up when John walked in—he was a handsome kid. Eddie introduced them to everyone, much like he did when Ripley and I showed up, all of us standing up and shaking their hands.

Once we all settled in, Eddie got down to business. "I'd like to take a few minutes to tell y'all what to expect from me and this club. Would that be okay with y'all?"

Everybody said yes, so he went on. "First, I will not be preachin' at y'all. That's not my purpose here. Yeah, you're gonna hear about Jesus, but nobody is gonna try and force you into somethin' y'all aren't ready for—that's a promise. Secondly, what's said in this room stays in this room unless it's somethin' that could really hurt you or somebody else. Is that understood?"

Ripley (who else) asked, "What does that mean, exactly?"

Smiling, Eddie said, "Well, suppose you said you were gonna go home and shoot your family tonight, or that you were gonna go home and hurt yourself in some way. I couldn't, and wouldn't, just let that pass. Does that make sense?"

"Yeah, that makes sense," Ripley allowed.

"Good. Everyone else understand? I know how tough it can be sometimes when you're a teenager—how tough school can be at times, right? I'm not talking about grades or stuff like that, although that can be tough. I'm talking about relationships—relationships with your friends or with someone in your family."

Linda and I glanced at each other.

"I want you to close your eyes for a minute, okay? Just for a minute. Now, be honest—how many in this room have ever felt 'less than' your friends? Not good enough? Even a failure? How many of you have ever felt like you weren't as handsome or pretty as your friends or family members, or somehow you just didn't measure up? Now, with all eyes closed, if any of y'all ever felt this way, raise your hand. Come on, be honest."

Embarrassed, I raised my hand thinking I was the only fool in this meeting, but then Eddie said something that changed my mind. "Okay, keep y'all's hands up and open your eyes."

I was shocked to see that everyone in the room had their hand up, including Eddie. "I'll bet all y'all thought you were the only one who raised your hand, didn't y'all?" We all laughed nervously. Eddie was right.

"If y'all come back to this meetin' every Wednesday, if you're brave enough, I believe you will find the answers your lookin' for because we all are lookin' for answers. You'll find that God loves you exactly the way you are right now. He isn't waitin' for you to be good enough because, to be real honest, you will never be good enough. Neither will I."

Things got quiet for a few minutes while everyone took that in. "We'll have a lot of fun here too—games, burgers and pizza night, make your own milkshake night, stuff like that!"

After the meeting, most of us hung around outside, discussing what we'd heard and getting to know each other. Ripley chatted up the girls there, although most of them seemed interested in John, much to his dismay.

Walking home later, I asked Rip his thoughts on the group. "Well, what did y'all think about that?"

"It was okay."

"Wanna go back next week? I think I will."

"Yeah, let's give it another try."

We went the following Wednesday and the next. Eddie announced that we'd take a break for Christmas and that we would start up again in the new year. I had been wanting to talk to Eddie alone for a while and knowing that it would be such a long time before I saw him again, I asked if he would stay after and talk to me. He said he would. I told Ripley to go on home without me. He gave me a funny look but then walked away without another word.

Eddie and I sat alone in the youth room, sitting backward on our chairs facing each other. He offered me a soda, and we chatted about school and plans for the holidays for a while. Then Eddie asked, "What ya want to talk to me about, Mickey?"

I felt my face heat up, a little embarrassed, then started talking. "Ya know about what happened at my house a while back, right?"

Eddie nodded. "I heard somethin' about a terrible fight between you and your dad."

"Right. Charlie, the man I thought was my daddy attacked my family."

"Yes. And you protected them."

I sighed. Hot tears came to my eyes. "Yeah, that's one way to look at it."

"What's the other way of lookin' at it?"

"I wanted to kill that bastard. Oh, sorry."

Eddie smiled. "Don't worry about that, Mickey. I grew up around here. There is no judgment here, you can say what ya need to say, okay?"

"Okay, thanks. The thing is, if my Uncle Bobby, who's a deputy around here, hadn't stopped me, I would'a killed him. The sheriff was even gonna charge me, but my uncle talked 'im out of it."

Eddie nodded. "Because it was self-defense."

"Yeah, it was. He was gonna hurt my Grandmama and everybody else that was there. But the truth is, I wanted to kill 'im. I wanted it more than anythin'. I blacked out during the fight, and when I came out of it, I was so disappointed he was still alive. And I feel so guilty for feelin' this way. I can hardly carry this guilt around anymore.

"How can God love me for wantin' to kill someone? Hatin' someone as much as I hated—and still hate—Charlie? Ya keep talkin' about God's forgiveness. How can God love someone like me? Forgive me? Knowin' what's in my heart?"

"Well, that's a good question, Mickey. Of course that's what God's love is all about. Knowin' the darkness that's in our hearts and forgivin' us. He makes our hearts clean."

I took a deep breath. "Eddie, that's what I want. I want a clean heart. I wanna be forgiven."

Eddie put his hand on my shoulder and gently squeezed. "I was hopin' you'd say that."

The world changed color after I prayed with Eddie. I swear it did. The sky was bluer, and the grass was greener. The Christmas holidays had been brighter, and I felt lighter, more peaceful than I'd ever felt. Nineteen-sixty-five had been one of the worst years of my life, but now everything seemed to be changing. Charlie was gone, school was good, and Harley seemed happy, making new friends, including girls! I was still worried about Mama, but I had hope that might change too.

THIRTY-EIGHT

PRESENT
APRIL 22, 1972
9:56 P.M.

I was lost in memories of Mama, Harley, Uncle Bobby, and me, and before I knew it, I was only a few miles from home. Like magic, a Florida Highway Patrol car turned on his lights and toggled on his siren for a short burst, just to make sure I got the message. I did, so I pulled over and stopped the car, rolling down my window as I did so.

"Good evenin' sir. Let's see your license and registration please."

"Sure, officer. What's the problem?"

"Just let me see your license and registration."

"Sure, I got it right here." I handed him the documents.

"The speed limit here is thirty-five, an' you was goin' over fifty."

"Really? I had no idea. I got a lot on my mind." He pointed his flashlight at the documents. Checking out my license, he said, "Yo' right taillight is out as well. Wait a minute. Mickey Crow. Any relationship to Charlie and Dixie Mae Crow?"

"Yeah."

"No shit?!"

"No shit." This felt so weird.

"Damn, I cain't believe it. I used to hang out with Charlie and Bobby Bailey when we was all in high school. Hell, we played football together. Yo' mama was the prettiest girl in school—everybody thought so. She and Charlie were inseparable. None o' the rest of us had a chance. How's she doin'?"

I had no interest in talking about my family with this guy, but I didn't want a ticket either. "Mama's doing as good as ever."

"Ain't that somethin'? I lost track of Bobby. Haven't heard much about him for a while. How's he doin'?"

CHAPTER THIRTY-NINE

Uncle Bobby kept coming by, often for dinner, and couldn't do enough to help out around the house when things needed fixing. I could see in Uncle Bobby's eyes that he was more in love with Mama than ever before. Perhaps knowing that Charlie was truly out of the picture gave him hope.

Mama seemed comfortable around him, and it was easy for us all to be together, but Mama never gave off any romantic vibe that I could tell. School was good, and home was good enough. Ripley and I were having a great year. Nineteen-sixty-six found the Dixie Mae household as healthy as it had ever been.

Uncle Bobby drove Mama to the courthouse to meet with Charlie's attorney a year or so after she'd filed for divorce. She signed the final papers and returned home a single woman. I was so delighted that I wanted to have a party, but Uncle Bobby told me that would be in bad taste. Maybe so, but it was a red-letter day for me.

Bobby stayed and we had dinner together as usual. Afterward, Harley went to his room, and I sat watching television. Mama and Uncle Bobby went out on the porch to talk, which was unusual, so of course, I got myself in a better position to eavesdrop. It wasn't my fault that I had excellent hearing.

"Bobby, thank y'all for always being here to help. It means a lot. I don't know what I'd do without you. I really don't."

"Dixie Mae, that's another reason I came down to visit today. There's something on my mind that I need to talk to you about." Bobby sounded quite nervous.

"Well, go on and say what needs to be said, then."

"All right. It's ain't no secret that I love you, Dixie Mae—always have, ever since we were kids in high school. Hell, maybe even before that. I didn't say anythin' because you were in love with Charlie, and he was my best friend. I thought you and him would get married, but then you up and married Jack McCarthy. Charlie went nuts over that, wanted to kill Jack, and wanted me to help him. But I said no."

"Good Lord, Bobby, I didn't know that. Thank God y'all said no."

"I didn't do it for Charlie, I did it for you, Dixie Mae. I did it so you wouldn't be hurt. Next thing I know, y'all are back in town and startin' up with Charlie again, then I heard that you was pregnant with Harley and Jack was outta the picture."

"I know, Bobby. I was crazy in love with Charlie. Jack was a big mistake, but at least I got Mickey out o' the deal."

Yes! I knew it! Jack is my daddy and Charlie is Harley's!

"I know, I always did. Every time Charlie left you, after those fights y'all had, I thought—hoped—that I might finally have a chance with you, but then he came back. Y'all renewed yo' vows. I don't mind tellin' y'all, that damn near broke me."

"Bobby, I'm so sorry. I really am." I could hear in her voice that she was tearing up.

"Thanks, Dixie Mae, but I ain't lookin' for sympathy. Charlie's gone, for good. Your divorce is final and he's in prison. All I'm saying is that I love you, and if there's any chance for me, now that Charlie's gone, I wanna take it."

Taking his hand and looking into his eyes, Mama got very serious. "Bobby, I cain't even think 'bout somethin' like this right now. I'm damaged goods, broken—have been for a long time." She stared down at their hands for a moment. "Bobby, y'all really are the best man I've ever known. I mean that I really do."

"Dixie Mae," he gently put his arms on her shoulders. "Will ya just consider it?"

She nodded. "Okay, Bobby, I will. I promise. But I need time right now. I've always acted so quickly on things. Can y'all understand that? I need time."

He moved in closer. "Lovin' you is a hard thing, Dixie Mae. It really is. I wish I could walk away from it, but I can't, so yeah, I can do that. How long do you need?"

Mama took a long time to answer. "I don't want to put my boys through anythin' that won't work out. So, you're welcome to come round any time, like usual. School's about to start for the boys. Let's get through the fall and let's talk after Christmas."

"Oh." Bobby was disappointed. Christmas was five months away.

"Can you wait that long, Bobby?" Mama asked hesitantly, as if afraid that he would say no.

He took her hands in his. "Dixie Mae, I've waited for you since we was kids. What's a few more months?"

She kissed him gently on the cheek. And the deal was struck.

We spent Christmas with Grandmama and Tootie at the Right Reverend Snowden's church, and even Mama was in attendance— miracle of miracles. After church, we all packed into Grandmama's light blue Dodge Dart for the ride to her house to pick up the yummy goodness that Grandmama, Tootie, and Mama had made the night before. It was the perfect winter's day in Florida, chilly, but not cold, and decorated for the holidays in Quincy's town square.

Mama invited Uncle Bobby to be her date for the festival. He'd come around still, but a little less than usual. I think it was hard for him to see her and be waiting for an answer. But Mama said she'd think about it, and apparently, she had.

I hadn't told Harley or anyone else about the conversation I'd overheard, so I was the only one who knew that if Mama wanted to see Uncle Bobby today, it could mean that we'd soon have a new daddy. Everyone ate, played games, and was caught up in the moment.

When Mama found herself alone, she approached Uncle Bobby and asked him to walk around the park with her. I watched them take each step, trying hard to read their body language. Uncle Bobby walked with his head down and his hands in his pockets, clearly edgy in anticipation of what she would say. Mama must have caught a chill because Bobby took off his jacket and wrapped it around her shoulders. She seemed nervous, too, without the sassy confidence she usually displayed around men. She talked for quite a while, moving her hands around a lot, and then she looked up at him and asked him a question. He stood there, as if stunned. *Uh-oh, she's told him no.*

I saw Uncle Bobby reach down and grab Mama by the waist and spin her around in a circle. I could hear her laughter from the other side of the park.

She had said yes!

They came back to the group holding hands with goofy grins on their faces. The closer they came, the more people looked up and realized what they were witnessing. Uncle Bobby and Dixie Mae holding hands in public! By the time they got back to where we were gathered, everyone was staring at the two of them.

Uncle Bobby cleared his voice and said loudly, "As you all know, I've been crazy about this woman since the first time I met her when we were nothin' but kids. It's taken a while, but I finally got the nerve to ask her to marry me." He looked down at Dixie Mae.

Not willing to be left out of this dramatic moment, Mama shouted, "We're havin' a weddin'!"

Grandmama teared up. "Well, it's 'bout damn time!" Then the rest of us erupted in joyful cheering and laughter. We'd all been waiting a damn long time for this. I know I had.

When we got home later that night, we crawled up on the couch together—me, Harley, and Mama. We wanted to hear the details. "Y'all really gonna do this, Mama?" I asked.

She grinned. "For better or worse, Mickey. For better or worse."

"Do y'all love 'im, Mama? I know I do."

"Mickey, y'all know I loved Charlie since I first saw 'im. What I feel for Bobby is different. I trust him, and I do love him. Maybe different from how he loves me, but I told 'im if he wants me, knowin' me like he does, I'll try hard to be a good wife to 'im. Would that be all right with y'all?" Her smile was the most beautiful I'd ever seen it!

"That's good, Mama, it really is."

"I think it's great, too, Mama. Uncle Bobby's been nothin' but good to us our whole lives," Harley said.

"Yeah, Harley, he's always been good to us," I said. "And now, he's finally gonna be our daddy!"

Mama wanted to be a June bride, so a date was set for Friday, June 3rd. She got busy making plans, as there wasn't a whole lot of time before it would be here. It had been a long time since I'd seen Mama so happy, so carefree—it almost made me cry. It really did. This was a dream come true for me. I had always wanted this very thing for my mama, Harley, and me. The cloud of despair that seemed to hover over our family disappeared as Winter drifted into Spring.

Grandmama and Tootie were caught up in the excitement as well, helping to plan the food for the wedding and sending out the invitations to as many family members as they could think of no matter how distant the relations. We were going to have a June wedding and Reverend Snowden agreed to perform the wedding on the condition he could attend the reception. Bless his heart, we all knew what that was about. He never missed an opportunity to sit at Tootie's and Grandmama's table.

CHAPTER FORTY

I woke up early that Friday morning. My first thought was that after Harley and I got home from school, we'd all get together and have a rehearsal for the wedding. I was nervous about being best man. I was the one who would take care of the ring. What if I dropped it? I had a big responsibility.

But then I noticed something strange. I could hear voices in the house. Mama never got up early because she worked so late. Harley and I had been getting ourselves up, dressed, fed, and off to school for years now. The house was always silent when I got up each school day.

Harley was still asleep, so I tip-toed out of bed to see who Mama was talkin' to. I found Mama, Grandmama, and Tootie all sitting around the kitchen table. Mama looked like she was in a trance. Aunt Tootie had her head in her hands. Grandmama sat and wept. They all looked up when I entered the room. Mama held out her arms to me and even though I was fourteen, I let her fold me into her lap. She sobbed into my shoulder.

Grandmama said, "Mickey, I have some very bad news."

"It's Uncle Bobby, isn't it?"

"Yes."

"Is he hurt?" I could barely breathe.

"No, baby. He died last night. He was shot while on duty."

I crumbled into my mama's arms and felt my world spin out of control.

Grandmama had been the first to be told about what happened to Uncle Bobby. She later told us that the County Sheriff, Dylan McKnight, walked in the front door of the Blue Star, and she knew immediately that something awful had happened to someone she loved. She knew he and Doris well because they'd been eating at the Café for years.

She said he walked over to the counter where she was folding clean napkins and said in his deep southern baritone voice, "Good evenin' Miss Colee."

"I asked 'im what he was doin' out here at this time of night, and he said to me, 'Colee, is there somewhere we can talk, privately?' I said, 'Sure, we can go to the storage room in the back o' the Cafe,' and he followed me back there. He closed the door and tol' me to sit down, he had some bad news. He proceeded to tell me the whole story."

Deputy Bobby Bailey was on duty Thursday night performing speed checks on the highway coming into Quincy—the last duty before his wedding on Friday when he would marry the love of his life, Dixie Mae Crow. After the wedding, he and his new bride were going to honeymoon in the Florida Keys for two weeks. Two weeks of sun, warm sand, and clear blue-green water. Two weeks of fishing, snorkeling, and doing what honeymooners have done for thousands of years. He could hardly wait.

"Bobby, this is dispatch," his radio blared, interrupting his daydream.

"Dispatch, Deputy Bailey here. What's up?"

"Bobby, we got a silent 211 call in progress at Hankins Guns and Tackle. I'd like for you to go check it out. Over."

"Will do. Where's Deputy Peterson? Can he back me up? Over."

"Deputy Peterson is finishing up a call out in the county. It'll take 'im fifteen to get up to Hankins. Looks like y'all on yo' own, Bobby, so be careful. Over."

"Roger that, Dispatch. I'm rollin' now. Out."

Hankins Guns and Tackle was only two miles south from his position, off Highway 267 and the newly named Martin Luther King Boulevard. He rolled his cruiser along 267 without his siren, not wanting to spook anyone that might have broken inside the store. Hankins had been robbed a few times over the years, usually a "smash and grab" netting the thief some ammo or tackle. Old man Hankins kept his shotguns, rifles, and handguns locked up in his walk-in safe every night. He claimed he was the only one that knew the combination to the safe—bragged about it sometimes down at the Better Days Tavern, around the corner from his shop. Every call the Sheriff's Department had been on at Hankins was after the thief had left the building with the loot. Most times they got caught later, but not every time.

Deputy Bailey pulled in, off to the side of the store, not wanting to be seen in the lights in the small parking lot in front of Hankins. He turned on his spotlight and immediately saw that the side door was opened slightly. Turning off the light, he called dispatch.

"Dispatch, Officer Bailey here."

"Officer Bailey, Dispatch, over."

"I'm over at Hankins. Looks like the side door is open. Proceeding inside. Any idea when backup will be on scene? Over."

"He's still ten out. Proceed with caution. Over."

"Roger, out."

Bobby stepped out of the cruiser before reaching back in to get the shotgun he had stored in a rack connected to his dashboard. He flipped the strap that kept his service revolver in its holster and racked a shell in his scattergun, then proceeded to the open door. It was dark inside, and it took a few seconds for Deputy Bailey's eyes to adjust. With his shotgun up and at the ready, he proceeded to clear the store. First, he checked the front area by the counters, and then went aisle by aisle, working his way to the back of the store, where the walk-in safe was. As he cleared the final aisle, he slowly rounded the corner to where the safe would be visible. As he did, he noticed the shape of a man standing there.

Flipping on his flashlight, which he was holding on the side of the shotgun, he yelled, "Freeze, Sheriff's Department!" The first thing he noticed was Mr. Hankins staring back at him. Confused, he lowered his shotgun a bit. "Mr. Hankins, what are you doing here tonight?" Someone pushed Hankins to the floor, but before Deputy Bobby Bailey could pull his shotgun up to open fire, he was shot between the eyes—dead before he hit the floor.

Five minutes later, Deputy Joe Peterson entered the store where after completing a search, he found the bodies of Hankins and Deputy Bobby Bailey. Later, they found the thief, and now murderer, who confessed that he kidnapped old man Hankins so he could open the safe. Deputy Bailey had caught him just as the last number in the code was entered into the keypad.

"It was the hardest thing I've ever done," Grandmama said, "telling my baby girl that the man she was going to marry died. Dixie Mae was still pulling her shift at Southwood. Tootie drove me out to the club. It was the first time I'd ever been there. As we walked in that big ornate front door, the hostess came over, looked at us funny, and asked, 'How can I help you ladies?'

"'We need to speak to Dixie Mae Crow,' I said. 'She works in the bar. It's an emergency.'

"She showed us to a sitting area and took our names. Said she'd be right back, but I'd had enough of her snootiness, and said, 'Why don't y'all just tell Dixie Mae her mama's out here waitin' on her. Can y'all do that, sugar?'

"She finally went to tell yo' mama. A minute later, Dixie Mae came out with a worried look on her face. 'Mama,' she yelled, 'What's wrong? The boys all right?'

"Tootie started to say somethin' but broke down in tears. Dixie Mae, now in full on panic mode said, 'Mama, what the hell has happened?'

"'It ain't the boys. They all right. It's—it's Bobby.' I sobbed. I just hated telling her.

"The hostess changed her attitude. She came over and asked, 'Would y'all like to use the office right over there? It'll give y'all a little more privacy.' Then she led us to the office. 'Thank you, darlin',' I said to her.

"Once the door was shut, yo' mama demanded to know what had happened. 'What 'bout Bobby, Mama? What's wrong with Bobby?'

"'Dixie Mae, Bobby was shot earlier tonight by a thief over at old man Hankins's store. He dead, honey, Bobby is dead.'

"Dixie Mae was overcome," Grandmama said. "I could see her world fallin' out from 'neath her. All she could say to me was, 'Bobby's dead?'

"'Yes, Dixie Mae, he is,' was all I could say.

"'What will the boys say?' Dixie Mae asked. She just sat there and rocked back and forth, her arms around her knees, tryin' desperately, and failin', to shut out the devastatin' truth.

"We came here together so that when you two boys woke up, we could tell y'all together."

Thankfully, Grandmama filled in all the empty places where my imagination had been trying on different scenarios—none of them comforting. It took a very long time for it all to sink in.

My mama, Dixie Mae, loved Charlie Crow—of that there was no doubt. Though she loved Bobby Bailey in a different way, she did love him, and the prospect of becoming his wife filled her with hope and joy. He had always been there for her, no matter what her condition, all the while loving her with the same intensity she'd loved Charlie. But he was never able to say so until a few months ago. He'd won her over, and he not only loved her, but he was a loyal friend, the best kind of friend. Always there when she needed him—yet not so much as to smother her. Now he was dead, and along with him, her hope, her joy, her future.

How could God do this to us? How? Maybe He's punishing Mama—or me.

There was no wedding on Friday, June 3rd. Instead, in the late afternoon on Sunday, June 5th, every pew and every space where a person could stand at the Calvary Baptist Church out on Stewart Street in Quincy was occupied by the people who knew and loved Deputy Bobby Bailey. Mama, Grandmama, Grandpa Hank, Tootie, Harley, and me all sat in the front row. All of us were there to say our goodbyes to a good uncle, a good friend, a good man, the best of us. Whatever would we do now?

FORTY-ONE

PRESENT
APRIL 22, 1972
10:05 P.M.

What are the chances I would be pulled over by some cop who knew Bobby? It triggered all of those horrible memories again. A strange look must have flashed across my face because Officer Wallace took a step back. "Are you okay, son?"

I nodded. "I'm sorry, sir. That's a painful subject for me. Bobby Bailey died in 1967, the day before he was gonna marry my Mama."

"Oh God, I'm sorry to hear that. I'm sorry to bring up something so sad."

I kept talking to avoid any more direct questions. "Bobby was a deputy, here in Quincy. He was shot during a robbery."

"I didn't know he was a deputy. I'd left for the Army right outta high school and served four years before comin' home. I've only been back a little over a year. It makes sense that he would be a deputy in Quincy. He loved this town, and he loved helping people, that's just the kind of guy he was. I'm sorry he's gone."

"Me too," I said. "I miss 'im every day."

"Look, I ain't gonna give y'all a ticket. Just slow down and make sure you get that light fixed, okay?"

"I will, sir, first thing tomorrow."

"When y'all talk to your Mama or Charlie, tell 'em John Wallace said hi."

"I will, and thanks for not giving me a ticket." I started the car, and he walked back to his vehicle.

After Officer Wallace pulled out, I made my way back on the highway home. I pulled up in the driveway, turned off the car, and just sat there staring off into space. The next thing I knew, I was slamming my hands on the steering wheel as a rush of rage at God flooded over me. It was like everything awful in my life was being thrown in my face at one time.

God, why? Why the hell are You doin' this to me! Why did you let Bobby die? Don't you know that he was our only hope?

I was spent—physically, spiritually, and emotionally. I had nothing left. I fell into bed and dreamt the dreams of a troubled soul. I woke on Sunday morning and was surprised to find my clothes still on from the previous night. I sat up and threw my legs over the side of the bed, sitting there for a few minutes clearing my head.

Finally, I stood up and made my way to the bathroom. I undressed and left my clothes where they fell. After passing the water that had accumulated during the night, I turned on the shower and got in. I made it as hot as I could handle, then stood under the soothing stream, hoping it would wash all my pain away.

I dragged myself out of the shower and threw on some clean pajama pants and a T-shirt. I was exhausted, emotionally and physically, and needed a day of rest. Taking my pillow and blanket out to the living room, I made coffee, and brought it to the sofa where I lounged and sipped on my hot coffee. A few minutes later, I made a decision. I would lay there all day and watch television, sleep, think, maybe call a friend—whatever—for the whole day.

Later that Sunday afternoon, the emotions of the previous day infiltrated my dreams again. I woke up in a sweat, remembering every detail. Time lost all meaning as I thought back to the time after Uncle Bobby died.

CHAPTER FORTY-TWO

None of us were the same after Uncle Bobby died, but Mama was gutted. She seemed broken beyond repair. She never cried, not through the details of canceling the wedding, planning the funeral, or getting through the burial. Her eyes were dark and lifeless, as if all the hope she'd been able to muster for finally finding happiness with a good man served to mock her into a kind of madness.

For the first time in anyone's memory, Mama couldn't work. After all of the details of Bobby's passing were taken care of, she fell hard into a bottle of vodka trying her hardest to drown there. We were used to her long benders, but her emotional absence added layers of pain to the suffering Harley, and I were dealing with. We turned to Aunt Tootie and Grandmama for comfort. In their arms we wept and fell asleep when we had worn ourselves out with grief.

I refused to go to church. Eddie reached out to me, and I shot him down. I didn't want anything to do with a God who would taunt us with the possibility of such joy and then snatch it away with utter cruelty. I don't remember much about that time except one gray day of anguish followed by the next unbearable one.

Sometime in the middle of July, Mama sat Harley and I down at the kitchen table and said she had something important to discuss.

She seemed a little nervous, fidgety even. "Boys, I cain't stay in this house anymore—in fact, I cain't stay anywhere near here anymore. Just too many bad memories—so many, I cain't breathe. If I'm ever gonna have a chance to get better, we gotta move."

"Where we gonna live, Mama, if we cain't live here?" I asked. I was thinking we'd just find another place in Quincy or maybe Tallahassee.

Boy, I was way off. "No Mickey, we gotta move as far away from here as we can. We are movin' to Key West."

"Key West? Where the hell is that?"

"Mickey! How many times I gotta tell y'all—aww, hell, never mind."

Mama was prepared and pulled out a map of Florida, laying it across the coffee table. "Look here. Y'all remember when we visited my Aunt Berta down in Miami?" We both nodded our heads yes. Aunt Berta, our great aunt, had a nice home near the Intercoastal Waterway in the Miami area. She pointed on the map and moved her finger from Miami south all the way to the very tip of Florida. "See here?" She was pointing at Key Largo and moving her hand down. "These are all islands, and Key West is the last island in the whole United States. Y'all will love it down there, I promise."

I just couldn't stop myself. "Why? Why would y'all take us all the way down there? We don't know nobody. Besides, I'm about to go into my Junior year. I want to play football and be with my friends here, and Grandmama and Tootie's not that far away. I ain't goin'!" I was defiant.

Harley got up. "No!" he yelled and ran out of the living room to his room, slamming his door. "See that? Harley don't wanna go either. I just don't understand why we have to go!"

Starting to get angry now, Mama snapped at me. "We goin', Mickey, and that's all there is to it. We goin'."

"Well, I ain't goin'. You can go by yo'self, if y'all want. I ain't goin' and neither is Harley. Mama, we lost Uncle Bobby too! We still hurtin' over it. Why can't we stay here, where we got family and friends who care about us? It's not fair. We ain't goin'!"

"We'll see 'bout that, shithead. We'll see 'bout that. Y'all are my sons. Y'all go where I tell y'all to go, and that's that!" She got up from the table, grabbed her keys and purse, walked out the door, and drove off. We didn't see her for the rest of the day.

I was in bed, not able to sleep, when I heard Mama's car pull in the driveway, sometime around midnight. By the way she slammed the front door when she came in, and kept bumping into hallway walls, I was pretty sure she was drunk, but at least she was home safe. Knowing that, I finally let sleep overtake me.

I spent the day at Ripley's, but I didn't tell him anything. I was too upset to talk about it. Later in the day, Ripley walked with me back home. When we walked outside, we both noticed a sign in my front yard. Walking across the street and up to the sign, we saw that it said in big letters, "For Sale."

"What the hell's goin' on, Mickey? Y'all movin'?" Upset at seeing the sign in our front yard, I pulled it out of the ground and threw it down, looking at me he said, "All right, what in the hell is goin' on?" I hadn't said anything all day about the conversation Harley and I'd had with Mama about moving to Key West. I didn't really believe she'd do it.

"C'mon in, and I'll tell y'all the whole story."

I explained everything to him. "That ain't right, Mickey, that just ain't right!"

"I know, it ain't right. But there ain't much I can do 'bout it. Mama's got her mind made up."

"Dammit! How long 'fore y'all gotta go?"

"I dunno. However long it takes to sell the house, I s'pose."

"Dammit!" He got up to go home.

"I'm sorry, Rip. It's not what I want. We'll still see each other." I said lamely.

He wouldn't even listen. Stomping out, he yelled back, "Y'all know that ain't true, Mickey."

I realized in that moment that I would go with Mama and Harley to Key West, like it or not. I couldn't let Harley go to Key West with Mama by himself. He was the one person who I really trusted and loved. I cared more about him than anyone else. He was a good boy, and I felt he needed me. I was turning sixteen in a few days and Harley would be fourteen the next month—and a young fourteen at that. How could I take care of either of them if I were up here and they were down there? She'd never let him stay behind with me. I simply could not, and would not let him to go through this move alone.

Mama got the house as part of the divorce settlement from Charlie, so she didn't have to split any of the proceeds from the sale with anyone. She'd also kept her real estate license current from when she'd sold houses in Quincy before we moved to Crawfordville. She signed on with a broker in the neighborhood so she could be the selling agent and earn the sales commission on her own house as well. Nobody said Mama was dumb. With the commission she'd earn from selling the house, and the money she'd make selling every stick of furniture in the house, except for her beloved console stereo, she would amass a nice little nest egg for our new venture.

Turned out, it only took a month to sell the place. That didn't give us much time to say goodbye to all our friends, but we managed it, though saying goodbye to Ripley was one of the hardest things I'd ever done. We both tried to hold back tears, unsuccessfully.

"You the best friend I ever had, Mickey. Truly, the best." Ripley had tears streaming down his cheeks as we stood out in the middle of the street between our houses.

"Quit cryin', dumbass. Only babies cry. I'll give ya a call after we settle in down there. Promise." I was no more successful at holding back my own tears than Rip was.

"Y'all better, shithead."

Just then, his youngest sister, Suzy, came out of his house and walked over to us in the street. She gave me a big hug—her perfect breasts pushing into my chest. "Goodbye, Mickey. We gonna miss y'all 'round here." She turned and walked back home.

Just for a minute, I forgot where I was—I felt a little dizzy, and my throat was kind of dry.

"I just thought y'all might like a little partin' gift." Rip said, cracking up. "That's gonna cost me, but it was worth it just to see the look on yo' stupid face."

Damn it all, I was really going to miss Ripley! Hugging awkwardly, we said our final goodbyes.

Sitting on the floor in my room, it hit me how painful it was going to be to leave Ripley. Not only Rip, but Linda and my other friends, not to mention Grandmama and Tootie. It seemed like I was forever leaving people I cared about. At sixteen years old, I felt beaten down by life, and it had hardly started. I couldn't seem to find hope or joy with two hands and a compass. And at that point, all my compass was saying was, *You're going South.*

The car was packed, along with the U-Haul trailer Mama rented, so we were ready to go. We drove to Quincy and spent the day and night at Grandmama's house. Saying goodbye to her and Grandpa Hank was hard enough, but saying goodbye to Tootie—that broke my heart. There were more tears and hugs the next morning, then we were off on our little family's next adventure. For better, or for worse, we headed south.

CHAPTER FORTY-THREE

We arrived in Key West in the middle of August. I thought I knew what humidity felt like, but this was next-level humidity—oppressive and suffocating—like hitting a brick wall at sixty miles per hour. Mama and Harley loved it immediately. Water was everywhere, along with tropical breezes, and very friendly people. I refused to enjoy myself. All I wanted to do was go back home.

Mama found a nice little double-wide mobile home next to the bay on Stock Island, less than three miles from Key West. It was a working waterfront and port for shrimpers, lobstermen, and commercial fishermen, but had some residential areas spread all over the island, too, like ours.

The Keys are made up of eight-hundred-and-eighty-two charted islands, thirty of which are inhabited, connected by one-hundred-and-twenty-seven miles of bridges, the longest being Seven Mile Bridge. I have to say, when we crossed over that bridge for the first time, it was scary as hell. By the time you got to the middle of it, you couldn't see land behind you, or in front of you. Spooky—real spooky.

"Mama, we gonna die out here?" I said, only half joking.

"Shut up, shithead. Y'all gonna scare yo' brother."

"I ain't scared one bit," Harley said nervously, eyes wide open, with what looked like abject fear to me.

One of the first things we noticed was mile markers. Key West was located at mile marker zero, Stock Island was located at mile marker four, and so on. That's how you gave directions in the Keys. "Yeah, look, you go down to mile marker eighteen, then turn left on the dirt road that's just after that"—typical directions around here.

Our trailer was in a park with maybe fifteen others, made up of mostly middle-aged and senior folks. Kids our age were hard to find, so I felt isolated, adding to the misery I felt at leaving behind everything and everyone I knew. But Harley got me interested in exploring the place, like all of the other neighborhoods we'd moved to. So before long, I got into the spirit. There was so much to explore, and Harley and I were determined to explore it all.

I got a job on a shrimp boat for a month, hardest job I ever had—before or since—but damn if I didn't learn a lot from those crusty old Conchs, including a few new cuss words. Those folks took profanity to a whole new level. By the end of the day I was bone tired, so not a lot of time to sit around feeling sorry for myself.

Conchs is what you called the folks that were either born in the Keys or had lived there so long they couldn't remember not living there. They were a stubborn bunch and took a lot of pride in being native-born. Even Key West High School's mascot was a Conch, which I found hilarious, seeing how my new high school mascot was named after something so slow and ugly!

Harley worked on a small lobster boat that summer and learned where all the great fishing and lobster grounds were. He worked hard, too, taking to the job like a natural, becoming a tanned and muscled kid. In fact, both of us had gotten almost as dark as some of the Conchs. We lost any weight we might have gained during the winter and spring earlier that year, and gained quite a bit of muscle, working the nets and traps of the fleet.

Even though Mama was still suffering from Uncle Bobby's death, she did what she had to do and got a job as a bartender at a local dive called The Ambassador Lounge on Key West. I didn't like it at all. It was dark and seedy looking, filled with drunks and desperation.

She also got a job at the Naval Air Station Officer's Club. I liked the Officer's Club, though. It reminded me of The Savannah, where Mama worked back home, with its white tablecloths and waiters wearing tuxedos—it was a classy look.

Mama threw herself into the jobs, which meant Harley and I were back where we started before she was going to marry Bobby—alone. Mama made friends easily, especially of the male variety, but there was no joy in her eyes. I wondered if I'd ever see her come to life again. I wasn't holding out much hope.

School started soon enough, and both Harley and I began attending Key West High School, me as a Junior and Harley as a Freshman. It was a brand-new school with a beautiful campus and water views. It didn't take Harley long to begin making friends at school, and I was happy about that.

On the other hand, I was miserable, having to continuously keep an eye on Mama, her relationship with Vodka becoming stronger and stronger. I didn't understand how she was able to stay sober long enough to work two jobs, but somehow she pulled it off. For me, her alcoholism was soul-crushing and the resentment I felt, alongside my own sadness and grief, was becoming too heavy to bear.

Since Mama worked the Ambassador during the afternoon and the Officer's Club at night, she slept until we were off to school. When the bus dropped us off in the afternoon, Mama was at work until eleven at night.

I'm surprised Harley and I didn't starve to death. I was no cook, but I could boil water, open a can, or make a sandwich. Canned spaghetti, macaroni with beef, and onion sandwiches made up most of our diet, in the early days in the Keys.

I sure missed Grandmama and Tootie's cooking. No matter how hard I tried, I couldn't convince my taste buds that pasta from a can tasted like fried chicken and biscuits, but we made do.

In October, Grandmama got really sick with pneumonia. Aunt Tootie called on a Friday night and begged Mama to come up for a week or so to help out. She couldn't run the Blue Star and take care of Grandmama by herself. Grandpa Hank was helping where he could, but he worked all day too. Based on how worried Mama was, and how quickly she made plans to leave, I think they were afraid Grandmama might die, but no one told us, probably to keep us from worrying.

It nearly was seven hundred miles to Quincy and would take Mama two days to get there and two days to get back. She expected to be gone for ten days total. That was a long time to leave me and Harley alone, especially since Tropical Storm Inez was gaining strength out near the Bahamas. People were saying it might turn into a hurricane.

Harley didn't want her to go and neither did I.

"Mama, I'm worried 'bout this storm out in the Atlantic. Cain't y'all wait 'til it's passed us by?" I asked.

"Mickey, Tootie said Mama is real sick, and she needs my help. I gotta' go, besides, the radio says it's gonna go north, to the Carolinas. And you boys won't be alone. Bud and Doris said they'd watch out for y'all 'til I get back." Bud and Doris French were our neighbors, both retired cops from Rhode Island and real good people.

"All right, Mama, I understand. Harley and I'll be all right. Just please be careful drivin' those bridges. It's already windy."

"Boy, ya worry too much. I'll be fine." She seemed sober as a judge, so I hoped she was right.

Later that day, Mama packed a bag and hugged us goodbye. "Y'all stay close to home 'til I get back, understand? Here's some money for groceries and things. Make it last, okay?"

"Okay, Mama."

"And don't give no trouble to Bud and Doris while I'm gone."

"Yes, ma'am," Harley said.

She climbed into her trusty old Bug, now getting a little long in the tooth, and waved at us, Bud, and Doris, then drove out onto Highway 101 to Miami.

A day after Mama left the Keys, the wind picked up considerably and was shaking our double-wide more than I liked. Harley and I flipped on our old black and white TV to see what the storm was up to. We didn't have cable in our trailer like a lot of people did, but we did have a big antenna strapped to the side of the doublewide. All the programming came from Miami, so our signal was weak and fuzzy, but we could hear and see well enough. We didn't like what we were hearing one bit.

The weatherman said, "Well, folks, it looks like Inez has been declared the first hurricane of the season. Forecasters are now saying that Hurricane Inez has changed direction and is expected to hit the Keys after all. Last night, after ravaging the Bahamas, all indications pointed to Inez making a turn to the northeast. She's now making a southeasterly turn towards Key West and is expected to make landfall around Marathon sometime tonight. There is a Hurricane Warning now in effect until further notice."

Marathon Key was about forty miles north of us, not far enough to be safe.

"Damn, Mickey, what we gonna do now?" Harley asked.

Before I could answer, there was a knock on our front door. Opening it, with Harley leaning over my shoulder, I found Mr. French standing there yelling over the wind. "Boys, everyone in the park is evacuating to higher ground. You and your brother have gotta come with us." I guess I hesitated a little too long, so Bud yelled again, "You hear me, Mickey? Grab Harley and let's go! I promised your mother we'd look after you until she got back from Quincy, and I aim to keep that promise. Get whatever you need and meet us out front in ten minutes, you got that? Ten minutes!"

"Yes, sir, Mr. French. Ten minutes, got it." I was now alarmed. "Harley, grab some clothes and put 'em in yo' pillowcase." I grabbed the case off my pillow and stuffed some clothes into it along with the money Mama gave us. That done, I turned off all the lights and the TV, pushed Harley out the door, and got our asses over to the French's, who were already in their station wagon waiting on us.

Sitting in the back seat, holding onto our little pillowcases filled with clothes, Harley was worried. "You think Mama's all right?"

I'd been wondering the same thing. She said she'd call us when she got to her motel room in Melbourne, three hundred and fifty miles away, but we hadn't heard from her.

Both Harley and I had experienced hurricanes before, living through Hurricane Donna in 1960 while living in Quincy, but this was far scarier, especially with Mama gone. The rain was coming down in sheets and with so much force that the station wagon's wipers couldn't keep up. There was only one road going into and coming out of Key West. There was water on both sides, so in addition to the rain, the growing strength of the winds—now gusting to eighty miles per hour—were whipping up saltwater spray with enough intensity to completely cover the car in places, and Inez hadn't even hit yet.

Harley and I were terrified, as was Doris French who screamed every time the wind pushed the heavy station wagon around. It was like riding in a bumper car at the county fair and being hit by the bully who targeted you for the entire ride.

The plan was to get to a motel or hotel with multiple floors. The French's chose a motel on Highway 1A1, across the street from Smathers Beach. This was a good choice because the waters along the shores of Smathers were shallow and on the Gulf side of the island, instead of the Atlantic side with its deeper waters. Thankfully, we made it through the deluge of water and wind, pulling into the driveway of the two-story motel. As we exited the car, a strong gust of wind hit Mrs. French so hard, she fell to the ground in a heap. Harley and I ran over and grabbed the horrified woman, pulling her to her feet and helping her to the stairs where she hung on for dear life.

"Harley, stay here and hold on to Mrs. French while I go back to the car and get our stuff." I had to scream over the howling wind for him to hear me. He nodded his head in understanding, so I raced back to grab our pillowcases. When I got to the car, I grabbed them and looked over at Harley and Doris French. I was struck by the realization that Mr. French wasn't with them. I looked over the hood of the car but still didn't see him. Running around to the other side, I found Bud French lying next to the wide-open driver side door.

"Mr. French!" I yelled as I kneeled down next to him. "Bud, Bud, ya all right?"

He looked at me dazed and confused. "What the hell happened?"

"I dunno. I ran over here looking for ya and found ya on the ground. You don't look so good, Bud."

"I don't feel so good either, Mickey. How's Doris? She okay?"

"Yeah, she fell when she got outta the car. We got her over to the stairs, and Harley's there with her now. She's all right, just a little scared, is all."

"Help me up, son, and let's get out of this mess." I got my arm under his and held on to the car door to pull him up. He was still unsteady, but his eyes began to focus. When he turned around to get something off the front seat, I noticed he was bleeding from the back of his head.

"Mr. French, yo' bleeding from the back of yo' head. Must'a hit it when you fell." Reaching his hand back to feel his wound, it came away heavily bloodied.

"Help me over to the railing with Doris and Harley. I'll tell you what you've got to do after that, okay?"

"Let's go." I helped him over to where Harley was standing and Doris was sitting on the steps, both of them holding on to the rails.

Seeing me helping Bud to the stairs, Doris stood up and yelled into the wind. "Bud! What happened?" She quickly looked him over. "Bud, you're bleeding. What the hell happened?"

"Got no time for that right now, Doris. Let's get to the room, and I'll tell you all about it."

She looked at him sternly for a moment. "All right, for now."

"Mr. French, sit here a minute while Harley and I help Mrs. French up the stairs to the room. Is that okay? Then we'll come back to get ya."

"I came down here last night and got the room, just in case we needed it." He took the room key from his pocket and handed it to me. I put it in my pocket and helped Harley get Doris to the right door. Letting her go for a moment, I unlocked the door and helped her inside. After she was settled, Harley and I went back down to get Bud.

Once we had him in the room, he had some instructions for me. "Mickey, here's my car keys. There's a first aid kit in the back of the wagon, along with some water, food, flashlights, candles, and other stuff. Can you and Harley go down and bring those supplies up here?"

"Yessir, no problem."

"Just be careful, boys. We don't need you hurt too." He flashed us a reassuring smile.

Harley and I were able to retrieve the supplies without incident. By the time we got back up to our shelter, we were soaked from head to toe and thankful we'd brought some dry clothes with us. The four of us snacked on cheese and crackers, a few cookies, and some water while we listened to a small transistor radio Mr. French had thought to bring along. The man on the radio was talking about the hurricane. "...sustained winds of one-hundred-forty miles per hour in places up and down the Keys. There's also been widespread flooding reported on the Atlantic side as the storm surge rises. Get to the highest ground you can find, stay inside, and for God's sake, be safe."

"Mr. French, yo' think our Mama's okay?" Harley asked with tears glistening through his eyelashes.

"Oh, yeah, Harley, I'm sure she's fine. Probably doing exactly what we're doing—just hunkering down 'til this thing passes. Besides, she's way north of here by now, probably up near Melbourne."

"It's just that she said she'd call us last night, is all, and she didn't." Poor Harley was so worried, and so was I. Worried sick.

"Phone lines are the first thing to go down in winds like this, son. This will all be over tomorrow, and I'm sure she'll call you as soon as it is. Why don't we all try and get some sleep, and see what things look like tomorrow? What do you say?" We both nodded in agreement.

There were two beds in the small room. The Frenches took one, and Harley and I slept in the other. It seemed as if Bud and Doris fell right off to sleep—same with Harley. I had just finally drifted off when I heard something that sounded an awful lot like a gun shot. It woke me, and then Harley, but the Frenches didn't budge.

"What's that?" Harley sounded a little panicky.

"I don't know, but I'm gonna find out." I jumped out of bed.

CHAPTER FORTY-FOUR

The first thing I noticed as I headed for the door was that one of the glass slats from the louvered windows in the door was missing. I found it when I stepped on one of the shards of glass that had erupted from its frame, crunching it underfoot. Thank God I'd laid down with my shoes on in case we had to evacuate in a hurry.

I got a towel from the bathroom and scooped up as much of the broken glass as possible. The wind, which had been howling through the broken glass frame, suddenly stopped. I couldn't help myself and opened the door to see what things looked like outside. It was weirdly quiet and calm. No wind, no rain, and even the moon came out as the clouds parted, lending an otherworldly look to the landscape. In that half-light cast by the moon, I was amazed and horrified by what I saw.

The water was more than halfway up the side of the French's station wagon. I couldn't tell if it was actually floating or not, but I saw there were other cars that were floating. Some had already crashed into other cars and the exterior of our little motel—or were in the process of it. That explained the gunshot-like noise I'd heard earlier. I was so engrossed in what I was witnessing, I didn't hear Harley or Mr. French walk up behind me.

"Son of a bitch," I heard Bud say. "Would you look at that. I knew buying that tank would pay off one day."

"Is it over?" Harley asked.

We both turned to look at Harley, but Bud spoke first. "No, just the eye of the storm. In a bit, it'll start up again. They say the second half is usually the worst. Why don't we see what the radio has to tell us?" Bud turned to go back inside while I shut the door. I found some other towels and packed them in the space left by the shattered slat to keep the rain and wind out when the eye passed over.

We listened to the radio for a little while, keeping it low so as not to wake Doris. The man on the radio was saying much the same thing as before—lots of flooding and wind damage. There were reports that several homes had lost their roofs and several mobile homes had been picked up and tossed into the bay on Stock Island where we lived. I looked at Bud, my eyes asking the question I was too afraid to pose.

"I wouldn't worry too much about that. All those trailers in our park have hurricane tie-downs, most of them anyway." Bud may have been right, but I honestly didn't know if we had tie-downs or not—I never noticed. Still, I let his optimistic words wash over me and soothe my worried mind.

Shortly after that, we heard the winds begin to pick up. Then the rain started to fall, in earnest. It didn't take long for the howling to begin again. The rain sounded like it would punch holes into the roof above us.

"Why don't we try to get a little more sleep if we can. Okay?" Bud asked.

Harley and I headed for our bed. I laid down, but Harley grabbed his pillow and headed for the bathroom.

"Where the hell you goin', Harley?" I asked.

"I'm gonna sleep in the bathtub in case the water gets up here."

I don't think we got much sleep the rest of the night. The wind had gotten stronger, and the power of it caused the windows on the door to rattle in a kind of high-pitched hum from hell. It was awful and loud, waking even Mrs. French. But finally, sometime after sunrise, the humming and the wind began to diminish. Around noon, the clouds parted, the rain stopped, and the sun came out. Even the storm surge had receded a little, leaving the cars wherever they landed, except for Bud and Doris's big beautiful station wagon! It hadn't moved an inch and was waiting to take us home!

"Mickey, how about you and me taking a trip to the park to get the lay of the land before we all go back?" Bud asked.

"Sure, let's go. Harley can y'all stay here with Mrs. French while we gone?"

I could see he really wanted to go with us, but he just nodded his head in the affirmative.

Most of A1A was clear of water, although there was considerable damage to buildings and cars, some of which, along with lots of palm fronds, were blocking the highway in places. Mr. French expertly traveled around them, and it wasn't long before we made the few miles to Stock Island and our little trailer park. Driving through the open gate to the property left me speechless, and I began to cry. Most of the trailers were firmly in place, but not all; not ours. It was gone, swept clean, as though it had never been there at all.

Bud parked his car near his trailer, and we got out of the wagon. We slowly walked over to the sea wall that, until recently, had sat directly behind our home. We surveyed the bay and its new additions. Sitting not more than fifty feet offshore was our trailer, and everything we owned in it, bobbing up and down like a cork on a fishing line waiting for a bite. We didn't have much, but Mama's beloved stereo console was lost forever, as was her entire record collection.

We drove silently back to the motel and retrieved Harley and Doris. Harley took one look at me and knew something wasn't right.

"What's goin' on, Mickey? What happened?"

"Let's get in the car, and I'll tell ya everthin'." I could barely keep it together. By the time we got back to the park, he knew the whole story.

"What's going to happen now?" he asked.

Before I could answer, Mr. French spoke up. "Right now, you boys will stay with us until your mother gets back. Then we'll figure out what to do next."

Mama didn't get home that night but showed up the next morning. We heard the Bug slide to a stop and ran outside to greet her. Mama bounded from the VW and grabbed us both in her arms, all of us crying and trying to talk.

"Oh my God! I thought I'd lost y'all! I thought I'd lost y'all!" She just repeated it over and over.

"We fine, Mama," Harley said first.

"Yes, Mama, we're fine, thanks to the Frenches."

Mama walked over and gave both Bud and Doris a big hug and kiss. "I just cain't thank y'all enough for takin' care of my boys. They all I got in this world. They all I got." She wept tears of relief.

"Mama, there's bad news," I said.

"What's that?"

"Look at our place." She spun around and saw the empty concrete pad.

Mama turned white as a sheet. "Whe-where did it go?" She sounded almost childlike.

I pointed to the bay. "It's out there, Mama. See it bobbing up and down? That's ours."

She dropped to her knees. "That's everythin', everythin' we own. Our clothes, pots and pans, oh God, and my console." She broke down and wept so much, it broke my heart. How much more loss could she, or we, take?

After surveying the damage, we all went inside to Bud and Doris' place. Mama told us that she'd gotten as far as Ft. Lauderdale when she heard on the news that Inez had turned and was going to hit the Keys after all. She turned around but only got as far as Key Largo when she was stopped by the Florida Highway Patrol. She said she tried to call but the phone lines were down. She had to stay at a shelter there until the next morning. When the winds died down, she high-tailed it to Stock Island.

We stayed with the Frenches for a week while Mama figured out what to do next.

One day at supper, Bud French came home with a huge smile on his face. "Dixie Mae, have a seat. I think I've got some good news for you and the boys."

"Bud, we'd love some good news right 'bout now." Mama sat next to Doris.

"I was talking to a lawyer friend of mine that I've known for forty years. He and his wife retired last year and moved to Big Pine Key. I had lunch with him today, and he told me something interesting."

"Well, what is it, Bud? Don't keep us in suspense." Doris said, giving him the *look*.

"He said in order to own a mobile home in the Keys, you have to have tie-downs. It's the law. You know what that means, Dixie Mae?" Bud was grinning from ear to ear.

Mama got it immediately. "I might be blonde, Bud, but I ain't dumb."

Bud went on. "If you give me the name and address of your landlord, a phone number if you've got it, my friend said he'd make a call on your behalf as a favor to me, so it won't cost you a dime!"

"Y'all gotta be shittin' me, Bud!" Mama smiled so big that her eyes disappeared. "If Doris wasn't sittin' right here, I'd give you a big kiss right on the mouth!"

"Oh, go ahead, Dixie Mae. It'll probably give the geezer a heart attack!" Doris quipped.

Mama jumped up from the table and planted a big wet kiss right on Mr. French's mouth, then turned and did the same to Doris, who almost did have a heart attack, turning bright red. Every one of us burst out laughing.

Bud's friend was as good as his word. A couple of days later, our landlord, Mr. Jenkins, called with the good news. In return for not suing him for damages and loss due to his failure to use tie-downs on the trailer he rented to us, Mama got a check for five thousand dollars! She gave Bud and Doris French five hundred dollars for their help with getting her the money and for taking care of Harley and me during the hurricane. Bud refused to take it, so Mama slipped it to Doris in an envelope a few days later when we left for our new place on Bay Point, ten miles north of Stock Island.

Mama still had some of the money from the sale of the house and furniture up in Quincy, and now, with the money from the recent settlement, it was enough to start over. Bay Point was a small little island divided by a canal that led to the bay. One side of the island was populated by mobile homes of one kind or another, and the other side by the much more expensive block-and-mortar homes. There wasn't much inventory in the way of trailer rentals, and there was no way we could afford the block-and-mortar homes. However, Mama found us a small, thirty-foot travel trailer with a large cabana attached. It was one of several owned by our eighty-year-old land-lord, Reba, who lived next door.

Right off, I noticed Reba was a real animal lover. She owned five little poodles, an old chimpanzee named Brutus, and had a penchant for wearing leopard print bikinis everywhere, including while maintaining her properties and collecting rent. She even wore a bikini to the store.

Our trailer wasn't much to look at, but it was on the canal, and for the time being, it was home.

A few days after we moved in, I was out in the cabana around dinner time doing homework and listening to music. Suddenly, I smelled the aroma of steak cooking on a grill. Harley did too.

"Whoa, that smells good," Harley said.

"Sure does." My mouth was watering. I walked outside and saw Reba, in a leopard skin bikini, cooking something on her grill. Her poodles were at her feet.

"Smells great, Miss Reba. Y'all havin' steak tonight? Sure smells good."

"Oh, hell no, son. I don't eat no meat. This here's fo' my babies." She meant the five fluffy little white rats running in circles excitedly. "There ain't nothin' too good for my kids. They won't eat nothin' else—just steak, pork, and chicken."

I groaned as I thought about the canned Italian food Harley and I would be eatin' shortly. "Them's mighty lucky pups, Miss Reba," I said.

"Don't you know it, I done spoiled 'em—spoiled 'em rotten." Hell, I couldn't have agreed more. "Well, y'all have a good evenin'." She went back to finishing her work on the grill.

Harley and I looked at each other mournfully, then walked inside the trailer and opened a couple of cans of spaghetti. "Maybe it'll taste better with some parmesan cheese on it," Harley said.

"Pro'bly not," I said.

"Pro'bly not."

A day or two later, Harley came rushing into the cabana. "Mickey, y'all gotta come out to the canal with me. C'mon!"

"What the hell, Harley?"

"Just come on!" He was running out the door.

I followed him and found him at the seawall overlooking the canal behind our trailer. "Look! Look down to the bottom!"

I did as I was commanded and was rewarded with a wonderful sight. Running around on the bottom of our crystal clear canal were at least a dozen spiney lobsters! We'd lived long enough in the Keys to know how good they were to eat—almost as good as steak, and a hell of a lot better than canned pasta.

"How we gonna get 'em, Mickey?"

"Go get our fish net and goggles. We eatin' good tonight." I was excited.

He left and was back in a flash with the gear. I took the goggles, spit in them to keep the fog off the glass, grabbed the net, and jumped in. When I came up, I had two of the delicious crustaceans in my net. I handed it to Harley, who emptied the two lobsters into a bag and handed the net back to me. I went down a second time and came up with two more. Handing the net and goggles to Harley, I climbed up the ladder attached to the seawall.

Fortunately, it doesn't take a lot of skill to cook lobsters—just boil water in a pot and throw them in. In the time it takes to melt some butter, they are done and ready to eat. And eat, we did, every last morsel. Damn, that was one of the best meals we'd had in a long time. We didn't share any of it with Reba's spoiled little brats either.

CHAPTER FORTY-FIVE

Thank God Christmas was over. It would've been the first Christmas with Bobby as our stepdaddy—a happy celebration for the newly wedded Dixie Mae and her boys. But this Christmas only served to highlight the fact that Bobby wasn't here and never would be. No one was happy or in any kind of mood to celebrate the birth of Jesus. The stench of Uncle Bobby's death hung in the air like some terrible, ugly vulture, ready to pick our emotional bones clean.

Mama had a few days off after Christmas and spent them at the bottom of a bottle, crying and cussing God. We tried to console her, even as we were fighting off our own despair and pain.

Finally, a few days after New Year's, she emerged. Her eyes were swollen, her hair was dirty and greasy, and her complexion was as white as the beaches around us. In short, she looked like death warmed over.

There was always a fear flirting around the edges of my consciousness that made it hard to concentrate or feel like I could focus on myself. No matter how much I begged her, she was drinking more, smoking more, and staying out late, if not all night long, when she wasn't working. I didn't know how much longer I could watch her fall down that rabbit hole.

When the burden became too much, I would jump into the little skiff Mama bought for us not long after we moved to Bay Point. I'd start up the engine and run her as fast as I could along the waters of the bay. The ocean breeze and salt water spray covered my face and filled up my senses, cleansing my spirit and breathing freshness into my soul. I availed myself of the healing power of our skiff many times, only to find myself needing it more and more, like a drug addict needing a fix.

Harley and I both became increasingly worried about Mama driving the narrow bridges from Key West to our little trailer in Bay Point, knowing she would be drunk. She didn't drink while she worked at the Officer's Club on the Naval Air Station—she was the model of sobriety and responsibility, else they would have fired her. But once she was at the Ambassador, sobriety became a distant memory. Many nights, I woke up at one or two in the morning to find an empty space where her Bug should've been, then lay awake, unable to find sleep again until I heard her VW pull onto our lot. I listened with a mixture of fear and anger as she stumbled her way to the cabana door, then fumbled with the door handle to the trailer, finally making contact and entrance.

One night, I woke up at 2:00 a.m. to find Mama missing in action, like so many times before. I stayed awake for as long as I could, hoping she would come home safely, but eventually, sleep overtook me.

"What the hell's goin' on?" I grumbled, as I again slowly rose through the layers of unconsciousness. Looking at the bedside clock, I could hardly see the time, but when I finally focused in on it, I saw it was 4:30 in the morning.

Another knock on the cabana door told me to turn on the light, which I did, then moved to the door and opened it. "You Mickey

Crow, son?" asked the police officer. He and his partner were holding up Mama. I could see that they were holding Mama up because she was so drunk, she couldn't stand on her own.

"Yes, sir!" I said with anger and relief. "What's wrong with my mama?"

"She's okay now, but we found her passed out in her car in a ditch just before the Rockland Channel Bridge, just before Mile Marker nine. You know it?"

"Yessir, I know right where it's at."

"We could've taken her in, but we know Dixie Mae from the Ambassador and didn't wanna put her in the system. Know what I mean?"

"Yeah, we like Dixie Mae," the other officer said. "She's always good to us cops. Treats us with respect. Where's her room? We'll set her on her bed and then take off. That okay with you?"

"Yessir, come on in. I'll show y'all where it's at."

In a few minutes, they had Mama inside and laid her gently on her bed located at the back of the trailer. "Yo' Mama is a real good woman, son," officer number one said. "Don't think badly 'bout her 'cause of this. It could happen to anyone." He handed me his card. "Look, if Dixie Mae needs anything, just have her call me, okay?"

Just then, Harley woke up, startled at seeing cops in the cabana.

"Why they here, Mickey?"

I looked over at the bed. "Just a second, and I'll tell you every-thin', okay?"

"We were able to get her car out of the ditch and my partner drove it here. Needs some cleaning up, but no real harm done."

"Thank y'all for bringing Mama home, officers. I'm just glad she's okay."

"Me too," one of them said, and they left the way they came.

Listening to the conversation, Harley asked, "Mama drove the Bug into a ditch? Is she okay?"

I told him the whole story. "She's fine. Bet she won't feel so good tomorrow, though. What y'all think?"

"I 'spect yo' right. Mickey, it seems to me Mama's comin' home drunk more and more, an' I'm really worried 'bout her. I tried to talk to her 'bout it a while back. Did I ever tell you that? Maybe not, but I did try. She tol' me to shut the hell up and mind my own business."

"No, I didn't know you said anythin' to her, but it sounds like somethin' she'd say alright."

Making my way back to my bed, I said, "Tell ya what. Let's try to get some more sleep, okay? We'll try to talk to her when she sobers up." I reached over to turn the lights out.

Harley turned over and went back to sleep.

I slept a little, but mostly just tossed and turned. Finally, I got up when sun shone in the cabana. I put on my shorts and walked out to the front to see what the VW looked like. It was a mess—mud and seaweed all over it. Going back inside, I grabbed some rags, towels, a bucket, and soap. Back at the Bug, I grabbed a nearby hose, filled the bucket with water, then washed the slimy business off the car, drying it with the towels. As I was washing the bug, I noticed that there was a sizable dent in the right front fender that hadn't been there yesterday, and the mirror on the driver's side was missing, ripped from where it had previously been attached to the car door. Looking it over, I was glad Mama's precious and beloved VW Bug had been wounded.

"Maybe showin' Mama this'll wake her the hell up," I mumbled to myself. I heard Harley moving around in the cabana and walked over to the window. "Harley, get yo' lazy ass out here. I got somethin' to show ya."

Still wiping sleep from his eyes, he quickly looked over the Bug. "Shit! This gonna be real bad when Mama sees this—real bad."

"I know. Might be the right time to talk to her 'bout her drinkin'. What y'all think?"

"Just might be, but it ain't gonna be pretty. Know what I mean?"

I sure as hell did know what he meant.

This was Sunday, so Mama didn't have to work. We decided to let her sleep, and sleep she did, not stirring until three in the afternoon. Walking to the open doorway to her room, I couldn't help but notice that it smelled like a distillery.

"Mama, after you get up and eat somethin', me and Harley got somethin' to show you, okay?"

"All right. Give me an hour. I gotta take a shower and clean up first, then I'll eat somethin' and come out, okay?"

"Sure. See y'all in an hour."

After what seemed like an eternity, Mama opened the door from the trailer to the cabana. She looked better than last night, but she had bruises on her arms and legs as well as a cut on her forehead.

Harley, not having seen Mama when the cops brought her home, acted surprised. "Mama, how'd y'all get them cuts on yo' head and those bruises on your arms?"

Looking at the bruises, she said, "I don't rightly know, Harley. I cain't 'member."

"I'm pretty sure I know where they come from." I pointed to the front of the trailer. "Mama, follow me out to the Bug, and I think that'll explain it all."

The three of us marched to the front yard where the now clean Bug was parked. Spotting the dent in the fender, she yelled, "What the hell did y'all do to my Bug?" She ran over to it to get a closer look. "Goddammit, what happened to my side mirror! Damn, Mickey, you been drivin' my car without my permission again?"

It was true—I had *borrowed* Mama's VW from time to time when she was passed out after coming home drunk, without her knowledge. "Ain't true, Mama. I didn't do this. You did."

"I'll be damned if I did!"

"Mama, the police brought you home last night, after four in the mornin'. They said they found you passed out, in a ditch, near Mile Marker nine. You know, just before the Rockland Bridge."

"That's a goddamn lie, Mickey. Why would you say somethin' like that?"

Looking straight into her eyes, I reached into my pocket and handed her the business card the officer gave me. "Here's the policeman's card." I looked down long enough to see his name. "Officer Tyler gave me this last night. Why don't you call 'im and tell 'im I'm lyin'?"

"I will, smartass." She snatched the card from my hand and almost ran to the phone in the trailer.

Harley and I just looked at each other and shook our heads. "Let's just sit here and wait."

He nodded his agreement.

About fifteen minutes later, Mama opened the trailer door and walked out to where Harley and I were sitting. "Sorry I called y'all a liar, Mickey. I don't 'member nothin' about it—nothin at all."

"Okay, Mama, but Harley and I got somethin' to say, and we need you to listen, okay?"

"Go on ahead, speak yo' mind, both y'all." She was looking at Harley as she said it.

"Mama, Harley and I are worried 'bout you like never befo'."

"Yeah, Mama, like never befo'."

"You drinkin' too much, Mama." She tried to protest but, before she could, I continued. "Mama, y'all know it's true! What happens to me and Harley if you get killed drivin' home one night? We don't have a daddy to take care of us if you get splattered out there on OSH. So, what happens to us?" I worried that I sounded more forceful than I intended or maybe not forceful enough. I wasn't sure.

I kept up my argument. "We barely get to see y'all anymore, and when we do, you either drinking or drunk. Mama, I know I ain't no adult, but I ain't stupid. We been through enough, Mama. Ain't we been through enough?" Tears began rolling down my cheeks, again.

Harley, now crying a bit, had something to add. "Yeah, Mama, ain't we been through enough? I don't want y'all to die. We need y'all here, Mama." As the words poured out of him, he practically threw himself in Mama's arms. "We. Need. You. Here." He over-emphasized each word.

When we finished, all three of us were crying and hugging each other. Finally, Mama said her piece. "I know life ain't always been kind to you two boys. It sure as hell ain't turned out the way I thought it would, way back when I was yo' age, Mickey. I swear, I'm doin' the best I can to keep a roof over our heads, clothes on our backs, and food in our bellies. That's why I'm workin' two jobs, y'all know that?"

Honestly, I'd heard this speech before. "I understand that Mama. I know y'all are workin' hard, an' both o' us appreciate it a lot, but we worried 'bout yo' drinkin'. How many more times will the police find y'all in some ditch 'cause you passed out from drinkin?" On a roll, I continued. "Mama, my friend Blake says his Mama is an alcoholic. Not sure what that means, except she drinks too much and passes out. Says she's sick and cain't help herself. Are you an alcoholic, Mama? Are you sick?"

I might have pushed it a little too far because Mama got mad. "Hell, no, I ain't no goddamn alkie! I know I drink too much some-times—hell, everybody does—but I can control it. I can stop anytime I want to. Alkies cain't. Don't ever let me hear y'all say that again, hear me boy? Never let me hear y'all say that again!" Calming down a bit, she added, "I promise I'll dial it back some, okay? I ain't gonna promise I won't drink no more, but I will cut it down. That's a promise." She walked back inside the trailer.

Harley looked at me and asked, "Y'all think she'll do it, Mickey? Think she'll cut back some?"

"Not a chance, Harley. Not a chance in hell."

To be honest, Mama did try. She usually did when she said she would—for a short time. She didn't stop drinking, not by a long shot, but she did seem to slow down a bit. At least the police hadn't brought her home in some time, and life went on as usual. Harley, nor I, would ever stop worrying about her driving home drunk.

FORTY-SIX

Most of the country was obsessed with the war in Vietnam, both supporters and detractors. The Beatles' "Hello Goodbye" and "Judy in Disguise," along with Marvin Gaye's "I Heard It Through the Grape Vine" and Aretha Franklin's "Chain of Fools" played constantly on our local radio station, WFYN. Our football team may have failed to inspire the faithful, losing twenty-six to six to Coral Gables High back in November—in the Orange Bowl, no less—but our basketball team had set the islands from Big Pine to Key West on fire, beating Miami's Curley High in the state championship in March. The school, and the town, threw them a parade down Duval Street, and it was great!

While race relations in the country were strained at best, Martin Luther King's assassination shocked the entire nation, including our small corner of the world. Key West in 1968 was, among other things, a Navy town. As such, our school had always been integrated. White, Black, Cuban, and others worked and played together daily. That's not to say that bias and prejudice were eliminated—this was the "Deep South," after all.

Mama was still working at the Ambassador Lounge, now as the head bartender, and the Officer's Club on the Naval Air Station, where she had also been promoted to Bar Supervisor. I never knew how she did it, drinking the way she did, but miraculously, she flourished in her work life.

Early one Saturday morning in March, I was awakened by the phone ringing. Looking at the clock next to my bed in the cabana, I saw that it was three o'clock in the morning. I got up and answered the phone. "Hello?"

The voice on the other end of the line asked, "Is this Mickey Crow?"

I was on full alert now. "Yeah, this is Mickey. Who's this?"

"This is Officer Tyler with KYPD. I believe we met a while back. You remember that?"

"Yessir." Now panicked, I asked, "Is my mama all right? I-is she dead?" What other reason would the KYPD be calling us at three in the morning?

"No, son, yo' Mama ain't dead, but she is hurt. She's in Fisherman's Hospital."

"What happened, Officer Tyler?"

"She was drivin' home from work and when she crossed Saddle Bunch Key Bridge, her Vee Dub caught fire, right in the middle of the bridge, where she stopped. Luckily, a man in a pick-up goin' the opposite direction saw her car on fire and pulled yo' mama out of it just before it blew up."

"Oh God!" I yelled, waking Harley.

"Sorry to say, Mickey, but there ain't much of that VW left—just a pile of smokin' metal."

"How bad is Mama hurt?"

"Mama's hurt?" cried Harley.

"Hold on Harley, let me find out."

"She's fine. Got some cuts on her arms and legs, and her hands got second-degree burns—not much worse than a bad sunburn, I'm told."

Breathing a sigh of relief, I asked *the* question. "Was she drunk?"

He hesitated a moment. "Afraid so, Mickey. She was pretty much out of it. Since no one else was involved, we're not pressin' charges of any kind. Now if y'all need a ride to the hospital, I can send someone to pick you up, but I was told she'll be sent home sometime tomorrow if y'all wanna wait. The nurse said she's sleepin', so not much you can do if y'all decide to come."

"Well, if she ain't bad hurt, and she's comin' home tomorrow, I'll wait."

"Sounds good. Write down this number to Fisherman's, and they can connect you to her room when you call."

"Thank you, Officer Tyler, I 'preciate you callin'. You got the name of the man that pulled her out?"

"He said he didn't want nobody makin' a fuss over what he did. Said anyone would've done the same thing."

"Okay, thanks again for lettin' us know what happened."

I told Harley what Officer Tyler said.

"Thank God she didn't die, Mickey."

"I don't know, Harley, it don't seem like God gives a damn about us."

"You shouldn't say that, Mickey, it ain't right."

"Fine, let's get back to bed. I think it might be a long day tomorrow."

I didn't sleep a wink. When the sun came up, I walked to the little store just south of OSH to get some milk and cereal for breakfast. Lucy, the owner of the store, was sitting behind the register waiting on customers as always. "Damn, Mickey, sorry to hear 'bout y'all's mama. Is she all right?"

"What you talkin' 'bout, Miss Lucy?"

Pushing the local newspaper toward me, she said, "Says right here in the fish wrapper that y'all's mama's car caught fire on Saddle Bunch Bridge and blowed the hell up. Says a man named, let's see.

Oh, yeah, here it is. A man named James Trent pulled her from her Bug just 'fo' it blowed up." Again, shoving the paper in front of me, I saw a picture of what was left of Mama's beloved VW Bug. It was awful and gave me chills thinking about how close Mama had come to dying.

"She's okay, Lucy, just cuts and bruises is all. She'll be comin' home later today."

"That's great news. Glad to hear it. So, what you need today, boy?"

"Just came up for some milk and cereal for breakfast. We're almost out."

"Tell y' all what. Get the milk and a big box of cereal. It's on me, today. Y'all got 'nough on yo' plate right now. And tell yo' mama I'll be prayin' for her, okay?"

"I sure will, Miss Lucy. I cain't thank y'all 'nough for the milk and cereal. Yo' the best!"

"Oh, go on now, 'fo' you make me cry." She smiled and I smiled back, grabbed the goods, and left for the walk back home.

Late in the afternoon, Mama's friend and co-worker, Maggie, pulled onto our lot with Mama in her car. Harley and I ran outside to help her out of the car and into her bedroom. Everything she had was in a little paper bag with "Fisherman's Hospital" printed on both sides. After we got her settled, it didn't take long for her to fall asleep. I walked Maggie out into the cabana.

"That was a close call, Mickey—a real close call. Besides the cuts and bruises, the pain she has from the burns is bad, so her doctors gave her some real strong pain pills. She'll be sleeping a lot over the next week or so, okay? Also, there's a jar of ointment inside the bag that should be used three times a day on her burns. Doc says not to miss it, 'cause it's very important."

"Got it, Maggie, thanks for bringin' her home. Yo' a good friend."

She blushed a bit. "No big deal. Yo' mama would do the same for me. In fact, she has done the same for me." She didn't elaborate, and I did not ask. "Doc says she needs to be off work for at least a week, so do yo' best to keep her off her feet. The club owner loves yo' mama and said he'd pay her for the hours she missed. That's good 'cause Dixie Mae's gonna need some time to get a new car. I helped her file a claim this morning, so it shouldn't take too long. Call me if y'all need anythin'. I mean it. Call me if you need me."

Mama slept all day Saturday, so Harley and I kept an ear out for her, taking turns napping on and off throughout the day. I kept checking in on her, worried she might not wake up, although she finally did late Sunday morning. We got calls from our friends throughout the day who'd read the story of the fire.

"Heard y'all's mama almost burned up," Mark Brazzini said. He was now my best friend in the Keys, although I still missed old Rip.

"That's true."

"How she doin'? She hurt bad?"

"Bad 'nough—cuts and bruises. Got burned pretty bad on her hands, but the doctor said she gonna be all right after a while."

"She drinkin'?"

"Yeah, she was. She ain't never gonna stop, Mark. Never. Mama gonna drink 'til she's dead."

"I hear ya. Well, call me if I can help at all, hear me?"

"Thanks, man, I will."

A few days later, I ventured into Mama's lair. "Y'all wanna talk 'bout it, Mama?"

"No, I don't need you preachin' to me right now, Mickey. Just leave me alone for a while."

That made me angry. "Mama, I'm done preachin'. You wanna kill yo'self, then go on, do it, 'cause y'all sure as hell don't give a damn about Harley and me. It won't be long, and I'm gonna graduate high school, and when I do, I'm gone. If I can find a way to take Harley with me, I will. Ever'body up and down the Keys knows y'all were drunk when that man pulled you out of the car. Ever'body! Cain't hide it anymore. Now ever'body knows Dixie Mae Crow is an alkie, nothin' but a drunk. So, no, I ain't gonna preach to y'all ever again, cause I'm done!"

"Get out my goddamn room, you little sumbitch! Get out!"

It was a long week. At least it was quiet.

Mama was healing faster than anyone thought. She got a check from her insurance company ten days after the *accident* and bought herself a shiny new red VW Bug with a tan ragtop. I have to say, it looked good, and she looked good in it. A few days later, she went back to work. She slowed down the drinking for a while, like she always did when something like this happened. I didn't think it would last long. It didn't.

FORTY-SEVEN

OCTOBER 1968

I'd turned seventeen in July and Harley turned fifteen. We'd been in Key West for more than a year, and I had made a few close friends.

I told Mama I was through worrying about her, and if she wanted to kill herself, go ahead. But that was a lie I realized because even though I felt a lot of resentment towards Mama, I still felt like I had to keep a close eye on her.

However, I'd managed to give myself permission to have some kind of a life that didn't include worrying about Mama every minute. I didn't realize it at the time, but I was beginning to separate myself from her emotionally—at least a little.

When school started in September, both Harley and I got busy—me with football and schoolwork, Harley with girls and, well, girls. Before we knew it, Halloween was upon us and November was on the horizon, which meant Homecoming and Thanksgiving. I'd been dating a pretty girl named Darlene with long brown hair and longer tanned legs.

While I'd had a few girlfriends along the way, I'd made it to my junior year as a virgin. Don't get me wrong, there was lots of heavy petting and such, but I refused to go all the way. I'd like to say it was because of some moral code, and it was to a degree. I mean, I knew what the Bible said about having sex outside of marriage. But the real reason is I didn't want to get a girl pregnant. I'd seen a friend of mine, who shall remain nameless, get a girl pregnant. She left somewhere to have her baby and when she came back, my friend dropped out of school, married her, and got a job working with Mark at the tire shop. No way was that gonna be my future. Truthfully, I'd dry hump like a rabbit, but there was always gonna be something between me and the young lady, period. Funny, though, my reputation was that I'd gone all the way with a few girls, taking their virtue, but it was a damn lie.

Darlene was a virgin, she said, and she desperately wanted to have sex for the first time. And she wanted it to be with me. It was becoming more and more difficult to say no to her. On her birthday, in early November, I stopped by her house to give her a present. When I opened the door, I was met by a beautiful girl, completely naked.

"You just gonna stand there with yo' mouth open, Mickey, or come inside? My mother and father are up in Miami for the weekend and won't be back 'til Sunday night, so get yo' ass in here!"

Being a red-blooded, hormonal teenage boy, I went in. "I brought y'all this present for yo' birthday," I said, handing over the wrapped gift, and trying and failing to keep my eyes off her perfect breasts and everything else the south had to offer.

"Mickey, all I want for my birthday is you!" She reached out for me.

"Darlene, we've talked 'bout this. I don't wanna be no daddy right now! Y'all really wanna be a mama right now?"

"I cain't get pregnant right now, Mickey, it's impossible."

I was feeling my self-control beginning to falter. "You cain't know that for sure."

"Sure do. It's what's called my cycle."

Damn, I really wish I'd listened better in health class.

She took my hand and walked me into her bedroom, shutting the door behind us. We began making out and petting, and somewhere along the way I found myself in my underwear. I was on top of her and grinding away like a maniac. Darlene, in the meantime, was trying her best to get my tidy-whities off, to no avail. I finished, my underwear full of, well, the results of my efforts, so to speak. I fell off Darlene and onto my back. I looked up to find her crying and red-faced.

"What's a matter? Why you cryin'?"

"Mickey, I want you to leave. Just get out!"

"Why, what's goin' on? Why you mad?"

"You's just a child, Mickey. I need to be with a man—a man who wants me as much as I want him, and that ain't you!"

I put my clothes back on and headed for the front door. "Fine, this is fine with me. I tol' ya all along that I wasn't gonna find myself leavin' school and havin' to marry someone 'cause we were stupid. So, fine, we done." I opened the door, slamming it behind me as I left her house for the last time.

On a Friday, a couple of weeks later, I was called down to Mr. Brazzini's office, Mark's dad, who was Dean of Boys. "Have a seat, Mickey," he said, pointing to a chair next to his desk.

"Yessir."

"Son, I got a visit today from a young lady I think you know—Darlene Sealy?"

"Yessir, I know her. We was datin' but broke up a couple of weeks ago."

"Yeah, that's what she told me. Mickey, Darlene said that she's pregnant and you're the daddy."

The blood drained from my face, and I felt faint and dizzy. "She said she's pregnant and I'm the daddy?" I almost screamed. "That's a lie, Mr. Brazzini! A damn lie!" Thinking, again, that I should've listened better in health class. "Mr. Brazzini, we fooled around and stuff—dry humped, y'all know, but I never put my—my pecker inside her. Never, ever!

"I believe you, Mickey, however, I'm gonna need to see your mama and Darlene's parents in my office. Take this letter to Dixie Mae, have her sign it, and bring it back to me on Monday. Understand?"

"Yessir, I will."

"Good, now get your ass back to class." Mark's dad always liked me, and as a rule, was very kind to both me and Harley. "What are you waiting for? Get out!" He didn't have to tell me a third time.

Since Mama had to work on Saturday, I waited until Sunday to approach her with the letter. Handing it over, she read it, then asked, "What the hell's this all 'bout, Mickey? What have y'all done now?" It wasn't like I brought home a letter from school on a weekly basis! Damn.

Harley, overhearing the comment, came over to sit next to me. "Go 'head, Mickey. Tell Mama what that letter's all 'bout."

I had shared the contents of the letter with him on the bus coming home. Shooting him a murderous look, I decided to just rip the band-aid off. "'Member Darlene, my ex-girlfriend?"

"Yeah, I think so. What of it?"

"Well, Darlene says she's pregnant, and I'm the daddy."

Mama sat there, stunned for a minute, turning white, then gray, and finally red with rage. Sputtering, she began to yell at me, then ran over to where I was sitting and began hitting me. "How could y'all screw that pig, you dumb little shit?" She hit me again. "You done ruined yo' life, Mickey. Ruined yo' life. How could y'all be so goddamn stupid? Didn't y'all use a rubber?" She went on, slapping me upside my head one last time.

Finally, I recovered from the shock of her response. "Mama, I didn't do it. If she's pregnant, it ain't by me! We messed 'round plenty, but I never screwed her—never!"

'You lyin', Mickey! Quit lyin' an' tell the truth. Y'all screwed her and y'all know it."

"I didn't, that's the truth. And I don't give a damn whether y'all believe me or not! Anyway, you gotta sign that letter and call Mr. Brazzini tomorrow. He wants to see you and Darlene's parents in his office next week."

"I just cain't believe the trouble you done got yo'self in. I just cain't believe it."

Harley's eyes found mine. He put his arm around me and said conspiratorially, "Did y'all screw her, Mickey? You can tell me. Did y'all do it?"

"No, dammit, I didn't!"

"Then damn, y'all a bigger idiot than I thought 'cause I would'a done it."

I gave the signed letter to Mr. Brazzini first thing when I got to school on Monday. Later that day, he caught me outside the gym and told me that a meeting with Darlene, her parents, my Mama, and me had been set up for Wednesday at eleven in the morning. When the day came, I was as nervous as cat in a room full of rocking chairs, even though I knew I was innocent. The thought of facing Darlene's father and mother was frightening. Her dad was a big man and known for his temper, and her mother was a humorless shrew. Add my mama to the mix, and well, fiery hell was about to rain down on us all.

I was the first to arrive and was directed to a seat in the small conference room in the administrative building. Darlene and her parents walked in five minutes later. Glaring, her daddy practically snarled when he saw me. Mr. Brazzini's secretary seated them as far away as possible from me, hoping to avoid a murder she might have to clean up later. Shortly, Mr. Brazzini walked in, all smiles and handshakes. "Looks like we're all here except your mama," he said, looking at me.

Just then, Dixie Mae Crow walked in dressed in tight fitting capri pants, high heels, a flowered print blouse that showed ample amounts of cleavage, and wearing enough perfume to outfit an entire French whorehouse. Walking over to where Mr. Brazzini was sitting, she leaned over to shake his hand, holding it a moment longer than necessary, giving him a good look down her blouse. In her best southern belle accent, she said, "Good mornin', everyone. How are y'all today?"

"Well, good, Dixie Mae," he choked out.

Mama turned to greet Darlene and her parents. "Bless yo' heart, Darlene. It's sure is an unfortunate set of events that done brought us here today, ain't it, sugar?" Darlene quickly looked away.

She approached Darlene's father next, also flashing her cleavage. "Hi there, I'm Mickey's mama, Dixie Mae. What's yo' name, darlin'?"

Stammering, this tough looking man was thrown for a loop. "David, Dave, Dave Sealey." Almost as if it were an afterthought, he said a little too quickly, "Darla, this is my wife, Darla," not taking his eyes off my mama.

"Nice to meet y'all, Darla." Mama's eyes, though, were saying just the opposite.

Looking at me and nodding, a little stiffly I thought, she acknowledged my presence. "Mickey." Then she walked around the table and sat next to me.

"All right, then, we're all here, so let's get started," Mr. Brazzini said. "We're here today because Darlene has confessed that she's pregnant and claims Mickey's the father." Everyone tensed, except Mama. Her gaze was glued to Darlene, who was fidgeting. Darlene's father was turning a deep purple, ready to explode.

Mama interrupted. "Why don't we just dispense with all the bullshit, shall we?" She sounded as sweet as could be. "I believe the boy did diddle y'all's *innocent* daughter. Y'all know, my mama always told me that every nasty, dirty thing a boy knows, he learned from a girl."

"You bitch!" Darlene's mama yelled, standing up and ready to fight for her little girl's honor.

"Calm down, the both of you!" Mr. Brazzini said. He was attempting to hold the meeting to a certain standard.

"So sorry, Marcus," Mama said. "Please let me finish. I say, let's just get a pregnancy test, and if it shows Darlene's gonna have a baby, then we can get a paternity test. That way we'll soon know who the liar is. Y'all agree?"

Everyone stopped talking. "Paternity test? What the hell is that?" Dave Sealy was obviously behind the times.

"Oh, Dave, sugar, it's simple, really. A doctor takes a little blood from Mickey, here, and some from y'all's little princess. Nothing to it. Now, have y'all already taken her to a doctor, you know, to see if she really is gonna have a baby?" Mama behaved like an expert witness.

"No, not yet. Why would she lie 'bout somethin' like this?" Darla asked.

"We don't know if she is lyin', Darla. Hell, little Darlene here pro'bly' is tellin' the truth. Mickey's done this befo', you know," Mama said.

"What the hell," I said, looking at my mama like she was crazy.

"Well, everybody, that sounds like the best idea to me. Why don't you folks take her to her doctor today, and we'll see what's what?" Mr. Brazzini said. "If it turns out she *is* with child, then we'll go to the next step and get a paternity test. If it turns out Micky is the father, then we'll deal with that at the time. What do y'all think of that plan?"

Darlene's father was obviously uncomfortable with how this was going. "Hell, no, we ain't gonna put Darlene through all that! Just forget the whole damn thing! We outta here!" As they got up to leave, Darlene just glared at me, hate radiating off her like an oven. But the jig was up, and she knew it.

I never saw Darlene again after that day, but I did get a letter from her a few months later that rocked me to my core. She included a picture with the letter. It showed a very pregnant Darlene. She apologized for all she had put me through, and said the baby was actually her daddy's. She said that even though she did want to have sex, it was her daddy who was pushing her to do it with me. He didn't want her mother, the Navy, and anyone else finding out it was his. She went on to say that she told her mama the whole story, and the two of them moved out of their house. Her mama filed for divorce the same week.

I was just glad it was over, and the truth was out, though my reputation took a major hit. The rumors swirled around the whole affair, like flies on a cow patty, spreading their stink far and wide.

I showed Mama the letter, along with the picture of Darlene. I don't know what reaction I expected to get when she read it, but I was unprepared for the reaction I got. Mama teared up. "That poor, poor child. I hope they shoot that sumbitch for what he done to his own little girl. Shit, give me a gun, and I'll shoot the bastard m'self!" She got up and walked to her bedroom, slamming the door loudly. I leaned against her door, listening as she fell to the floor next to the bed and wept bitterly.

It confused me, to tell the truth. Mama cried for herself, but rarely because she felt sorry for someone else's pain. I didn't understand how something that happened to Darlene, someone she barely knew, would move her so deeply. I wondered if what Charlie had said was true—that Tootie had had an abortion and that was what set her off. There was no point in asking her to tell me the truth. The only thing I could be sure of is whatever she would say would be something she made up.

FORTY-EIGHT

PRESENT
MONDAY, APRIL 24, 1972
11:35 P.M.

It was close to noon, and my American history class at FSU with Professor Cooper started at 1:00. She was brutal to students who were late. I hadn't eaten breakfast and my stomach was insistent on me feeding it, so I pulled into the parking lot of Gordo's for a quick bite before her class.

It was packed, as usual, with FSU students all late for class and looking for nourishment, just like me. I got in line behind this pretty brunette and the minutes flew by as I chatted up the lovely co-ed. Soon I was at the counter ordering a large coffee and bagel with cream cheese.

I paid the girl at the register, found an empty stool by the door, and waited for my name to come up as I reviewed Professor Cooper's lesson plan for today. "Ripley, Ripley, your order is ready." Ripley? That got my attention, so I looked up to see the back of a young man reaching for his order. As he turned around, I almost fell off my stool! It had been six years since I'd last seen Ronnie Ripley, but I'd know his mischievous and devious face anywhere. I watched as he made his way over to a booth where a few other students were sitting.

Walking up to his booth I said, "Your sisters still datin' sailors?"

Rip looked up and seeing me standing there, virtually exploded out of the booth. "Mickey Crow! Is that really you boy?" He hugged me so hard I thought I heard a bone break somewhere deep inside. Before I could get my breath back to answer, he announced to everyone in the booth, "This is my best friend, Mickey. We went to school together in Crawfordville. I ain't seen 'im in six years. Scoot over y'all so he can sit down."

Everybody scooched over to make room, and I sat down, half on and half off the seat. "It's great to see you, too, Rip. What you doin' here?"

"Hell, son, I'm an honest-to-God, genuine Seminole. I'll be a Senior in the fall. You go here too?"

"I'm a freshman. This is my first year here."

"Freshman? Aren't you a little old to be a freshman?"

"Long story, Rip."

"Well, hell, let's go someplace and catch up boy."

I glanced at my watch. "I'd love to, but I cain't right now. I got a history class with Cooper at 1:00."

"Oh hell, you don't wanna be late for her class—she'll beat you down like a rented mule. What ya doin' tonight? Wanna grab a drink over at Potbelly's and catch up?" Potbelly's was an FSU legend.

Standing up to leave, I nodded to everyone at the table. "Let's do it, say six? That work for you?"

"Groovy. I'll see you then."

At 6:25 that evening, I found a parking space across the street from the popular bar. The front patio was already crowded with young men looking for cold beer and hot co-eds. From what I could see, both were in plentiful supply. Walking inside, I spotted Ripley

sitting at a small table in back of the bar next to the jukebox. He saw me and began waving me over.

When I approached the table, he stood up and gave me another bear hug. I felt another bone break but hugged him back. "Damn Mickey, I cain't tell you how good it is to see ya. I honestly thought I'd never see you again."

"I know what ya mean, Rip. I felt the same way, and you don't know how good it is to see y'all again."

He called the bar girl over and we ordered a couple of beers. When she left, Ripley and I began catching up.

"So tell me, how come yo' just a freshman? What happened?"

"Rip, you know I moved down to the Keys when we left Crawfordville, right?"

"Yeah, I remember."

"The day I graduated Key West High, I joined the Navy. I was in for two years and got out just in time for the fall semester in September."

"What made you come back here?" Rip asked.

"Quincy's home. It's where my Grandmama and Aunt Tootie live. It's where I'm from. It's where I belong."

"What about yo' mama and Harley? How they doin'? They live here too?"

"Nope," I said. "Mama married a Navy officer a few months before I graduated high school, and they moved to Long Beach, California. Took Harley with her."

"She just left you there?" Clearly the thought of that happening was incredulous to him.

"Yeah, but there's more to that story..."

FORTY-NINE

I am a quick learner and started playing the guitar to pass the time when I came to the Keys. I got good really fast. I was asked, from time to time, to fill in for a member of one band or another who couldn't make it to a gig. As it happened, I was asked to fill in for a friend of mine who belonged to a band that was booked to play on the Friday after Thanksgiving at, of all places, the Officer's Club on base—the same Officer's Club where Mama worked. The band was to play from eight to eleven, so I asked Mama for a ride to the Club.

Her shift started at six, so I hung around the base, visiting some friends of mine, until seven or so when I met up with the band back at the Club. It took about an hour to set up the equipment and then we were ready to play. The place was full of Naval officers and their wives, who just wanted to get out after spending all day on Thanksgiving cooking and cleaning. The mood was light and fun, and I even got to sing a couple of tunes. During our breaks, I watched Mama work. As always, she was the consummate professional, keeping her operation running smoothly. I have to say, I was proud of her, thinking how much better life would be if she always acted like this.

After the band's last set, Mama pulled me aside. "If y'all wait for me, after I help clean up, I can give y'all a ride home. Just got to stop off at the Ambassador for a minute and pick up my paycheck."

"That'd be great, Mama!"

We left the Club about 11:45 and headed to the Ambassador Lounge. She parked and looked at me. "I'll only be a minute Mickey—be right back."

While I was waiting, I fell asleep in the Bug. Waking up, I realized I'd been sleeping for over an hour. The VW's clock showed 1:15 a.m., and there was no sign of Mama. I sat there for a minute, trying to figure out what to do, a little miffed that Mama wasn't back yet. Making a decision, I got out and entered the back door of the bar. I found Mama sitting on a bar stool next to a man I'd never met before. She'd clearly been drinking but wasn't too drunk yet. I walked up and touched her on the shoulder. "Mama, y'all said you'd only be a minute, and it's been over an hour. I'm tired—let's go home."

She looked surprised. "Oh, Mickey, okay. Go on back to the car, and I'll be there in a minute."

"C'mon, Mama, let's go home now."

The man next to her was a short, stocky, muscled Italian who looked like he'd been there for a while. He didn't say anything, but gave me a look that I read as, "Beat it, punk, before I squash you like a bug."

"So, y'all comin' in a minute, then?"

"Yeah, I told y'all so, didn't I? In a minute. Just go on and get back to the car."

Defeated, I made my way back to the VW and turned on the radio. Soon enough, I fell asleep again, waking up at nearly 2:30 in the morning. Full-on angry now, I made my way back to the bar. There she was, still sitting next to Al Capone and in a rather intimate way—their heads were touching.

"Mama!" I was loud. "Y'all said you'd be right out, and that was over an hour ago! It's 2:30 in the mornin'! Let's go now."

She wasn't "just high" anymore—she was full-on *drunk*. She slurred her angry response to my interruption. "Dammit, Mickey, I told y'all I'd be out in a minute, didn't I?"

"Yeah, and that was over an hour ago. Let's go home, now!"

"Just go back to the car, boy. I'll be out when I'm good n' god-damn ready! Now go on, get out!"

The Italian looked like he was ready to kick my ass but didn't say anything. As I was leaving, I heard Mama say, "Little shithead. He's worse than my mama."

I trundled back to the Bug, fuming and mumbling curses to my-self. I got back in the car, turned on the radio, and fell asleep again. I woke up at 3:45 to the sounds of my mama trying and failing to get her keys out of her purse. When she did finally fish them out, she promptly dropped them on the ground. I watched as she bent over to pick them up and proceeded to fall face first on the tarmac with a sickening thud. I jumped out of the car and raced over to where she had fallen.

"Damn, Mama, you okay?"

She mumbled something I couldn't quite understand about her driving. I took her by the arm and lifted her. I let go for a second to open the driver's side door, and she intentionally fell on her ass. She wouldn't budge.

"Mama, you ain't drivin' this car home tonight. You'll get us killed, for sure." Even though I was seventeen, I still had my learner's permit, not a license. There was no rush to get one since there was no way we could afford to buy me a car, and Mama would never, know-ingly, let me drive her car. Of course, what she didn't know was I'd *borrowed* it many times over the last couple of years. Anyway, I figured I had a better chance of getting us home alive than she did. I took the keys from her and began guiding her over to the passenger side.

When I tried again to get her into the car, she pushed me away. "Y'all just a kid, and yo' ain't drivin' this here car, you little shit." She grabbed for the keys.

"Mama, I'm drivin' us home, and that's all there is to it. If that ain't good enough, then I'm gonna call the cops. They gonna put yo' ass in the drunk tank, then take me home. Is that what y'all want? Is it!"

"Oh, all right, shithead! You drive us, ya little bastard. Y'all know that's what y'all are."

"Yeah, I know, but at least I'll be a live bastard when we get home tonight."

I started the Bug and off we went. Mama passed out before long. There weren't many cars on the road at that time in the morning, and I was grateful for it, though I kept my eyes out for police cars—both local and Florida Highway Patrol. I didn't have a license, after all. We were just about to Big Coppit Key, about five miles from home.

We were just a minute from crossing the Rockland Channel Bridge when Mama woke up suddenly. "Pull over, Mickey. I'm gonna drive!"

"I ain't gonna pull over, Mama. Yo' too drunk to drive."

"Yo' pull this goddamn car over, now! This is my car! Now pull over!"

Thirty seconds from the entrance to the bridge, she grabbed the wheel, jerking us toward its abutment.

"Let go, Mama, let go! Yo' gonna kill us!" I fought her for the steering wheel and forced the VW back on the road.

Mama went nuts. She was grabbing the wheel with one hand and hitting me with the other. "Stop this goddamn car! It's my car, you bastard! It's my car!" She was screaming at me so loud it made my ears hurt. We barely made it onto the bridge, just missing the abutment, but she didn't calm down.

Trying to keep my eyes on the road and pushing her away, I saw headlights coming toward us from the other side of the bridge. "Mama, stop!" I pushed her off me again.

She began pulling my hair and scratching my face as the headlights were coming closer. Not knowing what to do, I backhanded her across the face to make her stop. She paused for a moment, then launched herself at me, all fist and fingernails. She grabbed my hair wherever she could find any and pulled with all her might, all the while screaming at me like a banshee.

I tried my best to push her off me before the oncoming car reached us. Then, before I could stop her, she grabbed the wheel one last time and violently pulled it toward her. The little VW began to swerve up onto the bridge, missing the oncoming car by inches. I lost my temper. I pushed her so hard her head hit the passenger window, splintering it, cutting her forehead, and leaving a deep gash. Finally, she moved as far as could to the passenger door, almost becoming a part of it—curling herself into a little ball and whimpering.

I got the Bug under control, but not before it clipped the bridge, leaving a dent on the right front fender. I stopped the car in the middle of the bridge, trying hard and failing to regain my composure. I sat there, numb in the driver's seat, and realized I had wet myself. I just glared at Mama but said nothing.

After a few minutes, I was calm enough to start the car and head for home. Mama didn't say anything to me the rest of the way home. She just continued to whimper. The moment I drove onto our lot, she opened the door and promptly fell out of the bug and onto her knees.

I ran over to help her up, but she pushed me away. "Get away from me! You hit me! Don't touch me, you sumbitch. Yo' just like Charlie. Don't ever touch me again!"

It felt like I'd been hit in the head with a baseball bat. I stumbled back against the car, feeling sick and ashamed, then vomited. I'd hit my Mama. I'd actually done the thing I'd most feared my whole life. I couldn't move. I'd become Charlie Crow.

Mama finally got up and stumbled her way to the cabana and into the trailer. A few minutes later, I came out of my stupor and followed her inside. She'd already passed out on her bed. I got a wet washcloth and cleaned her bloody forehead, applied some iodine to the cut, and finished it off with a bandage. After taking off her shoes, I pulled a blanket over her, leaving her to sober up.

The adrenaline from the fight dissipated rapidly after that, and I barely made it back to my bed before I crashed. I didn't get up until late morning. Harley was already gone, doing whatever, but Mama was still asleep. I made coffee, cooked some bacon and eggs, and ate some, leaving the rest for Mama to eat when she finally woke up. I was sitting out in the cabana when I heard the door to the trailer open. Mama walked out, holding a cup of hot coffee, and sat across from me.

"Look what y'all did to yo' mama, Mickey." She was pointing to the black eye and bruise on her cheek where I'd hit her. Then, touching the bandage on her forehead, she said, "Yo' just like Charlie, after all." Without saying another word, she walked back into the trailer and shut the door, leaving me feeling like the biggest asshole in the world.

I was devastated, crushed to the core, and so ashamed. I left the cabana, walked out back to where our little boat was tied up, and jumped in. I quickly had the little Johnson engine fired up, untied the mooring lines, and headed out, hoping I could get some peace and comfort from the skiff that had given me both so many times before.

The bay was calm, the water smooth as glass, but there was no peace or comfort that day. The breeze was a little cool, but I put the little motor in neutral and drifted along with the current for a while.

Beginning to weep, I looked up at the heavens. *It's true, I am just like Charlie Crow.* Weeping harder, I spoke to the only one who knew the truth about me. "God, please forgive me for hittin' my mama. I don't wanna be like Charlie Crow, I really don't. I truly don't. Please forgive me. I didn't mean it. I didn't mean it. I was just tryin' to keep us alive, is all. Just tryin' to keep us alive."

After about an hour, I put the Johnson in gear and headed back home, my soul still troubled. After securing the boat, I walked into the cabana. I went straight to my room and closed the door.

Shortly after I returned, there was a knock on the cabana door. Opening it, I was surprised and shocked to find the man Mama had been sitting next to at the Ambassador the night before. "You must be Mickey."

"Yeah, that's me. What can I help y'all with, sir?"

"I just wanted to check on your mother to make sure she got home last night. My name's Sal Benetti." He was holding out his hand for me to shake. I looked at it for a moment before I finally shook it.

"Come on in. I'll get her." I went inside the trailer and found Mama getting dressed.

"Mama, there's some man out in the cabana named Sal who wants to see you."

"Tell 'im I'll be out in minute." I shut her door and walked back to where Sal was standing.

"Said she'd be here in a minute," I said, as I shut the door to the trailer behind me.

He sat down on a chair and thanked me. I waited with him, and a minute later Mama walked through the trailer door.

Sal stood up and looked at Mama in disbelief. "What the hell happened to you, Dixie Mae? You look like hell!"

Mama pointed to her black eye, bruised face, and injured forehead. "My son did this to me. Just look at what my son did to me."

Sal turned to look at me with disgust and anger on his face. "You hit your own mother?"

I felt like a worm. I was supposed to protect my Mama, not hit her, even though I knew on some level I'd had too. I couldn't speak, couldn't defend myself, and couldn't give an answer to Sal Benetti's question. I pushed past him and walked out the cabana door. I walked and then ran to no place in particular. I just wanted to find someplace where I could hide my disgrace, shame, and disappointment in myself.

FIFTY

DECEMBER 1968

Mama and I didn't talk much after that until a few days before Christmas when she called me and Harley into the trailer. "Boys, I got excitin' news." She seemed a little lighter than I'd seen her in a while, but what I heard next completely blew me away. "Sal, y'all 'member Sal?" Hell, how could I forget Sal—the look he gave me could have melted glass. "Sal's been transferred to Long Beach— that's in California, y'all know—by the Navy. He's asked me to marry 'im and go with 'im to California. Ain't that great?"

Almost speechless, I managed a few words. "What in the hell are y'all talkin' 'bout, Mama?"

I hadn't even seen Sal since the day after the incident, and that was thirty days ago. Damn, I didn't even know that they were dating.

Harley seemed as shocked as I was. "Yo' gonna marry 'im, Mama? Why? You barely know the man."

"Oh, Harley, he's a good man and he's gotta great job. He's an officer in the Navy, did y'all know that?"

"Hell, no, we didn't know that. We don't know nothin' 'bout the man. Why y'all gonna marry someone y'all have only known for a month?" I got my voice back.

She held her chin up in defiance. "Boys, I'll marry whoever I want. I don't need your permission. Truth is…" she paused. *As if she'll ever tell us the truth!* "I've already married 'im."

"What?"

"We went to the courthouse yesterday. I drove him to the airport right after, and he's in California getting everything ready for us. We're married and we're movin'."

I was furious and silent. She had more to say. "Micky, y'all just know when y'all know, and I know. Besides, he won't never hit me." She looked at me a little side-eyed, causing shame to rise in my chest. "It's a done deal, Mickey. We movin' right after Christmas, so y'all can start school at the end of Christmas break in January. Time to pack and get ready."

"Mama, I ain't leavin'. I don't wanna go. I graduate the end of this year, and I don't wanna start a new school now—not this time. I'm stayin'." I knew Sal was never going to forget that I'd hit Mama that night in the car, even though it probably saved our lives. And I had no intention of having him try to be a stepdaddy to me.

Surprisingly, she looked thoughtful for a moment and answered calmly. "Hmm, let me think on that, Mickey. Might be the best thing for us if y'all didn't come right now. Umm, maybe my friend Maggie would let y'all stay at her house in Key West 'til you graduate. Let me talk to her, an' then we'll talk again, okay?"

"Okay, then."

"What 'bout me, Mama? Can I stay too?" Harley surprised me again.

"No, you comin' with me," Mama said. "And that's final!"

That's when it hit me that my mama might just not ever forgive me for hitting her. *She believes me to be just like Charlie, and obviously, I am. Will we ever be close again?*

⚸

Maggie owned a house on Key West, not too far from the high school. She was an attractive divorced woman with two kids—a six-year-old daughter, Tish, and a twelve-year-old boy named Kenny. Mama's friendship with Maggie was a lot like the ones she'd had with the divorced women in Quincy—lots of drinking and partying. She met with Maggie and told her the whole story about getting married and moving to California with Sal. Mama told her I didn't have long left in high school and wanted to stay and graduate.

Mama told me she had said to her friend, "Maggie, y'all think it'd be all right for Mickey to stay here with y'all 'til June? Sal told me we can pay you somethin' for his room and board. Hell, he can even babysit for y'all some."

Mama said it only took Maggie about a second to think about, then agree. She said she had an extra bedroom and could use the money. Mama told her they'd be around until New Years, and that's when I'd be moving in with her. It was all set.

Christmas came and went like melting snow on the Florida Turnpike, and before you knew what was happening, New Year's Day 1969 was here. Mama was busy packing up our meager belongings once more, like we'd done so many times before. Harley and I spent as much time together as we could, though he had lots of people to say goodbye to. I knew I was going to miss Harley a lot—we'd been through so much together over the years, clinging to each other like life jackets in a storm. Like most brothers who get older, life was going to lead us in different directions, but our bond was unshakable and unbreakable, and we both knew it. He loved me, and I loved him. No two brothers could have been closer. For the rest of his life, if he needed me, I'd be there no matter what. He knew he could count on that. And I knew the same about him.

Mama sold our little skiff to one of the kids on Bay Point, but before we turned it over to him, Harley and I took one last trip in that little boat, spending some time enjoying the cool breezes of a winter afternoon in the Keys. We fished a little, laughed a lot, and cried some, remembering many of the precious, and not-so-precious moments we'd shared as the children of Dixie Mae Crow. And we knew that our lives would never be the same again.

It was on this trip that Harley asked me something I'd been waiting for him to ask. "Mickey, how come y'all think Mama has never told us the truth 'bout who my daddy really is?"

"What ya mean?"

"C'mon, don't play dumb. I know Jack McCarthy's both our daddy."

"What the hell, Harley?"

"I know the truth 'cause I heard you and Mama talkin' 'bout it one time when we was livin' up in Quincy. You wanted her to tell me Jack McCarthy was both our daddy, but she wouldn't do it, on account she thought I was too young."

"Harley, that's true. Hell, she even showed me some birth certificates that said Jack was both yo' daddy and mine. I asked her back then to tell you the truth. She refused and said it'd confuse y'all, or some such bullshit.

"But look, Mama hasn't ever told me the truth about any of this. I still don't know for sure, to be honest. When we were nothin' but kids, we thought that Charlie was both our daddy, 'member that?"

"Yeah," Harley said.

"Later we found those ol' pictures at Grandmama's house. I dunno, maybe you was too young to remember?"

"Yeah, I kinda remember that. Mostly, though, I just remember Mama bein' mad at everybody when she got home."

"Well, Mama told me that Jack McCarthy was both our daddies, and said I could not tell you the truth—made me swear."

"So, you lied to me, Mickey."

It hurt like hell to hear him say that.

I didn't defend myself, but said, "Right after they got married again, Charlie told me that he was our daddy. I was so confused then, but here's what I suspect. Jack McCarthy is *my* daddy, there's no doubt about it, and Charlie Crow is *yo'* daddy. There were pictures in the album that I thought were of you, but they weren't. They was of Charlie as a kid. Didn't ya ever notice that you look just like him? In fact, you look so much like him now, it's spooky. You his boy, all right. Never doubt it. But Mama has never come clean with me."

He looked out over the water for a while. "So, you think that Jack is yo' daddy and Charlie is mine?"

"I dunno, but believe me, I've asked her a bunch o' times, and she just gets mad and starts yellin' at me. Who knows, maybe she'll tell us someday—wouldn't hold my breath, though." Harley and I both laughed, and then we headed back home, one last time.

On December 31, Mama, Harley, and I stood around the Bug in front of Maggie's house. The plan was for Mama and Harley to drive up to Quincy and, once she dropped off some things to store at Grandmama's house, she and Harley would fly to California on January 2. I had no say in the decision and had no words to say right then.

Mama broke the silence. "Mickey, we gotta get goin' if we wanna get to Quincy by tonight. Y'all know how your grandmama is if I don't get there when I tell her I will."

Nodding my head in understanding, I gave Mama a big hug, my voice beginning to thicken with emotion. "Mama, y'all be careful out there, okay? Please call me when y'all get there, an' let me know yo' safe."

"I will, son, promise." She had tears cascading down her cheeks. Things hadn't been good between us for quite a while now, but she was still my Mama and always would be.

Saying goodbye to Harley was the hardest. All I could see when I looked at him was this little six-year-old, tow-headed, Florida cracker, not the fifteen-year-old young man standing here in front of me. We hugged each other with a genuine affection borne of many of life's shared experiences.

"I love you, brother," he said.

"Me, too, always will," I said back.

Harley got in and the Bug rang to life. "See y'all in a few months," I said, as they pulled out into the street and drove away. It felt so strange standing there, watching them drive off. Since I was nine years old, when Charlie first left my Mama, I'd felt like I was the man of the family, and it was my job to protect them both and keep them safe. Now, they were leaving to live with a man I didn't know in a place three thousand miles away that I'd never even seen. And it was my fault. If I hadn't hit her, she'd never have married Sal. She was afraid of me now. So she turned to Sal instead of me. He was her protector now. I'd never felt more distant from my mama.

CHAPTER FIFTY-ONE

JUNE 1969

"So, you're not coming out for my graduation?" I asked.

"No, Mickey. It's too expensive and all." Just an excuse, I knew that. "But I've got a ticket for you to come out to stay with us in California."

"You didn't ask if I wanted to come to California, Mama. And I don't."

That set her off into a hysterical fit. "You better get on that plane, Mickey, and get yo' ass out here. Y'all hear me, boy?" she screamed through the phone.

"Mama, I turn eighteen in July, and I don't have to answer to you anymore. You have Sal now."

"What does that mean?"

"That I'm not taking care of you anymore. I'm joining the Navy."

"You what?"

"That's right. Already signed up. I'll damn well do what I want to, so yellin' at me and callin' me names ain't gonna change that."

"Yo' an ungrateful little shit, Mickey, y'all know that?"

"I'm ungrateful? That's a joke." *After all the sacrifices I made to protect her, and Harley.* "Call me what you want, Mama, but it's my life, and I'm gonna live it my way."

"Goddamn you, Mickey!" Mama screeched.

Rage, bitterness, and resentment exploded from my mouth, and I was powerless to stop it.

"Goddamn *me*? Too late, God damned me the moment you gave me birth and every day since! I've put up with yo' shit for years. I'll tell you this, I'm done. Do you hear me Mama? I'm done!"

She hung up on me. I stood there shaking, a wave of disgust flowing over me. I'd spent my life trying to protect this woman from her awful choices. But the bond between us finally cracked, then splintered into pieces, like a tree being struck by lightning. Shaking my head, I hung up the phone and walked out of Maggie's house.

While living with Maggie for the last semester of school, I worked a part-time job and saved enough money for a used car--graduation present for myself. It wasn't much, but it got me around and I was happy to have it. I attended my graduation without any family there, though Maggie and her kids came to see me get my diploma.

Watching the other grads celebrate with their families bit hard into my soul. Other than working and going to school, I'd kept to myself for the last month or two. I just wanted to graduate and get out of there.

My bags were packed, so I said goodbye to Mark and a few other good friends. After thanking Maggie for letting me live there for a semester, I jumped in my car and began the long drive to Quincy.

I'd been looking forward to getting back home with Aunt Tootie, Grandmama, and Grandpa Hank. It was a tearful, heartfelt reunion full of hugs and kisses.

After order was maintained, Grandmama said, "Mickey, you can move yo' stuff into the room next to Tootie's."

"Thanks, Grandmama, but I'll only be here for the few weeks until I report for duty in San Diego, California."

After I got settled, we gathered around the dinner table. Before I could take the first bite of the fried chicken Grandmama had made, Tootie burst out with, "Why'd y'all sign up for the Navy?"

I was immediately defensive. "What's wrong with the Navy?"

Grandmama looked startled. "Well, nothing, Mickey. It's just sort of a surprise, ya know what I mean?"

I took a bite of the best fried chicken ever made. "Damn, I sure did miss y'all's cookin'!"

Tootie smiled. "Look, boy, I didn't mean to criticize yo' decision."

"Tootie," I leaned over my plate, "I'm not a little boy anymore, so stop treatin' me like one. I've been on my own since Mama ran off with Sal and took Harley with 'em. I make my own decisions now. Understand?" Aunt Tootie shot a glance at Grandmama. I looked at their faces and realized I'd been too harsh with the people who'd loved and cared for me most of my life. "Sorry, that came out meaner than I meant it to."

Grandpa Hank spoke up, a rare occasion. "Of course, yo' a man now, Mickey. These ladies will get used to it soon enough. Just a shock is all. We ain't seen ya in two years. Lots has changed." Grandpa Hank didn't know just exactly how much had changed.

"Hank, I'm afraid you won't see me for another two years, maybe more. The Navy first, then after that, I don't know what'll come next. Just have to wait and see."

Aunt Tootie and Grandmama changed the subject and tried to keep the conversation going by giving me updates about people I didn't care about anymore.

I couldn't wait to get into the Navy and get as far away from Quincy as I could. I was afraid they see how ashamed I was of myself—of what I'd done and who I'd become.

It was the rough landing on August 7, 1971, that startled me from the dream I was having as the wheels touched the tarmac at Tallahassee International Airport. I'd returned from Adak, Alaska after being separated from "this man's Navy." I'd been gone for two years serving in Alaska, had lost touch with most of my family, and was back to go to college in Tallahassee.

I walked down the ramp from the government flight that brought me here and descended into what only could be described as hell. It was hot and humid, especially to a man arriving from a frigid place like Adak.

My temper was not tamed in the Navy. It had only grown into a beast that I could barely contain. I'd worried for years that I would wind up like Charlie—a mean, violent, and angry sumbitch. *He'd be proud of the man I was becoming.* My thoughts were jumbled as I headed for the baggage claim to pick up all of my worldly possessions. I didn't have much to show for my time in the service.

Shortly after I arrived in Adak, I'd taken and passed the 3rd Class Petty Officers Exam and received my stripe shortly thereafter. After getting into several fights and winding up in the brig a time or two, I was stripped of my rank and demoted back to Seaman, although I'd earned an Honorable Discharge. I just couldn't seem to get my anger under control. I tried. I really did. I just couldn't seem to find the key to unlocking all that rage inside me.

CHAPTER FIFTY-TWO

PRESENT
MONDAY, APRIL 24, 1972

Things were starting to quiet down at Potbelly's by the time I finished my narrative. Ripley sat back in his chair and didn't say anything for a long time. Finally, he said, "Damn, that's quite a story, Mickey."

"There's a lot I'm not proud of, Rip."

"You survived, Mickey. It's been one awful disappointment after 'nother. You cain't blame yo'self."

I smiled sadly. "Actually, I can." Then I told him about the meetings I'd had with Grandma Jean, and what she was asking me to do.

"Well, what are ya gonna do? You gonna meet with Charlie?"

"Hell, I don't know Rip. I been wrestling with it for days, and I still don't know."

"Listen here, Mickey. If you need t' talk to somebody or just vent, you call me. Anytime, an' I mean anytime. Y'all understand?"

"Thanks, Rip, I can use a friend 'bout now. I mean it, buddy, I'm glad we got together again."

"Me too, Mickey, me too."

FIFTY-THREE

SUNDAY, APRIL 30, 1972
MT. CALVARY BAPTIST CHURCH
GRANDMAMA'S CELEBRATION

Early Sunday morning I dragged myself out of bed, showered, dressed, ate some toast, and headed for Mt. Calvary Baptist Church. I dreaded having to walk back into that church. If I hadn't promised Grandmama, I'd never put myself through another caustic sermon.

When I arrived, I found a seat in the same pew that the family had occupied for more years than I could imagine. And as usual, Grandmama Colee sat on one end of the pew and Grandma Jean way down on the other. Aunt Tootie, who never came to church, was already there, sitting uncomfortably next to Grandpa Hank. She shot me a glance as I sat down, letting me know she didn't want to be there any more than I did. I tried not to make eye contact with Grandma Jean because I still hadn't made up my mind about seeing Charlie and didn't want to discuss it with her right then.

The Music Director stood up and walked to the podium to begin the service. "Good mornin' everybody! Would y'all please turn in yo' hymnals to page two-hundred-fifty-four and join me in singing, 'The Old Rugged Cross.'" To my surprise, I remembered most of the words, though I hadn't sung them in many years.

Pastor Snowden had aged well and looked regal when he stood up. "I'm so glad to see such a large turnout today for Miss Colee's celebration. I hope y'all are hungry because I've seen the food that y'all have brought to the potluck—especially Miss Tootie, who I'm glad to welcome here today."

I looked over at Tootie. She was practically snarling through gritted teeth. "I cain't wait to get the hell outta here."

Pastor Snowden pretended he didn't hear her. "We're fixin' to have ourselves an old-fashioned feast!"

"I'll be leavin' the tribute part of our morning for the reception after the service in Fellowship Hall, so please stay, share a great meal, and give your regards to Miss Colee at that time." Grandmama looked around and smiled, already basking in the wonderful things that would be said about her today.

Pastor Snowden sat down in a chair behind the podium, while Sister Angela read the announcements for the week and gave the attendance numbers and offerings for last week's service. That business completed, the Music Director led us in a couple more songs. As the last note of the last song rang out, Pastor Snowden stood up and approached the podium.

He gave a decent three-point sermon, and we ended with the alter call hymn, *Just As I Am*. I loved that old song, which touched me unexpectedly, but I was also agitated and ready to get to the feast before somebody beat me to it. I thought I'd stop by the men's room on the way to the Fellowship Hall.

As I opened the bathroom door to leave, I ran smack into Mr. Leon Mann! He was older now, of course, his hair was almost as white as his mustache, which edged up on the sides when he broke into that big smile of his. Suddenly, I was eight years old and sitting in his Sunday School class hanging on his every word as he told us one of the great Bible stories.

"Well, Mickey, you gonna stand there, son, or let me pass before I wet my trousers?"

Jolted to the present, I said, "Oh, sorry Mr. Mann, so sorry. I just didn't expect to run into you here."

Chuckling, he said, "I'm old, Mickey, but I ain't that old—not dead yet."

"No sir, y'all sure ain't." I laughed aloud.

"You gonna be at yo' grandmama's reception?"

"Yessir, I was on my way when I ran into you."

"Very well. Will you save me a place, son? I'd like to catch up. Would you mind?"

Surprised at his request, I couldn't resist the idea of time with him. "Yes, Mr. Mann. I'd be happy to save ya a spot." Patting me on the shoulder, he disappeared into the men's room.

Entering Fellowship Hall, I saw Tootie and Grandmama sitting at a round table with eight chairs near the front where a podium had been set up. Delicious looking food sat on long tables along the walls of the building. My mouth began to water as I took in the aromas that wafted through the air like an early summer morning mist, rising from Apalachicola Bay. I made my way over to where they sat. "Sit here next to me, Mickey," Tootie said.

"I ran into Mr. Mann," I said as I sat down.

Tootie looked at me quizzically. "You know, the old Sunday School teacher Harley and I had when we came here as kids."

"Oh, yes, I saw Leon sittin' just behind us at the service this mornin'," Grandmama said. "He's such a sweet and carin' man." She leaned over Tootie's chest and whispered conspiratorially, "His wife, Joy, just died, you know. She was a wonderful woman—a real lady."

"I don't remember 'im," Tootie said.

"Well, I ran into 'im comin' outta the john, and he asked me to save 'im a seat so we can catch up. Y'all don't mind, do ya?" Tootie looked nonplussed, and Grandmama seemed pleased that he would sit at her table.

A few minutes later, Mr. Mann walked in and sidled over to where we were sitting. Leaning down to hug Grandmama, he said, "This should'a happened a long time ago, Colee. A long time ago—you surely deserve it."

Grandmama had the grace to blush. "Thank you, Leon, that means a lot comin' from y'all."

Righting himself, he approached Tootie and offered his hand. "You must be Miss Tootie. I remember seein' you when ya dropped off Mickey and Harley when they was just boys."

Tootie looked at his outstretched hand, then took it in hers. and gave him a genuine smile. "That's right, Mr. Mann, that was me all right. Y'all got a great memory."

"Well, you must be so proud of your mama this morning."

"I sure am, but then, I'm proud of her every day." Then she bent to the side and gave Grandmama a hug.

"I hope y'all don't mind if I sit at yo' table."

"Not at all, Leon. Hank will be here shortly, but there is plenty o' room." Mr. Mann sat down next to me and began asking me questions about my life.

Soon the hall was packed with well-wishers and admirers. It hurt my heart not to see my mama there. She made some excuse about Sal having some big Navy thing to go to, but I knew it was just an excuse. She didn't exactly hide her disdain for me these days. But I felt bad for Grandmama. Harley was in the Navy, and she understood why he couldn't come, but I'm sure she expected her daughter to be there. Still, she never mentioned it.

Pastor Snowden gave a funny and warm tribute to Grandmama, and several others in the congregation spoke as well. When all was said, Pastor Snowden said a quick prayer, then announced that Grandmama and her guests would be first in line. I remembered it was always good to be the first Baptist in line at a potluck.

After I delivered my plate to the table, I made my way to the sweet tea pitchers. I saw Grandma Jean standing there and really couldn't avoid her without being rude. "Grandma Jean, glad you made it. I'm sure Grandmama is happy that yo' here."

"I doubt it, but I've known yo' Grandmama since we was girls, and she really does deserve this."

"Well, thanks for comin'. I gotta deliver these sweet teas to the table."

She looked down at her watch, then up at me. "Tic toc, Mickey. Time is runnin' out, boy."

"I know, Grandma Jean, I know. I won't keep you waitin' much longer, I promise."

After a while, slowly, folks began to depart, leaving others to gather in smaller groups, talking, laughing, and enjoying another slice of pie or cake. Tootie finally had enough of righteousness and left for home. Grandmama and Hank were off at another table visiting, leaving Mr. Mann and me alone at the table.

"Mickey, if y'all don't mind me sayin' so, you looked like a man with a burden today in church."

I looked up at him in surprise. "Why do ya say that, Mr. Mann?"

"Let's just say I'm good at readin' people. Body language, things like that. I also noticed you talkin' with your Grandma Jean at the drink table. Both of yo' bodies were practically screamin'." Then he smiled that smile—a smile that says, "You can trust me. I won't judge you."

"You wanna tell me about it? I've been told I'm a pretty good listener." Looking around at the people in the hall, he said, "Looks like we got plenty of time, and I got nowhere to go."

What can I say, I trusted the man. Damn, I couldn't shut up. I told him everything.

"Now Grandma Jean says Charlie is dyin' and wants to meet with me to make amends. Says it's the Christian thing to do." As I said this, all the old thoughts and feelings came flooding in. "I was still so mad at God for letting a good man like Uncle Bobby die after the hell we went through with Charlie. Why would He give Mama, Harley, and me hope for a better life, only to snatch it away at the last minute? By doing so, he allowed Mama to circle the drain of life, as a drunk. Didn't He care enough about us to keep these things from happening? Mr. Mann, Charlie wants forgiveness, and I just don't have any to give—not even for God."

He hesitated for a minute. "Do ya mind if I tell you a story? It might help."

I didn't think there was anything he could say that would help, but, what the hell, it couldn't hurt. "Sure, I wanna hear it."

Something flashed in his eyes as he looked directly into mine.

"Mickey, I've sat where you're sittin' right now. Believe it or not, I've been where you are, right now, in yo' heart. I hated God with a burnin' passion. I didn't want nothin' to do with Jesus, the Holy Spirit, or the Father—none of it."

The way he said this really got my attention. It was hard to believe this kind, warm, gentle soul could ever have felt that way.

"I don't think you ever met my wife, Joy. She passed a few months ago, and I really miss her. We had a great life together. Raised two great kids."

"I wish I could've known her," I said.

"Me. too, as I think you would've liked her. Mickey, most people here don't know what I'm about to tell you. Never felt the need to tell 'em, but I'm gonna tell you. They all think Joy and I had two children. What they don't know is that we had another child, Julianne. She was our first, and she was a beautiful, happy, child—so full of life. When she was three years old, we found out she had a rare, incurable blood disease. The doctors told us she had a year at the most to live.

"We were devastated, as you might guess. As believers in leadership roles at our church, we prayed, and we prayed hard." Mr. Mann held back for a moment here, tears forming in his eyes at the memory.

"There was no doubt in my mind that she would recover because God wouldn't let her die. He'd hear our prayers and heal this beautiful child." Now tears were streaming down his face. "Julianne died six months after the diagnosis. Joy and I were heartbroken and bereft.

"Joy turned to God for consolation and comfort in her immense grief. I did not. I told God He was a liar and a bastard for lettin' my little girl die, and I was done with Him. I began to drink, heavily, and was drunk most days."

I sat there stunned into silence at what I was hearing, believing every word was true.

He continued. "I couldn't work, and I couldn't be around Joy and listen to her prayers. I even tried finding comfort in the arms of other women. I knew it hurt Joy at a time when she needed me most, but I didn't care.

"Eventually, I lost my job, and one by one, we lost our savings, house, car, everything. We lost everything! Joy tried so hard to reach me, but I was lost and so angry. Finally, Joy gave up and moved into her parents' home."

He took a break for a moment to retrieve a handkerchief from his pocket. Wiping tears from his cheeks he went on.

"I was at my lowest point. I'd been stayin' at my brother's home. He was a police officer and had several guns around the house. While he was at work one day, I stole one of his pistols, jumped in an old car he gave me to use, and headed out to this closed phosphorus mine I knew about.

"Mickey, I just couldn't stand the pain anymore. I couldn't bear the loss of my beautiful little girl, my wife, or the life we'd been buildin'. I felt I was worthless and like I—and everybody else—would be better off if I was dead. I put the cold, blue-steel barrel of the gun under my chin and pulled the trigger."

I gulped loudly. "Oh my God!"

"The click of the empty chamber was so loud it jarred me to the bone."

"It didn't go off?"

Mr. Mann shook his head as tears streamed down his cheeks, unchecked, causing him to take a breather. After a minute or so, he regained his composure.

"I couldn't believe I was still here! I cried out from the deepest depths of my soul, 'My God, my God, why have you forsaken me!'"

Suddenly, tears burned my eyes as they spilled onto my warm cheeks. I tried to stop, but I couldn't. I'd never had anyone be this honest and vulnerable with me. I sat there, shocked at what this man was saying. That's what I felt after Uncle Bobby was killed, along with all of my hopes and dreams.

Whispering, I said, "That's exactly the way I feel—forsaken."

He patted my hand gently. "I know, son, I know." We sat there in silence for some time. Me, trying to take it all in. Mr. Mann most likely preparing his heart to tell the rest.

"Then, as I knelt there with that gun still in my hand, I heard this still, quiet voice in my mind say, 'I love you son, I always will, no matter what you think of me. You are forgiven, please come home.'

"I had cried hard, especially after Julianne died, but I'd never wept like this before. When I was done, I was wrung out—there was nothin' left, no anger, no hate, nothin'. I realized in that moment that God was not my genie in a bottle. That havin' faith in Him was not some kind of insurance policy against hardship. Everyone in the world feels pain, hardship, and even loss as some point in their lives. It's part of what it means to be human.

"I realized that I was angry because I thought God owed me somethin'. Listen to me, Mickey, when I say this: He owed me nothin'. And He don't owe you nothin' either. And I finally realized that God knows what pain and suffering feels like, just like you and I do."

He stopped again to let that sink in for a minute. "I ain't gonna preach to y'all, Mickey. Every man's gotta make up his mind about what he believes about God. It's not for me to judge 'em, one way or the other. Sittin' there with that gun in my hand, I realized that God was not someone lookin' down, just waitin' for me to do something wrong so he could send my sorry ass to hell, if He were, there would've been a bullet in the chamber. No, what I'd experienced that day wasn't judgement, fear, or damnation. What I felt was love, acceptance, and forgiveness."

I shook my head, "You said God knew what pain was. What kind of pain has God ever had to deal with?"

"Well, Mickey, you don't think He didn't feel the pain that Jesus suffered on this earth; on the cross? Don't you think it broke His heart when he heard Jesus cry out, 'Father, Father, Why have you forsaken me?'"

Shaken, I flashed back to Mr. Mann's Sunday school class all those years ago, where he could tell a story so vividly I felt I was watching the event with my own eyes.

"I never thought about it that way before, Mr. Mann."

"Well, I don't know what you believe, but as a father, I believe He did. Think about it, Mickey. It broke His heart, but He had to let it happen. Why?"

"I don't know," I admitted.

"Love, Mickey. Simply because he loves us. Somebody had to pay, so He offered up his son as payment, and because he did, you and I are forgiven. Do you know what the result of forgiveness is, son?"

"No sir, I don't," I said, barely above a whisper.

"Freedom, balance, peace, and most of all, love.

"So, I ask you, how can we ever understand love so profound, so powerful, so selfless? How can we know a love like that?"

"I don't know, Mr. Mann. I certainly cain't."

"I don't know either, Mickey.

"So, here's the thing, the point of my story. If God can forgive me for all I did when my daughter died, he can forgive you. If God can forgive the people that beat and killed his Son, he can forgive you, and if He can forgive you, then you have in you to forgive those that hurt you.

"If yo' angry with God, even if you hate Him, hear this: You cain't outrun God's love for you. Believe me, I tried, and I couldn't do it. I'm quite sure you cain't either."

I was stunned by this man's story. My heart was in my throat, and it was so hard to breathe that I felt like I'd been gut-punched. Mr. Mann put his hand on my shoulder and spoke in the kindest voice I'd ever heard.

"Mickey, you didn't lose yo' faith, son. You made the decision to reject it. It's entirely up to you to decide how you'll move forward from here. It ain't for me to tell you what to do. I can say that your anger and pain can define you and the darkness that dwells in you, or you can forgive and live a life of freedom, joy, peace, and love. It's entirely up to you."

CHAPTER FIFTY-FOUR

Sunday night turned into Monday morning, and I could not find enough peace to fall asleep. It wasn't for lack of trying, but my heart, soul, or whatever, could not be settled, and sleep remained elusive.

Finally, in the early morning, just before dawn, I decided to do something I hadn't done in a long time. Slipping out of bed, I found myself on my knees, my head buried in my hands. I began to talk aloud. "Lord, I've been so mad at you, and I've been carryin' around this anger, this hate and pain so long that I've become just like Charlie Crow."

My voice began to rise, and I cried out, "Please, God, forgive me and help me to forgive him!" I don't know how long I knelt there, weeping and groaning, purging the anger, hate, and pain from my heart, like pus oozing from a rancid wound.

At last, spent and wrung out, the sun began to rise over the heart of Dixie, and pushed the darkness and shadows from my room. When I rose from the side of my bed, I was no longer the same man I was when I knelt just a short while before.

The heaviness that I'd always felt was gone. The sadness that was just underneath the surface was no longer in residence. Without a doubt, I'd been forgiven, and knew that in turn, I was now able to forgive.

The clock next to my bed said 6:45 a.m. I slowly walked to the kitchen to put some coffee on, and while it was brewing I headed to the bathroom to take a quick shave and shower.

After I was dressed, I headed back to the kitchen, grabbed a cup, and filled it with the rich, dark brown liquid gold. Sitting at the counter, coffee in hand, I dialed the number. "Grandma Jean, I've decided to meet with Charlie."

"Thank the Lord, Mickey. Thank the Lord."

"Grandma Jean, you don't know just how right you are."

"Well, you can tell me about that later. Charlie can be here in an hour. Will that work for you?"

"Yes, ma'am, I'll see ya in an hour."

When I turned onto Harrison Road, I could clearly see Grandma Jean's farmhouse ahead and someone sitting in the front yard in one of the two old Adirondack chairs underneath the old bean tree. Bumping down Grandma Jean's long, dirt driveway, my heart began to beat faster, and I noticed beads of sweat forming on my forehead. *Wait, I've made a mistake! What am I doing here? I can't do this.*

Then something Mr. Mann had said announced itself with total clarity and assurance: "Who am I to hold back forgiveness when I've been forgiven so much?"

I braked the truck and got out. Standing there for a moment, I watched this beaten, frail old man waving me over. I took a deep breath, let it out slowly, and began the most significant journey of my life with one step.

I remember Charlie being the strong man of my childhood. Now, I saw an elderly, weak, sick man sitting under Grandma Jean's huge tree drinking sweet tea and smoking a cigarette.

I offered my hand and Charlie shook it as he stared me up and down with a look of disbelief on his face. "Won't y'all sit down, son?" He pointed to an old, but solid and sturdy chair on the other side of a small round wooden table from his. He adjusted his chair to face me, and I followed his lead.

"Want some tea? Mama just made it fresh."

"Yes, sir, I believe I do." He grabbed a glass and a small pitcher from the table and poured me a glass. I couldn't help but notice his hands shaking as I reached out to take the sweet tea.

He took a sip and then said, "You look good, Mickey, really good."

Charlie reached into his shirt pocket and pulled out another Camel. Lighting it slowly, he took a draw and let it out. "The doctor says I ain't supposed to have these anymore, but what the hell does he know? I'm dying anyway, so screw it." As he pulled more of the foul smoke into his lungs, he immediately began to have a coughing fit so violent, I thought he might cough up one of his diseased lungs.

"You okay, Charlie?" I was alarmed and reached over to try to help him.

Waving me off, he finally recovered enough to continue speaking. "I'm fine, I'm fine, don't worry. I ain't gonna die today." He laughed, and I couldn't help but think that maybe laughter was helping him through this dying process. "Hell, maybe the doctor's right, but it's too late now." He took another, shorter drag, thankfully without incident.

"Mickey, I cain't tell you enough how much I appreciate y'all comin' over here today. I know y'all got no reason to—" He began to say something, but then stopped to collect his thoughts. "I didn't wanna die without reaching out to you and Harley, and y'all's mama, of course. I've been in touch with Harley for some time and made my peace with him."

It appeared that Charlie was reluctant to say what he wanted to say next. He sat there, staring out at the farmland, blinking fast and sort of shaking his head real slow. Just as I was about the break the awkward silence, he spoke up.

"I reached out to your mama, Dixie Mae, but she just told me to hurry up and die." Once again, he laughed, but his eyes weren't in it. "Cain't say I blame her, Mickey. I told her I was working on it and she said, 'Work harder,' and then hung up on me." There was a painful silence.

"That sounds like Mama, all right. She ain't the forgivin' kind."

"I surely hope that y'all didn't inherit that from her, Mickey, because it's gonna be important to this here conversation.

"You know, that's one of the things I loved about Dixie Mae—her fire along with her passion. You know, Mickey, I always loved yo' mama. Hell, I still do. I think that's why I never got married again. I just never met a woman that could measure up to y'all's mama."

Looking at the ground, he said, "Just one o' many regrets I have, and there are so many, I'm afraid. And that brings me to why I asked to see you."

Things got quiet again, for a long while, same posture as before, same look on his face—like he was thinking hard about how to say what he needed to say next. But then, it just all came gushing out of him.

"I just want you to know that I'm real sorry for the way I treated you. Truly I am. I was a real sumbitch to all y'all, but especially to you, Mickey." He coughed again but recovered quickly.

"You know, I had a terrible relationship with my daddy when I was a boy. He got real mean and violent when he was drunk, and he was drunk all the time. He beat my mama senseless more times than I can count. When he wasn't beatin' her, he was beatin' me or my brother Jimmy. You remember Jimmy? He was a good boy; died a couple of years ago, bless his soul. Mickey, when I got outta the Air Force, I made sure he never beat any of us again."

Charlie paused for just a few seconds, and when he resumed there was a lot of emotion in his voice. "I promised myself that I'd never be like that good-for-nothing sumbitch, I'd never beat my wife or kids—no way, I would never do it! But, as you know, I did do it, and I turned out just like him—hell, maybe worse."

I sat there, my heart beginning to beat faster—so fast I thought it would jump through my chest. Charlie was talking about his daddy's impact on the man he'd become in the same way I'd feared his influence would have on me. Making me just like them, violent and mean. I had to take a few deep breaths to calm down.

Looking at me straight in the eyes, he said, "I've never told anybody what really happened out there in that swamp. But I'd like to tell you, Mickey, if you wanna know—if you care to hear it."

"I'd like y'all to tell me, Charlie. I've heard so many versions of that story. I'd really like it if you'd tell me the truth."

"Well, we were trying to launch Daddy's shallow, flat bottom, wooden jon boat, before it tipped over and filled with swamp water. It was just like any other day out fishing with my daddy, except he was a little drunker than usual, if that's even possible. He was cussin' at me, sayin' I was a worthless piece o' shit. I could take it better than Jimmy. But then he started after him too.

"He cuffed Jimmy upside his head and yelled, 'Grab hold of the front of this boat like I told y'all to or I'll slap yo' head off, boy! Quit screwin' around and get in the goddamn boat, da both of y'all. We wastin' time, an' the fish'll stop bitin' 'fore we get a line in da water.'

"The only thing my daddy, Jimmy, and me all had in common was fishing. Hell, we loved to fish, and did so often, but I hadn't been on one of those fishing trips since joinin' the Air Force. I'd grown up a lot in the service, sort of stepped into my manhood, if y'all know what I mean. And this was the first time I'd been around Daddy since I'd come back. Didn't realize how much I'd changed till that day, and how much meaner Daddy had gotten. Saw him beat my mama so much I thought I'd puke.

"That day Daddy started drinking earlier than usual, stoppin' at the Qwik Shoppe to fill the cooler with beer before drivin' out to the swamp. A couple of hours after the three of us launched the boat, the sun began to rise and the swamp came to life. It was kinda eerie, like it always was that time in the mornin'. I remember there was mist hoverin' above its black waters, and I could hear the red-throated loons singin' their mornin' call.

"Daddy had drank several more beers on the ride out. When we got to his favorite fishin' hole, he pulled this old Colt 45 pistol he'd had since childhood old, worn-out, burlap sack carried on these fishin' trips. He said he brought it in case he needed it to chase off gators, wildcats, and others living in the swamp.

"I'll never forget how he laughed when he pointed the gun at Jimmy's head and what he said to him. 'You know, boy, I never liked you much. Did I ever tell you that? What with that red hair and those big ol' freckles, yo' too ugly to be one of my kids.' He went on, waving that damn gun around in Jimmy's direction. 'In fact, I don't even think yo' mine.'

"Finally, I'd had enough and spoke up. 'Put the gun down, Daddy, and leave 'im alone.'

"'What ya say to me, boy?' he shouted at me, then pointed the gun at my head. I didn't even flinch. 'Put the gun down, you old piece of shit! Y'all ain't nothin' but a goddamn drunk!'

"I almost pissed myself when the gun went off. Damn bullet only missed my head by a whisper. Daddy fell backward from the shock of the gun going off and dropped it on the bottom of the jon boat. Jimmy moved first and grabbed the gun from where it landed, just a few inches from where Daddy sat.

"'I'll never forget the look on Jimmy's face when he lifted that Colt and pointed it at Daddy. He started to cry. 'I'm gonna kill ya, Daddy, and y'all will never hurt any of us again.'

"'I said calmly but firmly, 'Jimmy, gimme that gun.' I held out my hand and told Jimmy, 'He ain't worth killin', brother, so please, just gimme that pistol.' I didn't take my eyes off Daddy when I reached over and took the gun from Jimmy. His hand was shakin' like a leaf.

"'Right then, I saw Daddy let out the breath he was holdin'. Then he shouted at me. 'Y'all better gimme that friggin' gun, boy, right now!'

"'I looked at Daddy, his brown eyes burnin' with hate and rage, and I pointed the gun at his head. I told 'im, 'Jimmy's right, Daddy. You are gonna die today.'"

FIFTY-FIVE

"Daddy started laughin' at me, but he didn't get far. I shot our daddy twice in the head. Jimmy took one look at Daddy's head, turned around, and vomited over the side of the boat. I just stood there, the gun steady in my hand. I watched smoke from the end of the Colt mix with the mornin' mist. With nothin' left in his stomach, Jimmy asked me, 'Charlie, is Daddy dead?'

"I moved on over to where Daddy was lyin'. Lookin' down, I saw Daddy's eyes, wide open, drained of the life force that was present there just moments before, along with two bloody holes in the middle of his forehead.

"'He's dead, Jimmy. The sumbitch is dead.'

"Jimmy freaked out. 'What we gonna do now, Charlie? What we going to do now?' He was so scared, just whimperin' and shakin'.

"I took him by the shoulders, looked him straight in the eyes, and told him as coldly as I could, 'You stop that shit right now, Jimmy. Right now, you hear me?'

"I watched him choke back tears. 'Okay, Charlie, okay. I'm all right now.'

"'Listen Jimmy, we gotta get rid of Daddy's body and clean this boat. Then we gotta get our stories straight. Before that, though, we need to find just the right place to hide Daddy's body—someplace where only the gators can get at him—so keep a sharp eye out, okay?'

"After an hour of looking, I pointed to a spot. 'Jimmy, look over there, next to that egret.' I used his oar to turn the boat. 'See that old cypress tree that's broken on top? Y'all can see that tree that's fallen down in front of it? See it?'

"Jimmy turned in the direction that I was pointing. 'Yeah, I see it. You think that's a good place?'

"'Yeah, I do. Let's paddle on over there.' We reached the shore where this huge cypress tree and had fallen over into the water—I guess during a storm a while back. As we got closer, the egret that was standin' by the fallen tree, flew off, cussin' us all the way." Charlie laughed at his funny and stopped to take a sip of sweet tea.

"When we got next to the tree, I tol' Jimmy to get out in the water and pull Daddy's body underneath the tree.'

"He panicked. 'Uh, I ain't gettin' in that water, Charlie! No way!'

"That made me mad. I picked up the Colt and held it to the side of his head. I said, 'Jimmy, yo' my brother, and I love y'all and all, but if you don't help me, I swear there will be two bodies for the gators to eat today. Understand?' I don't think I'd have actually shot Jimmy. But I had to get him to help.

"Jimmy wasn't about to cross me. 'All right, all right, I'll do it, but there's a lot of snakes and gators 'round here—y'all can see 'em all over the place.'

"I told 'im to shut the hell up and grab daddy's head. I grabbed his feet and then we slid his body into the water.

"Just as I started to move Daddy's feet over the side, it hit me that we didn't have the keys to the truck back at the ramp. 'Jimmy, stop, we gotta get the keys to Daddy's truck. We can't get home without 'em!'

"We got to work going through Daddy's pockets looking for his car keys, wallet, and such. When we didn't find anythin', I remembered he always placed any items like that into the same burlap sack where he'd kept the Colt. Grabbin' the bag, and digging inside, Jimmy found the keys.

"'Here they are. And so is the rest of his stuff.'

"It didn't take long to get Daddy's body over the side of the shallow boat. I jumped into that murky, black water, and it turned orange all around me due to the rottin' vegetation in the swamp. I held on to his body with one hand and the side of the boat with the other. I yelled at Jimmy, 'Hand me that line over there and jump in!' I let go of the body long enough to point to the rope.

"Grabbin' the rope, Jimmy jumped in the water with me. 'Let's hurry up, Charlie. Bein' in here really gives me the creeps, ya know?'

"I pretended not to hear 'im. 'Okay, here's the deal. Yo' gonna dive under this tree and tie Daddy's body to the branches on the bottom. Got it?'

"'I got it, but Charlie, there's a couple of gators on the other side comin' over this way.' He was scared and startin' to panic. Hell, so was I.

"'Well, you'd better get yo' ass movin' then. Get under there and tie 'im up, and I'll watch the gators out here. Now, hurry!'

"Jimmy did what I told him to do and pulled Daddy's body under the old tree while I helped by pushing on it. After a minute or so, Jimmy was still under that damned tree. Those two gators were big, looked like dinosaurs, and they was gettin' closer and closer. I lost sight of them under the water, so I grabbed Jimmy by the legs to get his attention. He shot up from under that old tree screaming, his mouth fillin' with swamp water. When the gators came up again, I could see 'em comin' right at us.

"I screamed, 'Jimmy get in the boat now! Right now!'

"Both Jimmy and I scrambled for all we were worth trying to pull ourselves out of the water and into the boat. We did it, too, just as the pair of 'em disappeared under the water right where we had been. I still get the chills at night when I think about how close we came to bein' gator bait. Jimmy was out of breath and still coughing up swamp water when he started laughin' like a crazy man. 'I done thought a gator got me by the legs!' he yelled. 'Tellin' the truth, I thought I was a goner, Charlie. I really did!'

"'We almost were. Those gators didn't miss us by much! What in the hell took you so long?'

"There were lots of roots down there, and I was tryin' to tie 'im so he wouldn't get loose and float to the top.'

"As soon as he said that, we both heard a commotion by the tree where we'd just hidden Daddy's body. We leaned over the side of the jon boat and witnessed something I'll never forget—not fo' the rest of my life. It has haunted me every day since I saw it.

"Those two giant gators had ripped Daddy's body from the bottom of that old cypress tree and were fightin' over his remains— ripping, tearing, and swallowing, until there was nothing left. I mean there was no pants, no shoes, nothin' but black water stained with Daddy's blood. We sat back in horror, screamin' at the top of our lungs, tryin' and failin' to push the sight of it out of our minds.

"We closed our eyes and lay in the bottom of that boat for a long time. I kept playin' the day's events over and over again in my mind. I think Jimmy was, too, because he was silent and looked really pale and shaken. Finally, after what seemed like hours, we untied the jon boat and headed back to the dock where the truck and trailer were waitin' for us.

"On the way back, Jimmy asked, 'What we gonna tell Mama, Charlie? How we gonna explain to her why Daddy didn't come home with us?'

"'I'd been thinking about it. 'We're gonna tell her the truth, Jimmy. Daddy got drunk again and pulled his gun out and was goin' t' shoot ya because he didn't believe you was his boy. I tried to stop 'im from killin' you, we fought, and he fell out of the boat. We tried to pull 'im back in, but before we could, a gator got hold of 'im and pulled 'im under. Another gator came up and the two fought over Daddy, killed 'im, and ate 'im.'

"But that ain't the truth, Charlie. You killed Daddy.'

"I reached over, grabbed him by the hair, and pulled his head way back. 'You ever mention that to anyone, Jimmy, and I'll kill y'all and feed your dead body to the gators, too, hear me, boy? Do y'all?' My voice was calm but menacin', and he knew I was capable of it.

"He started crying, 'Charlie, I'll never tell, I promise! You saved my life. I was sure Daddy was gonna kill me when he pointed his gun at my head. I really was. I wanted to kill him myself, but I was too afraid. I'm glad he's dead, Charlie. He can never hurt Mama or us again!' I agreed with every word of it. Daddy had been a cruel and bitter man. He'd done terrible things to all of us. I justified his death because of it. I still do.

"We began to row the jon boat back in silence, not sayin' a word. The sun began to set over the Apalachicola swamp, and I heard the birds, frogs, and crickets take up their evenin' symphony. They didn't notice or care about the murder of our daddy, not one bit."

I let out a deep breath, not realizing until then that I'd been holding it through the entire story. "That's not what you told Bobby, is it?" I stated it as fact, not a question.

"Nope, it was hard for me to lie to Bobby. He was my best friend. But I knew it was best for 'im not to know, even though I think he would've seen it as self-defense. Y'all never know with those sheriff types, though." Charlie chuckled. "It seemed like a burden he didn't need to share.

"So, yes, Mickey, I killed my own daddy." I just sat there in silence, looking past him at nothing at all. "I'd hated him because of the way he'd treated Jimmy and Mama, but I didn't plan to shoot 'im that day. I wouldn't have if he hadn't have pulled his old Colt on Jimmy. I decided right then that he would die. I didn't have to kill him, I'd gotten the gun away from 'im. But I hated him. I feared him. I wanted this nightmare to end. So I pulled the trigger."

I watched the afternoon breeze push the hair back from Charlie's forehead. His once handsome face was furrowed, with deep cracks and lines filled with the yellow pallor of someone who didn't have long to live.

I knew it was my turn to talk.

"Charlie, I know we ain't blood, but I thought you were my daddy for most of my growin' up years, and I'd heard lots of stories about how mean yo' daddy was. For years I believed that I would be as mean and violent as you and Grandpa Willie were. After the fight we had the last time we saw each other, I was sure I would be doomed to that life. And I've gotten into more than my share of fights."

Tears started rolling down Charlie's cheeks. Through his tears, his voice shook with pain and grief. "Oh Mickey, Mickey, y'all were never like me. Never could be, boy, y'all hear me? You were a good boy, only trying to protect yo' mama and yo' brother. Your grand-mama too. I pushed you into those fights, son, because y'all weren't like me and never would be. I resented y'all 'cause ya weren't my boy, and that would never change.

"Lookin' at you was a reminder every day that you were Jack's boy, not mine. I knew hurtin' you would hurt your mama, so when I was mad at her, I took it out on you!"

Charlie was weeping now. "I'm so sorry, Mickey. I'm so sorry. I wish I could take it all back. Don't let the anger take you down like it took me."

I put my hand on his shoulder, surprised at how bony and sunken his frame had become. "Charlie, let's be honest, I would'a killed you that day in the street if Bobby hadn't stopped me."

His eyes got big, and he looked at me for a long time, then grinned. "We did try to kill each other, didn't we?"

"We surely did. But God saved us from that fate." Forgiveness filled my heart—completely and utterly. I forgave Charlie. I forgave myself. All the pain, all the fear, all the hate, fell from me like water over a gentle waterfall. Tears stung my eyes, and the emotion of the moment filled my chest with—well, with joy. I took a deep breath in, then exhaled out all the poison our shared past had brought into my life, leaving it all behind in that singular moment.

"Charlie, I hated you when I first drove up here. And now I don't. You and I are good."

Charlie's eyes filled with tears one last time. He put his scrawny arms around me and held on like he was drowning. He shook with relief and then let me go. "Thank you, Mickey."

Charlie and I talked a while longer. I caught him up on my life. He listened, nodded, and smiled. It was so strange. I couldn't believe what God was doing in my heart. I didn't know how to share what Mr. Mann told me about forgiving and being forgiven, but I did begin to pray that very day that Charlie would find peace with God before he passed. The sun faded over the back of the house, and I could tell Charlie was tired.

As I waved goodbye to him to head back to Quincy, I thought of the lyrics to one of my favorite hymns. "And Lord, haste the day when my faith shall be sight, the clouds be rolled back as a scroll; His trump shall resound, and the Lord shall descend, even so, it is well, with my soul, *it is well with my soul.*"

FIFTY-SIX

On my drive back home, I realized that this wasn't the last conversation I needed to have. That evening I called Grandma Jean. "Sorry, Grandma Jean, but I didn't have the time to talk to you after I spoke to Charlie."

"That's all right, Charlie told me some before he went home. I cain't tell ya enough how much it meant to him and me that you came."

"I got more to say, Grandma Jean. I want to come over tomorrow and talk with y'all about it."

"What about?" She was curious, but what I had to say couldn't be summed up in a short retort.

"Tomorrow, okay, Grandma Jean?"

"See ya then, Mickey."

The next morning, I drove up to Grandma Jean's house and found her under the bean tree snapping beans. For the next hour, I filled her in on my conversation with Charlie.

When I told her that Charlie shot Grandpa Willie, she cried. "Oh, Charlie, my po' son. Willie was such a mean and violent sum-bitch. I'm sure he felt like the only way to protect us was to kill his daddy. Hell, he was pro'bly right."

I nodded. "And it broke him, Grandma Jean." The compassion I felt surprised me. I had hated Charlie for so long, it was odd to have any other feeling toward him.

I waited for Grandma Jean to say more about Charlie, but a peace had settled over her. I took a deep breath and said, "I've got another question for y'all, but it's even a harder one, Grandma Jean."

She stopped snapping and sat back to give me her full attention.

"Charlie once told me that Tootie had an abortion and that you told him this was so."

She looked pained. "Charlie said I told him that?"

I nodded. "And as best I can tell, he spread that rumor around town and taunted Aunt Tootie with it. I haven't had the nerve to ask her directly. I know that Charlie can lie, so I wondered if there's some truth in this, or did he just make the whole damn thing up."

Her eyes filled up and she quickly rubbed away tears, her large chest rising and falling as she fought back emotion. I waited until she gained control over herself. "Lord Almighty, I've done a terrible thing. A terrible thing." She put her face in her hands and silently shook as the tears exploded from her eyes. "Lord have mercy on my soul."

It took her a full five minutes to regain her composure. She pushed back her hair, straightened her shoulders, and put her chin up as if to face the truth. "It was a long, long time ago, Mickey. I was a midwife and helped most of the women around here give birth back then. I was good at it too. Never lost one woman, although some of the babies didn't make it back when we was too poor to have proper health care." She took a deep breath.

"One night I got a call from yo' Grandmama Colee. She was in a panic. Said that Dixie Mae was bleedin' to death and begged me to come help her. She went on about how she'd sent Nash, yo' grandaddy, to come fetch me, but he disappeared so she decided to call instead. I told her I'd be right over.

"When I got there, Dixie Mae was in the bathtub, and it was filled with her blood. Some backroom butcher botched her abortion. She was only thirteen years old at the time."

I was shocked. "Mama got pregnant at thirteen? Who was the daddy?" I was ready to track down that sumbitch and beat him to a pulp.

"I never asked. But I knew just what to do. I got the bleedin' stopped and calmed Colee and Tootie, who were nearly hysterical. I told 'em to clean the mess up.

"About that time, a sheriff came to the door and said that Nash had been killed in a car accident. He was drunk when Colee sent him out to come fetch me, and he drove his car right into a tree. Dead on impact. That was a horrible night, it surely was.

"Colee lost her husband and almost watched her daughter bleed to death in the same evenin'. It was overwhelmin' to me, so I left." Grandma Jean started crying again. "What you must think o' me now."

"I've got no stones to throw, Grandma Jean."

"I was so upset that Colee's girls were promiscuous at such an early age, and that Nash was drunk and killed himself, that I got real judgmental. Before this happened, Colee and I was good friends. We went to the same church, sat together on that same pew we do today. Only then she and I sat side by side. But, after that night, I thought they were all a sinful bunch, and I didn't want much to do with 'em anymore."

"I suspect that hurt Grandmama quite a bit." I said gently, but I knew it would hurt.

"Yeah, I know it did." She waited a moment. "I'd all but forgotten this until a few years later when Charlie started datin' Dixie Mae. I thought we were too good for her and her family. I know this must be so painful for you to hear."

"It is, but go on."

"Well, I was so angry at Charlie when he decided he wanted to marry her, in a fit of anger, I said, 'Those girls are just whores.' I went on to say that I'd helped with an abortion on the night Nash died. Charlie could do the math and couldn't imagine that Dixie Mae had been havin' sex at the age of twelve or thirteen. So he naturally assumed it was Tootie. I knew I created a mess, but I was too proud to fix it. Poor Tootie. Poor Dixie Mae. It's all so sad."

I sat there shaking. I don't know if I was angry at Grandma Jean, Charlie, Mama, or who. But I was furious that all of these secrets had hurt so many people. I stood up and yelled, "Can anybody in this damn family tell the truth?"

Grandma Jean cried in earnest at my outburst, and I sat down, ashamed of myself.

We sat in silence until we both calmed down, lost in our own thoughts.

I finally spoke up. "Grandma Jean, you challenged me to do the hardest thing I've ever tried to do—talk with Charlie and see if I could forgive him. And with God's help, I have. So now, I'm gonna challenge you. It would make a world of difference if you talked to Grandmama Colee and Aunt Tootie and made peace with them."

She stopped crying and looked at me with fear in her eyes. "Ah, I see, now the shoe's on the other foot."

"It's ain't easy, is it?"

She took a deep breath and her eyes grew calm. "I won't promise you I'll do it, Mickey. But I promise to think on it real hard."

"Pray about it, Grandma Jean. Thinkin won't get you where you ought to be."

FIFTY-SEVEN

I had hoped that having met with Charlie and Grandma Jean was all that I needed to do. But there were questions that still swirled through my mind that weren't answered. I needed to talk with Tootie. A few days later, I stopped by Grandmama's place after dinner, just as the sun fell past the horizon and night began.

I was hoping that Grandmama and Hank would already be in bed, so I was relieved when I walked in and found Aunt Tootie by herself in the kitchen washing dishes. "You working on your own?" I asked.

Tootie smiled. "They're in bed. You missed them."

I picked up a towel and started drying. We worked silently together for a while until I got the nerve to say what I needed to say. Once we put the last dish into the cupboard, I confessed. "I'm here to talk to you, anyway."

Tootie gave me a sideways glance. "About what?."

I asked, "Y'all got any sweet tea in the fridge?"

"Sure do." I got a couple glasses from the cupboard, pulled the iced tea pitcher out of the icebox, and brought everything over to the table, and sat down.

Looking at me with suspicion, she asked, "What's the occasion?"

I smiled and poured us both a glass. "Come sit with me, Aunt Tootie. I think we need to talk."

She knew something big was coming. I could tell she wasn't so sure she wanted to participate. She didn't sit down. "C'mon," I said, pushing one of the chairs out beneath the kitchen table with my foot. "I got some questions I think you have answers to."

She sighed and plopped into the chair. "I knew this day would come someday, ya know."

I smiled. "Well, I guess today's the day."

She started before me. "I suppose you want to know about Jack, right?"

I nodded. "Mama says he abandoned us when Harley was a little baby, and Charlie stepped in, took us in, and adopted us."

Aunt Tootie laughed as loud as I've ever heard her. "She did, did she? Charlie swooped in and saved the day—is that the story she's tellin'?"

That brought a grin to my face. "Yep, didn't sound right to me either."

"Well sit back, Mickey. It's a long story. Well, the first thing y'all need to know is that yo' Mama and Charlie Crow was absolutely crazy in love with each other and had been for a long time. It didn't matter how the rest of us felt about Charlie or his mama, Jean. We all figured they'd get married soon as they graduated high school, but that didn't happen because Charlie joined the Air Force right away. I think he was eighteen at the time. He didn't come back 'til he was near twenty. Dixie Mae was a mess and mad—you know how she gets when she's mad, right?"

I nodded. I did know, and it wasn't pretty.

"Anyways, I was twenty-four and Dixie Mae was eighteen. Seemed like we worked all the time at the Blue Star Café. All the truck drivers, comin' or goin', who stopped to eat there, always called it Mama's Place. We was open twenty-four hours a day, seven days a week. It was gruelin' work. Mama would hire a few other girls to help out from time to time. Me and Dixie Mae waitressed there on and off ever since we could see over the counter. Mama's was a popular place back then 'cause Dixie Mae was pretty, and she filled the truckers cups with strong, hot coffee and their bellies with lots of good ol' southern food. I worked the kitchen 'cause I ain't as pretty or smart as Dixie Mae."

"I think you're beautiful, Aunt Tootie, and smart too!"

"Thanks, Mickey, you just done made my day." She blushed. "Anyways, one day this young Air Force man in his twenties came in for breakfast. He was so sharp in his uniform. We all thought so, 'specially yo' Mama. I think it was the spring of 1950, and we all was working and joshin' around with the truckers, like always.

"Anyways, she thought Jack was the cat's meow and flirted with him shamelessly. Nothin' serious, understand, just havin' fun. Mickey, yo' Mama is pretty now, but she was a real beauty back then. Dixie Mae waited on him that mornin', and to be real honest, I think Jack was smitten immediately. He fell in love with her before she finished sayin', 'What ya gonna have this mornin', sugar?'" Tootie giggled like a schoolgirl. But there was more to tell so she pulled herself together.

"Jack was goin' to Korea in a few months, but they started datin' anyway, and a few weeks later, yo' daddy asked Dixie Mae to marry him. He said she was too beautiful to be stuck in a small town like Quincy—she was destined for bigger things. Dixie Mae thought so, too, and he had money, which didn't hurt none. Dixie Mae told Jack he had to ask Mama, since Daddy was dead by then, if she'd give her permission to marry him. Mama did, though she wasn't too happy 'bout it, and they got married at the end of May, or first of June. I cain't remember."

"How did you feel about it?"

She frowned. "It wasn't my finest hour, to be honest, Mickey. I didn't like him. Jealous a bit, maybe. But also, I didn't like it one bit that he wanted to take Dixie Mae away from here—from me. But there was nothin' I could do about it. Still, I always resented him for that."

I sat there mesmerized by her accounting of the whole story.

"After their honeymoon, Jack moved her to Valdosta, Georgia, where he trained at Moody Air Force Base, 'bout a hundred miles away. Dixie Mae had never been that far from home before, and she was bad homesick.

"Soon, yo' Mama was pregnant with you, Mickey, and the next July, y'all was born—a beautiful baby boy. Sometime in the winter of 1952, Jack got told he had to go to the war in Korea in order to fight those bastards, so's we wouldn't have to fight 'em on the beaches of Florida. He moved y'all back here to Quincy so Dixie Mae wouldn't be alone while he was away."

"Wow, my daddy went to war, Tootie?" It was amazing to me.

"Yes, he did. Once yo' mama got back to town, she went back to work with me at the Blue Star. Charlie Crow walked into the café a few days afterward. He was one smooth operator; I have to admit. He seemed bigger, somehow, more of a man than before joining the Air Force. Some folks thought Charlie was ignorant because of his southern accent and vocabulary, but they was wrong. Now, y'all know I don't like sayin' anythin' good about Charlie Crow, but I gotta be truthful. He was smart. He'd learned how to fly all kinds of airplanes, from jets to crop dusters in the Air Force."

Aunt Tootie got back on track. "Like I said, he was smart, handsome, funny, and as cool as a spring breeze on a warm Quincy night. I do believe yo' mama never really loved Jack. He was just a way fo' her to get out of Quincy, and she took it. An' also a way fo' her to punish Charlie fo' leavin' her. That's just a guess. She never talked 'bout it. Anyways, she fell ass over tea kettle in love with Charlie, again, the minute he walked into the Blue Star. It was almos' like he bewitched her, somehow.

"Anyway, when she wasn't workin', she was out with Charlie, and I have to say, it caused some problems with the rest o' us 'cause she wasn't spendin' 'nough time with you. She even hired a Negro woman to take care of you. It wasn't long and Dixie Mae got pregnant with Charlie's baby, yo' brother, Harley."

I sat there with my mouth wide open, having a hard time getting my mind around everything Tootie was telling me. My mind and heart were racing. I'm guessing she saw it on my face.

"I 'spect this is a lot to take in. Do you want me to stop?"

"No, I wanna hear more. Please, Tootie, tell me more." Besides, she was on a roll, and I didn't think she wanted to stop either.

"Well, let's see. Yo' daddy, Jack McCarthy, came home from Korea the very same day yo' Mama was in the hospital givin' birth to yo' baby brother, Harley."

"What? He did? How can that be?"

"Yes siree, he surely did."

"What happened then?"

"Well, Mama was at the hospital with Dixie Mae and Charlie. I was workin' the Blue Star, just startin' the supper shift when yo' daddy walks through the front door. You could'a knocked me over with a feather! He came up to the counter where I was workin'. 'How y'all doin' today, Tootie?'

"'What are you doin' here, Jack?' I couldn't hide my surprise, and I wasn't too happy to see him, neither. I was worried that he'd take her away from me again.

"He said, 'Didn't Dixie Mae tell you I was comin' today? She was s'posed to pick me up in Pensacola this mornin' but she didn't show up. It took me a while to get a taxi to bring me all the way to Quincy.' And then he asked me if she was okay and why she didn't come to meet him."

I sat there shaking my head and mumbling, "Wow," every few seconds.

"I stood there starin' at him, not knowin' what to say. Then I blurted out somethin' really mean. I said, 'Why, Jack, Dixie Mae's down at Quincy Memorial havin' Charlie Crow's baby. Didn't she tell y'all?'

"At first, he just stood there, kinda like a statue, then he turned and ran out of the Café. A little bit later, Lettie, our babysitter, and maid, called the Café' and told me that Jack had come to the house an' took you and all yo' stuff with 'im in a taxi—said he wouldn't tell her where they was goin'. He just up and took you away!

"I called yo' mama at Quincy Memorial and told her 'bout Jack comin' home, and how he went to the house and took you with 'im."

By now I was drenched in my own sweat, just overwhelmed with all the information, plus the dramatic unfolding of this whole part of my own past, but I had to ask what happened next. I didn't want her to stop.

"Well, y'all's mama went crazy after that. She told Bobby to find you, no matter what it took. I heard she told 'im to find y'all and bring ya back, even if he had to kill yo' daddy to do it."

I sat there in shock. "So, wait, my daddy didn't abandon me?"

"Hell no! He wanted you so much he took y'all and went across state lines with ya. Y'all was kidnapped, is how Dixie Mae looked at it."

"How long was I gone, Tootie? Did Uncle Bobby kill my daddy for takin' me?" I wondered if that was why I'd never met him.

"Let's see, I think you was gone four months before Bobby found y'all and brought ya back."

"Four months? Wow, I don't remember any of it."

Tootie stood up and got what was left of an apple pie from the icebox and cut us both a piece while I sat there in a daze. I've got to say, this story felt like a time bomb sitting right in my lap, ready to go off. She slid the plate over to me and waited.

I leaned back in my chair and asked, "Do you know where Jack is now?"

She shook her head no. "I never heard from 'im or about 'im again. Dixie Mae and Charlie married about a year later, so I guess it took that long to get a divorce. Dixie Mae made us all swear that we'd never speak Jack's name and that we'd all say that Charlie was both of y'all's daddy. And that's what we did, until—"

"I found the pictures."

"That's right. I was hopin' to tell you someday. But y'all saw what happened when Dixie Mae felt we betrayed her. Once she gets you to go along with her tales, it's hard to say no."

"Don't I know it!"

"Do you have any more questions, Mickey?"

"Not about this, though I'm sure I'll have plenty of questions as time goes on. But there's somethin' else that's really hard to talk about that Grandma Jean told me a couple days ago. I hope you'll be willing to tell me about."

A dark look came over her face. "What kind of lies did Grandma Jean tell you, boy? That woman has caused me nothin' but trouble."

"I know, Aunt Tootie. I want to talk to you about my mama's abortion."

FIFTY-EIGHT

Tootie slammed her hand on the table and stood up in a rage. "She told ya about the abortion? That bitch!" She stormed out the back door and slammed it behind her. I followed and found her out behind the garage, crying and cussin'.

"Aunt Tootie," I reached out to touch her, and expected her to pull away, but, instead, she fell into my arms and sobbed. I let her cry it out, not knowing what else to do. When she stopped, my shirt was drenched and her face was wet and puffy. I pulled out a handkerchief and she wiped her face and nose. She mopped up my shoulder with it. "Sorry, Mickey."

"It's okay, Aunt Tootie."

She looked back toward the house. "I don't wanna talk about this here in case Mama and Hank overhears us."

"Then let's go for a drive in my car."

We took off together, and I drove aimlessly for a while until we ended up at a diner on the other side of town. "This place is shit compared to the Blue Star," Tootie said. I agreed. Once we'd ordered coffee and a burger, she started in. "Ya sure y'all really want to know the truth, Mickey? It's ugly."

I took a deep breath and nodded. "Tootie, all the damn secrets in this family have torn me to pieces. I wanna know everythin', no matter what."

"Okay, then, here it is. The harsh truth. Nash, y'all's granddaddy, raped Dixie Mae and me."

I stared at her, as my stomach lurched into my throat. "He what?"

"And not just once." She closed her eyes as if trying to block out the memory but kept talking. "He started on me once I developed, around twelve or so. I hated it. I hated him. I was desperate and tried everythin' I could to get 'im off me. I put on weight. I wouldn't bathe. I talked back to him, but nothin' I did stopped him."

"You didn't tell Grandmama?"

"She wouldn't have believed me now, would she?"

"I suppose not."

"So, I kept puttin' on weight to drive him away, but he still wouldn't stop. Then somethin' else happened that got him to stop."

"What was that?"

"Yo' mama."

I was speechless. "She developed earlier than I did. Around the age of eleven, I think. Once he liked her shape, he left me alone. I never saw 'em together, but I knew that if he wasn't forcin' me, then he was forcin' her."

"That's disgutin', Aunt Tootie."

She started to cry. "See why I cain't go to church? God could never forgive me for what I did—or didn't do. I didn't protect her, Mickey. I didn't protect my little sister. I didn't tell anybody, and I didn't try to stop him. I was just so relieved that he didn't drag me to the garage or drive me to the woods and do that shit to me anymore."

I was enraged. "That sumbitch! That bastard!"

"It gets worse. He got her pregnant, and po' Dixie Mae didn't know what was goin' on. She started showin' and Mama just assumed she was havin' sex with some boy. Mama didn't care who it was, she just called Dixie Mae a slut and a whore and…" Aunt Tootie started to cry again. "It was horrible. I knew the truth and didn't say nothin'."

I reached out for her hand. "Aunt Tootie, you were so young yo'self. You can't blame yo'self for that!"

She pulled her hand back. "The hell I cain't, and I do! Why do y'all think I've tried to help yo' mama so much? I love you boys, I do. But I would do anythin' to make up for my part in that horrible thing."

It took her a while to control her emotions and I waited for a time, but then had to know the rest. "So, what happened next?"

"Well, Mama took her out of town for an abortion. It was against the law, of course, and it was a botched job. Mama brought her in from the car and there was blood comin' down her legs, all over floor. Mama put her in the tub and told me to hold towels 'tween her legs, but the blood just kept comin'. I almost passed out I was so scared. Dixie Mae went in and out of consciousness. I was terrified she'd bleed to death right in front of me.

"As usual, Daddy was drunk and didn't give a shit anyway. Mama screamed at him to drive over to Jean's. She and Mama were friends back then and Jean was a midwife. Daddy grumbled but staggered to the car and took off.

"Since Jean never showed up, Mama called her. Jean said Daddy hadn't come over to get her. Said she'd come right over. I don't know exactly what she did 'cause they threw me out of the bathroom. But soon yo' mama was in her own bed, sleepin' and the bleedin' had stopped. Right after that, the highway patrol came and told us that Daddy was dead. He'd done drove the car into a tree and killed himself."

While Grandma Jean had told me much of this, I could barely take it all in hearing Aunt Tootie share it.

"Now ya see why nobody wants to tell the truth in this family?" Aunt Tootie asked. "We're an awful bunch."

I took a sip of water trying to settle my stomach.

"Let me ask you somethin'. What did Jean tell you about the abortion? Did she say that I was the one who had it?"

I shook my head no. "Grandma Jean told me the truth, and said she was embarrassed and ashamed about how she'd treated y'all since."

"She should be ashamed, spreadin' all those rumors and lies about me."

"No, that was Charlie. He couldn't imagine that Dixie Mae bein' so young, could've been the one who was pregnant. So, he decided you were the one and spread those rumors about you."

"Goddamn it, Mickey! He made my life a livin' hell!"

"Yes, he did. How come you never set him straight?"

"Well, hell, boy, how could I do that? Say, 'No, Charlie Crow. It wasn't me. It was Dixie Mae? And oh, by the way the father is our daddy?' That just wasn't possible, not in those days."

I sighed, knowing it was the truth.

She sat back, looking tired and beaten down. "Your mama has no memory of that night, the abortion, or daddy dyin'."

"What ya mean?"

"Ask her yo'self."

I laughed. "Look, Aunt Tootie. She's the last person I would ask to tell me what really happened. She can't keep her stories straight even now."

"Well, if you did ask her, you'd see something weird. I tried to talk to her about it once, you know, tryin' to apologize or somethin', and she looked me in the eye and said she don't remember her daddy ever touchin' her, the abortion, or the night he died."

"She always lies, Tootie, you know that."

Aunt Tootie leaned into me, putting her face close to mine. "You ain't gettin' what I'm sayin' to you, boy. She actually don't remember any of it. She's never said a bad word about Daddy. Have you ever heard her say anythin'?"

I'd never noticed that before. "No, she never has, good or bad."

"That's because she's blocked it from her mind. In fact, she don't remember hardly anything of her childhood. Her memory starts once Daddy was dead and buried. Around the time she met Bobby and Charlie."

That suddenly made sense to me. The pieces fell into place.

"Is that why she keeps twistin' the truth?"

Aunt Tootie nodded. "I don't think yo' mama has any idea what the truth is, other than she's loved Charlie Crow as far back as she can remember."

It was so late when Tootie and I finished talking I just decided to spend the night at Grandmama's house. Grandmama and Tootie were both up before me.

"Hey ladies, what's for breakfast?" I said, walking into the kitchen.

"We got some bacon and some biscuits ready. If y'all can wait a minute, I'll make you some eggs," said Grandmama.

"I'll just take some bacon and a biscuit. I got a class this mornin' and need to move my ass before I'm late."

Tootie wrapped everything up for me and put it in a paper lunch bag. I grabbed the bag, and ran out the door, almost running over Grandma Jean standing at the door ready to ring the doorbell. Smiling, I said, "Good mornin' Grandma Jean. Gotta go, late for class." I put my hand on her shoulder, whispered, "Good luck," and ran for the car.

FIFTY-NINE

SATURDAY, MAY 6, 1972
FINDING JACK

The next morning, I called Harley in California. I filled him in on the secrets our family had kept hidden all these many years. He was stunned and amazed.

"So, are you gonna go find your daddy?"

"Jack? I have no idea how to find him."

"Mickey, you been haunted by this situation damn near yo' whole life. Do somethin' about it. Go find 'im, damnit."

I froze with doubt for a minute. "What if he don't wanna be found. I don't wanna—"

"If he don't want anybody to know about you, then at least you'll know that much. But one way or another, you gotta get on with your life, Mickey. So, what do you know about 'im?"

"I know he was in the Air Force, but I don't know fo' how long. I know that he moved Mama to Valdosta when he trained at Moody Air Force Base, and we know he's a Korean War Vet."

"Is that all? Not a lot to go on."

"Oh, I remember one time when I asked Mama about where he lived, she said somethin' like, Shitland, Maryland." We laughed. "I'm not sure that was the actual name."

"If Jack retired from the Air Force, he pro'bly gets benefits of some kind. If that's true, then somebody, somewhere knows where he lives, right?"

"Yeah, so what?"

"They'd have records, dumbass. Don't you know anybody who could help?"

"I don't know anybody, Harley—not off the top of my head. I'll have to think on it some."

Later that evening, I met with Ripley for drinks at Potbelly's again. I told him about the conversation I'd had with Harley earlier. "How the hell is Harley? He doin' okay."

"Yeah, he's great. He's in the Navy now, seems to like it. I haven't seen 'im in a while, though. I told 'im about meeting you again after all these years."

"Really, what'd he say?"

"Just wanted to know if you were the same old smart ass that he knew back in Crawfordville."

"You said I was, right?"

"Of course I did!" We laughed, and it felt like no time had passed since those days back in our neighborhood in Crawfordville.

Eventually the conversation came back around to Jack McCarthy. I said, "I just don't know anybody in the Air Force, or who I should even talk to or ask for if I did."

"Mickey, you remember my sister Suzy?"

Is he serious? Hell, yes, I remembered Suzy! "Yeah, I remember Suzy, Rip."

"Suzy works for the Air Force, if you can believe that!"

"That's great, but what's that gotta do with finding Jack?"

"Suzy is a civilian contractor, working in the Records Department in Texas."

"Wait, what?"

"Yeah, she works in the records department. I don't know what she does there, but I can ask, if you think that might help."

"Are kidding me? Yeah, please ask her! That would be great! Thanks Rip."

"Hey, don't thank me yet. I got no idea if she can help us or not."

"I understand, but at least it's a place to start."

We finished our drinks and headed for the exit. "Look, Mickey, I'll check with Suzy tomorrow and give ya a call when I hear something, okay?"

"That'll be fine, Ripley. I'll wait for yo' call. Oh, and tell yo' sister that I've never forgotten her and never will."

Laughing, Rip said, "I'll make sure and send along yo' greetin'."

Rip called me late the next day. "Hey boy, I just got off the phone with Suzy."

My heart began to race in anticipation. "Cool, what did she say?"

"She actually works in the office that sends out checks to Air Force retirees!"

"Wow, that's great. Does she think she can help?"

"Well, she said that they ain't allowed to give out addresses, names, phone numbers, you know, personal stuff. Said she could get fired if they found out."

"Well, I don't want her to lose her job over it. I'll just have to figure out another way. Can she tell us if a Jack McCarthy even gets a retirement check from the Air Force?"

"Way ahead of you buddy. She checked and yes, there is a check that gets mailed out every month."

"Okay, at least that's a place to start, anyway."

"There's more. She said that if you wrote a letter to Jack McCarthy and put it in a sealed envelope, she'd send it to the address listed in the file. If it's the right McCarthy, and he wants to contact you, then that would be within the rules."

"Damn, Rip! That's great news!"

"Write it, give it to me, and I'll send it on to Suzy."

"I'll write it tonight. Wanna meet over at Potbelly's tomorrow, say five-ish?"

"That works. Oh, and Mickey, Suzy says she remembers the hug she gave you when you were movin' to the Keys."

Damn, could this day get any better?

I wrote the letter and gave it to Ripley the next evening. I wrote all the information I could think of to prove I might be Jack's son.

Days passed with no reply. After ten days, I gave up hope and got on with life.

On a Monday afternoon, I got a phone call.

"Mickey? Mickey Crow? My name is Jack, Jack McCarthy, and I'm your father."

A week later, I was driving to his house on a nice, tree-lined street, a couple miles west of interstate seventy-five, just outside Sarasota. My nerves felt like guitar strings wound so tight they were ready to break as I pulled into his driveway. He must have been anxious, too, because before I could get out of the car, he was out his front door and headed toward me.

"Mickey!"

"Daddy!" We embraced, both of us blubbering like drunken fools. Just then I heard a door open, and a beautiful middle-aged woman came out and introduced herself as Joyce, his wife. Soon we were all laughing, then crying, then laughing some more.

"Why don't we go inside where it's cooler and have some iced tea," Joyce said. We followed her into the house and didn't come out until it was late in the evening. It was glorious!

They invited me to spend the night. As I lay there in the guest room on a queen-sized bed, I was astounded that I was indeed there with my biological daddy in the next room. I tried to remind myself that I needed to be careful not to get my hopes up about where this would lead.

After breakfast, Daddy and I spent some time alone out by his screened-in pool. I spoke first. "I don't know much about what happened between you and Mama. Can you fill me in? She won't talk about it."

"I imagine she wouldn't. Are you sure you want to hear the story? I don't want to talk bad about your Mama."

"Yes. The good, bad, and the ugly. I want to hear what happened. I need to hear what happened."

"Okay, then. I tell you, son, your mama was the most beautiful woman I had ever met. I had no idea I would fall in love when I walked into your Grandmama's café that day. She seemed to love me, too, and before long we got married. I had joined the Air Force around the time the Korean War started. We knew I would eventually go to Korea, but we decided to get married anyway. After the honeymoon, I moved Dixie Mae up to Valdosta, Georgia, while I trained to be a radioman on a bomber."

I sat there enthralled with my real daddy's story of my birth. I think I may have said an "uh-huh" and a "no kidding" now and then as he shared, but mostly I just nodded my head.

"Soon your mama was pregnant with you. When you were a little one year old, I got my orders to go with a bomber squadron to Korea, so I moved you and your mama back to Quincy to live with her mama while I was gone. I was there for a year. You were so little when I left, and I missed you so much. I knew you were growing, and I was missing it all. When Dixie didn't meet me at the airport, I got a taxi ride to the Blue Star Café from Pensacola. When I walked in, Tootie was the first one to greet me."

I stopped him. "Aunt Tootie told me she wasn't particularly happy to see you."

"Yeah, your Aunt Tootie didn't like the fact that I took Dixie Mae away from her."

"She feels bad about that now."

"Water under the bridge, Mickey. But when I heard that your mama was in the hospital having Charlie Crow's baby. I was shocked and so terribly hurt that I could barely breathe. Then I got angry."

According to my daddy, after he left the Blue Star, he ran over to a cabbie he saw filling up his gas tank at the Phillips 66 next door and got in. He gave the driver the address of Grandmama's house figuring his baby boy would be there. Sitting in the back seat of that taxi, his emotions ran wild. As the shock of the news began to wear off, he became extremely hurt and confused. Then hurt and confusion gave way to anger, and finally blinding fury.

"I told the taxi driver to keep the meter running, and that I'd be back in a minute. Without really thinking things through, I banged on your grandmama's front door until Lettie, their longtime maid and babysitter, finally opened the door. Her eyes flew wide open as she asked me what I was doing there. I told her I was home from the war, and I wanted to see my boy—you! I pushed her aside, and she yelled, 'I don't think that's a real good idea, Mr. Jack! Mizz Dixie and her mama aren't here right now, and they left the boy in my care.' I just looked at her and let her know that I didn't give a good goddamn what she thought. I told her you were my boy, and I would take you wherever I wanted to."

Jack said that Lettie showed him to the room where I was sleeping. He packed my stuff in a bag knowing Lettie was upset. "I told her that you were my boy just as much as Dixie Mae's, and I was taking you no matter what.

"She wrapped you up in your favorite blanket, and as she handed you to me, she asked where I was going to take you." Daddy stopped a minute to take a long drink of his sweet tea. "I told her it was none of her business, and I took you and your things out to the taxi. I sat in that taxi with you in my arms watching Lettie cry as we drove off, and I honestly felt that I was doing the right thing by you.

"Lettie called Tootie at the Café and told her what had happened. She called the hospital where your mama had just given birth to your little brother with Charlie Crow and your grandmama present. She informed them all that I was home from Korea and that I had taken you away. They were all understandably upset.

"You were with me for four months. What I found out later is that your mama, in full panic mode, had Charlie Crow call a cop friend of theirs, and he began trying to track us down. But it took a while. Four months later, a Deputy Bailey showed up on the front porch of our little house in Redbud, Illinois, less than an hour south of St. Louis. My cousin, Jimmy, lived there and had agreed to let me and you hide out there for a while. When I opened the front door, this large deputy was standing there."

I could not believe my ears. My Uncle Bobby, always looking after me. "Yeah, Uncle Bobby was a big man. He died a couple years back. Please continue, Ja—Daddy."

"Oh, okay. Well, he asked, 'You Jack McCarthy?' I asked who he was, and he gave me his name, along with the fact that he was a friend of your mama, and he didn't mince any words. I guess he had tried to find me through my parents, but they had died years before, and it was my granddaddy who then raised me on a farm in Iowa. Bailey had found him and questioned him, but he wouldn't tell him anything. Investigating all my family, he found my cousin and the house I had taken you to.

"I told him I didn't care and to get off my front porch. He told me that he didn't have an arrest warrant and was just searching for me on his own. He stepped toward me, and I blocked his way, but he said something like, 'We can do this the hard way or the easy way.'

He sounded awful menacing. He also threatened me. Said I could hand you over and not go to jail, or he could take you by force and arrest and charge me, and then I wouldn't see you anyway. I told him I was your daddy! I had a right to you! But he began to grab me, and I was afraid of you seeing what was going to happen if I fought him. I just didn't want you to get hurt."

Daddy stopped and tears flooded his eyes. He said it was hard to tell me the rest. I told him to pause a bit until he felt better able to finish. He did just that, offering to refill my glass of tea. The emotions I was feeling caused my mouth to dry out, so I needed that drink. But in just a few minutes, he was ready to carry on.

"Mickey, I agreed to hand you over to him. It was the second hardest thing I ever did, son. I cried as I carried you over to him, and I told you how much I loved you and that I would be seeing you soon. You began squirming and screaming for me as the deputy put you in his car and started to back out of the driveway. But then he stopped suddenly and stepped out of the cruiser. I will never forget what he said to me. 'Jack, don't let me or Charlie Crow find your lily white ass in the State of Florida ever again. Y'all hear me, boy?' Then he left along with my boy."

We sat there in tears for a short while—me trying to imagine what it must have been like for every one of us there that day, and Daddy looking terribly sad. He began again, this time his voice softer with a note of shame.

"Signing the papers to let Charlie Crow adopt you was the hardest thing I ever did, son."

"What? Charlie actually adopted me?"

"You didn't know?"

"I can't believe how many secrets there are in my family. Mama told me that he adopted me once, but it was part of another lie, so I believed the whole thing was a lie. Plus, Tootie laughed when I told her Mama said it."

Jack paused. I could tell he was getting emotional. "Mickey, there hasn't been a day in the last twenty years that I haven't thought about you—where you were, what you looked like, what kind of childhood you were having, what kind of man you turned out to be. When Deputy Bailey took you from me, I should have come back to Quincy to fight for you, but I was scared. Then your Mama called me and asked me to relinquish custody. She begged me. Then she threatened to have me arrested for kidnapping you. She was right. I had kidnapped you, according to the law, and I would have had to face charges. So I gave in.

"I knew Dixie Mae would follow through on her threat. Then the Air Force transferred me to Germany, where I spent four years. I met Joyce, fell in love, got married, and had a couple of our own kids." He saw the astonished look on my face and stopped for a second. "Oh, that's right! You've got two half-sisters, and they are dying to meet you! They've heard about you all their lives. Anyway, life got in the way, but never doubt that you were loved and missed. There was always this hole in my heart until the day I got your letter."

We spent the day catching up. I told him all about Charlie Crow, Harley, and Uncle Bobby. I told him about my recent meeting with Charlie. When I finished, he was sobbing. "You've always got a home here, now. I'm your daddy. I'm so sorry, Mickey. I'm so sorry you had to go through all of that."

"I'm not, Daddy, not anymore. All of it has led me here, back to you."

The next day, back in Quincy, I made a trip over to the county courthouse and filled out the forms to change my name to Mickey McCarthy.

SIXTY

The sun shone through the moss-covered coastal oaks that lined the patio at Cora's Seafood Restaurant—my mama Dixie Mae's favorite place—staining the water with golden bits of light. With the humidity unseasonably low at this time of year, it was comfortable, so there was some relief. The warm breeze gently moved through Mama's still blonde hair. She managed to look pretty, in spite of the years of smoking four packs a day and fighting a losing battle with the demon drink. It was a month after I met with Jack McCarthy.

Once seated, Mama, Harley, and I ordered some beers and oysters on the half-shell and settled in for the long haul. It had been a while since the three of us had sat down together, and Cora's turned out to be the perfect place for it.

The waitress arrived with our drinks, and we sat there in silence for a while looking at those beers like they held the family's secrets, and I guess they did. Harley lit up a cancer stick and offered one to mama, who took it.

"Well, Mickey, this was a great idea," Mama said, taking a hit off her cigarette and blowing out blue smoke that circled overhead like a coiled snake.

"Thanks, Mama. Glad we got the chance to spend some time together. It's been too long." I truly meant it. Sal had been shipped out for one last sea duty tour before retiring. Mama had called to tell me she was coming out to visit Grandmama and Tootie for a few weeks while he was away. Harley, who was still in the Navy, had a month of leave and wanted to come. I couldn't have been more pleased. I had a lot to tell them.

"Too damn long," Harley agreed.

Our oysters arrived, accompanied by God's own nectar, Tabasco Sauce. Placing the sea's goodness on a saltine cracker, we sucked them down with gusto and delight. Mama eventually switched to her favorite drink, vodka and orange juice, but didn't get drunk. I offered no judgment, and she seemed to sense that and relaxed. We spent hours there, on the deck of Cora's, telling stories of times gone by. We laughed, we cried, we hugged, and kissed each other. It was the best day I'd spent with my mama since the Sunday barbeques we enjoyed together, along with Tootie, when we lived in that little house on Lake Irene in Quincy. It was magical, damn magical, and I was so glad they'd come.

We'd spent a couple of very pleasant hours together, and I'd had three or four beers, something I never did. I was feeling good. And with all the stories and the emotions that followed them, I had a thought. *Maybe this would be a good time to ask Mama about finally admitting who Harley's daddy really was.*

"Mama, I don't know if I told y'all, but I met with Charlie a few months back."

"You what?" She stared at me with a mixture of disbelief and disgust.

"Yeah, he asked Grandma Jean to contact me and ask if I'd see him before he…." my voice trailed off as I glanced at Harley.

"I know, Mickey. He's dyin'."

Mama took a long drag on her Marlboro. "Good, I never wanna see that sumbitch again—never."

"Well, he asked for my forgiveness, Mama, and I gave it to 'im."

She gripped the sides of the table as if I'd slapped her across the face. "You *forgave* Charlie? After all he did to me? To you?"

"Yes ma'am, I did."

I looked over at Harley, and then we both looked at mama, who was looking down at her drink.

"Don't you think it's time for us to put the past to rest, once and for all, Mama?"

Her hands started shaking. "What ya mean, Mickey?"

Harley immediately looked up from raking another oyster onto a saltine with terror in his eyes. "Mickey, I don't think that's somethin' we should be talkin' 'bout now. How 'bout another time." His eyes were pleading with me to stop. I didn't.

"Mama, I've met Jack McCarthy." She gasped and looked up with something akin to fear in her eyes. "Yeah, a friend of mine helped me track 'im down. About a month ago, I went to his house. And he told me everythin'. He told me that Charlie is Harley's daddy, and he is mine."

Slowly, deliberately, she looked up, rage now filling her jade-green eyes. "Whatever he said, it was a goddamn lie, and y'all can tell him I said so. Mickey, y'all don't know a damn thing 'bout what really went on back then—not a goddamn thing."

I said gently, "Mama, I don't need to know everythin' that went on back then. Honestly, I don't. All I ever wanted was the truth about our daddies. That's all. Just the truth."

Mama shot out of her chair and looked down at my little brother. "Harley, take me back to the hotel, if y'all don't mind!"

I said, "Mama, don't leave like this."

She picked up her purse and spun on her heels. Harley said, "I'll take you, just give me a second. Why don't you go to the lady's room, and I'll meet you out front?"

"Fine," Mama said, then gave me a look that could've set a glacier on fire. "Goodbye, Mickey, hope you're happy." She turned and headed for the restroom.

After she was out of sight, Harley let out a sarcastic laugh. "The truth, Mickey? What good is the truth if it destroys everybody? And you lied, too, Mickey. Y'all didn't tell me the truth about Charlie until I was leaving the Keys. You kept that *secret* from me fo' years."

"You're right, little brother, I did, and you know why I did, right?"

"Yeah, Mama made ya swear not to tell me."

"Right! I wanted to tell you, I tried for years to get Mama to tell us both what the truth was, but just like today, she won't, or can't do it."

Harley stood up, and I was about to do the same when he sat back down. "Micky, I've done my best to be a good brother to y'all and a good son to Mama. I have, right?"

I nodded, a bit shocked by his direct question.

"And you did yo' best to take care of me, Mickey. I know that, and I'm grateful."

I kept nodding, waiting for the other shoe to drop.

"But..." *there it was* "you made it yo' business to try to fix everythin' for us."

I got defensive, "That's right, I was tryin' to protect y'all."

Harley rocked back in his chair, lifting the front legs off the ground. He looked at the ceiling, as if searching for the words. Before he could speak, I asked, "Didn't you care about what Charlie was doin' to Mama?"

Bam! The chair legs struck the floor and Harley put his hands on the table, eyes ablaze at me. "Of course I cared. And I loved her the best I could. That's all I've ever tried to do, was love y'all."

Not knowing what to say, I said nothing. He continued. "Every family has secrets, but you made it yo' business to poke around and stir up so much pain for everybody."

I couldn't tell if I was more shocked by the fact that Harley felt this way, or that he was actually telling me that he felt this way.

"You came here today knowin' the truth about Jack and Daddy—everythin', and yet you pestered Mama to do what, confess? You tryin' to rub her nose in her mistakes?"

"No, Harley. I wanted her to…" I stared at my hands, trying to hold back hot tears.

Harley stood up and put his hand on my shoulder. "I know, Mickey. You wanted Mama to say she's sorry for all of the ways she hurt y'all growin' up, and all the ways she let Daddy hurt ya too. But if you're ever gonna forgive her, you'll have to do it without Mama askin' for it."

His words cut through my heart like a knife. He was right. I'd forgiven everyone—Grandma Jean, Aunt Tootie, Grandmama, Jack, even Charlie. But they'd acknowledged the hurt they'd caused. Mama did not.

Harley turned to leave. "If ya wait for that to happen, Mickey, you'll never be at peace."

I stood up and grabbed Harley, giving him a bear hug that probably scared the hell out of him. I cried and said, "Thank y'all, Harley."

When he pulled away, he had tears in his eyes too. "I love ya, Mickey." He turned and headed to the front of the restaurant to look for Mama.

I sat down and watched Harley's car drive away with Mama and all her secrets. He was right. It was time to forgive Mama, even though she would never know. She forgave no one. Sadly, she never experienced the freedom that comes with knowing you are forgiven. I couldn't force it on her. This would be the last time I would try.

Sitting on the patio at Cora's, right there on the shores of Ochlockonee Bay, I forgave my mama. I let go of the last residue of resentment and disappointment I was holding on to. I knew the truth. And knowing that, was finally enough for me.

EPILOGUE

SUNDAY, NOVEMBER 5, 1972

The next time I saw Harley was at Mama's funeral, a few months after our visit to Cora's Seafood Restaurant on the Ochlockonee Bay. She'd developed a bad case of emphysema from smoking four packs of carcinogens every day and didn't tell anyone until it was too late.

But Mama didn't die without a fight—didn't give death an inch—and fought the Reaper until her last breath. It wasn't so much her losing her life as death ripping it from her.

Grandmama insisted that Mama's funeral be held at Mt. Calvary Baptist Church, Pastor Snowden presiding. Harley and I looked at each other and shared a knowing smile. He leaned over and said, "Mama would'a hated this, ya know."

"I know she would, brother. She'd rather us be sittin' out on the patio at Cora's where we would all be tipping back a vodka tonic in her honor."

"Oh well, funerals are for the livin' and the grievin', not for the dead."

The church was filled in honor of Grandmama, not Mama. As usual, we all sat together in the family row, but this time with a significant difference—Grandmama Colee and Grandma Jean sat side by side in the middle of the row, with the rest of us flanking them on the pew.

After the service, we made it out to the gravesite. It was hard watching that coffin being lowered into the ground. Once done, everyone left for a small reception at Grandmama's house, leaving Sal and 'Dixie's boys' alone with her one last time. After a few minutes Sal, with tears in his eyes, said goodbye to his wife for the last time and left for the reception, leaving me and Harley standing by Mama's final resting place. Harley wept as he held onto me, so tight I couldn't breathe. Then again, maybe it was me holding onto him. It was hard to tell. We stood there over that open scar in the ground for a long time. "Damn, Mickey, I'm gonna miss her so much."

My emotions were raw, wrenching my insides like sandpaper on a rough piece of wood. "Me too, Harley." My voice trembled with the pain of loss.

Dixie Mae was my mother. I loved her. I hated her. And I loved her again. Mama kept a lot of secrets, she surely did. I did everything I could over the years to get her to open the vault to her heart and come clean. In the end, she had it her way. Mama took her private thoughts and secrets with her on her eternal journey. When I really thought about it, I realized that her secrets were *hers* to tell—or to keep, as it turned out.

ABOUT THE AUTHOR

Mike Reynolds writes fictionally about what he knows, where he's lived, and what he's experienced with an ease that comes with familiarity. Born in the small town of Bainbridge, Georgia—which is just over the Florida Panhandle line where Georgia and Florida come together—and raised in Florida, Mike's blue collar upbringing exposed him to a lot of hard working honest people, but also to the seedier side of life there. He grew up in a violent and abusive home, and one in which alcoholism played a major role in day-to-day life. But Mike was able to break free of the abusive cycle and become a successful business owner and entrepreneur.

As the child of an Air Force flight instructor, Mike's family moved around a lot, creating even more fodder for his stories. He served in the Navy for six years, married young and had three daughters, but the marriage ended in divorce. Later, marrying a woman with three sons, Mike's family kept him busy.

Mike worked in the mortgage industry for 40 years, eventually opening his own mortgage company, which he ran for 10 years and employed scores of people. He finds it humorous that it was in his position in that company where his talent for writing was honed. He had always been a good storyteller—people invited him to dinner parties because they wanted to hear his stories—but writing daily to weekly inspirational memos to his many employees garnered a lot of positive response. This added to his confidence. Mike retired in 2016 and began writing in earnest.

Now enjoying retirement, when Mike's not writing, he's spending time with his six kids and sixteen grandchildren. Having been in a Christian rock band for many years, he still plays guitar and is teaching himself to play the blues. He and his beloved Annette enjoy their many friends in the beautiful hamlet of Glendora, California.

A NOTE FROM THE PUBLISHER

We at Berry Powell Press are proud to publish *Darkness Dwells in Dixie* by Mike E Reynolds. This raw and riveting story, fictionalized yet drawn from actual events, embodies our vision of authentic storytelling of pain, loss, and hard-won redemption.

First, Mike E Reynolds is a remarkable storyteller who is ruthlessly honest about his characters. They are multi-faceted and engaging, evoking both anger and compassion. His writing style immediately engages and whisks you away to Mickey's childhood marked with violence, Southern humor, and his insatiable curiosity for uncovering the highly protected family secrets.

Second, the book defies category. It's a story of faith and yet doesn't naturally fit alongside traditional Christian fiction due to the rawness of the dialog, the sexual elements, and the realistic depiction of some destructive teachings of the church. At the same time, the book is unapologetically a redemption story revealing the power of forgiveness in our lives. We at BPP are motivated to publish books that challenge the status quo, and Darkness Dwells in Dixie fully hits that mark.

Lastly, because Mike based the story on his experiences, it rings true—the harshness and the healing. We at BPP have read books that have shifted our paradigms, challenged our cliches, and caused us to pivot. We hope that *this* book will be *that* book for someone who needs a word of hope at a critical moment in their lives.

If you have life experiences or insights to share with the world but you don't know how to do so, please contact us...at www.berry-powellpress.com.

Berry Powell Press is a hybrid publishing house that publishes authors with transformational perspectives on timely personal and societal challenges. We provide our authors with in-depth mentorship and collaborative assistance to create life-changing books. Additionally, we assist them in building book-based businesses that can impact the largest audience possible. We publish fiction and non-fiction for adults and children.

Made in the USA
Las Vegas, NV
09 December 2022